SHERIDAN HAY grew up in Australia and worked in bookshops and in publishing for many years. She holds an MFA in writing and literature and lives in Irvington, New York.

From the reviews of *The Secret of Lost Things*:

'A brilliant version of the coming-to-adulthood-in-Manhattan story with a page-turner of a plot about a lost manuscript for which the people around the charming heroine are willing to do very nasty things . . . Pacy, confident, and beautifully written, *Lost Things* satisfies on every level'
NUALA O'FAOLAIN, author of Are You Somebody?

'Sheridan Hay's first novel is a romantic fantasy fired by actual experience . . . The assortment of endearingly eccentric characters that Rosemary runs into could sustain an urban-hipster blog for weeks'
USA Today

'With this eccentric cast of characters (some of them worthy of Muriel Spark), Hay constructs a touching story of displaced passion . . . an original first novel'
Scotland on Sunday

'This insightful literary debut satisfyingly leaves room for readers to unearth for themselves the psyches of both the Arcade characters and the tormented soul of Melville himself'
Irish Examiner

SHERIDAN HAY

The Secret of Lost Things

HARPER PERENNIAL

London, New York, Toronto, Sydney and New Delhi

Harper Perennial
An imprint of HarperCollins*Publishers*
77–85 Fulham Palace Road, Hammersmith, London W6 8JB

www.harperperennial.co.uk
Visit our authors' blog at www.fifthestate.co.uk

This Harper Perennial edition published 2008
1

First published in Great Britain by Fourth Estate in 2007

Copyright © Sheridan Hay 2006

PS Section copyright © Rose Gaete 2008, except 'How I Came to Write' by
Sheridan Hay © Sheridan Hay 2008

PS™ is a trademark of HarperCollins*Publishers* Ltd

Sheridan Hay asserts the moral right
to be identified as the author of this work

A catalogue record for this book is available from the British Library

ISBN 978-0-00-724392-1

Lines from 'The Sea and the Mirror' by W. H. Auden reproduced by
permission of Faber and Faber Ltd.

Printed and bound in Great Britain by Clays Ltd, St Ives plc

Mixed Sources
Product group from well-managed
forests and other controlled sources
www.fsc.org   Cert no. SW-COC-1806
© 1996 Forest Stewardship Council

FSC is a non-profit international organisation established to promote the
responsible management of the world's forests. Products carrying the FSC
label are independently certified to assure consumers that they come
from forests that are managed to meet the social, economic and
ecological needs of present and future generations.

Find out more about HarperCollins and the environment at
www.harpercollins.co.uk/green

FOR MICHAEL,

my own tempest

"...for experience, the only true knowledge..."

Herman Melville, *The Confidence Man*

THE
SECRET
OF
LOST THINGS

PART
ONE
∽

I was born before this story starts, before I dreamed of such a place as the Arcade, before I imagined men like Walter Geist existed outside of fables, outside of fairy tales. My time at the Arcade would have gone very differently but for him, for his blindness. His eyes were nearly useless when I met him, and were it not for his condition, I would never have known about Herman Melville's lost book. Walter Geist's blindness is important, but it's my own, with regard to him, that remains a lasting regret. It's the reason for this story. If I start with my own beginning you will understand how I came to the Arcade, and how it came to mean so much to me.

I was born on April twenty-fifth, never mind what year precisely; I'm not so young that I care to put my age about, but not so old now that I forget the girl I was.

My birth date, however, is significant in another sense. April twenty-fifth is Anzac Day, the most important day of commemoration on the Australian calendar. It is the day when Australians pin sprigs of rosemary to their breasts to remember those lost to war, to remember that first great loss, at Gallipoli, where rosemary grows wild on the beaches. "There's rosemary, that's for remembrance," says Ophelia, once she's lost her mind to grief. "Pray you, love, remember."

It was April twenty-fifth on the island state of Tasmania, when my mother saw stalks of spiky rosemary pinned over hearts, the day she walked to the free public hospital to give birth to me, walked through the crowded Square trying to avoid the ragged annual parade of veterans and gawking locals. That hardy plant stayed in her mind through a difficult labor, not as the symbol of loss, for she was gaining me, but as an emblem of memory.

Anzac Day, then, determined my name—Rosemary. And given along with my name, the occupation I practice here—to remember. After all, memory is a kind of obligation, perhaps the last duty owed anyone.

I have only one other name. My last—Savage. And Mother too gave me this name, only Mother. She brought me home to the small flat she rented above the shop off the central town Square. Remarkable Hats was the only store of its kind on the island of Tasmania, and we grew up in that shop, Mother and me. But like a pair of goldfish, we grew only so much as the bowl allowed. We came to fit it, but we lived in a bowl of separateness, a transparent wall between us and the rest of the town. Mother had come from the mainland, she was an outsider, and everyone knew that "Mrs." Savage was a prefix that didn't disguise one single defining fact: there wasn't a husband in sight.

But disguise, in a way, was Mother's business. Hats, after all, can cover up a good deal of what one might not want revealed. Hats can even grant a measure of acceptance to a woman who'd appeared from the mainland to establish a small, decent business—pregnant, without an apparent partner.

"It's hats that saved us," Mother often said. "That's why I call these hats remarkable. They made me unavoidable to respectable people."

It was imagination that saved us. Hers, in particular. And I like to think imagination was her gift to me.

Remarkable Hats made Mother something of an arbiter of taste in our town as well as wise to vanity. She could guess the hat size of customers within moments of laying eyes on them. The measurements of regular customers she memorized, along with a characteristic that, to her, matched the circumference of their head.

If she saw our prosperous and ambitious landlord, Mr. Frank, in the Square she'd say: "That Mr. Frank, no wonder he's a nine-and-three-quarters. With all those big ideas, he certainly needs the space."

Or she'd mention that Mrs. Pym, the florist, had been trying on hats to wear to the Cup: "Of course, Rosemary, nothing I had was right. Pym is one of those five-and-a-halfs. Practically a pinhead. No room in there for a thought, let alone a decision."

Hats were oracles, divining rods to behavior, and while Mother's way of judging her fellow Tasmanians was often accurate, matching the opprobrium of a small town with her own brand of snobbishness did little to relieve our isolation. Of course, isolation itself worked on our imaginations, our illusions, separating us even more. We were only glancingly acknowledged, and never included. I helped in the store after school. Friends were discouraged, if they'd ever been interested, or more precisely, curious.

We had each other.

"Better to do well in school," Mother advised. "Keep up your reading." And she'd tap her temple with her index finger for emphasis. "All your future's there beneath your hat."

She didn't mention my body. She never did, except in the most perfunctory way, imparting only biological information. As Mother knew firsthand, bodies caused trouble.

She did have one close friend, Esther Chapman, a mentor to me and the owner of Chapman's, the only shop in the village that sold books. Miss Chapman (I called her Chaps from early on) helped to educate me, taking me to any theater that made its way to our small town, favoring the rare Shakespeare troupe that occasionally washed ashore in Tasmania. Chaps taught me to read before I started school, endowing my purposes with words she would have said, quoting from her favorite play. Chaps held that books were essential, whereas hats were a kind of ephemera, a fancy, objects that ultimately wouldn't provide Mother or me with security.

She worried for us.

"Books aren't lumps of paper, but minds on shelves," she urged Mother. "After all, hats aren't books—people don't need them."

"Tell that to a bald man in the summer," Mother teased back. "Or to a plain-faced woman."

But Chaps was right to be concerned.

By the time I finished school, Remarkable Hats was mostly remarkable in that it was still in business. Hats were no longer fashionable, no longer the article of differentiation between decent people and ill-bred ones. Hats went the way of gloves and stockings. Eventually, even regular customers were infrequent, not immune to the whims of fashion or mortality. The town itself was waning.

Mother's own health had been in steady decline for some time, linked as it was to the dwindling business. She was a small woman, and dark, and she grew thin and pale with worry. As I grew older, Mother diminished. In the absence of customers, Mother had me try on hats after school. I had the height, she liked to tell me. It cheered her up.

I'd find her dozing on her stool behind the high serving counter in the afternoon. She said she could only rest in daylight, that she was most comfortable in the opened store, and that nights were spent endlessly waiting for day. When I finally discovered how deeply in debt we were, Mother's insomnia was all at once explained.

Late morning one April day, a few months after I'd finished

school, I came down the back stairs which joined our small flat to the shop, and found Mother collapsed behind the counter. Her breath was halted, her face the livid color of a bruise, as if she'd been beaten.

Mother died a day later, in the same free hospital where she'd given birth to me. By grotesque coincidence then, it appeared that the town, the state, and the whole of Australia commemorated my private loss publicly, the day I turned eighteen. Anzac Day. I didn't consider the rosemary pinned to lapels an admonition to remember.

I would never forget.

∽

Mother's funeral was a short, unsentimental proceeding the following week. I stood in disbelief at the copper door of the mock tomb, a deco affair, that housed the crematorium, set on the highest hill above town. Five old regulars were good enough to come. Both men respectfully held hats to their chests, while the women thoughtfully appeared in Remarkable chapeaus. I thanked them along with Chaps, now my unofficial guardian.

The service was impoverished. Mother and I possessed no religion, save the worship of imagination, of living a kind of fiction, which death, in all its realness, had made a mockery of.

Afterward, we gathered awkwardly in the parking lot outside the tomb until the regulars departed solemnly in their cars, single file, down the steep road. I watched them grow smaller as they separated at the crossroads, the town below just a handful of scattered red tiles, haphazardly thrown across low green hills, without order or pattern, carelessly. It was a narrow, ugly spot on an island of tremendous beauty. The village had never seemed smaller or more unremarkable.

"She's gone, Chaps," was all I could manage, feeling short of breath.

The funeral director approached after a while, handing me Mother's ashes sealed inside a wooden box.

"You said you wanted the simplest one, Miss Rosemary. And this here is the simplest. It's a native timber, Huon pine. Tasmanian heartwood. Very strong and durable."

He rapped the box with his knuckles. I winced. Chaps knew him, and, helpfully, the one funeral director in town who wasn't too unctuous was also the least expensive. But he was nervous for his line of work, and oddly unpracticed in handling grief. He chatted away, not oblivious to my distress but perhaps made so anxious by it that he sought to fend it off with information.

"My supplier told me once that Huon pines can live a thousand years. Practically forever. Isn't that something?" He went on: "The wood has a very distinctive perfume, too—strong." He sniffed. "It's usually found on the west coast of the island—"

"Yes. Thank you," Chaps said, cutting him off. She took me by the elbow and tried to lead me toward her car. I appeared fixed to the spot.

I held the box of Huon pine with both hands spread beneath, unable to move. The box was warm and smelled faintly corrupt. My eyes began to tear, the water on my face as startling to me as to the nervous director.

Chaps finally pushed me to her car and drove me to her little house. I couldn't get out, or really move at all, so we set off again, driving in silence down long Tasmanian roads all the way to the coast.

"The ocean," Chaps said by way of explanation when, eventually, the paved road ended in sand and the sea stretched away, white-capped and vast, before us.

Chaps rolled down the windows so I could smell the salt and feel the pure, fresh Roaring Forties blow their way west to the bottom of the world, to the end of the great globe itself. My throat choked in the cleanest air that exists and I tried to catch my breath. Staring at the ocean, I felt at once surrounded and alone. Between me, there on the Tasmanian island, and ice-covered Antarctica lay nothing but empty, open sea, unpeopled and unknowing. I bent over the Huon box, but couldn't utter a word until night came in, cold and complete, carried across the Great Southern Ocean by those same prevailing winds.

"What will I do?" I finally breathed aloud.

Chaps, who always had an aphorism to hand, was silent.

Chapter

Two

For nearly every year of my early life I went with Mother to Sydney, on the mainland, to buy hats and the materials milliners use to dress hats. We made sure to spend my birthday in the city; it was, of course, a public holiday. At first, we stayed in a boardinghouse in Surry Hills, on Sophia Street. Mother had known the landlady, Merle, before she'd moved to Tasmania, when she lived a life I know nothing about. Her own life before mine.

Merle was a fat, angry woman with small eyes and dyed hair. She resembled a magpie, all black and white and on the lookout for morsels. Her rooming house was cheap, smelled of boiled vegetables; and until I was five and old enough to go with Mother to suppliers, I was left there with Merle for several hours.

Those early hours away from Mother are circumscribed in my memory by a shortage of breath. I can't have actually held my breath, but the sensation of breathlessness is attached to Mother's absence like a keepsake. Afraid to upset an invented balance that would result in Mother's continued nonappearance, I stayed as quiet as possible in the stale-smelling sitting room. Her return was marked with great intakes of breath and tremendous exhales: life restored to the small cadaver I'd become.

"That's the quietest child I've ever seen, Mrs. Savage," Merle would say, tutting, and shaking her big, smooth head. "It's not natural to be so good. I'm happy to watch her, she's no trouble, but it's like she only exists for you."

"I'm all she's got," Mother said, often.

∽

"*Next year, Rosemary* love, you can come with me and do the rounds," Mother promised. "I don't want to leave you any more than you want me to."

So began annual encounters with haberdashery and notions, with felt workrooms full of rabbit pelts and beaver furs, with polished wooden heads and metal blocks (screws protruding from their necks), devices that formed crowns and shaped hats. The storefront shops were bright and cool, but the workrooms behind them were vaporous and warm, the air thick with condensation from steam used to mold and clean hats.

Every supplier indulged me. I was distracted, entertained with bright buttons and lengths of silk ribbon while Mother placed her orders and reviewed new styles. Like a bower bird, everything that sparkled caught my eye. I was served triangular sandwiches, and drank milk from a frosted glass with a striped paper straw. I was a small sultana, my treasure counted in the currency of trifles.

Foys supplied all the biggest department stores with accessories. The notion display room was lined with a wall of slim wooden drawers, built half a century before, that opened to reveal a collection of bric-a-brac: zippers, buttons, samples of fur and skins, silk flowers, sequins translucent as fish scales, glass beads, dye samples, feathers from unimaginable birds, sweets and fruit made from wax. The wall of drawers held hundreds of brilliantly colored trinkets designed to trim hats, to dress lapels or shoes or belts. Ornaments came from all over the world: marcasite stones from

Czechoslovakia, brilliant as metallic diamonds, and rhinestone pins, direct from France, were stored in deep lower drawers, pirate's chests unearthed.

I used to imagine that the endlessly varied objects contained in the drawers appeared only moments before the knob was pulled and the drawer opened, as if conjured by my wish to see them. The wall of drawers appeared to my small self to hold everything; and "things," of course, were the sum of the world.

Workroom girls told Mother I would be beautiful one day, "What with that hair," they'd say. Mother looked dubious. My hair was thick and red, and seemed hardly to belong to me. I must have favored my father, and likely shared as well his green eyes and freckled skin, for Mother's dark hair set off fathomless blue eyes, and her skin was flawless, the color of very milky tea. She was bird-boned and compact, her bosom high. It seems barely credible that I was her child, so little did we resemble each other.

At Foys, and at other suppliers, rabbit fur was pressed into fine felt: fur felt, for bowlers, fedoras, and the peculiarly Australian work hats with old-fashioned names like the Drover or the Squatter. The most expensive used imported beaver and were never worn to work but kept for best, for show.

In the very rear of Foys's workroom was a dim adjoining chamber, piled with skins and smelling sharply of lye, frightening even to pass. I held a strange empathy for the mounds of lifeless pelts, waiting to be shaped into something purposeful. I had felt just as empty, as breathless, as those flayed furs during the hours Mother had left me with Merle. The other side of glimmering bric-a-brac was this grim sepulchre. Evidently, appearances deceived.

Yet Sydney made me happy. I loved the city. We were anonymous, and even then I had the sense that cities were yielding; that they moved over and made room. In the city, I wasn't a girl without a father. I wasn't outside of things. I wasn't even Rosemary. In a city there is no one who can tell you who they think you are, who they want you to be. Once a year we were special and complete.

Here was the start of my scrapbook full of city scenes, any city, decorated with buttons and ribbon collected from suppliers, and painstakingly glued onto the oversized pages.

Peculiar to Sydney, in those days, was a single word written in chalk in beautiful, looping copperplate on street corners. Sydney was known for it, the word chalked at the feet of the inhabitants and visitors, like a letter consisting of a lone word, but personally addressed to each member of a crowd.

"What does it say?" I asked Mother, pointing to what I took to be scribble, the year I was five. The letters didn't resemble any in the books that Chaps had given me.

"It says '*Eternity,*' love," Mother replied, taking my hand. "A man has been writing that word in chalk for thirty years. It's famous now. I don't remember a time when I didn't see it, written there on the street." She put her arms around me.

"What does it mean?"

"We'll never know it, Rosemary. It's a word that means something going on always and forever. And you know, nothing does. Not a human thing, anyway. Everything ends eventually. That's something you should remember, love."

She looked absently up the crowded city street, staring past my face and into the distance.

"Remember, Rosemary," she said. "Nothing lasts."

∽

It was weeks after Mother's death before I slowed from the manic activity that marked the days following the funeral. A madness held me. I quickly closed Remarkable Hats, sold off the stock or returned it to suppliers for credit against accumulated debt. I was helped and advised by Chaps, and by Mr. Frank (the nine-and-three-quarters).

There was no other decision to be made. It isn't true that he who dies pays all debts: I couldn't preserve the store any more than I could our life together. Mother and I had depended on a complex web of credit and postponed payments, revealed once she was gone as a great tangle of insolvency.

I cleaned the flat, the three rooms I'd lived in my entire life. I couldn't tolerate the space without her; every article reflected her absence. I kept the only photograph I had of her, taken before I was born. After that, she'd always been behind the camera with me as subject.

Those first days I was a somnambulist, but it wasn't like living a waking dream, even a nightmare, it was its opposite. My whole life up until her death had been the dream, and this reality— the one without Mother, the one where every object I thought mine was either sold or returned, where everything familiar to me disappeared—had waited, hidden behind all I loved.

Suppliers were kind but businesslike. Only the girls at Foys sent a condolence card. I sold off the furniture and the contents of the flat, but after settling accounts, there was little money left. Chaps moved me into her spare bedroom and encouraged me to rest. As my mania subsided, stupor took its place. Chaps urged me to come into her bookstore, where I had worked before, usually stock-taking, during school holidays. Chapman's Bookshop was cozy, safe; and the small tasks we performed together helped stave off a wave of terrible passivity.

"No one dies so poor that something isn't left behind," Chaps said one afternoon, as we unpacked a box of books together. "You are what your mother left, Rosemary. You've got to make good on that legacy. I know you will."

Her talks became daily affairs. I just listened.

"You have to think of your mother's passing as the way to get out. To escape. You have to begin your life," Chaps would urge.

Esther Chapman took very seriously the opportunity to advise me. She'd always been a sort of maiden aunt, and I loved her. But after all I'd taken care of in the past weeks, after what I'd lost, I was languid with grief. Before Mother's death, I hadn't any idea of real despair, even while I'd been hurtling toward it for eighteen years.

Chaps was stoic, and that helped. She'd lost her own mother after a long illness, and lived in her childhood home. Her father—an Anzac, as it happens—had been killed in the Great War. When called a spinster, Chaps would say: "And far better off that way, not that it's anyone's business." She shared a similar social position to that of Mother (invisibility), and their recognition of this was what had first made them friends. They were oddities, marginal and not exactly respectable. For her part, Chaps was too well read to be considered entirely proper. Books had made her unreasonably independent.

Judging by photographs in her neat house, with age, Chaps resembled her own mother. Both had pigeon-breasted bodies, small gray heads, large light eyes full of candor. I set my only picture of Mother beside one of Chaps's mother in the living room. The silver frame wasn't terribly old, but there was something timeless in Mother's photograph. Black-and-white, it had been taken when she was around eighteen, my age exactly at the time, but taken by whom I would never know. Her youthful face looked out at me vivid with the secrets of her past, her future, and, I fancied, more alive than I was in that same unformed moment.

∞

At the end of that first month, sick with my own drowsy sorrow, I took the Huon box outside Chaps's tiny house and sat in the neat square of her garden, bordered with flowers that repeated themselves on three sides. The orange, red, and yellow heads worked against melancholy; their unopened leaves, like little green tongues, reproached me. I picked a few red ones, Mother's favorite color, and put them on top of the box.

I knelt down to inspect a large, open leaf, an almost perfect circle. A silver drop of water balanced on its surface, shiny as a ball of mercury. Carefully, I picked the leaf and spun the bead of water inside its green world—a tiny ball of order, isolated and contained. Focusing on the drop relieved an increment of anguish, about the same size, near my heart.

"Help me," I prayed to the water drop. "I want Mother. I want it all back. I want my life."

Chaps arrived home early from the shop. I heard her fussing with the kettle, making tea in the kitchen. She called through the little house.

"I'm out here, Chaps!" I replied.

"Ah, I wondered, dear," she said, coming outside. "Lovely here in the garden. What are you doing on your knees? You look as if you're praying to the flowers."

"It makes me feel better," I said, embarrassed. "They look so happy, with their bright faces. They smell like ants, though, these flowers . . ."

"Nasturtium is their variety, and I'm sure I don't know what ants smell like." She raised her eyebrows. "But I've no doubt you do."

The tea kettle whistled and she went in briefly to turn it off and brew the tea.

"I see you have her ashes with you," she said, coming out with a tray.

Perhaps she considered a talk about the maudlin nature of my attachment to the Huon box, but let it go. She sat down on a wrought-iron chair, after laying the tray on the matching table.

"I've something to talk with you about," she said, growing serious.

"I know what you're going to say, Chaps."

"You only think you know," she said, pouring out two cups.

"You're going to tell me again that ambivalence is fatal," I said to the leaf.

She had been saying such things all week.

"You'll tell me to give sorrow words. You're going to say that I must choose, decide, begin to make my way. You're going to suggest I bury these ashes—"

"Well, I certainly would say all those things," Chaps cut in. "And have said all those things, but that's not what I have to tell you."

She sat up straighter, filled with the drama of surprise. She hesitated, then took a deep breath.

"I bought you a ticket today. An airplane ticket. I want no argument about it—I had the money saved. Guess where you're going?"

I stared at her, unable to answer. Did she want me gone? Was she sending me away?

"Can't guess," she said. "I thought it would be easy."

I was silent.

"You love cities, but the only one you've ever been to is Sydney. It's not to there, so don't consider that one."

I couldn't imagine what she'd done, or what I'd done to want her rid of me. I had no money for school. I had no means to travel. I had nothing, so far as I could see, but her affection for me, a box of ashes, and a black-and-white photograph of someone I had loved more than life.

"Come on, why don't you guess?"

I couldn't guess. I had that new, hurtling feeling again, the rapid and unpredictable movement of events coming toward me, like getting into a car after a lifetime spent walking. I thought I'd just stay in Tasmania with Chaps, that she'd teach me the book trade. That I'd live as she did, quietly and in my head.

"I've bought you a ticket to . . ." She paused dramatically, and with an uncharacteristic flourish.

"New York!"

I dropped the leaf, sat back on my heels and, after a confusing moment, burst into tears.

"Now, now. I'm not throwing you out, my dear Rosemary." Chaps bent across and patted my shoulder, my back. She was awkward with affectionate gestures. Her voice remained firm.

"Out of tears, plans!" she said, and handed me the handkerchief she kept folded and tucked inside the sleeve of her cardigan. I never carried one.

I wiped my eyes and nose.

"There now, dear. If you really think about it you'll see you're ready to go. The best is not past. Your mother's death is a break in your life but your life is not broken. You can mend it by living it, by living a different life than either you or your mother imagined."

"I have imagined it though, Chaps," I said, thickly. I had, but I was afraid. More than I'd ever been. "I want to leave and travel. I want to discover things, to know things. But I'm frightened. And now you've gone and sorted it out for me. You've taken away my excuse." I blew my nose on her handkerchief.

"I've done nothing but make the decision for you about where to start, Rosemary. And that was easy because of your scrapbook, all those pictures of New York, of cities. I thought you must have always intended to go there, making a fetish of the place, collecting up clippings and things since you were small. All I've done is give you a push. I'm sure your mother would have done the same thing."

Chaps herself became a little teary. But she was vehement, too.

"You have to get away, Rosemary. You must go abroad! It's what I would have done, my girl, in a minute, if I'd had the chance."

Her filmy gray eyes locked on mine. Chaps could be fierce. "It never came for me, Rosemary. The chance to really make a break, to leave and not look back. Now you must go. You must begin! It's what your mother would want for you, my dear Rosemary. What I want for you. A larger world. You know now where to start. We've a couple of weeks left together to arrange everything."

∽

New York was a fantasy. It was Sydney multiplied, which was all I could imagine then of a great city from the peculiar vantage of Tasmania. It was true I had kept a scrapbook of images since I was small, and many were of New York, but that fact was secondary to the freedom the pictures represented. Liberation was in the very scale of the city: a goldfish bowl one could never grow to fit. I had postcards of tall buildings sharp against the sky, of the magnificent interiors of train stations and libraries illuminated by slanting shafts of light. Spaces between pictures I had filled with bits of ribbon, buttons, and flakes of colored felt.

I hadn't consciously imagined traveling to New York, or to any other city but Sydney, while Mother was alive. But Chaps had guessed the shape of my deepest wish: I thought my father lived in a city. I didn't know where. A place free and anonymous and far away. The opposite of Mother. Father could only be foreign. Unknown and mysterious.

My father was a city; the scrapbook my attempt to make him real. In the absence of an actual photograph, any one of the faceless men in the postcards or newspaper clippings of cities could be him. Many of the images were old street scenes, and Mother used to say, "Look at all the men wearing hats! Those were the days to be in business!"

She never guessed at my real interest—I didn't know it myself. My father was in a city, any city, and I was collecting evidence, clues to his existence. He had long before suffered a sea change.

As Mother gave me no tangible detail of him to build upon,

19

my fancy was as real to me as any fact. She barely knew him, and what she did know she'd kept to herself, would keep to herself, forever.

How much Esther Chapman did for me, letting me go as she did! As a reader of fables, she must have recognized that I would need one of my own. An antidote to catastrophe. My world had been emptied of all its contents, save her, and she knew a city would be the cure to the small life I had lived, the one I'd lost.

But it was myself I was calling into being.

CHAPTER

THREE

⁓ I arrived in New York late at night, unprepared for a life I only dimly suspected might be found there. A storm caused the plane to land roughly. I never saw my destination; clouds covered the city, the ground visible only moments before the plane's wheels struck it. I felt myself land hard, as if thrown to earth.

I had three hundred dollars. In my suitcase, underneath my clothes, lay my scrapbook and Mother's photograph. At the airport, with tears on her cheeks, Chaps had pressed upon me two presents: a green stone necklace (the color of my eyes) which she assured me was an amulet against further heartbreak, and a small book—her very favorite, she claimed—wrapped in her store's bluish paper. I couldn't bear to open the package, the Chapman's Bookshop paper as dear and familiar to me as the wallpaper in my childhood bedroom, in fact, its surrogate. I told Chaps that I would keep her parcel intact, waiting for the day that I desperately needed a present. I didn't doubt it would come, and for the moment, travel was gift enough. The necklace, though, I put on immediately. A guard against heartbreak couldn't wait.

Mother's ashes were covered in an orange scarf at the bottom of a carry-on I was reluctant to put down.

My arrival was not auspicious. The rain continued, veiling the city, and when the taxi I took from the airport tried to deposit me in front of the residential hotel Chaps had booked, it appeared to no longer be in business. I couldn't have known it, but I had arrived in the final year of a difficult decade for the city. New York itself was stirring from years of financial hardship, and many inexpensive hotels then housed residents permanently courtesy of the state.

Terrified, I agreed to an additional fare and the driver took me farther downtown to a hotel he knew was cheap and, he said, safe. The Martha Washington Hotel for Women had a dingier address (29 East Twenty-ninth Street or 30 East Thirtieth Street, depending on the entrance), but it was open, with a room vacant at the right price. There was little evidence that it had once been an impressive establishment, even prosperous, with many rooms. Built in 1902, the hotel was now dilapidated. More than seven decades after it opened, the upper floors were closed off for repairs that would never eventuate. The restaurant had been shuttered for thirty years.

A woman sat behind the battered reception counter watching a tiny black-and-white television, connected by twin earplugs. She was striking and dark, about sixty, with aristocratic features. After I had her attention, she explained the hotel requirements in heavily accented English: payment a week in advance, linens changed once a week, no guests in the rooms, no smoking, no cooking, no noise.

I had no intention of breaking any rules. I was barely eighteen years old, absent Mother and country, soaking wet, and so bereft that I sagged inside my damp clothes, shrunken and childlike.

I paid the taxi driver, handed over one week's rent, and staggered to my room at the end of a shadowy corridor. I took the Huon box from my bag and placed it beside my pillow.

"Come back," I said aloud to Mother, my voice thin and trembling. "Come to me here."

It was hours before I slept, kept awake by sadness, by anxiety, and by cars passing on the avenue, their headlights flashing in the room like counterfeit lightning, tires plashing into potholes where rainwater pooled.

∼

A *hot June* sun appeared the following day, the weather surprisingly steamy. I spent that early summer week trying to stay out of the dun-colored room as much as possible. The room was fetid by early afternoon. A single, clouded window, with bars across it, faced the bed. I had to keep the window closed against the street noise and also because this wing of the Martha Washington was downwind from an Indian restaurant on the next block.

At first, I shared a grubby bathroom with two women along the same corridor, although they might as well have been phantoms. They banged around slamming doors and drawers, but I never once saw either of them except from behind—in retreat. They soon disappeared altogether, a fate I feared awaited every fresh arrival to the city. If I sat in the room during hot daylight hours I felt I had been sealed into my predicament, held inside a shrinking box, with no escape but sleep. I woke early, claimed the bathroom first, and promptly ventured out. My life depended on it.

The dark lady of the reception desk appeared to live at the Martha Washington. I heard her speak Spanish to a stern man I gathered was the owner, and I called hello to her each day as I left to investigate the city, as much to speak aloud as for politeness. But after several days without acknowledgment, I stopped. She was either too intent on the television or hard of hearing. Or perhaps she simply didn't care to answer.

The labyrinthine city waited. It anticipated me. I was swallowed whole, surrounded by a populace buzzing and purposeful, a remedy for grief and a goad to it. I was utterly alone, and lived at first without the imposition of order, too scattered and overwhelmed to effect any. I recognized no vista. No building was familiar, apart from the iconic Empire State and the Chrysler (motifs of my scrapbook), but even those were unrecognizable from my altered perspective on the ground. I forgot to eat, and an entire day would pass before I spoke out loud. Even then it might just be an acknowledgment of thanks, or a plain request: "Could I have milk in my tea, please?" My own voice was alien and took my ear strangely. No one addressed me, no one knew my name, and my anonymity was at times a raw joy in my chest, freedom at its most literal, while at others, a source of paralyzing fear. I didn't know then that this was how deep emotion most often comes, from opposite directions and at once, when you are least aware and farthest from yourself.

I did know profound dislocation, and had to remind myself that the young woman I caught sight of in store windows was me. She had no family. No one expected her home. Yet she existed. There she was reflected in the glass, her wild red hair on end as if with fright.

∽

I needed money and I needed work. I had to know who I might become. I walked and walked around the immediate neighborhood, tracing a large circle, the Martha Washington and Twenty-ninth Street the fixed foot of my compass. I was searching for something I recognized, apart from what I found in my own face, for a sense of the familiar in the unaccustomed.

By odd happenstance I had landed at the eastern edge of New York's garment district. The streets surrounding the Martha Washington were known for their small accessory suppliers, and tiny storefronts displayed crowded windows full of hats and caps, wigs and handbags, sparkling appliqués and notions of all kinds. It was as if Mother had herself selected the location of my first residence without her. There was a looking-glass quality, almost antipodean, to my immediate location. Mother and Remarkable Hats, the Foys workroom, were far away on the other side of all things, and yet in New York I was surrounded by their emblems.

I ventured farther downtown and actually walked past the Arcade on several occasions without realizing what it was—the largest used-book store in the city. I hadn't heard of its reputation for housing lost things: books once possessed and missed or never possessed and longed for. I hadn't read Herman Melville; only his famous name was familiar (just another on the rather limited stock list at Chapman's Bookshop). And I knew nothing whatsoever of the value of rare manuscripts. I fancied bookstores were generally similar to each other, in their way. But the Arcade was of an altogether different order; and because then I was in every sense lost, once I was inside, it proved irresistible.

The Arcade's charm is oddly absolute, but that day it was also intensely personal. Walking into the store, I had walked into an image from my postcard collection, into a picture pasted in my scrapbook. I was inhabiting space I thought imaginary. In this way, I had the distinct impression that I had conjured the Arcade up, had made it appear, a whole cloth woven from unexpressed need.

From the unimpressive entrance, the ceiling rises in an enormous curve toward the rear of the store, a sweep of space that lifts one's eyes upward in search of another firmament. Of course, there isn't one; the ceiling is just a deep, dusty dome, like the inside of a skull. (Both are vaults, both repositories of knowledge.) How could so slight a portal reveal so impressive a space? It occurred to me that I had been tricked into entering.

Understand, the Arcade is itself a city; itself an island. That bookstores are such places is always hoped for, but the Arcade is like the original wish behind such hopes. In that first visit New York was made actual. The Arcade was population, mass, was the accomplishment of a city. Books were stacked like the teeming New Yorkers, invisible inside their buildings, but sensed as bees in a hive. The

25

hum of life issuing from the crowds that filled the city I had begun to experience, but in the Arcade that buzzing life was made calculable in things. Chaps always told Mother and me books were minds on the shelf. Here it was true: books didn't seem inanimate; a kind of life rose from the piles heaped on tables before me.

I moved toward a laden table and placed my hand upon the closest stack, listening, waiting. I recall it exactly. An opening, a beginning. I must work here, I thought. I will. Less an act of confidence than of desperation. I surprised myself.

I looked around in the soft, faded light. I wasn't startled by the Arcade's shabby randomness, by the small areas of order within a more general chaos; by its filth, its quiet, and its occasional bursts of jarring sound. Or by the precariousness of book stacks which seemed to lean, without regard to gravity, toward some apprehended but unseen center. I was at home. Dust filtered what sunlight made its way through two dirty windows. Huge, dim lights hung by heavy chains above customers' heads, bent in concentration.

Turning to the entrance, I checked that outside on the avenue it was actually a sunny, ordinary day in late June. Inside, it was cool and obscurely timeless.

I edged along goat-track passages winding between stacks, only navigable foot in front of foot, a few inches at a time, trying to avoid piles of titles stacked and leaning against spine-out-only shelves. I stopped before a raised platform, an oasis of space amid the clutter. A small man stood behind its oak railing, elevated higher than even the tallest customer. He was pricing old books, but his compelling gestures suggested a priest at a lectern. The brass nameplate that faced the store from his oak desk shone: GEORGE PIKE, PROPRIETOR.

His gestures were practiced and repetitive. A stack of volumes sat to Pike's left. He took a book from the top of that pile, frowned, ran his eyes over the binding, checking for rips or nicks. Then, quickly and elegantly, he flipped to the title page, his eyes scanned the copyright, his thumb fanned rapidly along the edges of the entire book. Reaching the end, he closed the volume, only to reopen it at the first page. He took a pencil from behind his ear and lightly scribbled in the upper-right-hand corner, tracing a looping filigree. He returned the pencil above his ear and rubbed his index finger beneath his nose. He then unfrowned his forehead, set the volume to his right and, having priced the book, immediately reached for another at his left.

He repeated these actions as a single gesture, without variation. It was unconscious; a rough magic. There seemed no moment for contemplation, for the weighing of competing possibilities. Pike alone appeared the arbiter, the heart of the enterprise.

I had made my pledge to work in the Arcade, Pike was evidently its captain. I wanted proximity to such mastery, such certainty. I seized upon the existence of the place like a buoy floating in the middle of the sea.

"Excuse me, sir. My name is Rosemary Savage," I said to Pike, my own accent peculiar, nasal in my ears.

He was unaccustomed to interruption. I went on hurriedly, shocked at my own boldness, at how sharp was the desperation that prodded me forward.

"I have worked in a bookstore before, Mr. Pike. And I must work here."

He looked up from his task to register my temerity. Raised eyebrows were the only indication of affront on his rather unremarkable face. He was an anachronistic figure. His striped waistcoat, his shirt bunched above the elbows by armbands, suggested a man that hadn't altered his style of dress in decades. He wore a waxy-looking mustache, a darker shade than his whitish-gray hair, and he ran his finger over it before lowering his eyebrows to return his gaze to the book in his hand.

"You *must* work here?" he said in an odd, thin voice. He appeared to address the book in his hand rather than me, asking the cheeky thing if it really had the gall. "Do you imagine this an infrequent request?" he asked the book.

I didn't know what to say. Too much was already at stake. I looked up at him and calculated that his platform was a good twenty-four inches higher than where I stood. It was designed to meet the floor at an angle, masking its height and disguising its purpose. It was a stage. I guessed Pike a full head shorter than my own five feet ten, but recognizing this didn't reduce his stature. He loomed, flanked by books.

But I had given Pike my future, and I wonder now if he saw this himself. There was a long pause as he made his way through his litany of gestures. His movements seemed the process by which he could figure the book's price, winding himself up to calculating its value.

He set the volume to his left.

I waited. He drew a long breath.

"What we want here is the mild boredom of order. Don't try to be too interesting, girl." He read me as easily as the book he had put down.

"Find the Poetry section and begin to shelve what remains on the floor." He waved his hand in a shooing gesture. "You're probably ripe for poetry," he added, in a lower voice.

Was he hiring me on the spot?

"Order by poet, mind you. Only by poet. Don't give a damn about editors and translators—that's all a charade. You will shelve by poet or you will not be employed by George Pike. Remove all anthologies! Alphabetical, that is all. There are a few things that should be predictable."

I had followed this breathlessly, even while it didn't appear to be directed at me. Had he said "ripe"?

"Ah, yes, sir. Mr. Pike . . . ah, alphabetical, of course."

"Find Poetry and my manager will assess your competency shortly."

He picked up the next unvalued volume to his right.

I hurried deeper into the Arcade and found the Poetry section halfway down a tower that leaned dangerously toward the public toilet, in a far corner. Quickly I began the task of rearranging books that had apparently never been shelved in any order. The section began at eye level. Above it appeared to be books on Occult Practices. The juxtaposition of subjects struck me as deliberate, only accidentally alphabetical. To reach the shelf I had to lean across a tall pile of books on the floor, awkwardly moving volumes around, my arms stiffly extended. I decided to take handfuls off the shelf and sort them while sitting on the floor. This too proved pointless, as I had to constantly reorder each section, accomplishing only what amounted to tidying up. Was this a test of my patience, of my real interest, a practical lesson in the overwhelming nature of bringing even the slightest amount of order to the Arcade?

After half an hour I'd barely managed to complete a single shelf, and was standing with my back to the aisle, wresting another few volumes off the shelf, when I had the sensation of being watched. I heard a sibilant whisper and turned, promptly dropping the books in my hand.

An albino man of uncertain age was no more than two feet from me, his pale eyes moving involuntarily behind pince-nez glasses. From the first it was his eyes. His eyes could not be caught. He stepped back and knocked over several books I had set aside. Ig-

noring his clumsiness, he took in my surprise with practiced unsur-
prise. I had never seen anyone like him, nor any face more marked
with defensive disdain.

"Walter Geist, the Arcade's manager," he whispered, turning.
"Follow me, girl."

I picked up the books I'd dropped, forced them onto the shelf,
and caught up with him as his stooped shoulder disappeared around
a corner stack.

As I trailed behind his quaint figure, I had the fleeting fantasy
that this man was what someone would look like if he'd been born
inside the Arcade, never having left its dim confines. Pigment
would disappear and eyesight would be ruined beneath weak light,
until one lay passively, like a flounder on the ocean floor.

In fact, as I walked behind him, Geist's white ears reminded
me of delicate sea creatures suddenly exposed to light, vulnerable
and nude. There was a shrinking quality to him, a retraction from
attention like an instinctual retreat from exposure. I was fascinated
and repulsed in equal measure, a contradiction that was never to
leave me. As I follow him there in my memory, I feel again that
charge to his strangeness, a shock that compelled.

He led me to a small office in the very rear of the store, built
high into the corner of the vast ceiling like a reef. I followed him up
a narrow flight of wooden stairs, the handrail loose and broken.

"Wait here, girl."

He indicated the patch of landing at the entrance to the office.

"My name is Rosemary, Mr. Geist. Rosemary Savage," I said,
tired of his anonymous address. I extended my hand then, thinking
it appropriate, brave even, as I had seen Americans do. His hands remained clasped behind his back. He entered the office and
reemerged holding several forms.

"Please fill these out. Print only."

He handed me a pen and stood examining the activity on the

floor below. From that high landing the chaos of the Arcade was fully evident, with the exception of Pike's platform, where he moved as if choreographed, a small flicker of concentrated activity. I leaned over the rail, following the inclination of Geist's head, to see what drew his attention. An obese man sat on the floor in a cul-de-sac made by piles of books, his legs splayed out like a toddler's. He was turning the pages of a large photography book with one hand, his other hidden beneath the heavy covers opened across his lap. Even from the landing I could tell the images in the book were nudes.

"What are you looking at?" Geist asked me.

"Ah, just looking down where you were," I said nervously.

"I don't mean that," he said. "What do you see?"

I described the fat man studying the photographs.

"Arthur!" Geist called down from the landing. "You should be shelving."

"Just familiarizing myself with my inventory, Walter," Arthur returned sardonically, his accent British and articulate.

He looked up at me and put a thick finger to his lips, indicating silence. Had I informed on him? Couldn't Geist see what I had seen? Arthur returned to his nudes, his hand beneath the book's cover moved rhythmically.

Geist stomped his small foot with impatience, and I noticed he was wearing elegant, polished boots, their smooth black shape nosing from his pant legs like the shiny heads of tiny seals.

"Mr. Geist, could I have something to lean on?" I asked, finding it difficult to write legibly without the support of a desk, and wishing to distract him, and myself, from Arthur.

"No," he replied, his shifting eyes still directed over the rickety railing. He removed his glasses, placed them in his breast pocket, and continued to wait for me to complete the forms, his manner uncanny as his appearance.

Now that I was closer to him I could see Geist was younger than I at first thought, perhaps twenty years Pike's junior, in his late forties. He was an unfinished version, a poor copy, of the masterful Pike, yet equally a creature from another time. Every feature was pallid. His hair was white and fleecy, the sheepish outcome of his soft face. His clothes were not as fastidiously kept as his boots, his trousers slightly frayed along the pockets. I completed the forms and handed them back to him.

"You will begin work tomorrow morning at nine," he instructed without seeming to actually address me, a tactic he perhaps learned from Pike.

"You will finish for the day at six. Your responsibilities at the Arcade will, for the time being, be that of a floater. This means you do not belong in a specific section, as you have no expertise, but will float between tasks that are assigned to you. Do not concern yourself with assisting customers, you will only frustrate them with your ignorance."

"I have worked in a bookstore before, Mr. Geist," I said, defensively.

He replaced his glasses, lodging them in the wrinkles of his forehead and frowning to keep them in place—or frowning because he thought me impudent. He leaned in toward my face, and his nostrils twitched as he appeared to take in my scent.

"Not in this one, Miss Savage," he said. "Please do not interrupt. You will receive a salary of seventy dollars per week. There are no advances on wages. Do you have any questions?"

"No," I said, afraid to lose the opportunity.

"Good. There is one more condition of employment you must understand." Geist's pink ears shifted back delicately. "George Pike will not tolerate the theft of money or books. Immediate termination of employment will result if theft is suspected." This last admonition was said in an emphatic whisper.

Later, I saw the statement printed in placard capitals on a sign in the women's bathroom, and again over the clock all employees punched when the day began and ended. Another sign was located directly in the line of vision on the wall in front of the staircase that descended to the cavernous basement. Reading these signs was like being regularly rebuked, and so they paradoxically served to remind patrons and staff alike that theft was in some sense assumed.

George Pike himself called to me as, newly hired, I passed his platform on my way out.

"George Pike will not tolerate the theft of money or books!" he cried, characteristically speaking of himself in the third person.

Theft was a problem, as I would discover. The Arcade was regularly scouted by shoplifters; but more seriously, there had been several scandals involving ludicrously overpriced volumes whose provenance had been fictitiously embellished, resulting in what Pike defended as imaginative pricing. Scandals only increased the number of customers, both sellers and buyers. In other words, theft ran both ways at the Arcade.

∽

"Why you stopped saying hello to me?" the dark lady of the front desk asked loudly when I returned to the Martha Washington. She had taken the earplugs attached to the television from her ears, and I could hear a tinny whining, the sound of cartoons speaking cartoon language.

"I'm sorry," I said, trying to be pleasant. "But I stopped saying hello to you because you didn't respond. I just gave up."

"Don't give up!" she said, enigmatically. "You just got here. That's what can happen in New York. You give up. I know. I come to this country from Argentina. My brother, he own this hotel. My name is Lillian. Lillian La Paco. Still say hello, miss. You the only one who does."

"All right, Lillian," I promised. "I'm Rosemary," and for the second time that day I stuck out my hand, only this time it was taken.

"Rosemary Savage," I told her as we shook hands. "Nice to meet you, Lillian, and I'll still say hello. I'm certainly not about to give up. I just got a job. My first proper job ever."

"Ah," Lillian said wisely. "Then you begin!"

"Yes," I nodded, pleased with her pronouncement. "Yes, now it all begins."

I went to my room at the end of the corridor and locked the door. I'd bought a pound of cherries from a street vendor to celebrate my employment, and I sat on the single bed savoring them. I felt optimistic; felt breath coming back into my flattened-out self.

Now that I had work, surely someone would notice if I died tragically at eighteen, having, say, choked to death on a cherrystone I might have neglected to spit out. I could stop fantasizing about what terrible things might befall me and write home to Chaps, reassuring her and myself. I could stop searching the streets for a sign. I had already found more than I could have imagined.

I pulled the Huon box from its silk scarf and recounted what had happened that day: how strange Pike was but how commanding; how bizarre Geist, and how I was already sure he disliked me; Arthur sitting with his nudes in the art section like a great obscene baby.

I missed Mother with an ache that could only be managed by a sort of separation from ache. A pain so deep that I came to observe its presence at a slant, sensing it crouched, and off to one side. If I could contain the pain in something like a transparent globe, it wouldn't overwhelm me. If I didn't look at it in its dark entirety, I could manage. Speaking to her helped. Chaps had told me I must give sorrow words.

I kissed the smooth Tasmanian heartwood, set it aside, and sat back against the pillows to relish more cherries. I spat a stone across the room, aiming at the metal bucket that served as a garbage bin, and heard a satisfying ping as it hit home.

"This is the beginning," I told Mother. "Don't you worry and I won't either."

I had a job to go to, and was expected at nine. They would know Rosemary Savage there, and notice me gone if I happened to disappear. I was an inhabitant of a great, perhaps the greatest, city. And what was more, I would always have books to read.

CHAPTER

FOUR

～∾ The Arcade existed according to a logic all its own, governed by a set of arbitrary rules invented and maintained by George Pike. Paperbacks were never shelved. As the poor relations of hardcovers, they were heaped without order upon tables near the store's entrance and priced identically—one dollar and fifty cents—whether fiction or history, a thousand pages or barely more than a hundred.

Pike was unimpressed by innovation. Any "new" book (one published within the past two years and hardbound) would never cross his oak table but was immediately sent to a vast, low-ceilinged basement, to be priced by Walter Geist. These books Pike cared nothing for, although he received a daily accounting of their acquisition, at one-quarter of the publisher's list price, and subsequent sale, at one-half of that same price. So if a reviewer brought in a book that the publisher listed at sixteen dollars, Geist would give him a quarter of that, four dollars, and the book would go on the Arcade's shelf in the basement priced at eight dollars.

Every other hardcover book in the Arcade, Pike had held in his hands at one time, remembering more of them than seemed humanly possible.

Pike employed a considerable number of eccentric individuals, Geist aside, and it remained a mystery why he had employed me. I was not eccentric, unless being an eighteen-year-old orphan from Tasmania made me so. As well, a number of the Arcade's employees had rather dramatic aspirations. They were variously failed writers, poets, musicians, singers, and were marked with the clerkish frustration of the unacknowledged, the unpublished. The Arcade's thousands of volumes mocked, in particular, literary aspirations. The out-of-print status of most of the stock was further proof of the futile dream of publication. As a monument to literature, the Arcade had an air of the tombstone about it.

"You will work this morning with Oscar Jarno in Nonfiction," Geist directed, my first morning. "You will follow his orders."

"Oh, that's all right, Walter," Oscar said, his voice mild and confident.

He had approached us soundlessly. He smiled then and touched my arm, almost imperceptibly. I was struck by his appearance, and moved by his gesture, the first indication of kindness since my arrival. Oscar's extraordinary eyes were brass-colored and large; warm as the sun that never reached the Arcade's interior.

"Don't mind Walter," Oscar confided, steering me away from the manager and toward the rear of the store, my elbow cupped in his hand. His touch left me a little breathless; eager to catch every word he spoke.

"He really can't help his officious manner," Oscar went on. "It's important to Walter that he appear in charge. Obviously, he requires all sorts of allowances."

Immediately then, I imagined Oscar Jarno took me into his confidence. He released my elbow once we reached the Nonfiction section, and ran his hand over his pale brow, leaving it to rest at his temple, as if he had a slight headache.

"Your blouse, Rosemary, is made from a type of polished cotton not commonly available in this country. I am interested to see how well it takes the dye."

He fingered my sleeve gently and I thought in that moment that I'd do anything to keep his attention.

"Lovely," he said into my face. "A type of faille."

Oscar was slightly taller than me, and handsome in a poetic sort of way. His head was perfectly shaped, as if sculpted, and the contrast of his golden eyes against the pallor of his skin was dramatic. There was little else dramatic about him—he was soft-spoken, articulate—but there was a magnetism to his face: in the smooth planes of his cheekbones, the wide brow above rich eyes.

When I met him, Oscar had been at the Arcade for five years, and because he was quiet and reliable, Pike had come to accept that he worked only in the Nonfiction section and that whatever Oscar was doing in that suburb of twelve tall stacks would be accomplished with a minimum of fuss. More than a few customers were devoted to him. Oscar passed most of his day seated on a stool, writing in a black notebook, exempt from the loading and unloading of heavy boxes of books. No one questioned his special status.

He knew a great deal about many subjects, but his personal interest was cloth. His mother had been a dressmaker and had introduced him to fabrics—their names and properties.

Pike had occasional use for Oscar's knowledge; he'd ask him to check rare bindings and speculate on their provenance or even how they might best be repaired. Oscar had had some experience with restoration, and with arcane materials like vellum. I witnessed his value to the Arcade during the first days he was training me. Pike called for Oscar from his platform, and I followed as he hurried to respond (the only time Oscar moved quickly).

"Ah, Oscar," Pike said sharply, gesturing to a customer at the base of his platform who held an old volume in his hands.

"We have here *Old Court Life in France*, which should be on its way to the Rare Book Room for repair but has been kidnapped by this fellow. At the risk of encouraging such practices, please examine."

Customers were always trying to snatch books before Pike had appraised them, before they had been allocated a value and destination. No doubt they wanted to believe that they had discovered something of greater worth than Pike would have reckoned.

As I watched, Oscar took the book gently in his hands, turning over the tattered binding, a smile cornering his mouth. Oscar was thin. His skin was so fine and dry it made a slight rustle when his hand moved across his brow, in an anxious sweep. His dark hair receded in a way I quickly loved, revealing, as it did, more of his remarkable face.

"This volume is bound in Chardonnet silk," Oscar said, his voice soft, authoritative. "A fabric named for the French chemist who invented a process to produce it."

Pike's eyes narrowed appreciatively, pleased at the opportunity to overprice the shabby volume based on Oscar's remarks.

"Chardonnet silk was first commercially produced in France in 1891," Oscar added unnecessarily, as the customer was already removing it from his hands in a proprietary way.

"Thank you, Oscar," Pike said, dismissing him.

Pike stretched down from his platform and took the volume from the customer. He then unconsciously proceeded through his ritual gestures—he flipped to the title page, scanned the copyright, his thumb fanned the edges of the entire book, he closed the volume, reopened it at the first page, took a pencil from behind his ear—and marked a reassessed price. He handed it down to the customer.

"But this is outrageous, Pike!" said the man furiously. "Nothing short of robbery!"

"Rosemary," Oscar whispered, as we returned to his section. "Do you know what the common name for Chardonnet silk is?"

"No," I said cautiously. "I've no idea."

"Rayon," he said, stifling a small chuckle. "Made from extruded wood pulp. Not silk at all, of course. Remind me to tell you the history of silk."

He covered his mouth with his fine, long hand and, sitting up on his tall stool, took out a black notebook and began to write in it rapidly.

Oscar's face appeared composed of layers of papier-mâché, and this quality made his face seem expressionless as he wrote. He gave the impression of a man-sized marionette: his head large and shaped upon a soft, slight body. When Oscar looked at me, his round eyes glowed as if they reflected light, but over time I came to understand that this was a trick of their splendid color. The irises were actually golden.

It was something of a trick also that Oscar often sought to engage in conversation by expressing an interest in clothing. He was reserved by nature, phlegmatic, but knew well that an interest in another's clothes flattered the wearer. I imagined this something his mother, the dressmaker, had taught him.

Oscar was sought after by regular customers looking for an insider watchful on their behalf, a staff person willing to perform special favors and engage in secret confidences. Oscar always played for both sides.

The Arcade was frequented daily by several bibliophiles who obsessively searched for fresh inventory: books that were stacked to be shelved after Pike had priced them. Oscar was especially favored by two competing Civil War buffs, both of whom bought his consideration with morning coffee, the occasional lunch. Small cloth-wrapped bundles (like Japanese favors) would appear at intervals, bribes for withholding books from sale. Oscar wasn't particularly interested in the Civil War, except for the uniforms, but he was knowledgeable about the volumes in his section and managed to conduct intense conversations with collectors in diverse subjects— history, biography, philosophy, anthropology, science.

I consciously chose to emulate him. Oscar was quick, and remembered most of what he'd heard or read. He wrote everything down. Impressionable as I was, I took to carrying a small notebook, determined to assume for myself Oscar's observant style.

It is through my own notebook that I recall these days, my first months in the city, my apprenticeship. And through my clear recollection of that girl who was so raw, so avid, that she ate up every detail, absorbing into her body whatever might later be needed as provision, whatever might sustain her should it all, once more, disappear.

∽

At the Martha Washington, I befriended Lillian slowly, in increments, for she was prickly.

"What are you watching there, Lillian?"

"I am not watching, Rosemary," she answered, her eyes flickering from the television screen for an instant.

"It looks like you're watching," I ventured.

"Everything not how it looks. Especially not here. I am not watching, but I am thinking. Watching help me to think, and sometimes not to think."

"I don't know how you can think with those things in your ears and the sound turned up so loud."

"I need that noise. I don't hear so well. But I'm thinking all the same," she said, removing the earplugs.

"What do you think about, Lillian?" I asked, wanting to know her, needing a friend. She was a little older than Mother, but younger than Chaps. She was the only person I knew outside the Arcade, and really the first person I met in New York.

Lillian heaved an enormous sigh, and closed her eyes against the tears that had filled them.

"I cannot say what I think of," she answered, thickly.

I couldn't understand what I had provoked with my question. Confused and embarrassed that I'd been unwittingly careless, that I'd upset her, I was about to apologize. But Lillian visibly collected herself, focused instead on the television, her expression changing rapidly into one of disdain.

"Well," she said, sniffing. "One thing I think from this television is that Americans are stupid!" She waved her hand at the small screen.

"Oh, I don't think Americans are stupid," I said, thinking of Pike, of Oscar. "I have a job now, at an enormous bookstore, and it's full of brilliant Americans. Readers!"

"Pah," Lillian said, smiling, recovered by the change in subject, by her sense of humor. "You only think they are brilliant," she imitated my accent, "because you are a child."

"Lillian, I'm eighteen years old," I said, indignant.

She nodded as if to say, "Exactly—you are a child."

"They have Spanish books in that store where you work?" she asked.

"I don't know, but I'll look for you. I think you can find anything in the world at the Arcade."

"You can't find what I'm looking for," she said, darkly. "But bring me Spanish books if you have. I will pay you for them. I maybe should be trying to read again. And to forget about these idiots."

Before she replaced the earplugs and turned her attention back to the television screen, she handed me a letter.

"This come for you," she said. "From your country."

"Thank you, Lillian."

The letter was from Chaps. I hurried to my room eager to read my first letter in America. It was disappointingly short.

July 5

Dearest Rosemary,

Thank you for your card. Tasmania is a lonely place without you, without your mother, but, as I like to say, loneliness is good practice for eternity.

I was heartened to hear from you and thrilled that you would so soon have found yourself employed—and in a bookshop! I couldn't wish a better occupation for you, my dear Rosemary. My own little shop has given me a dignified, ethical life, and work I believe meaningful. Selling books provided shape to my life, and reading them, a shape to my mind that I doubt I could have formed otherwise. That you are employed in such an extraordinary place gives me great satisfaction. (Perhaps I was training you all along!) The difference, though, is that you are also immersed in experience, and not just taken up with lines on a page.

You will find interesting people, you will read, you will be able to live the way you want. I have heard of the Arcade, of course, but never imagined you would find your way there.

I'm sure your mother is with you always, but her absence is perhaps at times unendurable. For me it is. Don't be frightened to love. Look for it. I want you to have the life I did not choose. Take it, Rosemary dear.

With all my love, I am your own,

Esther Chapman

P. S. Have you opened the package yet? Remember, a book is always a gift.

∽

George Pike was not a demonstrative man. As he worked on his platform in a reverie of pricing, his gestures were reverential, ritualistic. His intention was that he remain inaccessible, above us all. Geist was his foil and henchman. Pike had a deep love of books, but his motivation for maintaining the Arcade was not esoteric. His chief inducement was evident: Pike loved money.

In slow moments—when gathered together awaiting a shipment, or lining up on Fridays to receive our meager pay from Geist— the staff liked to pick over rumors of Pike's legendary wealth, his frugality, his stinginess. Each secondhand book passed through his elegant hands because he trusted no one but himself to assess its value. No one else could, the value being weighed not only against some actual market notion but against his very personal assessment of the book's worth to him: what it cost him to acquire, and what the volume's sale would put in his pocket. The margins and his profit were tabulated instantly, the result of years of obsessive deliberation, an abacus in his head shifting beads back and forth in a silent, urgent reconciliation.

That Pike was exceedingly rational didn't mean that his notion of value wasn't arbitrary. It was particular and absolute, almost adolescent in its despotic insistence.

At intervals throughout the day and at closing time, Pike would momentarily replace Pearl, the Arcade's rather arresting cashier, then a preoperative transsexual, at the single register. Pike would remove larger bills, checks, and credit-card receipts, then disappear up the broken wooden stairs to the office at the back, reappearing (as in a conjurer's trick) moments later upon his platform, behind his table, a book in his hand, a pencil behind his left ear, his meditative pricing resumed. Pike shrunk considerably whenever he left his platform, only to attain his previous consequence once he returned to the stage.

That there was a single cash register was an instance of the Arcade's antiquated operation and evidence of Pike's apprehensions with regard to money, with regard to theft. Contradiction was key, and efficiency mattered not at all.

Although there were lulls in customer purchases, for most of the Arcade's business hours a queue snaked single file through and past the tables of paperbacks. Customers would become impatient and occasionally abusive while waiting. It was something of a sport among the staff to inflame already angry customers while they waited in line, a game that shocked me at first, unfamiliar as I was with that sort of impoliteness, schooled as I had been by Mother and Chaps to treat customers obeisantly.

"I've been standing here for thirty minutes!" a disgruntled customer would complain.

"Today's your fucking lucky day then," Bruno Gurvich, a burly Ukrainian who sorted paperbacks at the front tables, would shoot back. "Pearl must be picking up the pace a bit! Yesterday you'd have been here an hour at least."

Bruno was a musician with the temperament of an anarchist and the breath of a bartender's dishrag. He gave the lie to book-selling as a genteel occupation, to Chaps's ideal.

Bruno winked at me when he noticed my horror at this sort of exchange.

"Don't look so shocked, girlie," he said, dumping paperbacks in front of me. "Pike doesn't care how you talk to the regulars so long as they're buying. I got two separate assault charges pending for roughing up customers over Christmas last year, when we were really busy. This is nothing."

No doubt he was trying to impress me.

"I wouldn't be boasting about that, Bruno, if I were interested in keeping my job."

Geist had appeared behind me; he was always sneaking around, his sibilant voice making the hair on my neck stand up, his whiteness like a visible reproach.

"That's Pike's concern, not yours," Bruno said contemptuously, and stalked off.

"I'd keep away from that one," Geist warned, standing uncomfortably close to me. "A n-nasty p-piece of work," he stuttered slightly. "Come to me if he gives you any trouble."

I watched him bump into a table as he headed back to the base-ment, and I imagined he was returning to the bottom of the sea.

∽

Pearl Baird, the cashier, was, apart from Geist, Pike's most trusted staff member on the main floor. I loved her. She had taken the name Pearl after the biblical parable, and indeed she gave everything she had to become her female self, to become Pearl. Sitting behind the register, the no-nonsense slash of her lips a brilliant vermilion, she was unconcerned by the repetitive nature of her task.

Life had taught her patience.

Although she had a loving nature, Pearl was steely in her con-tempt for restless customers who often hurled down the books they had been holding for far too long, belligerently tossing cash or credit cards at her. Pearl took her time to open each cover, look for the price, and punch it into the register, her extended finger tipped with a long nail. (She took pride in her nails and frequently changed the vivid polish.) She muttered things like "Swine before Pearl!" at the most unpleasant types, but her air of superiority was mostly comment enough.

"It's just us girls among all these weird men," Pearl first said to me by way of introduction in the ladies' bathroom. She was ag-gressively applying lipstick as I washed my hands. Our eyes met in the mirror above the sink, and we smiled simultaneously.

"We girls got to stick together, you and me," she said. "We're friends already, I can tell."

Pearl was large, with enormous hands and feet, a beautiful long, brown face, and a singing voice that rang in the bathroom like a fleshy bell. She was an aspiring opera singer, and spent most of her two fifteen-minute breaks sitting on a ruined vinyl couch in the anteroom of the ladies' bathroom, rifling through a large bag of sheet music or humming to a tape played on a portable player. She took rehearsal very seriously and would repeat a difficult phrase, working on her diction and pitch, over and over again. She took lessons from a professional opera teacher after work, paid for by her Italian boyfriend, Mario. He was mad about Pearl, and had promised to pay for her operation after she'd lived the requisite year as a woman.

Pearl earned the reluctant respect of George Pike through her diligence and consistency, but chiefly through her willingness to perform a job that no one else could tolerate for more than a day. Only Pike or Walter Geist relieved Pearl on her breaks. She could detect any attempts to alter Pike's scribbled prices, and was merciless on the few occasions when fraud was suspected. At her command, customers suspected of shoplifting had been sent sprawling on the sidewalk outside the Arcade by Bruno, ejected like drunks from a bar.

I understand now that Pearl's ferocious honesty derived in part from her mutable sexuality. Truth was crucial to her; she knew her own veracity and had no choice but to live it.

Oscar knew the odd details and sad stories of many of the Arcade's staff. He elicited confidences, chiefly through silence, and sometimes flattery. With the Reference section at his disposal, he looked up details that might further his understanding of an individual's personal history. A gifted researcher, curious to the point of voyeurism, Oscar like to say that the world existed to end up in a book, and that it might as well be his notebook.

He told me, for example, that Pearl's dream was to sing the role of Cherubino, the adolescent boy in Mozart's *Marriage of Figaro*, a role usually performed by a woman playing a man; but she knew that at thirty-five, she was perhaps too old, and that the hormones she took were wreaking havoc with her voice and her body. Oscar had implied that if Pearl thought she had a chance at opera, then it was her mind the medication had affected. It took me rather a long time to understand he could be vicious.

I imagined that, unlike my own poor attempts, Oscar's note-books contained a stream of never-completed biographies of people who struck his fancy or provided an interesting word, the starting point of an investigation. Under "Pearl" he might have written "Cherubino" in his crabbed handwriting, followed by a thumbnail sketch of Mozart's life, a summary of the opera's plot, or the details of gender-altering surgery. Oscar knew that Walter Geist had the kind of albinism known as oculocutaneous. He told me that Geist's eyes never stopped moving because of a condition called nystagmus. Oscar knew all about Gallipoli and the Anzacs, and, of course, I'd told him myself why I was named Rosemary. He knew the Tasma-nian tiger was extinct. He knew I longed for my mother; that I was often lonely.

He was my guide to the Arcade, translator of its strange his-tories and inhabitants. The entire store was his occupation in many ways, his means of making sense of the world. Eventually, I would come to know something of Oscar's own secrets. After we had worked together in his section for a month, he told me the story of his early fascination with cloth.

When Oscar was a child, he'd kept an old hatbox his mother had given him under his bed. It was filled with small pieces of lux-urious fabric she'd clipped from the seams and hems of dresses she made and repaired—fabric far richer and more exotic than anything they could afford. The hatbox was Oscar's treasure and favorite plaything.

He would take out the pieces of fabric—gossamer chiffon, lus-trous silk, thick velvet—and rub them across his face. The box was his source of comfort and pleasure, and although the adult Oscar al-ways dressed uniformly in black trousers and a crisp white shirt, he'd never lost his fascination with fabric. He knew all the fancy names and adjectives—organdy, tulle, crepe de chine, damask, moiré, zephyr, batiste. He knew how they were made: colored, processed, woven.

Scraps of fabric had been Oscar's only toys, but as he grew older he became increasingly bookish. He too had an absent father, was devoted to his mother, and had never lived alone until her death. Oscar's mother had emigrated from Poland as a girl with her parents, but had fallen out with them over Oscar's father, who'd deserted her sometime after his son's birth.

Although he was ten years older, I used to think that in Oscar I'd found my double, a counterpart accidentally born in America, so similar were our circumstances. I thought we matched perfectly—his eternal investigations the match to my endless curiosity. Through his mother's instruction, he'd learned everything important—how to read, how to live an orderly life, and the value of remembering as much as possible. Which is how he'd come to always keep a notebook; his mother had had a dressmaker's book, filled with the measurements and particularities of her customers. He had imitated her, as I copied him, inscribing a life from fragmentary items.

If I'd been older, or really a grown woman at all, I might not have been so moved by Oscar's life, by his story, by our resemblances and correspondences. I might not have clutched the idea of him to me as if it were a secret leaf fallen from a lover's book. But then, my heart escaped me.

George Pike had employed Robert Mitchell for forty years, but their long collaboration had done little to improve an essentially antagonistic relationship. That Mr. Mitchell worked four floors above Pike made their professional interaction possible. Pike himself limited their contact to frequent telephone exchanges, often petty squabbles over money and, in particular, the costs of repairing extremely old volumes and collections of papers, whose fragility found a devoted champion in Mr. Mitchell. The care he took over damaged volumes seemed an extension of the interest he took in the well-being of the motley staff, who gladly rode the cranky elevator up to his own small store-within-a-store. It was a task we bickered over. His presence filled the Rare Book Room with gentility, a trait I now associate with the enveloping reek of a pipe.

Accompanying customers up to the Rare Book Room on the store's fifth floor was my favorite task, once I was actually floating. It was an opportunity for conversation with collectors about their particular tastes and obsessions, and I learned something from every encounter. A trip to the Rare Book Room meant I could visit with Mr. Mitchell and breathe in the vanilla scent of his pipe. I adored him.

The first time I escorted a client up to the Rare Book Room, struggling with the elevator cage, Mr. Mitchell was waiting. Pike had called ahead of our arrival to clear the customer I accompanied for credit approval.

"What a pleasure, young lady! You must be our antipodean newcomer. Rosemary for remembrance, if I'm not mistaken. I am Robert Mitchell," he said with a courtly reach of his hand. "Pleased to meet you."

In his late sixties, with vertical peaks of snowy hair, he had the complexion of a man who didn't manage his blood pressure. He was large and seemed professorial in a saggy, postathletic way. Tall, with an enormous belly that sloped from his breastbone and disappeared into his high-belted trousers; his face reminded me of an amiable bird's. I was at once struck by the odd happenstance that he resembled a type of cockatoo I'd long wished to own (but which Mother had refused me on account of its noise, its mess). This bird too was large, pink and white, but native to Australia and coincidentally named after an historical personage, some early dignitary, a certain Major Mitchell.

"Oscar told me I would enjoy meeting you," I told him, far more comfortable in the Rare Book Room than four floors below. The contrast with the belligerent paperback fellows, Jack and Bruno, couldn't have been more stark.

"Oscar told me the same thing, my dear. And also that you are very far from home. Van Diemen's Land, no less. A rare and beautiful place, I understand. A wild island. We must be sure to make you welcome," he said, and repeated, "We must be sure to."

The warmth in his voice spread through me like the melancholy I carefully, daily, kept at bay. And perhaps because Mr. Mitchell caught me on a particularly homesick day, or because my own lost father could not in my imagination have been more kindly disposed to me, or simply because unexpected kindness exactly locates one's well of sadness, tears itched the corners of my eyes.

"Indeed, Rosemary, you are very far from home," Mr. Mitchell said again, noticing my upset, "but you must feel welcome here. And safe." He took my hand inside his and patted it affection-ately. I had to turn away.

"Now, then, who has accompanied you to my aerie?" he asked in a businesslike way, leaving me to compose myself. "Who has come to see the infinite riches in my little room?" He knew perfectly well, of course.

The customer cleared his throat, impatient to be attended to.

"Ah, Mr. Gosford! Yes, the Beckett first edition, if I'm not mistaken? I've been waiting for you to pick it up."

Mr. Mitchell and the collector, Gosford, moved from the ele-vator into the first of several rare rooms, crowded with volumes and folios.

"Where are we—*Whoroscope*?" he called, and reached toward a shelf to the right of his desk.

"Rosemary, are you interested in an opportunity for instruc-tion?" Mr. Mitchell inquired, still trying to locate the book.

Oscar had prepared me. One of Mr. Mitchell's favorite things to do was teach. (Oscar had said "lecture.") He never waited for as-sent from the prospective student, but would go on, searching for the volume, chatting all the while.

"Let me see, *Whoroscope*, *Whoroscope*. You are very lucky, Mr. Gosford," he said, finally finding the book. "Now, Rosemary, per-haps you are not aware that this," he ran on excitedly, "that this, Beckett's first published poem, was composed in a single night! He wanted to win a thousand francs in a competition which called for submissions of no more than one hundred lines. Yes, that's right. A poem on the subject of Time." He paused thoughtfully. "Time, you see? He won, evidently. Ah, there we are."

He handed the book to Mr. Gosford like his own prize, a re-ward for his patience. The little book had brick-red wrappers and a white band, printed with a note from the publisher. It was incidental to me that it was a book by Beckett, with whom I was unfamiliar. What struck me was that it was a small, beautiful object, and that both men wanted it.

"One of a hundred signed by Beckett, Mr. Gosford. A bit dusty, slight fading at the top edge, no foxing, and otherwise a fine copy. A steal at ten thousand dollars. I've spoken to Pike and your credit is excellent. The bill will be forthcoming."

He leaned away from Gosford, in a perfectly timed motion, as if to better appreciate the moment. He paused.

"Rosemary, no need for you to wait," he took up after a minute. "Mr. Gosford is good for it, I assure you."

I left him to secure the signature. It was the practice of the Rare Book Room that a customer who'd selected and wanted to purchase a book had to be accompanied down to the main floor of the Arcade and straight to Pearl at the register. The potential for theft was the obvious reason for this ritual; but in the case of extremely valuable items, approval was often granted in advance. Customers like Mr. Gosford were billed monthly, so frequent and so large were their acquisitions.

This first visit I rode the elevator down alone, but I was to welcome any opportunity to visit Mr. Mitchell and be warmed by his affection, his information; to be at once reminded of my loneliness and comforted by its acknowledgment.

The other role as escort was to descend to the basement. Walter Geist worked there beneath a single blinding globe of light suspended from a cord attached to the low ceiling, its bare bulb casting shadows along the creases of his face, the only darkness there the hollows of mouth and nostrils. I carried new books to Geist at least two or three times a day, accompanying book reviewers from the city's major newspapers and periodicals. They cast anxious, furtive looks about, hoping not to cross paths with one of their colleagues. It was a shifty business, not exactly stealing but hardly legitimate, either.

Selling copies of books that had been mailed free of charge was considered one of the perks of reviewing. It was impractical for reviewers to keep stacks of books around after reviewing them (or not reviewing them) for a newspaper or magazine, and publishers knew the activity was part of the Arcade's operation—knew that they too lined Pike's pockets—although it wasn't widely sanctioned. When customers requiring escort showed up, Pearl would bellow either "Review!" or "Rare Book Room!" and whoever was on the floor at the time had to scurry up front to meet the waiting customer. I didn't mind, preferring the task of escort to shelving.

I often chatted with the more familiar sellers, asking them for recommendations or whether they'd given the books I carried to the basement a positive or negative review. In this way I came to be on speaking terms with several literary journalists and publishing types. My notebook from that time is peppered with recommendations of books I'm certain I never read. But I much preferred collectors to those disposing of books. Collectors were passionate, at least; opportunistic, but in a different way. Their attachment to books as things, I believed then, had more to do with love than with money. The fact is, collecting has an erotic appeal.

After Geist had tallied up the total of the books sold to him in the basement, he scribbled the amount on a small yellow square of paper and the seller returned upstairs to wait in line at the register. Pearl took the yellow square and dispensed the specified amount in cash. Certain journalists then retired to one of the nearby taverns and drank their unearned dividend, each glass an ironic toast to Pike's financial health.

He didn't return their deference. Pike referred to reviewers as "spivs" and directed Geist to handle the entire enterprise involving new books.

The basement was Walter Geist's domain; Mr. Mitchell's, the fifth floor. Heaven and hell, we used to joke. All of us on the main floor floating in a kind of limbo, Pike watching, raised omnipotently overhead.

Competing for my favorite task of a trip to the Rare Book Room was Bruno (who often had the distinct advantage of being near Pearl at the register, tending to the paperback tables) as well as his ragged-faced colleague, Jack. Pike had designated these two paperback people, and their proximity to Pearl's bellowed calls meant they were more often than not in either the basement or with Mr. Mitchell upstairs.

Jack Conway, an immigrant like me, was a musician, a traditional fiddler, and Irish. He'd had the end of his nose bitten off in a pub brawl and it was now an abrupt silvery edge. The scarred skin was shiny and pale, giving the impression of a punctuation mark in the center of his face that quickened the rest of his ruddy features. Jack seemed not to care how he looked, and his abbreviated nose had little effect on his attractiveness to women. He had a French girlfriend, Rowena, a sullen poet who often stopped in, but several women visited him during the course of a day.

I saw him, more than once, enter the single public toilet with various women. While they both remained inside for a good twenty minutes, customers in need jostled desperately with the locked doorknob.

Jack's hatchet look matched his manner. He was tough, and his thick accent often made him unintelligible to other staff members, including Geist (for all his facility with languages). I understood him perfectly, his Irish brogue not so thick to my Tasmanian ear. But I couldn't translate the filthy flirtatious remarks Jack directed at Pearl, who told me she found his inarticulate muttering exciting. Some I simply couldn't comprehend, but it wasn't a question of diction. It was a harmless attraction that upset Rowena, not because Jack was really interested in Pearl but because Pearl's fleshy laughter made a kind of triangle that included me. As the go-between, I was the one Rowena disliked, suspecting, as I came to, that Jack's mumbled obscenities were intended for my delight as much as for Pearl's.

I stayed clear of him. Mother had been overprotective to the point of mania about sex. Of course, I had my bookish fantasies, my adolescent ardors. But by then, Sidney Carton had been happily traded for Oscar Jarno, for an infatuation I mistook to be other than fictional. I was nervous around men, around all the displaced desire that ran beneath the surface of the Arcade. It wasn't that I ever thought they wanted me; simply that they wanted. I'd had no experience with men, and chose to deposit all ideas of romantic promise with the unattainable—with Oscar.

∽

Every morning but Sunday, mail was delivered to the Arcade by a mailman named Mercer. A rather elegant Trinidadian, he'd lived in New York for many years, and despite his uniform he looked more like a diplomat than a representative of the postal service. Chaps would have cast him as Othello in a minute. Mercer and Pearl were friends, and it was her custom to bellow to Pike across the huge store that the mail had arrived.

At the Arcade, mail was almost as coveted as books.

Letters brought requests for rare titles, offers from estate libraries, queries and contacts from all over the world. Mr. Mitchell would frequently appear right around the time Mercer showed up, and try to charm him into a quick glance through the day's mail. It was a slightly silly exercise, unworthy of him. Mercer wouldn't part with the letters until they were in George Pike's hand, as if he were more courier than postman. And Pike actually ceased his pricing to greet Mercer at his platform and formally receive the clutch of epistles.

Mr. Mitchell would follow, calling Mercer his "man of letters" and hovering about until Pike told him to go away, that any letters for him would be dispatched upstairs once Pike looked them over. It was a pantomime that made Mr. Mitchell appear childish, as if he had been waiting for a letter to drop from Mercer's hands so that he might snatch it up and read it before his magisterial employer.

∽

Shoplifting was a regular pastime for some, and I became familiar with one of the Arcade's more notorious thieves one morning after I answered Pearl's call of "Review books!" a couple of months after I'd started. Tall, about twenty-five, the shoplifter had hair as vivid as my own. He was waiting for me at the front register, leaning against the counter, his long legs crossed in jeans spattered with colored paint. Mr. Mitchell had christened this particular thief Redburn, although I didn't know that at the time.

"I was wondering when you'd accompany me to hell," the man said flirtatiously.

"I don't know you, do I?" I asked, taking several hardcover books from him, part of my job as escort.

"We haven't met before, but it's apparent what we have in common. They call me Redburn here because of it."

"Lots of people have red hair," I replied, ahead of him on the steep stairs. Pike's capitals fairly shouted in my face as I descended: GEORGE PIKE WILL NOT TOLERATE THE THEFT OF MONEY OR BOOKS!

"Pike overdoes that warning, don't you think?" he said, indicating the sign. "It's very threatening."

"Only if you're thinking of stealing," I returned.

We reached the bottom of the staircase.

"Some would say that buying review copies is stealing," Redburn developed. "New books may well have been shoplifted from a regular bookstore."

He challenged me with auburn eyebrows raised, conventionally attractive and confident of the fact.

"Are these stolen?" I asked him, stopping in the maze of stacks that wove through the basement. The low ceiling met the tall shelves, creating an oppressive tunnel through to Geist's lair in the rear.

"Why would you care?" he asked.

It was a question I didn't exactly know how to answer, so I ignored it. I resolved then to generally ignore Redburn as well.

"My guess is you don't approve of stealing, is that right?" he persisted, as we reached Geist's counter, starkly vacant beneath the blinding bulb.

"I don't approve of stealing, no," I replied, stacking the books on the counter. Geist stood some feet away, examining a book held close to his face, his back to us.

"Then give me my heart back," Redburn whispered, leaning toward me, his hands over his chest, feigning pain.

I couldn't help laughing out loud. Geist turned around abruptly, and I wondered if he'd overheard the man's request.

"Check the copyright, Rosemary, then read the list prices to me," he said, coming forward, all business, his glasses firmly in place.

"I wouldn't dream of cheating you, Geist," Redburn said slyly. "Not today at least."

I opened the covers of each book, confirming that they had been recently published, and read out the printed prices to Geist, who reduced them to quarters in his head, calculating what Redburn would receive. He scribbled the total on a yellow square of paper, sliding it across the counter.

"Want to tell me where you got these books?" Geist asked, his finger securing the note.

"Nope," the shoplifter answered, snatching it up.

"I didn't think so," said Geist. "Rosemary, in future you're not to escort this man anywhere in the Arcade. He is banned from the store."

Redburn smiled at me mischievously and headed back upstairs to redeem his yellow slip with Pearl.

I had begun to understand that a significant part of the Arcade's operation was based on deception; few questions were asked about the provenance of books. Whole libraries were bought in bulk sight unseen, and once priced individually by Pike, a few items often earned back what had been spent on the sum. It wasn't cheating exactly, or stealing; it was the canny leveraging of desire. Manipulating the lust for things that retained or lost value depended on whose hands held them.

"Mr. Geist," I asked, before returning upstairs. "Did that man steal the books you just bought?"

"Most likely," he said. "No concern of yours, of course. Just tell Jack or Bruno to throw him out if you see him in here again."

Oscar told me later that Mr. Mitchell had coined Redburn's name for him, and not only because his red hair was vivid enough to be ablaze. Wellingborough Redburn was the protagonist in a novel by Herman Melville, a first edition of which Mr. Mitchell had discovered beneath the thief's tatty shirt, tucked into the waistband of his trousers.

The valuable copy of *Redburn* had been set aside for the Arcade's most prodigious collector, a man who'd never set foot inside the store. Julian Peabody owned the largest private library in the country, and Mr. Mitchell was expecting his librarian, Samuel Metcalf, to pick up the volume from Pike's stage. He had been awaiting that gentleman, along with Walter Geist, an old friend of Metcalf's, when both were distracted by Pike, who chose that moment to argue for an increase in the book's price. While they bickered, Redburn audaciously pilfered it right off Pike's desk. The volume was dislodged accidentally when Bruno slammed into the thief as he hurried from the store.

Peabody acquired the book, and added it to his large collection of nineteenth-century American authors, the most significant outside any private institution. Herman Melville was a Peabody favorite and, shortly after I knew of this incident, Melville would become my favorite as well.

CHAPTER

SIX

I returned in the evenings to the Martha Washington, to Lillian and to the closet of my rented room. After several weeks, the Arcade had become my home, and the city that housed it the larger world Chaps had wished for me and, I realized, that I'd wanted for myself. Tasmania was remote indeed, an ideal of home that merged over time with Mother, with her absence, and with the contradiction of her occasionally overwhelming presence. In the framed photograph, her face at my age returned my own green gaze with dark eyes, projecting a confidence I still hadn't found.

I dreamed she lived often enough to wake with the kind of longing that makes memory eloquent. While I slept she had lived, and the pain upon waking was as much a fleeting uncertainty of her state as anguish over the clear fact of my own life continuing without her. We are never so aware of those we have lost, and dreamt of, than in that waking moment.

I developed the habit of walking for hours in the early evening after leaving work at six, and invented a zigzagging pattern of one block up, one across, to vary my route, reversing the pattern to return downtown. Something soothing in the process reminded me of picking up a practical skill, like learning letters so as to read, or learning steps so as to dance. It was light for hours then, and hot.

The city's grid ordered my mind. I walked as a way of thinking and, walking, I felt as sturdy and sensible as the shoes I'd change into before setting off.

Following a pattern gave me an assurance I often hadn't felt during the working day. My lack of knowledge of the Arcade's vast contents nagged at me, but through my walks I remembered, took note, and played out the day's events. I was determined not to be lost in the city, and through my walks I mapped more than locations and points of reference. I found a way to manage. I let the city work on me, into me, and I learned that I wanted the freedom it held out.

In the evenings, when the city cleared out, there was room for me in the geometry of emptiness that took over certain neighborhoods. The varied architecture taught me a sense of proportion, a contradictory sense even of scale. As I'd learned in Sydney, there was room in cities. Yes, I was a mote inside New York's great, swirling energy, but I was there. At twilight, I was even outlined against buildings, my shadow tall and attenuated upon century-old facades. Using zigzagging increments, I measured myself against blocks, buildings, streetlights. Of course, I was overwhelmed by New York, but was at once oddly freed of any requirement to agency. Although my shadow quickly disappeared as night fell, I carried a memory of its shape long against the great buildings: animated and free.

One hot July evening, I ran down an empty street as the peppery smell of city rain rose up from where the rain fell, spotting the pavement. The sharp scent set me sneezing. Seconds later huge heavy drops began to pelt my head and back. I took shelter beneath an awning and watched the storm through an amnion of water. Ten minutes later the rain ceased, as abruptly as it had started. The temperature dropped a few degrees, and I felt the materiality of weather, impervious to the great constructed landscape. Manhattan was at once sealed and, as I watched filthy rainwater disappear into subway grates and down street drains, as permeable as anything in nature. It absorbed everything, as I was learning.

Summer kept me out quite late into August. I worked at the Arcade every day of the week but one. Evenings I walked. I awaited the delicacy of the approaching fall as a seasonal shift I'd never before experienced. Toward September I felt a kind of unfamiliar anticipation. A dirty park on my way to the Arcade, around Twenty-third Street, became my bellwether, its trees gushed out greenly amid the traffic and surrounding buildings. Several people were permanent residents of the park and sat beside their possessions. I just visited.

Beneath the trees, inside their shallow shade, was my only constant reminder that nature was marking time, that trees at least were routine and predictable. Even though, for me, the cycle was reversed and more defined than it ever was at home, the trees in my park were committed to seasons, as I must become as well.

∽

When I returned from walking, Lillian would ask what I'd been looking at, what I had found. Our tentative friendship grew as she used me as her emissary to the larger city. She did not want to go anywhere, except (on certain days) back to Argentina.

"Where my Spanish books, Rosemary? You said you'd find."

"I'm sorry, Lillian, I'm still looking."

"Pah, my brother say you can't find nothing there in that place where you work."

"I'm sure there's something there for you, Lillian, I just have to find it. What did you read when you lived in Argentina?"

"I read Borges. Jorge Luis Borges. He think he too good for me, but I love him," she said. "He was a blind man who see better than anyone."

"I'll look," I promised. "Write his name down for me."

"You never heard of him?" she scoffed. "What do they read there in Tasmania?"

"They read lots of things, Lillian. But everyone has gaps."

She laughed out loud. Lillian had a warm, deep laugh, velvety with intimacy, with experience.

"Then you find Borges for me, but mostly for yourself. For your gaps. He will fill them, I promise!"

∽

That Walter Geist was an albino was a distinction he could neither hide nor help. And he could be difficult. He was consistently unpleasant to both staff and all but a few select customers. He was even unpleasantly obsequious on the few occasions that called for mild pleasantness, mostly in his dealings with collectors whose large libraries Pike was trying to acquire.

But toward me he behaved differently.

I am ashamed now, when I remember how I shrank from him, and from his whiteness. Ashamed, too, of my fascination. Or perhaps just guilty that I longed to stare at him.

At first, Geist would not meet my eyes and spoke to me with such particularity that I became fixed upon his strange speech patterns and upon his lips with their sibilant consonants. He spoke to me very little in the beginning, addressing me only when he was called upon to give directions for the removal of Pike's priced pile, to instruct me to wait at the rear door to help unload a delivery, or to tell me where to place the "new" books I'd brought down to him in the basement. I suppose a fascination with his appearance was not unusual; he seemed to almost have a dry expectation of it. He was sadly practiced at subjection to close inspection.

Walter Geist's parents had been refugees from Germany; this much Oscar had told me, but he hadn't gathered much more of

Geist's personal details, at least that he ever shared. Geist had not, as my imagination initially proposed, been born in the basement of the Arcade, but in Berlin, in the old Kreuzberg section of the city. He'd grown up in Pennsylvania after immigrating with his parents when very young. Walter Geist had never married, and lived a largely solitary life outside of the Arcade.

Geist's slight lisp was not the result of any actual speech impediment but suggested the palimpsest of languages he had mastered, a hint of them all compressed and vaguely present in his whispered English. It wasn't an accent like mine, broad and flat and, I feared, ignorant. His diction was subtle, exquisite in its way. According to Oscar, Geist spoke five languages fluently, his father having been a linguist at the university. What Oscar didn't know of Walter Geist's personal history, he supplemented with research on albinism. Oscar had his preoccupations and, briefly, Geist had been one, as he would become mine.

Inside the Arcade, Geist affected the use of a thick pair of pince-nez glasses that sat in his shirtfront pocket, attached to a silver chain around his neck. More often, though, they were miraculously affixed to the bridge of his nose, held in place by the folds of skin that his squint made about his eyes and forehead. Geist's eyes were of an undetermined color, but in some lights, particularly bright sunlight, they appeared violet.

"Actually, Rosemary," Oscar told me when I mentioned this odd fact to him, "Walter's eyes are colorless. I looked it up. The violet color is caused by blood vessels in the retina. You can see the blood because his retina is without the color of an iris. I suppose you could say Walter's eyes are transparent."

"Transparent," I repeated, fascinated. Oscar's golden eyes were beautiful but opaque; the idea that Geist's eyes were transparent was too whimsical, too curious, not to captivate me.

And yet, the wobbling movement of his eyes confused me as to where exactly to look—how to meet him. His eyes swam. Weak muscles caused this vacillation, and the constant motion gave the impression that his eyes were perpetually averted in a kind of deflection. I wanted to follow his shifting gaze into some other, quieter space—to see what he saw. He appeared particularly sensitive to light and shadow, and to scent.

"Yes, transparent. Interesting, isn't it?" Oscar smiled, and took out his notebook to write down something that had occurred to him. "I have quite a bit of information about Walter's condition."

"Do you?" I asked, curious. "It seems as if Mr. Geist doesn't want me to look at his eyes. They always move away. I want to look, though. It's as if I'll be able to stare right into his brain."

"Really? How odd," Oscar said, momentarily considering me.

"I imagine his thoughts might have color, even if his eyes don't." I could have added that he was entirely without color, but that would have sounded cruel. I did picture Geist's thoughts, however, as bright and secret things, moving just behind the transparent plane of his retina like exotic fish.

"I saw him looking at my hair outside yesterday," I told Oscar. "While we were waiting for that library. When I asked him if something was wrong, he cleared his throat and pretended he hadn't been looking."

"Well, Rosemary," Oscar said matter-of-factly, "perhaps Walter thinks your hair is beautiful."

Then, seeming to lose interest as quickly as he had found it, he continued to write in his notebook.

"Oscar," I ventured, my heart hot in my chest. "Do you think so?"

But he didn't answer or even acknowledge my question, absorbed as he was in his own note taking. I watched him, writing away, and felt ill with longing. His sculpted head bent over his task, his face expressionless.

∽

Occasionally, I would come upon Geist in the stacks of Oscar's section, holding books close to his face, his white fingers splayed against their covers like spread wings. The volumes he held at the tip of his nose had the compressed heft of textbooks, and their weight made him stoop with effort. Walter Geist was a lonely figure even within the world of the Arcade, and as Pike's designated other, he remained on the fringes of staff camaraderie. He was management, after all: George Pike's pale avatar, some variation of a shadow. But he also held himself separate, certain that he would always be distinct and removed from that which defined the lives of others. In this respect, he knew better than any of us the condition of his life, and I suppose, like everyone else, I assumed he was reconciled to that condition. It wasn't compassion on my part that made him so interesting to me. It was curiosity. My imagination was always overactive, and I made him a figure of significance in the fairy tale I was inventing, in the one I was living. Perhaps, as well, I just couldn't reckon with his humanity.

∽

The staff at the Arcade played a game to pass the time, a game prompted unwittingly when customers asked a question that was exceedingly difficult to answer. The game was called Who Knows? and it did make a long day pass more quickly, but it also served the practical purpose of sharpening the skills required to work in the Arcade. A sense of humor was necessary as well, particularly about the demands placed on one's memory.

There were no reference guides, save *Books in Print* (the place most likely *not* to list a book sought by a customer at the Arcade), so the only reliable source of reference was the staff and their collective memory. Memory was the yardstick of achievement at the Arcade, the measure of one's value to Pike. Memory housed the bookstore's contents like a constantly expanding index, an interior, private library organized by some internal, fleshy variation on the Dewey decimal system.

There were customers who knew only the title but not the author, or only the author but not the title, or even only the color and size of the volume but neither its author's name nor its title. A customer's hands might move apart as if to say "It's about this thick." The game became a way to address how difficult it could be to find anything in the Arcade. For the staff, each obscure question seemed like another bead in a string of non sequiturs. These inquiries demanded an equally nonsensical response, the standard Arcade response. Hence the name of the game: Who Knows?

Jack Conway, his friend Bruno, along with the huge Arthur (Pike seemed to think it amusing to have hired an Art for the Art section), liked to shout out, sometimes with real belligerence, the name of the game. At first I thought they were really serious, and angry, but I caught on eventually.

"Who knows?" they would call out to each other across the heads of inquiring customers, and then, if no echo returned, call with greater rancor, with a full, open throat: "Who the FUCK knows?"

I learned that this was actually a challenge, a call for others to help, and could even draw Oscar from his stacks if he wasn't already occupied. Oscar's recall of his section was practically infallible, but if the book didn't fall into the shapeless category of nonfiction, those with a slightly less remarkable memory needed to be found and consulted. Even Pike would participate, particularly as it often meant the certain sale of a book.

Where is the book I saw here once on the history and design of Russian nesting dolls? Can you tell me where I might begin to look for a monograph on Franz Boaz's dissertation entitled "Contributions to the Understanding of the Color of Water"? Do you have the classic gay novel *Der Puppenjunge* by Sagitta in English? I must have William D'Avenant's *Gondibert*—you know, it has fifteen hundred stanzas? Do you have a book of patterns for Redwork? Where are the decorative planispheres based on Mercator's projection? Listen, I know you have *Poems Chiefly in the Scottish Dialect* by Robert Burns, but where is it?

Customer inquiries were like cartoon thought balloons making visible what was on the mind of the city. They were as random, as subjective, as experience itself, and our only defense against the arbitrariness of the questions was our game.

Who Knows? helped find the most obscure books, and after several months even I became blasé about the astonishing capacity of longtime employees to place their hand on a slim volume, seven shelves down, nine books in—miraculously pulling out just the book a confounded customer had been seeking. Occasionally, I had seen Chaps performing in this way in her tiny, tidy shop in Tasmania, but the scale of this game was entirely different, as was the range and variety of interest. At the Arcade, finding the improbable was an act best accomplished with an impassive air, a bland repudiation of the feat of memory it displayed. The magical act of finding anything, let alone a specifically requested book, within the Arcade's repository was actually a point of pride. This rabbit-out-of-a-hat trick was the single exhibition the Arcade staff could perform that rivaled Pike's mysterious pricing.

⌒

"*I found this* for you, Lillian. But it's in English."

I handed her a small paperback by Borges, *The Book of Imagi-*

nary Beings, uncovered inadvertently while I waited at the paper-back tables.

"Ah, I like this one. I read it a long time ago. You and me, Rosemary, we are like this, no? Imaginary beings, here, no?"

"What do you mean?"

"It is like we are made up, like these creatures in here. See?" She opened the paperback at random. "The Lunar Hare—this is the man in the moon, you see? The Mandrake, the Manticore . . ." She smiled. "We are like these things. No one knows we exist, except a few people. And if we disappear, there is no Borges to make a little story of us, to remember us. Who knows you are here? No mother, no father. And look at you, already so different. You do not look like the girl that came here weeks ago. A girl from Tasmania." She screwed up her eyes, assessing me. "You look like a lion. Where is that other girl now, eh? Now she is imaginary being!"

I *had* changed. Tall, and long-boned, I'd become physically strong working at the Arcade, developing muscles in my arms and back for the first time in my largely sedentary life. Helping out in Remarkable Hats hadn't required much physical effort. But the cart-ing of boxes of books, mostly overpacked, strengthened me, as did my walking and the strictures of a diet confined to what could be bought cheaply, and eaten uncooked in my room at the Martha Washington.

"But we are real to each other, Lillian," I told her. "We aren't imaginary."

"You not know anything about me," Lillian said frankly, thumbing through the paperback.

"Nothing," she added, with a finality that hurt me. "I might not even exist."

"Well, it takes a while to know someone, Lillian, but I hope we will be friends."

"I am sorry, I don't want to read this in English. Thank you for the book," she said abruptly, and handed it back to me.

Perhaps reading the hurt on my face, she added, "You keep it. You read it for yourself. Fill up your gaps. I have no need of such things anymore."

Turning away, she put the television earplugs back into her ears.

I went to my room feeling rejected. I wanted friends, something I'd never had at home. Mother had discouraged such connections; she was fiercely private and secretive about our life. Although I loved the Arcade and New York, the other side of a teeming city was relentless isolation. There was nothing I had been to anyone, no impression I had made, no one to remember me. People here were tricky, and odd—sometimes deceitful. I needed to be careful. I fingered the green amulet at my throat that Chaps had given me.

The exchange with Lillian reminded me that I really needed to live elsewhere, to properly establish myself. Although I had been managing at the hotel for months, I longed for somewhere that didn't feel like a place of transition. The dirty park, my bellwether on the way to the Arcade, told me that fall was coming, and I knew little about the real winter that would follow. I wanted my own bathroom, free of grubby ghosts, and a stove to cook on, as well as a window I could open that didn't tease my hunger with the promise of Indian food I couldn't afford, despite its designation as cheapest cuisine in the city. The Martha Washington was also paralyzingly quiet, up until late evening. Then, the thump-thump of cars and taxis that failed to spot the large pothole directly outside the building's entrance began. The synchronized double-banging of the front and then the rear of each car, as its tires sank momentarily up to their hubcaps, was repetitive and deadening.

That evening I lay in bed, in darkness, and measured the

thump-thump of passing cars against the more predictable beat of my heart. I needed a place to make my own, and determined to ask around at the Arcade to see if anyone knew of an apartment to rent or to share.

Unable to sleep, I switched on the light and took up the Borges I'd found for Lillian, and which she insisted I keep. Why was Lillian so difficult to befriend? The little volume cheered me up. Lillian was right about Borges filling up gaps; he knew all about the lazy pleasure of useless and out-of-the-way erudition; all about the fertilizing quality of knowledge.

The book was arranged alphabetically, and so I started with Abtu and Anet, the Egyptian life-sized holy fish that swam on the lookout for danger before the prow of the sun god's ship. Theirs was an eternal journey, sailing across the sky from dawn to dusk, and by night traveling underground in the opposite direction.

I lay reading the short entries with interest, and passed the hardest part of the night forgetting about my larger concerns.

Some creatures were familiar, like the Minotaur, half bull and half man, born from the perverse passion of Pasiphaë, queen of Crete, for a pure white bull, and hidden within the Labyrinth because of its monstrousness.

The book's final entry was the Zaratan, the island that is actually a whale, "skilled in treachery," drowning sailors once they camped on its back, having mistaken the Zaratan for land.

I finally fell asleep with the book on my chest, my mind full of whales and white bulls, fish-men and girl-lions—a zoology of dreams with a cast made to populate the one I was living.

～

Arthur Pick was something altogether different. Another foreigner, an Englishman, he adored his Art section and was constantly examining photography books, in particular those that featured naked men, as I had seen him do the day I was hired. Arthur loved paintings as well, but photography was his passion. He gave me a nickname I hated, but he insisted on it, and insisted too that I look at photographs he fancied.

"Hello, my Tasmanian Devil, are you floating today? Are you busy? Come here and look, look at these pictures. Are they not lovely?"

"Well, yes, they're very, ah, powerful . . . But I think I prefer the paintings you showed me."

"Do you? I can't imagine why." Arthur turned several pages and my face reddened. I hadn't seen anything like these men. Ever.

"Don't you see that the photograph has made them innocent?" Arthur said. The question astonished me.

"They are frozen and unaware that they will change, or die, or even that they live at all," he went on.

"Innocent?" It was exactly what I thought of Mother's black-and-white photo, that she was captured in there before her life had overwhelmed her. But innocent? These men were hardly unwitting, they were complicit.

"Innocence is their appeal," Arthur explained. "Their nakedness is only part of it. I thought you'd see it, my Tasmanian Devil, because that's a bit like you."

"But how do you know I'm innocent?" I asked him, my face aflame.

"Ah, now you stretch credibility. It is what everyone here sees in you."

"I really don't understand you, Arthur . . . and I told you, please don't call me that name anymore." I knew he was being ironic calling me devilish, but just then I couldn't laugh it off.

Arthur continued to turn the pages of the large book. "It is my gaze that brings the nude alive. They live in my mind, you see. Isn't that marvelous?"

"So, will you stop calling me that name?"

"Tasmanian Devil? Of course, as you wish. Would you permit just TD then, for short?"

"But not, I hope, for long," I returned.

"Ah," Arthur said, surprised. "The stirrings of wit! Delightful! Perhaps, after all, you are not irreparably Tasmanian."

∽

One October evening, walking back to the Martha Washington, I first experienced a ritual of American fall. Passing my dirty park, I stood to watch as workers blew leaves into tall piles. Autumn leaves were collected up in colorful mounds of brown and orange, a few yellow edges fluttering out, like the slips of paper presented to Pearl for redemption at the register. Time was passing, heaped up on the path, blown into piles for carting off and burning to ash. I shivered.

Looking up into the trees, I noticed that one still had a few dark leaves clinging to the upper branches. Under my gaze, the leaves became a *semé* of birds, scattering upward and away in a salutary swoop, leaving only a plastic bag, caught and hanging listlessly in the bare limbs.

I hurried to the Martha Washington.

"I'm paying up for this week," I told Lillian when I arrived. "But I really want to find an apartment. I think it's time for me to move."

I had decided to look in earnest, despite a lack of funds.

"What's wrong with staying here?" said Lillian. "I keep my eye on you. I see you come and go. I make sure you not imaginary," she joked. "I see what you become after the lion."

She moved her hands around her head, simulating my messy mane.

I smiled.

"It's fine here, Lillian, but I'd like to have a place of my own. I want to cook, and feel more settled. Guests come and go here all the time. I'd like to think I had a home. The weather is changing. It's time I settled a bit more."

"I don't think you should go. Not yet. You are safer here," Lillian said, dropping her hands and looking fretful.

"People, they disappear," she said. "You have no idea . . ."

"What are you talking about, Lillian?" I said. "I'm not going away. Finding a proper place to live is the best way to become permanent. I'm not about to disappear."

Lillian shook her head, but not in disagreement.

∽

"*I hear you're* looking for somewhere to live," Jack muttered to me a few days later as I stood talking with Pearl up front. "I'd be happy to oblige . . ."

"Do you mean you know somewhere?"

"Me mate's just shot through, and I know somewhere cheap enough."

"It'll have to be cheap, Jack, on what they pay here," I said. "Is it far?"

"Walking distance," he answered. "If you're up for a walk. It's east of here." He waved his thick arm wildly, not specifying a direction.

East of the Arcade was a notoriously squalid section of the city; the neighborhood was known for its drug dealers and cold-water flats.

The following week Jack and Rowena took me to look at his friend's apartment after work. They led me down a block lined with several abandoned buildings, past a garbage-covered vacant lot to a dingy storefront, its windows clouded over with swirls of paint and wooden boards covered with graffiti. A battered-looking door opened on the side of what had once been a small grocery store. Inside the dank hall, I took in the hypodermic needles strewn under the stairwell, and the gray paint on the walls peeling off in damp flakes. The room was on the second floor. Jack had the key. His friend, a fellow musician, had left the apartment empty, although he retained the lease and wanted to sublet for only six months.

The door opened on a long, narrow space like a train carriage, with two dirty windows that faced the street. An oven, sink, and old claw-footed bathtub sat in the center against an exposed brick wall. A slightly narrower alcove with a tiny closet (and the toilet) was in the rear behind a filthy curtain. Worn, dark, wide planks on the floor were covered with the detritus of hasty departure: paper, rags, and clumps of clotted dust. The room was cold. The whole building was without heat.

"The boiler's out just now," said Jack, rubbing his hands together against the chill of the room. "Me mate used to turn the oven on and leave the door open when it got really cold in winter. Warm as toast after a while." He attempted a grizzled smile.

"There's even some pots under here you can boil up water when you need a bath," Rowena threw in.

After the Martha Washington, the squalid look of the place didn't bother me. In fact, in some perverse way it fit my developing ideas about bohemian life, about the requirements of adventure. Besides, I reasoned, I had always lived above a store, and while Mother would have been appalled at the place, something in its aspect reminded me of the flat above Remarkable Hats.

"I collect the rent," Jack said. "Fifty a week. But I need a deposit as well. Four hundred'll do up front. That's including the first month. Right? I'm to mail it to me friend."

I would need more than four hundred dollars to move in. I had to sleep on something, and clean the place. I didn't have the money.

"If you can't manage it, I know someone else who can," Rowena threatened, sealing the deal.

"I'll take it," I told them, wanting to move in right then, and lock the door against Jack and Rowena. Once I was alone I could worry about the fact that the small amount of money I had saved wouldn't cover what Jack wanted up front.

"Can you give me a few days to get the money together?" I asked.

"Sure, love." Jack grinned at me crookedly. "Day after tomorrow? So's we can start with November's rent."

∽

I couldn't ask Chaps for money. It would have taken too long to arrive, for one thing; and she'd done too much for me already, asking would only worry her. The day after I saw the apartment I discussed it, and my lack of funds, with Oscar.

"I'm not sure you want someone like Jack as a landlord," he warned. "How can you be sure he's honest?"

"But I haven't found anything else, and really, Oscar, it's perfect for me. I'll fix it up. I just have to figure out how to get the money."

"I shouldn't tell you this, but I have known, on rare occasions, of Walter Geist pressing Pike for an advance on behalf of an employee in need. You know, a small sum, a loan against future wages. You have to sign an agreement, and the amount is deducted in small increments on a weekly basis. Pike, of course, adds interest: ten percent of the loan, spread over the length of time the amount is to be paid."

Oscar sounded very familiar with what he had described as a rare practice. I suspect he was himself indentured by debt to Pike.

"I can't ask Mr. Geist for a loan," I said, loath to appeal to the store manager. But without a loan I couldn't leave the Martha Washington for several more months, and by that time the apartment would be gone.

∽

That afternoon, I came upon Walter Geist reading in Oscar's section. He stood holding a book no more than an inch from his face. Watching him, I thought he brought a certain amount of dignity to this close inspection. His dreadful eyesight made him appear momentarily vulnerable and, with his swimming eyes, peculiarly appealing.

He must have sensed he was being watched, for he closed the book with a thud, peered around nervously, and assumed his ill-favored demeanor. He hadn't seen me, but I had a fleeting glimpse of the expression on his face. He had the look of a child braced for a slap. Was it Pike who'd etched this expression on Geist's face, in the way a volatile parent draws pain as plainly as if with a crayon? Theirs was an intense relationship, often conducted in stage whispers and emphatic sentences. I couldn't have guessed at their bond, but knew that whatever held them, it was a fierce allegiance.

But in catching Walter Geist unawares, I had also seen something of his terrible defenselessness. His albinism, of course, meant that he was subject to all manner of vulnerability. He was trapped within a skin that appalled by its very perfection, but he was not without a strange draw. It was beneath another's gaze that distortion occurred. Contempt becomes stronger by becoming more precise, and Geist's whiteness served as a nexus for those that despised the strange.

My own experience with marginality didn't give me any insight into what Geist suffered. I was a willing émigré to New York, after all, whereas he was marked by birth to always be an exile. Like much of my understanding, it was through fiction that I gained a sense of his truth. And it was Herman Melville, in particular, that gave me an intimation of Geist's terrible distinction, and the abhorrence it evoked in others.

PART
TWO

CHAPTER

SEVEN

"They're a peculiar pair, Oscar, don't you think?" I asked after watching Geist, and puzzling over him. "Pike and Geist. A strange couple of fellows."

"Oh, Rosemary, d'you think they're any more peculiar than anyone else who works here? What's strange anyway?" Oscar asked rhetorically. "Perhaps it's all just strange to you because you're a stranger—in New York, I mean. To some people a young girl with wild red hair from Tasmania, with no parents, who lived above a hat shop her whole life, is unusual."

"I suppose," I said. "But I don't seem the least bit unusual to myself."

"Well, you wouldn't, of course. Any more than I seem odd to myself, or even Walter seems to himself. Really, though," Oscar conceded, "I suppose Walter truly is unusual. Can't help but be."

"I saw him in your section, reading with a book inches from his face," I said. "I thought I might ask him, you know, about the loan. But he seemed so intent, and so . . . well, vulnerable, I didn't want to disturb him. It occurred to me he needed privacy."

What I didn't tell Oscar was that I saw something in him revealed, as if I'd seen him naked.

"He's often in my section," Oscar confirmed. "But I can't help him much with the books he's after. I don't have much that's current on the brain, or neurology. He also wants books on anthropology, but anything current just doesn't come into a place like the Arcade. I have something intriguing on phrenology, but of course that's very out of date, although not without interest . . ."

His voice trailed off as if his mind was following another, more interesting thought, and his hand stroked his own head, perhaps attempting to read his prominent occipital bone. Was he feeling for indications of adhesiveness?

"How long has Mr. Geist been here, Oscar?" I asked, trying to bring him back to the subject.

Oscar didn't know exactly how long Geist had worked at the Arcade; but having spent his own adolescence in correspondence with either Pike or Mr. Mitchell, searching for books to satisfy his peculiar interests, he assumed Walter Geist was older than he was. Geist was actually not much past forty, despite the quaint figure he cut, which gave him an eternally aged aspect.

"Besides," Oscar said, "once I researched albinos, I found out that they often have a considerably shorter life span than most people, so Walter couldn't have lived long enough to have worked here for that many years, regardless of how old he looks. Albinos have always occurred in all human races, Rosemary."

Oscar turned then, quickly scanned a nearby shelf, and placed his hand on a large old volume. He extracted the book and expertly opened it on a Victorian-era photograph of two women, twin albino sisters, their long white hair so absent of color as to look like a flaw in the film. Hair overlapped their shapely silhouettes, as they leaned into each other's side. The whiteness of their hair dominated the photograph, its outline soft and blurred at the edges, hanging well past their cinched waists, loose and shocking beside the restriction of their black, heavily starched dresses. Their features were hardly discernible but for darker shadings at eyes, nose, mouth; and I was startled by the profuse hair, undone and on display—startled, too, because the women were beautiful, and something in the photograph was markedly erotic. I had a sense that theirs was an exhibition of unspeakable glory, but at the same time an inversion of propriety. The femininity of long hair was mocked by the absence of color and by the clear lack of pleasure taken in its exposure. Somehow, the photograph, or perhaps the photographer, betrayed them.

Oscar read to me from the text on the opposite page, his golden eyes moving back and forth hypnotically.

" 'The condition of albinism appeared frequently among certain Native American peoples of the Southwest, who believed albinos were messengers sent forth from divine entities, and who believed that the killing of an albino animal would result in a curse. Historically, albinos have been treated with the utmost suspicion, and many misconceptions persisted including the assumption that the poor vision that resulted from the condition indicated a low intellectual capacity or, conversely, that they possessed mysterious abilities like mind-reading. Albinos were at one time institutionalized at birth. In America in the nineteenth century, albinism was considered such a bizarre trait that people with the condition were exhibited in circus sideshows, or photographed as human curiosities.' "

He held the book up, although I'd shifted so as to see the picture over his shoulder. " 'See plate at right,' " he read, and pointed to the disturbing photograph.

I leaned in closer to examine it. He shut the book in my face with a dusty snap. I jumped.

"Quite a legacy, don't you think? Being considered a human curiosity."

His tone was matter-of-fact, and I wondered at his lack of sympathy; at my own. Certainly Geist was an oddity, but for Oscar he was just another subject for investigation.

I couldn't help being moved by what Oscar had read, and regarded myself harshly for what I had to admit was both repulsion and a sort of fascination with Geist. I suspected my own interest. Better to think of Geist as a messenger, like the Native Americans did, a messenger sent to remind me of my own incapacity, of my own lack of empathy. I determined then to warm my manner toward him, whether he loaned me money or not.

"I must find you a paperback of *Moby-Dick*," said Oscar, suddenly.

"Why?" I asked, clueless.

He reshelved the book.

"Because Melville has a lot to say about albinos, and you seem particularly interested. There's a whole chapter in there on it. One must always follow one's interests. And you're in America now. You should be reading Americans."

I was particularly interested in Walter Geist, although my odd preoccupation was fostered by Oscar's own fascination. I wanted to share whatever he would grant me. I would read whatever he told me to, and I was curious too, for here was Melville's name reappearing.

"Come on now, while I think of it, let's ask Jack and Bruno to keep an eye out for a paperback. Peabody's bought up everything of any value, but they must have an old paperback!"

We walked to the front of the store to search the chaotic tables. Mercer had arrived with the mail and was chatting to Pearl. When Oscar told the rough paperback pair that he was looking for *Moby-Dick*, and that it was for me, he unwittingly prompted a licentious boast from Jack with regard to his own (purportedly spectacular) anatomy. Bruno bluntly offered to, as he put it, "show the girlie me own Moby-Dick."

In any case, they didn't have a copy, but promised to set one aside when it turned up, as they assured me it often did.

❧

Lillian wasn't behind the reception counter when I returned to the Martha Washington that evening. I was surprised and disappointed, I had intended to ask her advice about the apartment. And she was worried about *me* disappearing!

"Where's Lillian?" I asked the small man who'd taken her place. He was quite elderly, with wrinkled dark skin that shone in patches on his forehead, cheeks, and chin.

"She didn't show up today, miss, so they called the agency and got me. Don't know what's wrong with her. Maybe she's sick? Very reliable, usually, I heard. Her brother, he's the owner, right? He went off to look for her. You have your key?"

I let myself into my room, concerned about Lillian and afraid she might be ill. But if she was sick, she'd be here at the hotel and her brother wouldn't have gone to look for her. I took off my shoes and lay on the sagging bed.

"Where is she?" I asked the Huon box aloud.

❧

I was stacking the titles that Pike had set aside for shelving beside his stage when I thought I caught sight again of Redburn. It made me jump to see a flash of red hair, as if I'd caught sight of myself in a mirror. I stood very still, waiting to see if whoever was hiding behind a corner of the Art department was in fact the shoplifter.

"Well, what do you have?" Pike was saying into the old telephone receiver as he stood behind his desk. "The man wants to buy, he has unlimited funds, and you've nothing to interest him?"

He was evidently berating Mr. Mitchell. I picked up a stack of volumes and watched the corner, but there was no movement.

"Peabody wants American. Metcalf said as much. But what about Melville? Remember that the library received those papers and you should have secured them for the Arcade?"

Redburn peeped his vivid head around the stack.

"You," I muttered.

He put his finger to his lips. He was listening as intently to Pike's conversation as, I had to admit, I was. I eavesdropped on Pike every chance I could get. Of course, I rationalized my rudeness by acknowledging how much I had to learn, how much he could teach me. Yet here was a common shoplifter stealing information that I wanted exclusively. How odd that Pike's subject was Melville.

"Peabody would have paid anything for those," George Pike continued. "Now Gosford tells you he can't manage that little Mandelstam at $45,000 . . ."

I turned away in search of Bruno or Jack. Geist had told me that Redburn should be thrown out, but by the time I returned with Jack in tow, the thief had disappeared.

"No one about. You're sure you aren't seeing things, love?" Jack asked, leaning into my face. "It happens here, after a while. We're all a bit mad, you know?"

He laughed and wandered back to the front of the Arcade.

It was a coincidence that Melville's name came up in what I overheard Pike discussing with Mr. Mitchell, but there is a way that coincidence coalesces, as if Providence itself conspires to alert one to significance. This feeling describes my experience in New York in general, and at the Arcade specifically: this idea of arranged happenstance. And, although there is regret associated with certain accidents, contingencies appeared to me then to be designed, and not a result of my undeveloped character. "Ourselves are fate,"

Melville whispers to that younger self. But that Rosemary wouldn't have understood.

∽

After escorting a reviewer downstairs to the basement the next day, I asked Geist if I could speak with him after work that evening. I smiled, trying to project as much warmth as I thought myself capable of. Geist studied me, his eye muscles relaxing slightly, his glasses sliding off his face and swinging to his chest, where the chain prevented them from falling farther. I imagined a mysterious thought passing across his brain, his transparent eyes a window to its workings. His hand went into his trouser pocket, where it audibly jostled loose change.

"Certainly, Rosemary, certainly I'll speak with you this evening. At six." He sounded surprised and stood a little straighter. "I'll meet you in the office upstairs."

He actually smiled slightly, and for the first time I noticed his small, even teeth, quite as white as the rest of him.

I ascended the rickety stairs to the rear office at six and waited in the doorway, taking in the tin desk, piled with invoices and correspondence and illuminated by a brilliant green-glass lamp. Geist sat hunched over a large, round magnifying glass. The glass was fixed inside a brass frame, an elegant scaffold designed to support the thick lens, leaving his hands free. The glass was an instrument for close work, more likely designed for use by a watchmaker, a silversmith, or perhaps a maker of maps. There was a quality to it that suggested a slower century, a time when objects demanded close inspection; when all of life might be captured and reproduced in miniature and made observable by just such a device.

For a second I saw Geist's face, transformed by magnification, grown monstrous and distorted; a white Moloch, the Minotaur in my little book. Bent over the lens, he poked rapidly at an adding machine with one pale finger, as if admonishing it. He shifted his head and the frightening image vanished.

The office was a shambles. Outside the triangle of light where Geist sat, a haphazard collection of papers and books, magazines, and letters, rivaling even the chaos of the store below, covered the room. As I stood in the doorway, Geist failed to notice my presence, so I knocked on the wooden door frame to attract his attention.

He immediately looked up and flinched. His delicate ears shifted back, his glasses falling. I wondered if it was me who had this effect on his glasses, that something in my appearance prevented them from remaining fixed on his nose. He knew to expect me at six.

"Sit down," he said, gesturing to an old wooden chair piled with newspapers. His hands were beautiful.

"Just move them over there," he instructed, and I bundled up the unread newspapers and placed them on top of another pile stacked on a metal file cabinet. Geist quickly reinserted his glasses into the folds of his face, pushed aside his magnifier, and sat forward.

"I was quite surprised by your request for a meeting. I meet infrequently with employees. What did you want to see me about?"

I was extremely nervous in Geist's presence, anxious that I not seem repulsed or inappropriately fascinated. I was determined to meet his colorless eyes directly, had steeled myself to do so, practicing on Oscar during an afternoon break, rehearsing my request. But Oscar's eyes invited staring into, like a golden mirror, while Geist's, hidden behind his glasses, were inscrutable, hermetic. I saw again his weirdly magnified face and my mind flashed to the image of those odd, exposed twin sisters haunting the sepia landscape of the photograph. My face grew hot.

"Well," I began, "in a conversation with Oscar, he mentioned to me—that is, Oscar mentioned to me—that a precedent exists at the Arcade . . . well, I mean that there is the possibility that, that . . . well, Oscar said that a small loan might be extended to staff members as an advance against wages. That is to say, Mr. Geist, I am interested in a small loan. That is to say, a cash advance . . . um . . ."

I sounded as false as I felt, prepared to the point of confusion, and clearly uncomfortable. I thought that if I used Oscar's name, it might recommend me to Geist. I was wrong. He faced me with his vacillating eyes. There was a lengthy pause. He recovered himself, dipping his head. The line of his mouth became flat and unpleasant, and I imagined his transparent eyes hardening, like water turning to ice.

"Am I correct in assuming you are not a citizen of this country?" he asked, beginning a line of inquiry I was at a loss to follow.

"That's correct," I admitted, bewildered.

"And I understand from my records that you have been employed by Mr. Pike at the Arcade for only a matter of months?" I nodded my assent, my hair falling forward into the light. Something in this irritated Geist further.

"And that you reside at the Martha Washington Hotel for Women—a . . . a transient hotel, at 29 East Twenty-ninth Street?" His alliteration of his *t*'s and *s*'s seemed cutting, cruel.

"Yes," I replied, confused. How did he know where I lived? Had he looked it up on my application? He paused and seemed to gather himself up.

"And do you consider yourself a worthy risk—a stable investment for Mr. Pike, Rosemary Savage? Do you plan to stay?"

I remembered the defenseless adding machine Geist had been jabbing at before the interview began.

"Well, Mr. Geist," I responded, "I consider myself a completely committed employee of the Arcade, I love working here . . . um . . . and have every intention of staying here and in this city. Mr.

Geist—" I faltered, not knowing what else to add. How could I tell him what the Arcade meant to me?

He looked down at the desk, brushing the clutter of papers with his pale hand. I was struck again by how beautiful his hands were, the fingers splayed like the flight feathers of a small bird, extended and separate. He noticed me watching his hand and, leaning forward, shoved it into his pocket. He moved the magnifying glass farther to one side.

"You can stop calling me Mr. Geist, Rosemary. My name is Walter. Most of the staff call me that."

I took from this a slight encouragement, although he had said it with some impatience.

As long as I knew him I would never once call him Walter.

The blue-red thoughts moved behind his eyes, no more explicable to me than the mind they passed across. His speaking voice required close attention; his sibilant consonants were distracting, and suggested he was searching the catalog of his brain, first for the right word and then for the appropriate language. But there was something deeply personal in his voice, something that addressed itself to me.

"It is true you seem a willing worker, but Mr. Pike is not a generous man, Rosemary, a fact I'm sure you have observed. He will certainly want to know why he should extend this courtesy to you. Can you suggest to me why you should be considered in any way unusual or exceptional in this regard? Why a loan of any amount could be considered a good investment? What do you offer as collateral?"

At this he looked up, scrutinizing me with his whole pallid being. The office was silent but for a faint hum rising from the Arcade below.

I had listened to his carefully chosen words—"worthy," "stable," that any loan was a "courtesy," and the person to whom it was extended needed to be "exceptional," "unusual," "a good investment."

His language was always deliberate and specific. What exactly was Walter Geist suggesting? Did he want to humiliate me?

I couldn't answer and only blinked, thinking of some way in which I was exceptional enough an employee to receive George Pike's trust—for him to extend to me the thing he valued above all: money. I sat silently abashed.

Gradually, I made out the purpose of his question. "I am not exceptional, Mr. . . . Geist, if that's what you're asking me."

"Ah." He leaned back, satisfied. "Not exceptional in any way?"

He paused. I blinked.

"I will take up your request with Mr. Pike, and will let you know his response tomorrow, Rosemary."

He moved his small body in the desk chair, and removed his hand from his pocket. His fleecy head was no longer illuminated beneath the triangular beam of the lamp. A moment passed. He repositioned his magnifier over the ledger open on his desk and resumed his vicious punching with one finger at the buttons on his adding machine.

I had been dismissed.

∽

Oscar was waiting for me at the bottom of the broken staircase, raking his hand across his face, his dark hair flattened to his sculpted head by repeated stroking. He seemed an actor, in that moment, awaiting his cue from the wings of the theater. Oscar was always poised, prepared to deliver his lines. His reserve was like a kind of readiness. He was on guard.

A casual observer might think more passed between Oscar and me than ever would, his waiting on the outcome of my meeting like that of one intimately engaged in the interests of another. But Oscar couldn't return to me anything except the reflection of my own longing. It didn't stop me from wanting more, but I would come to see that Oscar lacked the ability to connect to others in a tangible way. Instead, he had his investigations. And he had his notebooks: the repository of his longings, the narrative of his loss.

My face was still hot; I felt adrift, certain I'd made a horrible mistake asking Geist for help.

"Well?" he asked, his own eyes wide. "Did you get it?"

The thought that I had jeopardized what I had come to treasure—the world of the Arcade, its inhabitants, Oscar—rose up in my throat and filled my eyes. I turned from him and he followed me.

As we walked from the Arcade, I told him haltingly that I wouldn't know until tomorrow, but that Geist had not been pleasant about my request, suggesting I wasn't exactly a good risk for George Pike. I confessed too, my admission of being unexceptional. Oscar just smiled at this and tried to assure me this was Geist's way of testing me, and that Pike expected him to do so.

I was humiliated, and I knew, without understanding why, that humiliation had been Geist's objective. It was a provocation. A score off my naïveté. What collateral did I possess? All I had was my impecunious self. Did he mean what would I give? A flash of repugnance for the albino that immediately turned to shame was even more disconcerting. I was troubled by my willingness to even make such a request, encouraged as I was by Oscar. I realized how proud of my independence I'd become, how certain I was that I could look after myself.

"I found this for you," Oscar said, and handed me a dog-eared paperback of *Moby-Dick*. "To cheer you up!"

"Thank you, Oscar," I said, pleased at least that he wanted to give me something. "But actually, I think I've had enough of albinos for one day."

"Follow your interest," he said, reminding me that I had expressed some and handing me the book. "Besides, Melville was really a New Yorker. Think of it as a guide."

I dropped it into my bag.

Outside the Arcade, the darkening sky above the city was an inexplicable deep blue, familiar and close. We walked to the corner beyond the store and crossed the avenue. Oscar touched my arm in what I took to be a heartening gesture. He told me not to worry, that he felt certain Geist had taken a liking to me and that the loan would be forthcoming.

"He doesn't like me, Oscar," I insisted. "In fact, I think he hates me. He is very odd and peculiar toward me altogether. He was trying to embarrass me."

Oscar smiled slightly, his puppet's head molded in the twilight; his expression filled me with yearning.

"He's only odd toward you because he *does* like you, Rosemary, because you're pretty and nice, and maybe because of your red hair. And because you're so young. Walter is very lonely. It could be that kindness would be the end of him. Don't you see?"

Oscar turned then, told me over his shoulder that we would find out tomorrow, and walked to the subway station on the corner, leaving me astonished by what he'd said.

I wanted to tell Pearl, or Lillian. I wished Mother could tell me what to make of Oscar, what to make of men. Had Oscar actually told me I was pretty, or only that perhaps Geist thought so?

I watched his spare frame descend the subway stairs, his white shirt and black pants vanishing under the city street, and I touched the place on my arm where he'd briefly laid his hand, leaving it there.

"Oscar," I called softly.

But I was alone on the avenue and not immune to the night.

After Oscar left, I crossed the street and headed east, to begin an exploratory walk of what I so wished would be my new neighborhood. An examination of the area would, I thought, counter my pessimism, make me hopeful, would somehow improve the small chance of obtaining the means to move there. Walking has always helped me think.

East, at the end of the island, was as random and chaotic as the Arcade, but filled with even more marginal characters—drug dealers, poor immigrants, maverick squatters. The occasional art gallery or small café was an early sign of the transformation that was beginning to come to every corner of the city in its perpetual revision, its infinite reconfiguration. The neighborhood suited me, addressed my fresh pretensions, my growing predilection for the bohemian. It seemed full of the drowned searching for dry land. Full of orphans like myself.

I stood outside the ruined building Jack and Rowena had taken me to, staring up at the second floor. My pessimism increased, however, and I returned dejected to the Martha Washington, certain I'd found the perfect place to live, and equally certain that Walter Geist was no advocate on my behalf—that no advance would be forthcoming.

Lillian was still missing, the small man was again behind the reception counter, adding to my worries. I lay in my single bed thinking about Oscar, Geist, and George Pike, about the Arcade, and I listened to the repetitive thump-thump of cars hitting the hole in the street. How was I to escape the Martha Washington? Escape would, for now, have to come in the familiar way—the vertiginous fall into a book.

"No remedy but to read," I told the Huon box, shrouded in its orange scarf. Oscar would keep me company via Herman Melville. It appeared that everyone was interested in Melville, if Pike's telephone conversation was anything to go by. Some names just insist themselves.

I got out of bed and took from my bag the copy of *Moby-Dick*, holding the pages to my nose to see if they'd picked up any of Oscar's distinctively clean scent. The book smelled of sawdust and damp, but I knew I was bound to love Melville because Oscar had given him to me. Returning to bed and adjusting the shade to direct light on the small type, I scanned the table of contents, and turned first to the chapter he'd mentioned. Chapter 42: "The Whiteness of the Whale." I read aloud to the box of heartwood:

> What is it that in the Albino man so peculiarly repels and often shocks the eye, as that sometimes he is loathed by his own kith and kin? It is that whiteness which invests him, a thing expressed by the name he bears. The Albino is as well made as other men— has no substantive deformity—and yet this mere aspect of all-pervading whiteness makes him more strangely hideous than the ugliest abortion. Why should this be so?

"Indeed. Why?" I asked the empty air. I didn't find Walter Geist strangely hideous, just strange. Something in me answered that what Melville was saying need not be so. I had to agree with him, however, that whiteness exerted a kind of sorcery.

I turned back to the beginning then, to start the book properly, and was quickly smitten with Ishmael—orphan, traveler, and wanderer, like myself, of the insular city of the Manhattoes. But Ishmael had set off from that island bound for the Southern Hemisphere, for wild and distant seas, whereas I had reversed the journey and had traveled the other way. I had come from the watery part of the world, here, to Ishmael's nervous city. I felt as if his adventure had somehow met my own in mysterious recognition.

That night I dreamed of a long room with a bathtub at its center. The room ended in two windows, hard-edged eyes looking across a river that lapped gently just at the level of their sills. The tub was a porcelain boat, and climbing in, I passed through the wall and out to the river. The only possession I carried was the box of Huon pine, clutched beneath my arm. In the dream, I was certain I would find Lillian, Mother, my father—everything I had lost. In undertaking the voyage, all I ever wanted would be found.

The river opened into an ocean full of clusters of brilliant islands, islands made of buildings sunk up to their highest floors. I was adrift in the great submerged city, the molded tub floating in a twinkling sea. Watery avenues were lined with blazing lighthouses, which marked dangerous places to be avoided, hidden spots where whirlpools twisted, places where one might disappear. It crossed my mind that the islands might not be islands at all, but the treacherous Zaratans I'd read about, whales bent on deception. I paddled fitfully. The tub moved as if directed, and it was impossible for me to steer its course.

My boat sailed south while I lay back, staring up into the deep curve of the night sky: a theatrical firmament painted the fathomless blue of Mother's eyes. A haunted sky, alive with dark shadows cast by the city's bright buildings; a sky without stars but lit by two identical golden moons that watched, impassively, as a white fin broke the dark water, then submerged as it drew closer.

∽

The following day, Lillian still hadn't appeared. I arrived early at the Arcade, having slept little. While I waited on the street for Pike to show up and open the store, I took out *Moby-Dick*. The book had impressed an urgency upon me, even while I wanted to read it as slowly as possible. A few customers collected on the sidewalk. I felt a sharp sympathy for what the Arcade meant to them.

Exclusively male, these compulsive book buyers and collectors were neurotically convinced that a day missed was a volume possibly lost, or at least in someone else's hands. What were their lives made of, apart from books? The Arcade was their first destination, a quick stop to check on fresh inventory piled at the base of Pike's platform; an obligatory daily search for hidden treasure. Acquisitiveness drove them, and envy—the ingredients, I suppose, of any passion.

I wished a good morning to the customers I recognized and leaned against the store window. Nervousness took hold and I dropped *Moby-Dick* into my bag, pressing my cheek to the smeary glass.

Despite an October morning sun, the interior was dim, and dark passages between the stacks—discrete villages of categories, tall towns of subjects—drew me as magnetically as they had the first day I found the Arcade.

George Pike arrived. He opened the shuddering security grate. As I passed him I imagined him more dismissive of me than usual, although he was casually oblivious of me on most occasions. I took this to mean I would not be moving in the near future, that I'd disappointed him or, worse, angered him—that I would be fired as quickly as I'd been hired. Appalled at my presumption in asking to borrow money, tired from reading late and sleeping poorly, I went directly to the ladies' bathroom and locked myself in the single stall.

Pearl came in singing shortly after, looked under the door, and, recognizing my shoes, insisted I come out and tell her what was wrong.

I confessed.

She took me then and held me in her enormous arms, my head pressed against her improbably firm chest. She murmured to me that she would speak to Mario, her Italian boyfriend, who had piles of money and who would do anything she asked.

I had not been held since leaving home, and then rather dryly by Chaps when we parted at the airport. I was overwhelmed, and sobbed piteously. I couldn't borrow money from Pearl—her generosity, her kindness, only made it worse. I missed Mother, Tasmania, Chaps, my fledgling confidence. And where was Lillian? I cried harder into the exquisite luxury of Pearl's arms.

After a while, she put a tape of *Così fan tutte* into her player and insisted I sit on the vinyl couch and listen until I felt better. She hung up her coat in the locker, checked her makeup, and left to take her position at the register. Remarkably, after a while I did feel better. Deeply relieved, I washed my face and tidied myself up, and left the bathroom to look for Oscar in his stacks.

Oscar was certain I had imagined Pike's indifference, at least his greater indifference.

"I started the book you gave me," I told him. "It's incredible."

"I suppose, given your history, you'll fall in love with Ishmael," he said.

"Why do you say that?"

He shrugged, as if all my infatuations were obvious and predictable.

"This is entirely different," I told him.

He blinked without expression.

"Actually, I skipped ahead first and read that awful chapter called 'The Whiteness of the Whale.' "

"Funny you should mention that," Oscar said, lowering his voice and gesturing with a nod that someone was coming.

Geist advanced into Nonfiction.

"Rosemary, would you meet me in the office upstairs?" he hissed softly. "Now."

Again, I followed Geist and, accommodating some internal shift, I stared at his raw, sea-creature ears and questioned their delicacy. Given the memory of humiliation, I might have wanted to bash them, but Melville's chapter had worked on me. And I had copied into my notebook: "Whiteness . . . calls up a peculiar apparition to the soul." A peculiar apparition he was.

Geist took his seat behind the cluttered tin desk, glasses firmly in place.

"Rosemary, I have taken up your request with Mr. Pike. He is not inclined to advance you a loan against your wages," he said. My heart stopped in my chest.

"However," he developed, "I impressed upon Mr. Pike the fact that you are an industrious employee. One whom we should endeavor to keep. To train."

Geist cleared his throat, paused, and looked at me meaningfully.

"To that end I want to propose a compromise that would include extending you the loan."

"I'm not sure I follow you, Mr. Geist," I said, bewildered.

"Walter," he said. "Please."

"You said Mr. Pike was not inclined to give me the loan," I repeated.

"If you'll let me continue," Geist said. "I propose a compromise. A compromise that would change your job somewhat. In short, I could use an assistant. One who was responsible to me, to my particular . . . needs."

"But how does that affect the loan?" I asked.

"If you agree to become my assistant, I will ensure that you receive the loan."

I must have seemed particularly obtuse.

"But what does your need for an assistant have to do with the loan?"

"Come now, you are a bright young woman. You are either interested in these terms or you are not. Now, I can write a yellow slip for Pearl right now and the advance is yours. What I require is that you agree to work directly for me."

"I'm sorry, Mr. Geist . . . But I already do work for you. You give me my instructions, you tell me what section to work in. How would that change?"

"It won't change. I just want you to be aware that it is under my authority that you work here. That it is my requirements you are subject to. That you will be my assistant. I need you to—to look at things for me. This is a promotion of sorts, Rosemary. I am impatient with your hesitation," he said, taking up a pen and a yellow square of paper like those handed to customers in the basement and in the Rare Book Room for redemption at the register.

"Now, for what amount specifically is your request?"

"Five hundred dollars," I said uneasily.

"Fine. But Pearl cannot remove that amount this early in the day." He put down the pen and opened a drawer beneath the desk. He drew out a zippered leather pouch and counted from it five one-hundred-dollar bills. He put them on top of a printed sheet of paper and pushed it across the desk.

"What is this?" I asked, scanning the faintly printed lines.

"Just the terms of the loan," said Geist, smiling now. "Nothing unusual or extraordinary."

Nothing extraordinary. I took the money, the article of my liberation from the Martha Washington. He handed me a pen with his pale fingers and I signed the form. We rose together, as if on cue, after my signature was complete.

"You'll see," he said. "This will work out well. I've actually rescued you, in a way."

"Rescued me?" I repeated uneasily. "From what?"

"Why, from floating," he said. "Tedious, don't you think, to float about the floor, not knowing what's expected of you. This way, under me, you'll learn the correct way to do things."

I loved floating about the Arcade, and didn't ever want to stop. But I said nothing. I couldn't have. Mostly I was relieved that I had the money now to move.

He followed me to the door of the office. On the threshold of the landing, Walter Geist placed his hand against the small of my back, leaving it there a moment longer than seemed quite polite. I felt the heat of his hand on my back and the sensation surprised me. I supposed his hand would be cold, because his paleness suggested a kind of bloodlessness. It was the first time he touched me, and in recalling it, what I remember is his warmth—the heat of his hand through the thin fabric of my shirt.

"Rosemary," he said softly.

I said nothing but made my way down the stairs, shoved the money into my pocket, leaving him alone on the landing.

∽

Lillian sat watching her small television set, earplugs attached, as if she hadn't been gone for several days. I had found a book for her, Spanish poetry that a reviewer had brought in to sell, a bilingual edition of García Lorca.

"Where have you been?" I asked her immediately. "I've been so worried about you!"

"I was sick," Lillian said, not giving me her full attention. She spoke flatly, without affect. "I try to go home. I tell my brother to tell you."

"What! He didn't tell me anything," I said. "You tried to go back to Argentina? Why? They had another man here to fill in for you and he didn't know anything."

Lillian looked back at me, dispassionate. She removed the earplugs.

"Here, I've brought you something else to read," I handed her the heavy book. "It's in Spanish and English. I thought you might like it. García Lorca—I don't know if it makes a difference that he's a Spaniard. Lillian, are you all right? I was worried about you."

"Do not worry for me."

"Well, I *was* worried."

"You should not care."

"But I already do, Lillian. I can't take it back. Listen, I have to tell you something."

"Don't tell me nothing," she said, shaking her head.

"What?"

"Don't tell me, Rosemary. I don't want to care."

"I don't understand, Lillian. What don't you want to care about? Me?"

I couldn't keep up with Lillian's oblique way of speaking.

"This is a present?" Lillian asked, taking hold of the book but not opening it. She looked defensive, expecting disappointment, sus-picious.

"You are giving up? Going back? In that case, I don't want this." She shoved the book back at me.

"No, Lillian, I'm not going back to Tasmania. But I have found somewhere to live, and I'm moving there in a few days."

I pushed the book back across the counter.

"No!" she said, suddenly animated. "I not see you again! You will be lost as well . . ."

"Lost as well as who, Lillian?"

"*No quiero acordarme*," she said.

"Meaning, Lillian?"

She didn't answer.

"I've just found a small apartment. I can have you over, once I have some things. I'll invite you for dinner. And I'll come and see you here."

"How you get the money to move? You have saved?"

"Well, I had some saved, and I . . . Never mind, Lillian, I sorted it out myself."

"You should not leave here. I want you to stay. Please. You must promise on your honor."

"Lillian, what I promise is that I'll still see you," I took her hand and held it across the desk. "Don't worry. There's nothing to worry about."

Lillian shook her head, but said nothing more.

~

I *booked a* Checker cab and moved into the small apartment a week later. Lillian came out as far as the tatty awning of the Martha Washington to watch as I loaded the cab, but wouldn't help. I paid Jack, and with what was left, bought a pallet bed from a futon store several blocks away. I spent a good deal on cleaning supplies. Declining both Bruno's and Jack's offers to help, I cleaned for two nights straight. The claw-footed tub alone took almost an entire evening, until it gleamed dully against the rough brick wall. I slept in the back in the small alcove, placing Mother's ashes near my head on the scarf I'd brought from home. I told myself she was proud of my efforts, and walked her photograph around the place showing it off to her.

I began to accumulate objects. Many were rescued from the street, castoffs I polished up and made my own. I repaired a broken bookshelf of dark-stained wood and lined it with my few Arcade purchases. My favorites were *A Sentimental Education* bound in chartreuse silk (Oscar had particularly admired the binding); the dog-eared *Moby-Dick*; a paperback on mythology I'd bought from the dollar-fifty tables outside the Arcade; a Penguin Classic of James's *Portrait of a Lady*; along with the Borges Lillian had insisted upon to fill my "gaps." My scrapbook of cities, thick with clippings and bricolage, took up most of the bottom shelf, lying horizontally. Mother's photograph sat alone on top.

I still held on to Chaps's anonymous volume, wrapped in her blue bookshop paper. I continued to save her gift for a truly desperate moment, and now that things were looking up, I didn't imagine I would need it any time soon. Besides, I'd grown attached to the parcel as a parcel, and had almost ceased to wonder what it held inside. It was its own object, wrapped and nameless, on my repaired shelf.

The books housed in one's first adult bookshelf are the geological bed of who we wish to become. And when I think of my few acquisitions, I have to admit how fiercely the autodidact struggles for her education, and how incomplete that education remains. How illusory is any accumulation of knowledge!

I dragged a stained upholstered chair in from the street, wrestled it up the tiled stairway, and covered it with a bolt of bright cloth I'd bought from a fabric shop Oscar had recommended. From the same store, I found oddment pieces and hand-stitched some pillows in red, orange, and blue-green. I fashioned curtains for the two front windows and replaced the curtain partition with a fall of pink shot silk, a remnant of a longer piece perhaps intended to be worn as a sari.

I painted the lavatory in the rear a deep shade of French blue;

purchased a reading lamp and a green alarm clock, its face as bold and simple as a child's drawing. There was no mistaking the mechanical marking of time with the clock's incessant tick, tick. Jack's absent friend had left various small pots, along with mismatched crockery and glasses, all a bit grimy, in the couple of cabinets beneath the old porcelain sink.

Forever a collector of trinkets, of gimcracks, I lined the two deep windowsills with treasures. I'd found a couple of nice stones, and an arching piece of cobalt-blue glass from the vacant, garbage-strewn lot a block away. I'd kept a large brown autumn leaf from my park and purchased, from a local thrift shop, a dried starfish and a pretty enameled teapot that was only good for admiring. (Its spout had been imperfectly joined and leaked copiously.) Next to the teapot I placed a small salt shaker, shaped into a Cubist dog, that I pitied on account of it having lost its twin pepper, and a vase, with iridescent violet glaze, that had cracked along one side, but whose shape reminded me of an anemone. It was ugly, but then ugly objects as a general rule are the bravest.

In any case, these funny things gave me courage.

If I didn't ever physically resemble Mother, I had inherited something of her eye for shape, for pattern; and although eclectic and furnished mostly with leavings, the small apartment described me at the time—my optimism in particular. I'd made a bright, colorful room, open and surprisingly warm, despite the continued lack of any actual heat.

Finally, retrieved from the same thrift store, I hung a large, dark mirror, silver flaking at the edges, opposite the armchair. When I sat to read I felt I was keeping myself company, watching from the wall, verifying my existence. The old mirror wavered like a pool. On lonely days, as I readied for the Arcade, it seemed another resident of the apartment was forever falling back from me, a cloud of red hair above her turned shoulder. This other girl was always retreating. She walked away, not out into the city, brilliant with late fall light, but backwards, withdrawing into the mirror, where she was alone and it was always night.

∽

"*Girl, you understand*, don't you, what kind of a man Oscar is?" Pearl peered at me solicitously. She was sitting on the ruined couch in the ladies' bathroom, watching as I brushed my hair. I told her my intention to ask Oscar to have a sandwich with me during our lunch break.

"Did you hear me, Rosemary? You know what I'm asking here?"

"You mean, Pearl, that he's not the sort of man . . . not the sort of man that . . . that . . . can . . . that loves women?" I answered haltingly, blushing.

"You got that right," Pearl laughed. "Not that sort of man at all!" she said, mimicking my accent.

"Well," I said, teasing her back. "You're not that sort, either."

Pearl threw her arms up and guffawed. "I'm not any sort of man, Rosemary, girl. This ain't no travesty role. Don't you forget it!" She laughed, kicking her high-heeled foot in my direction.

I admired her long brown leg.

"Look, honey," she said. "I just don't want you to think that Oscar has anything to offer. Anyone can see you got yourself a great big crush on him there. And well, I . . ."

"You just want to make sure I'm aware of the situation," I finished for her.

Pearl was so kind to me, so sisterly.

"I know, Pearl. I'm not completely stupid." She looked unconvinced. "And what do you mean that anyone can see I've got a crush on Oscar?" I asked. "Do you think other people have noticed?"

Pearl cackled again.

"You got them all watching you, honey. They're all watching you. You can take your pick, Rosemary, but ya can't ever have Oscar. He wasn't made for loving back. But I would keep an eye on Walter Geist if I were you," she said.

"Geist hates me, Pearl," I told her. "But I'm supposed to be his assistant now, since the loan, so I'll just have to get used to it."

"It sure isn't anything like hate, Rosemary, I can tell you that. Pay attention, girl! I can practically smell the obsession. And what do you mean, 'assistant'? What does that have to do with the money? Wasn't the loan from Pike?"

"Geist wants me to help him out, Pearl. To be answerable just to him."

"Is that what he told you?" She pulled a face.

"What's the matter, Pearl?"

"I'd just like to know exactly what that white man has in mind."

CHAPTER

NINE

"Oscar, old chap, don't see enough of you. How goes the nonfictional world, the world of fact and not fancy?" Mr. Mitchell asked. "The real world," he chuckled.

Oscar looked pained. He and I were standing outside on the street. I was waiting for a shipment to arrive; Oscar was on his way to lunch—alone. Mr. Mitchell tipped his hat to me. (I identified the hat automatically, although I couldn't have guessed his size.) "Dear girl," he murmured, and I caught a whiff of vanilla pipe smoke and rum.

I loved to be called "dear girl."

"Fine, Mr. Mitchell," Oscar replied. "Haven't seen your shoplifter about for nearly a month. I can relax a bit now."

"I haven't seen him either," I told them, remembering the day Redburn and I both stood eavesdropping on Pike's conversation.

"Good. Good. No sign in my neck of the woods either, although there is a rather mysterious new collector I'll send your way . . . should be in today. Lots of money and quite excellent taste. Rather like that Mr. Gosford we've been sharing all this time."

"Well, Gosford spends his money on you, not me," Oscar smiled. "I don't think you could say we're sharing him. As he told me only last week—he's a collector of *rare* books, not just any old volumes."

"He said that?" asked Mr. Mitchell, matching Oscar's tone. "Then he's no collector, is he? What a fatuous thing to say. Only rare, old's not good enough?"

"What are you talking about?" I asked. "Why isn't he a real collector?"

"Oscar has plenty of things for Gosford, dear girl. But the man is collecting for price, not value. Cost, not worth, if you follow. Like valuing a gem only because of the degree of difficulty it took to extract."

"I don't really understand," I said. Wasn't that exactly how stones were valued? I knew the collector, Mr. Gosford, and remembered the Beckett he'd purchased for $10,000—an amount that astonished me then, although it was little enough in the context of the Rare Book Room. I'd taken him up there several times since then, when Bruno or Jack hadn't beaten me to Pearl's call. Gosford was supercilious, and mostly silent, in the elevator. I was beneath his consideration. He roamed about Oscar's section often. How keen did one have to be to warrant the classification "collector" at the Arcade?

"To a true collector, the acquisition of an old book is its rebirth," Oscar quoted, absent self-consciousness.

"A real collector is whimsical, after a fashion," said Mr. Mitchell, turning to me, seizing the moment as appropriate for instruction.

"That's not to say that I am whimsical, or Oscar here, or Pike, for heaven's sake. We are practical men. And serious." He smiled. "But we serve the whimsy of others, do we not, Oscar?"

"I think what you mean is that book collecting is only meaningful if it's personal," Oscar clarified. "If it's just another way of accumulating wealth, instead of for the books themselves, it isn't right. Collectors are trying to protect themselves. To separate themselves. It's a hierarchy. That's my complaint with Gosford. In a way

I'd rather Redburn steal the books—at least I know they mean something to him. He takes a risk to get what he wants."

I remembered Redburn's question about whether I cared if the books he sold were stolen. Surely Oscar cared? A collector, after all, wasn't a thief.

"Don't let Pike hear you say that, old chap! He loves to chide me about that Redburn incident," said Mr. Mitchell. "Pike, of course, has his own notions of ownership."

He spread his arms about us companionably.

"But that isn't our concern, my dears. Our business is to find homes for books with the hope they will be loved as we have loved them. My heart is broken every day I make a sale; then renewed again by the arrival of an unexpected replacement. I keep learning to love again—as I frequently tell Mrs. Mitchell." He chuckled at his own small joke. "After nearly fifty years my relationship to books remains mysterious to me, but I know from my own collection that ownership is the most intimate tie we can have to objects."

He let his expansive arms drop and felt around in his jacket for his pipe makings. Oscar rolled his eyes at me, while Mr. Mitchell was distracted, and made his hand into a talking scissors with thumb and fingers, silently parroting Mr. Mitchell's lecture. I laughed, because of the cockatoo that Oscar's hand brought to mind.

"All collections are, Rosemary, trying to elude time," the old bird went on, warming to his subject. "To stop time. To control it. Closest thing to immortality—which is, of course, the irony of it. Because the collector is physical, which is to say temporal. The collector is a childlike figure, dear girl, a prisoner of the eternal present. But you are too young, and too wise, to understand the meaning of such things. Nor should you care."

He smiled. Mercer, the mailman, was rounding the corner on the avenue and about to enter the Arcade's front door. Sensing an opportunity, Mr. Mitchell touched his hat again with his free hand and ducked into the south door.

∽

"*He does go* on," Oscar said. " 'A prisoner of the eternal present,' " he mimicked. "What rot! That lecturing is such a bore. You shouldn't let him patronize you like that."

"I think he's one of the most marvelous people I've ever met," I gushed.

"That's because you know so few. People, I mean."

Of course, Oscar patronized me himself, but then I didn't seem to notice, or care. I found both of them fascinating and studied them as if they were a new species. For me, they were.

Did Mr. Mitchell think I didn't understand time? Or death? Didn't I think of Mother every day? And I had my precious things, my own modest collection lined my windowsills. But it *did* seem that everyone at the Arcade knew vastly more than I did; every outbreak of Who Knows? confirmed it.

"That's a trilby," I said, referring to Mr. Mitchell's hat and trying to show off at least some expertise.

"Named from du Maurier's novel, later made into a play," said Oscar. "It was a style worn onstage."

"You mean *Rebecca*?"

"No, Rosemary. George du Maurier's *Trilby*. Not Daphne. That was his granddaughter. Now, *Trilby* also introduced into common usage the name Svengali. You see, it's a story about power, about control . . ."

And he too was off, leaving me behind, certain that I'd never catch up. I wanted to follow him, though, wherever he went.

"You're going for lunch now?" I asked him, interrupting.

"I am," he said, irritably. "And to stop in at my tailor's. I have my shirts made, you know. It's a habit I picked up. My mother always made my shirts."

"I suppose you're very particular," I said.

"I am." He ran his hand over his dark, thinning hair. "I know exactly what I want."

"And what's that?" I asked, genuinely curious. His shirts were beautiful, although only ever white. How many particulars could there be to a simple white shirt? Nothing about Oscar was simple.

"Well, if you must know, Rosemary," he sighed, "my shirts are made of one hundred percent Egyptian cotton, which is easy enough to find, but I require a 236-thread count per inch. I must have extra-long tails, and a two-piece hand-turned collar." He ran his own hand beneath the collar of his shirt, then turned around, continuing. "The yoke must be split across the shoulders, and because I'm slim, the cut is custom." He turned to face me. "I insist on seam tapes to prevent puckering, and ask for single-needle stitching. There's only one man in the city I've found that can manage the job properly and affordably."

My face showed my genuine surprise, not that only one tailor could manage it, but at the level of detail.

"Yes, surprising, isn't it?" he said, misinterpreting my expression. "You'd think everyone would ask for what they want and there'd be hundreds of tailors catering to specification. But most people don't know what they want, Rosemary. Whereas I always know exactly."

∽

"*Come here, you* Tasmanian Devil," called Arthur, from inside the fortress of the Art department.

"I wish you wouldn't call me that," I said for the hundredth time. "I told you, it might have been funny at first, but now it isn't. I'm not a bit like how it sounds."

"Why don't you like it?" he asked. "I'd think with all that red hair you'd be used to being described as devilish."

"Not everyone thinks like you, Arthur."

"Alas, you understate the case," he said complacently.

"In Australia if you have red hair some people call you Blue. It's a contrary place that way." He was similarly mocking me, calling me devilish because he thought me so proper.

But I liked Arthur. As we chatted I helped stack up overstocks of a large book on a painter named Soutine—all blood, meat, and inverted perspectives.

"Red equals blue—makes perfect sense to me," Arthur observed. "Like *Alice in Wonderland*. I like nicknames, actually. Well, some of them. Do you know what Mitchell calls me behind my back?"

He stopped his exertions and looked into my face. A sheen of sweat covered his wide forehead. I thought in that moment he looked exactly like an oversized Quilp, a giant dwarf, only benign, from *The Old Curiosity Shop*.

"Everyone is always making up names here, especially Mr. Mitchell. Who would know what he calls you behind your back?"

"Your crush told me—Oscar. We chat sometimes, though not as often as I'd like. That canny old coot Mitchell is a bit of a drunk, you know, and rather cruel, actually. Oscar told me that he calls me the Ape."

"What? I'm sure that's not true!" I couldn't believe it of Oscar or Mr. Mitchell.

"It is true, TD," Arthur laughed. "You don't get it, do you?"

"Is it because you're, well . . . large?"

"Fat, Rosemary. I'm fat, not large."

He drawled the word "large" in imitation of my flat vowels.

"The joke, if joke one thinks it, has to do with the expression 'Art is the ape of nature.' "

He looked at me for some sign of recognition.

"Do you see?"

And he was the ape of art?

"That's not funny," I said.

"Well, if it were about someone else I'd think it was quite good. But as it's about me, I'm appalled at Mitchell's insensitivity. Not surprised, though."

"It's cruel, Arthur, and you mustn't take it to heart," I said.

He sat heavily, and alarmingly, on a stack of coffee-table books on home decorating, and burped behind his hand. Arthur was plagued by indigestion.

"I'm used to cruel, Rosemary. I'm sure you've noticed that there are quite a few people here in the Arcade that have a familiarity with cruelty in common."

He burped again.

"I mean, look at Geist there, for pity's sake, and even the adorably peculiar Oscar. Then there's Pearl—hermaphrodites being but a fable! These people know all about what's cruel."

"But they're not cruel in themselves," I said firmly. "That's the difference. That's why it's safe here, for everyone."

"Don't be so sure. Cruelty is something everyone knows about, one way or another."

"What do you mean?"

"Look, my Tasmanian Devil—"

"Oh, stop!" I cried.

"Okay!" He held up his hands in mock protest. "Just don't insist on seeing only what you want to see. Try to see this place for what it is."

"And what's that, Arthur?"

"Well, a bookstore, but also a reliquary for the bones of strange creatures. Mermaids' tails, unicorn horns ... that sort of thing. You're looking at natural history in this place."

He swiveled his big head around.

"The books act to filter out the normal. The real. And we've changed shape in the isolation, like specimens from the Galapagos. We're isolatos—islands in an island, like the island you came from ..."

"Stop, Arthur, you are peculiar," I told him, impatient with not following his point, with his rambling.

"Exactly so. You've concluded my argument for me. I've no choice but to be peculiar."

He heaved himself up to stand and, turning his attention to a familiar customer, lumbered over to ask if he needed any help.

∽

"*Oscar, I want* you to see my apartment. I could make you dinner?"

We sat together on a bench in a corner of my dirty park, a few blocks north of the Arcade. Finally, he'd agreed to have a sandwich with me during lunch break. I'd been asking him for weeks.

It was really too cold now to eat outside, but Oscar apparently preferred my park to anything warmer or more comfortable. We were outside at his insistence, after we'd picked up sandwiches from a deli across the street. Gray November days were unfamiliar to me; in Tasmania, summer would have properly arrived.

My bellwether park was oddly still that day. The sky, the air, were both colorless and tired. The surrounding buildings looked archaeological. Pigeons pecked at filth beneath the benches, waiting for something more promising to fall.

I felt slightly giddy, away from the Arcade, alone in Oscar's company.

He chewed his sandwich and didn't answer my question

about dinner. I studied the muscular movements of his jaw. He swallowed loudly, looking about. We sat silently, and after a while I inspected my shoes.

Beneath the bench, beside my shoe, was a used condom. Had he seen it? What went on here at night? I mildly fantasized a squalid couple locked together on the bench, their mouths rapacious and working at each other's faces. Lovers, here, on this very bench in my dirty park! My skin went hot in the cold air. Oscar chewed his sandwich. I kicked the soiled thing under the seat and looked up to see if he'd noticed. Is there a more melancholy object?

Around us, the same ragged trees stood by and the same grubby plastic bags hung trapped in their branches, limp as pathetic phantoms; further remains of bad ideas and lonely dreams.

I cleared my throat, and when I began to speak, Oscar finally answered.

"Rosemary," he said slowly. "I, ah . . ."

"It's not a big deal, Oscar," I hurried to reassure him. "I just thought you might like to see where I'm living. It's quite nice, really."

I hadn't learned that my own silence had power, and prattled on.

"I bought some pieces of fabric, from that store you told me about," I ran on. "I've made pillows. And a curtain actually, from a piece of beautiful silk."

"Ah, yes?" said Oscar, relieved. "Do you know what kind of silk?"

"What kind? No, I didn't ask, but it looks a bit Indian. It might even have been from the end of a sari," I told him.

"Really," he said, putting his sandwich aside. "I'm very interested in Indian silks. They have marvelous names—I've written about them in my notebook. Great names: Kanjeevaram, Puttapakka, Baluchari. Very fancy silk comes from Benares—it's a holy city, you know . . . and ancient. Does your silk piece have a border?"

"Well, yes. The edge has some gold in it, but it wasn't expensive. It was just an end I found in a remnant bin."

"That's called the pallu, the end of the sari." He took up his sandwich again. "The ends can be quite ornate," he said with his mouth full. "They know about fabrics—Indians. They appreciate cloth. They understand its significance. Of course, the history of silk is itself fascinating, as is the cultural relevance of fabric. The Malagasy, for instance, believe that cloth actually makes people, in the sense that it gives them an identity. That people are woven . . ."

Mayonnaise limned the corner of Oscar's mouth as he spoke, and I longed to lick it; but I didn't want to be caught staring.

"So," I persisted, before he could recount the history of silk or the psychology of the Malagasy, "will you come to dinner? Oscar, you could see the fabric. Will you come?"

"No, Rosemary," he answered, his face a bleached bone in the strange light, petrified and dry. The rare color of his eyes appeared metallic, at once rich and hard. "I won't come. I don't really go out. I work on my notebooks when I get home. Or I go to the library. I have research to do. I really believe I can't spend my time any better. There is so much that requires investigation."

"Investigation?" I repeated, somewhat at a loss to his meaning.

He quoted then, from memory, something he'd noted down years before. He'd taken the quote as advice, as a recommendation on how best to live. It impressed me deeply, not because it was advice I thought worth taking but because of how fully it described him.

"'You could not employ your time better than by dissociating yourself from everything else and, in the solitude of your own room, peering into the kaleidoscope of this unknown world.'"

Oscar finished the recitation with as much of a flourish as he was capable of—a slight flick of his long hand.

"I like my solitude," he continued. "I don't go to people's

houses. I don't want anyone to expect anything, you see. You mustn't expect more from me. I won't come to dinner," he wound up. "I prefer not to."

He let this last sentence fall between us into silence, expecting, I suppose, that because I'd been reading Melville I could acknowledge a reference to *Bartleby*. But I couldn't have then, just as I couldn't join him in his solitude.

After a short while he looked up at the opaque sky, his expression abstract and impossible to read.

"I think it might actually snow," he said amiably.

I couldn't eat. I knew, from a fresh heat that began near my hairline and moved back toward my neck, that despite my increasing knowledge of the world, despite Pearl's protective advice, despite even his essential peculiarity, I was in love with Oscar. I knew it was pointless; that I deliberately chose not to hear what he told me quite explicitly.

Wanting him was a decision to yearn for what I would never have. But there was a way that choosing that actually helped. It revealed to me that there were other types of grief. And romantic grief can act as a rein on the extravagance of that other, eternal loss. It spread grief out, changing the finality of absence into something else—into desire that fed imagination. I had picked up the idea that the nature of love was unrequited, and that conviction forced me to imagine what it was I wished for. It was creative—although I never paused to imagine then what Oscar might want from me.

"I've never seen snow," I said, buttoning up my thin coat, though my face burned.

"Well, it's bound to disappoint," he said dismissively.

"Snow is useless," he followed up. "But how unusual not to have seen something so ordinary."

Almost imperceptibly, tiny flakes began falling without wind. I tilted my head back and watched snow fall as if materializing just above our heads. Its beauty was transporting. And the snow was like something made actual, a way to surround Oscar, to touch him, without his knowledge or permission. It seemed complicit in my wish.

"I suppose it's naive to call snow magical," I whispered, entranced.

"Not if you think it is," Oscar granted.

We watched the snow fall, particles of light inside gray atmosphere.

"It's all right, you know, Oscar," I offered. "I won't say I understand why you can't come to dinner, when we're sitting right here having a sandwich. Freezing!" I smiled. "But it's all right."

I wasn't looking for consolation. I wanted most of all to feel. To experience loss and restoration together, at once, like snow appearing to counter never having seen it before.

We stood up into the flecked air. I threw out the remainder of my sandwich and Oscar's empty paper bag. The dirty park was quickly changed, covered with a threadbare cloth of white, punctured with dark holes. I collected a tiny amount of snow and held it in my hand, my fingers turning pink.

"I thought it would be colder," I said, tossing the small clump away as we crossed the street, and wiping my palm against my trousers.

Oscar smiled slightly and turned his beautiful head toward the sky.

"Nothing is ever what you imagine, is it?" he said, to no one in particular.

∽

"*Rosemary*," *Geist called* from the base of the stairs leading to his office. "Are you there? Are you in Oscar's section?"

"Yes, I'm here." I placed the books I was shelving on the floor close to the shelf.

Geist was always calling for me now. For hours at a time I'd have to help him in the basement, reading off the printed prices of review copies while he calculated their prices in his head. Or he'd have me read out columns of numbers in his office while he jabbed accusingly at his innocuous adding machine. I longed to float about the floor, shelving books and helping customers, free of obligation.

He looked disheveled. Pike could be heard instructing a customer, and Geist listened intently, his head tilted in the direction of Pike's voice, like the dog in the old advertisement. He appeared to rely more on sound and smell than on sight.

"Did you need something?"

"Come up here to the office."

I ascended, meeting him on the landing. He turned to walk into the office and stumbled slightly on the threshold.

"Are you all right?" I asked.

He ignored me, sat behind his desk, falling into his chair. The magnifying glass lay, pushed aside, on top of loose papers and receipts.

"I want you to read something for me," Geist said, pulling open a drawer on the right side of his desk. "It's just a letter of inquiry. Here."

He handed me a letter, folded inside a torn envelope. There was no such thing as "just a letter" in the Arcade. Mail was precious, for it brought business. I'd never read any letters to Geist before. All the mail was delivered to George Pike's desk first, and daily, by the diplomatic courier, Mercer.

"Of course, Mr. Geist," I said. "But—"

He cut me off sharply. "Don't ask questions," he said. "Just read it aloud, that's all I'm asking."

"Yes, of course, Mr. Geist. Excuse me."

I removed the letter from the envelope. The paper was thick and heavy, silken paper I knew to be expensive. The letter was written in beautiful, looping copperplate. A delicate impression of character was conveyed in subtle shadings from light to dark, the pleasing inconsistencies of a fountain pen, pressure a key to temperament.

The handwriting triggered a chain of associations, bringing grief and pleasure together so keenly I couldn't catch my breath. I saw *"Eternity"* written in chalk on the sidewalk in Sydney, and felt the presence of Mother, like a rumor of her alive. I gasped, faltering for a moment.

Geist tapped his hand impatiently.

The wisp of her presence was quickly dispersed, iterating the hard fact of death. Against my heart, as the saying goes, I had yet to grow accustomed to grief's contradiction—here but not here. I hesitated, waiting for the fullness of the vision to pass into some less recognizable awareness.

"Well, go on," Geist demanded.

"Sorry," I said, my voice unsteady. I rubbed at my eye. "It's just that this handwriting reminds me of something. It's very, very beautiful."

"And impossible to read clearly—for me in any case. I've misplaced my glasses and this damned magnifier gives me a headache that makes me think my brain will split in two. I prefer typeface. Please continue."

The envelope was blank and without postage. Apparently it had been hand-delivered to the Arcade, and not by Mercer. I scanned the letter.

"What is it?" Geist demanded, his hand now a white fist on the desk.

"It's just that it begins, 'Dear Mr. Pike,' and I—"

"I am authorized to read all the inquiries that are sent to the Arcade. Do you think I'm not?" he whispered furiously. "Pike regularly has me handle correspondence!"

This was not true. I knew myself that Arcade mail was sacrosanct. Where had this letter come from? And how had Geist gotten hold of it? Had he taken Pike's mail? Had it been entrusted to him, to hand-deliver to Pike? Geist looked quite unwell, but I didn't dare ask him what the matter was.

" 'Dear Mr. Pike,' " I began, clearing my throat. " 'I have information to share with you in consideration of the Arcade's past contributions to my collection. I also trust your discretion. The subject of this letter concerns a lost manuscript of inestimable value by the American author Herman Melville. The manuscript is presently in my possession, but because I cannot honorably account for the way it came into my hands, I seek your assistance in authenticating and subsequently placing this rarest of finds. I am aware of several collectors who would be interested, but require you to act—' "

"That's enough!" Geist stood and snatched the letter so sharply that he tore a corner of the heavy paper, leaving the fragment between my fingertips.

"You've torn it," I said, stunned at his reaction. After looking at the ragged piece for a moment, I slipped it almost unconsciously into my pocket.

"Please, Rosemary," Geist stammered, clutching the letter, wadding it up like a rag. "I'm sorry to have troubled you. Please leave me alone."

He sat down. Then, leaning forward, he held his arm in a curve across his desk, his head down, like a child protecting his work from the avid eyes of a cheat.

CHAPTER

TEN

⌒⌒ I had never celebrated Thanksgiving before, and neither had Lillian. I wasn't sure of all the various rituals involved, but I knew it was an opportunity to invite her to dinner. Lillian's brother finally consented to giving her the evening off from sentinel duty at the Martha Washington. I splurged and bought a small turkey, and even stuffed it with lamb as a special treat, Oscar having told me that in Argentina they eat large quantities of meat. Preparing the meal warmed the apartment, but not enough to make taking off my coat necessary. Now that it was late November and practically winter, I often slept in it.

"Why it so cold?" Lillian complained when I let her in.

"There's no heat at the moment, but Jack tells me the landlord is going to fix it next week." He'd been saying that since I'd moved in.

"How long you live like this?"

"Since I moved in. It's not so bad, Lillian. I can afford it, and it's all my own."

"It will get even colder soon. Snow tonight maybe. You and me, we feel it more. We are from the warm side of the world. Our blood, it is thin."

"Don't worry about me, Lillian."

"I worry all the time."

"I know."

"I am alive because I worry. When I stop I die."

"That's a bit dramatic, don't you think?"

"No," she said flatly. "You know nothing about it."

"Well, you'll just have to tell me. Now please, I'm so glad you're here, sit down. You're my first guest ever. The first guest I've ever entertained in my life, so you'd better cooperate."

I laughed, and Lillian smiled slightly. I gave her a tour of the sleeping alcove; the toilet in the back.

"It's very small," Lillian said, poking her face around the silk curtain. "But so is a room at Martha Washington's. I like all these colors."

She returned to the front room and plumped up the pillows on the old armchair.

"This bath in here is like a little ship to sail away. A little boat to take you home." She laughed quietly, patting me. "You make it nice, Rosemary. Colorful. Like you."

"Thanks, Lillian. I'm so glad you came. I hope you'll come often."

We smiled at each other, equally glad to have a friend.

"Oh, I bring you something," Lillian said, jumping up and finding her large leather bag. She pulled out a bottle of wine. "From Mendoza," she said. "In Argentina. My brother, he has many bottles. Our father was from Mendoza, and he always have at home when we were small. He dead now. Like yours, yes?"

I took the bottle of wine.

"I told you I didn't know my father, Lillian," I said. "He might not be dead. I mean, I must have had one, but my mother never married, and she never named the man who'd gotten her pregnant. I somehow got it into my mind that he was from far away. Not from hints, really—more from just fantasies."

I set the bottle on the small table beside the chair.

"I used to dream that I'd come to a city and see someone who was unmistakably him—who was me, only a man, and older. Red hair, you know? Freckled like me. And tall. It's ridiculous, especially now that I'm here, but that's what I used to think."

I took two glasses from the shelf above the stove. I didn't have a corkscrew. I'd never had more than a few sips of wine in my life, but I wasn't going to admit that to Lillian, who liked to remind me I was a child.

"I used to think the same." She shifted in the armchair awkwardly.

"My Sergio, my son—I think I see the back of his head walking down the street in Buenos Aires, then in New York. I think he alive. That he escape—"

She broke off.

"I think I see him. It will be four years."

Lillian cleared her throat, determined now to speak.

"I know him, though, I love him, so it is different. He did exist. My husband and me, we raise him. He real." She touched the wine bottle on the table and looked across at me. "Your father is in your head only."

"Well, I suppose," I said, not wanting to contradict her. Wondering at her discomfort. This was the first time Lillian had mentioned Sergio. She did not do it casually but with great care.

I gave up. "I know there's a huge difference."

Lillian took out a pocket knife with a corkscrew. She opened the bottle expertly, poured two glasses; we clinked them together, and I took a large swallow. After a few more sips the wine went to my head, and although I didn't like the taste, I appreciated the effect.

"Lillian, you're helping me christen my apartment."

I moved a small side table closer to the armchair. It was my only chair, so I upended the suitcase Chaps had given me to serve as another chair. Sergio's name had called him into the room like a palpable presence. We had fallen silent at the sound of it. I stood and rinsed vegetables at the sink and, after a long silence, looked across at Lillian, who was staring out the window. She peered into the thick night, her own reflection staring back at me, unseeing.

"What are you thinking about, Lillian?"

"You have asked me that before. It is always the same," she said, with tremendous sadness. She drained her glass.

"What happened to Sergio, Lillian? Will you tell me?" I asked as gently as I could. I moved the suitcase closer to her, sat down, and touched her knee.

There was a long pause. Lillian leaned back against the chair and looked into the old mirror on the opposite wall.

"Where you get that?" she asked.

"You're always changing the subject," I observed, not unkindly. "I got it in a junk shop. It makes me certain I'm really here."

" 'I saw all the mirrors in the world and none reflected me.' That is Borges, you remember, the book you give me and I give you back?"

"I remember, Lillian. It's there on the shelf. What does it mean—'none reflected me'?"

"I don't know, but it make me think that no mirror in the world reflects now my son. He has fallen through." She stood up and then sat again. She stared at me with a kind of dull certainty.

"I will tell you the story of my Sergio, Rosemary. I do not wish to tell, but I must always tell. Otherwise I go crazy again. There is only me left now from my family—from the family of myself, my husband, Emilio, and our only son, Sergio."

She looked full into my face.

"First, I have more wine."

She refilled her glass and drained it.

"You know what means *desaparecidos*?" Lillian whispered. "What means *guerra Sucia*?"

The hot oven clicked loudly in the room, more obtrusive than the regular, softer tick of the green clock. The street door downstairs opened and slammed shut; footsteps on the tiled corridor ended with another slam. Lillian waited for silence. I had no idea what she was saying.

"He is one of the disappeared," she said with finality, as if this explained what I had asked. She read my confusion.

"You do not know what that means? Can you understand? You are a young girl from a young country. A safe place, I think, your Tasmania. You not know. Sergio was taken. Taken from his house at night. He was then twenty-five, older than you. Taken. Do you understand? Now he would be twenty-nine. His birthday last month . . . remember when I not go to work?"

She fidgeted with her collar, her hand at her throat.

"We send him to a good school. He graduate from university. He was going to marry his girlfriend. He begin to teach . . ." Lillian's voice dropped. She clutched at her throat and stared at the ceiling. She sighed.

"How to explain to you the difference between death and disappearance?"

In an instant she appeared angry, continuing in Spanish, thickly and with emotion. She stopped. After a while she began again, in English.

"You want to know, Rosemary, but you are a child. You cannot know. This kill me too, and yet I have to live, because my son did not come back. I'm still waiting for him. I wait to find out."

"You mean he was abducted, Lillian?" I asked, trying to make sense of what she was saying. "By who?"

"The army, the police. In Argentina, this the government. I

am Catholic, you understand? The church not help me. The priests do nothing. They maybe are involved. My brother left before this start to happen. He come to New York and he buy the hotel. He say that people will know soon what happening, but I think they always know, they just turn their face away. God turn his face away."

She stared into the mirror, and I met her eyes there inside her darker world.

"Four years ago, he disappear," Lillian said with finality. Her head falling back, she spoke to the ceiling.

"I not have practice telling the story of Sergio anymore. It make me tired. I start in too many places. It good you make me tell, because he takes with him the mystery of his end. It is good to tell. My brother, he sick to hear. He helped me, but he has had enough."

Lillian crossed herself reflexively.

"There are many such cases. Even now. Each day there are more. But I tell you from the start so you will know."

Lillian stood up and paced in front of me.

"It was organized. It start at eleven, in the evening—I know because on the same night they took six of Sergio's friends from university. They begin at eleven at one house. At one o'clock at another's, at three my son's place. He have a small apartment across from the park. The only witness was the doorman. The doorman he say they drag him out from behind his desk, they order him to open the door and then they scream for him to leave, but the doorman, he hide behind the stair, listening."

"Who did this, Lillian?"

"The doorman say several men, one in uniform. We never know who. They wreck the apartment, and after a while the doorman see them bring Sergio downstairs, already tied up. They put him in a van and drive away. That is all I ever know."

An ambulance or police car passed with diminishing sound

outside on the street. Lillian started at the sound of a siren. She rubbed her face.

"After they took him, I not sleep. I thought I was gone blind until Emilio take me to a doctor who told me I have to cry. Tears stop me from seeing. That doctor send me to a special doctor—you know the kind." She tapped her finger at her temple. "She help me to cry, and then, then I cannot stop. But I can see. After a while I try to read again, but this, all pleasure, is gone from me."

Lillian gestured to the few books lying on my repaired shelf. She twisted her hands together, the knuckles showing through her dark skin. She took up her glass and I refilled it.

"Emilio and I, we file a habeas corpus. You understand?"

I shook my head.

"We find a lawyer to help us. Where is his body, you know? This we are told to do. Our neighbors, their daughter disappear, they know a lawyer. Then the lawyer, he disappear too. We want an answer from the government. I am a mother. I need to know. I find the mothers who protest in the plaza. I join, we have meetings with officials—with liars. Nothing. We write letters. We tell. Now four years, my Sergio *desaparecido*. And more continue. Everyone need to know what happening there in my country. But nobody want to know. Understand this, Rosemary—my son, our children, they are very best. A generation who care, who see things different. Sergio study sociology, to help the poor. To change things. These are who disappeared. They took them. I not know where is my son. Is he dead?"

Lillian looked around my small apartment, her eyes ranging over all the small objects I had accumulated. The green clock with its relentless tick. The wine bottle, half empty.

"Lillian," I said softly. Her eyes swung to my face. There was an acknowledgment, and she began to speak again, very quickly, her voice grave, her accent thicker.

"I watch the TV. I not go out. He might come home, I not know. Maybe I am crazy? Emilio die, and my brother, he bring me here to petition the government. Emilio die broken, you understand? The absent child makes you to be absent. Can you understand, Rosemary?"

"No, Lillian. I can't really. I can only try to."

I took her hand and we looked into each other's eyes until I turned away, inadequate before her suffering.

"I don't know what to say. But I do understand that your pain makes you feel like you too have disappeared. That I think I can understand."

I felt my tears but stopped, ashamed. What had I to cry about? I stood up quickly. I tried to busy myself with dinner, I took out the turkey, leaving the oven door open for warmth. I buttered vegetables and arranged the overcooked food onto mismatched plates. Furtively, I checked on Lillian.

I couldn't have guessed why I assumed the weight of another's pain; I only know I did. At eighteen, I thought I was implicated in everything; I thought that because I had heard Lillian's story I could in some way mitigate it. That her suffering might be meaningless was more than I could ever allow. Who did allow such things?

Lillian did not weep. Her eyes scanned my apartment as if Sergio would appear. She stared at the claw-footed bathtub against the wall as if seeing his specter there wouldn't have surprised her, rising from it, a drowned man resurrected. Her mouth moved, murmuring in Spanish, her voice tender. She spoke on softly, smiling and even relaxing somewhat.

Perhaps she saw him there, lying back in the bath. It didn't frighten me, Lillian speaking to the air. After all, I talked to Mother every day. For all its poverty, it seemed that language was a thread.

I placed the plates on the small table. Lillian sat back in the armchair. She crossed her arms over her chest as if now she was ready to address me again, ready to speak English.

"It is gone from me too, child, that pleasure. Tears. My brother made me come and say I get help here. There is no help. I do nothing but watch on the TV. I work for him. I wait. Who can help? No one."

I ate the turkey mechanically, without appetite. Lillian ignored the food.

"What happened to your husband?"

"Emilio? He died. He was very depressed, you understand? He stop speaking."

Lillian leaned forward to speak.

"There are some films," she said. "They show because of pressure. I know from the mothers that secrets are being told. But I find out nothing more, nothing of Sergio. And then we see them on TV. They opened pits—graves without names. There are many bodies. They heave them into the air with bulldozers. Emilio, he stuck to the TV like me now, he see. How they can do this? He die after that. From a heart attack. My brother make me come here. New York, he say, you begin your life again. Get away from that place. Get away, he say. Escape. Sergio is dead for sure, he say. I leave because I can do nothing. I have no one. Many people tell me I am lucky because I can leave."

Lillian picked up her empty glass and stared through it: a spyglass, a periscope. Her face grew smaller from my vantage while mine, I imagine, was magnified and closer.

"But I don't want to lose my country too," she said, almost incidentally. "Like you."

∽

After Lillian left I couldn't sleep. I cleaned and tidied until I was hot with effort and emotion. In bed, with the Huon box near my pillow on the orange scarf, I told Mother about Sergio, and dozed fitfully.

"How?" I asked her. "How does this happen?"

I awoke in the early morning, the apartment icy and unaccountably bright. I untangled my legs from sheets heavy with nightmare, and wrapped myself in a blanket. I put on pots of water to boil and, waiting, stood at the front window. The street below was unrecognizable. Snow had fallen overnight, transfiguring the city. Outside was silent and blindingly white. Burial mounds along the street indicated entombed cars. The heavy snow was opposite that first, delicate dusting—the touching powder that had surrounded Oscar and me in the park. I pulled the blanket tighter and leaned my forehead against the chilled windowpane, thinking about Lillian, about her son. I knew well enough that a person was not a thing to lose, that a person could never be replaced. My breath was a faint apparition before my face, a visible exhalation that failed to reassure.

I remembered Chaps telling me about winter, prompted by an image in a picture book. "In winter with warm tears," went the verse she recited, "I'll melt the snow."

∽

"*Girl, you look* like you've seen a ghost," Pearl said in the Arcade bathroom later that morning. "What's happened? Are you all right?"

"I'm all right, Pearl. I just . . . it's just that I found out something very upsetting."

"It's that fucking Geist, isn't it? Maybe you literally *have* seen a ghost! What did he do to you?"

"What? No," I said, confused. For a minute I thought I'd told her about his hand on my back, or about the letter addressed to Pike. "No, Pearl. It's got nothing to do with him."

"What's happened, then?" she asked. "Here, sit down. Tell."

We sat together on the torn sofa in the ladies' room. Pearl took my hands into her large, dry ones. I tried to begin Lillian's story, but it seemed an invention of the night, like the snow that had buried the city. Pearl was patient.

"You know my friend Lillian? The one I met when I was staying at the Martha Washington?"

"I've heard you talk about her, but I haven't met her. You look for Spanish books for her?"

"That's right. She's not Spanish, though, she's from Argentina."

"Okay," said Pearl, encouraging me to continue.

"I've been trying to get her to come to my place for dinner. She was my first friend here really, and I'm very fond of her. She's about the same age as my mother, you see, and, well . . ."

"I understand," Pearl said.

"So she came over last night, for Thanksgiving, and I made dinner, and she brought a bottle of wine."

"So what's wrong?"

"Well, I don't know how much you know about this, but Lillian says her son was murdered by the Argentine government. That he is what she called 'disappeared,' and that her husband died as well, sort of from worry. And her brother sent for her to come to New York because he thought it would help her to get away, but all she thinks about is whether her son is really still alive or whether he was tortured or—"

I broke off, my eyes filling. Did I think it made any difference?

"I can't do anything, Pearl," I went on. "I just didn't expect to know this sort of thing about someone. What can I do for her? You know, Tasmania is very quiet and nothing bad really happens.

I mean, people die and that's terrible, but that's about the worst thing, and—"

"Welcome to the world, Rosemary girl," Pearl said without harshness or sarcasm, her voice deep with an unaccustomed seriousness. "Don't you read the newspaper there in Tasmania? There was a coup in Argentina a few years ago, and the government rounded up supposed subversives."

"I'm sure Lillian's son wasn't a subversive. He studied sociology."

"They're calling it the 'dirty war,' Rosemary. Look it up. Apparently thousands of people have been killed. There are stories of victims being drugged and pushed from planes into the sea. They called them disappeared because no one knows what happened to them, but it's not very hard to guess. They were murdered."

"But how could it happen? What's Lillian supposed to do? Why can't anyone stop them?"

"Oh, Rosemary," said Pearl wearily. "The world you want to know is worse than any nightmare you could imagine. Don't think you can hide here in the Arcade like the rest of us without encountering something of its ugliness. Books won't make it go away."

"I'm just so shocked, Pearl. I care about Lillian. I'm worried that she's a little unstable from grief and worry. Years of it. I thought she was a bit odd, but then so is everyone I've met here. I had no idea . . . I want to help her but I don't know how."

Pearl looked thoughtful.

"Mario's a lawyer, you know, and I think he might know some people who work in human rights," said Pearl. "I might be able to put her in touch with an organization here. I'm sure she's tried everything, but you never know. Mario knows lots of Italians, perhaps some in Argentina. I'll ask him tonight."

"It barely seems possible, Pearl. That someone can live with such horror. That such things go on—torture, murder. It hardly seems real."

"Reality is as thin as paper, girl," said Pearl, shaking her head. "I thought that was one thing you did know, what with an imagination like yours—as thin as paper, and as easily torn."

∽

"*Rosemary*," said Oscar. "Are you all right?"

"Yes, why?"

"Geist was looking for you."

"He was?!" The letter I'd read for Geist had been replaced in my mind by worry over Lillian. I had the torn corner in my pocket, and fingered it—a flake of paper snow. I had to tell Oscar.

"What's wrong?" he asked, his eyes full of interest. "Are you in trouble or something?"

I looked into his face. He blinked. It seemed that his golden eyes spilled light with each blink and that their light penetrated my skin, warming me. Melting me.

"Trouble? What do you mean?"

"Has someone, um, bothered you or something?" Oscar asked, dropping his voice.

"Bothered me? What are you talking about, Oscar?"

"You know, Rosemary," he said, a little impatient. "I'm very bad with that sort of thing . . ."

"What sort . . . ? Oh!" Did he think someone had attacked me? Had had sex with me?

"No, Oscar. For heaven's sake, I've just got a lot on my mind. I have to tell you something strange that happened . . ."

Oscar fidgeted for a minute with his notebook.

"Well, go on. What does Geist want? Is that one of the things on your mind? You've been spending a lot of time with him." He sat up on his high stool and leaned against one of his stacks. The awk-wardness abated. "I know you don't want advice from me, but you'd better be careful of him, Rosemary. He's quite taken with you."

"Geist?" I asked, confused. "No, my friend Lillian told me a terrible story. You won't believe it. Geist just wanted me to read a letter to him the other day, and perhaps he wants me to do that again. That's all."

"Reading letters? Where is he getting letters from?"

"It's very strange, I—"

Pearl bellowed from the register for an escort to the Rare Book Room, cutting me off. I waited, listening. She bellowed again.

"I'd better answer that. Jack and Bruno are always late in the morning. I'll be back in a minute."

I ran to the front counter, but missed the customer. Bruno had arrived and beat me to it. Another customer was waiting, though, a publishing type, chatting with Pearl, who stood filing a sharp green nail. He was an Arcade regular named Russell, first or last I didn't know then. He was middle-aged and kindly; his face had been rav-aged by acne, and deep scars pitted his cheeks. I'd escorted him downstairs several times before, and he visibly cheered at the sight of me. I knew he liked to talk with me and had taken something of an interest in my well-being. He'd traveled to Australia once, to work on a book, and we'd had a few conversations about the coun-try and its people. Even though I liked him, I didn't want to take the call, preferring to return to Oscar. But once Russell had seen me I had no choice. I had to escort him downstairs, and assumed Wal-ter Geist would be waiting in the basement.

"Still working here, I see, Rosemary," said Russell, handing me a bag filled with new books.

"Of course," I said. "Why wouldn't I be?"

"No reason. I just thought perhaps you'd be off on another adventure," he said, as we descended the stairs. "Not interested in a different job?"

"I like the one I have," I said.

"It can't pay much."

"It's enough for me. Plus I get to work with books."

"There are other jobs that involve working with books," he said. "I have one, for example. I'm an editor, you may remember."

"I love the Arcade," I told him.

"I can't imagine why," Russell answered. "A young woman like you . . ."

"It's a whole world in here."

We stood for a moment at the base of the stairs and he studied me.

"There's a whole world outside of here, too," he said with a smile. "As you must know, having come from the other side of the world."

"Have you read *Moby-Dick*?" I asked him.

He nodded.

"Well, the Arcade is like the ship to me. You know, people from everywhere, on a great adventure."

"Have you finished the book?"

"No, I'm deliberately reading it very slowly."

"Well, not to spoil it for you, but your ship sinks. You might want to find another metaphor, or at least consider other employment."

"The Arcade isn't going under," I said. "And thanks for ruining it for me."

He laughed. "There are other adventures, you know. How old are you, Rosemary?"

"Eighteen."

"You're smart. You should be in school."

"But that's exactly why I'm here," I said. "To learn."

"Aargh, don't tell me—the Arcade is your Harvard and your Yale!" Russell rolled his eyes, amused.

"Well, here I'm paid to learn. I'm even paid to read, if Mr. Pike doesn't catch me!"

"Look, when you want another job—like making books instead of selling them—let me know."

He handed me a business card printed with his name—Thomas Russell. The company symbol—a feather quill—matched the imprimatur on the spine of the books I held. I pointed this out to him.

"Why do you sell books from your own company?" I asked, wondering if he'd stolen them.

"They're publicity copies," he said, dismissive. "They're extras, if you like. And I've a few bad habits to support."

I was about to ask what they were, but we'd reached Geist's counter.

Arthur stood behind it, pleasantly surprising me.

"Where's Mr. Geist, Arthur, and why aren't you in Art?" I asked.

"Looks like I've gotten a promotion," he said ironically. "I'm just filling in, TD. Geist told me he had to return to his office briefly."

"Oscar said he was looking for me," I told him.

He shrugged.

Arthur took the books from Russell and, after checking the cover flap of each book and scribbling down several amounts and adding them, he handed him a yellow slip to cash in with Pearl at the register.

"Thanks, Art," said Thomas Russell. "Comes in handy."

"No doubt," Arthur returned.

"Let me know when you're ready to jump ship," Russell said to me as he left.

I just smiled and shook my head, turning back to Arthur.

"What do you think is the matter with him?" I asked.

"The matter with who?" he said, already pulling out a large book from beneath the counter, ready to pass the time until the next customer appeared.

"With Walter Geist, of course."

"Oh, I've no idea. I must say he did look rather the worse for wear. Bumping into things. Perhaps he had a bad night."

Arthur smiled slyly.

"I had rather a good night myself, TD."

"I don't really want to hear about it, Arthur."

"No, I suppose you don't," he chuckled. "'When Art is wanting, the beast is superior,'" he added, raising his eyebrows suggestively.

"What?"

"Yeats," he said.

I ignored him.

"I hope he's all right," I said. "Mr. Geist hasn't seemed himself."

"What self would that be? I'm surprised you're even interested. Such an impossible man. You have been spending rather a lot of time with him."

"I'm supposed to be his assistant or something," I said vaguely.

"Or something," Arthur echoed provocatively.

"What's that supposed to mean, Arthur?"

"Rosemary, guilelessness is charming only in children and animals. Just because Geist is the most peculiar man you're likely to ever come across . . . he is still a man. Desire exists, whether you choose to notice it or not. This place is full of it."

Arthur opened the book of photographs, nudes as usual. I felt sick to my stomach.

"For example," he said, pointing at a page.

"Arthur, I'm just concerned that he's not well, and I think it's affecting how he behaves."

"Well, illness makes one sensitive, like a photographic plate. No doubt Geist was born with a sickness we can't possibly understand. Perhaps it's just getting worse, that's all."

He turned the pages slowly, lingering over each picture. "Perhaps he's just fading away like an old photograph," he made out, dreamily. "Some images simply disappear and are lost. It's the chemicals."

He flipped around the book, opened at a double-page spread of a naked man, his face hidden in a shadow cast by someone standing outside the picture. The man's head was thrown back in ecstasy or pain, I couldn't tell which.

When I returned upstairs, Oscar had taken an early lunch and Pearl was busy with a long line at the register. I tried to help a few customers, but after seeing the huge piles left near Pike's platform for shelving, I wanted to visit the Rare Book Room. To escape.

Geist would come in search of me eventually, but first I wanted to see Mr. Mitchell. I needed comfort. Lillian, nightmares buried beneath snow, sinking ships, all had settled in my stomach like stones. The Rare Book Room felt safer than the Arcade below, heavenly in fact, and although I hadn't ever visited Mr. Mitchell without the pretext of escorting a customer, his paternal presence was the company I most wanted. Surely that wasn't breaking any rules?

CHAPTER

ELEVEN

∽ "Mr. Mitchell," I called after banging closed the cranky elevator cage.

"Over here, dear girl. Over here."

He was leaning on a tall ladder pushed against a high shelf, his feet several rungs above the floor.

"I'm looking for something, Rosemary, but as my mind and oblivion have much in common these days, I've actually forgotten what it was. I did find this rather wonderful edition of *Orlando Furioso*, and that set me to thinking about love and madness. But what I came up here for I've no idea. Perhaps if I stop trying to remember . . ." he descended the ladder steps. "I'll take a break with my pipe, and it will come to me.

"Ah," he said, sitting behind his small desk. "Whatever it was is forgotten, but here you are. My Rosemary for remembrance, yes?"

I smiled.

"You'll help me remember why I was up that damned ladder."

"No doubt you were looking for a book," I said, joining him at the cluttered desk.

"You won't make a detective with that sort of deduction."

He took a tobacco pouch from the pocket of his jacket, hung over the back of his chair.

"Let's leave it lost for the moment, and tell me why you're visiting—without the accompaniment of a customer, I see. A rare pleasure, my dear. Indeed, very rare."

I flushed to the roots of my hair.

"A pleasure for me as well, Mr. Mitchell. It's so nice and warm up here. I was so cold, and the snow . . ."

I didn't finish.

"The antipodes have left you unprepared," he said, referring, I assumed, to the weather.

We sat silently then, content. Mr. Mitchell pinched out some tobacco and tamped it into his pipe several times. I took in the room. It was like being inside a magic lamp. No vertical space was open or unlined with books, and the air was heavy with a leathery smell, mixed with vanilla. The old volumes themselves suggested a rough uniformity of color—from dun to brown to dusty claret, cloth covers of dull blues and greens. Something in the pattern of their spines, ordered in their way, gave the impression of fabric, a recurring weave or indentation like corduroy. I wondered if Oscar had ever noticed the resemblance. This subtle fabric was echoed and repeated in Mr. Mitchell himself, who dressed in tweeds and corduroys of the same colors, all of a piece with his rare room. His white hair stood up like the pages of an open book or a sheath of folio papers, such as were stacked in corners on the floor.

No doubt my fondness for the Rare Book Room came in part from a sense of familiarity. It was a version of Foys's hat workroom from childhood visits to Sydney. There were no piles of skins, no wall of drawers filled with bric-a-brac, but each old volume amounted to something like the same thing. A book was like a drawer: one opened it and notions flew out.

I had wanted to tell Mr. Mitchell about Lillian, but decided against it. I wondered if I should ask about the letter addressed to

Pike. The letter mentioned a manuscript of Melville's, and I remembered Pike asking him on the phone if Mr. Mitchell had anything for Peabody. The shoplifter, Redburn, had been listening, but so had I, and I couldn't admit to eavesdropping. I wanted Mr. Mitchell to believe in my better self.

I wanted his advice about many things but settled for soaking up the calm he exuded. He lit his pipe, and the match head in that room of paper and leather flared up like an idea. The small illumination from the pipe threw the room into a deeper dimness, and in that dimness everything appeared as if it were covered with a fine layer of ash, softened, as if in recollection.

"Something on your mind, dear girl?" Mr. Mitchell asked, interrupting my thoughts.

"Well, there's a lot on my mind, actually, but I don't want to bother you."

"No bother, Rosemary, not a bit. It can feel very isolating, this adventure you've set yourself on."

"What adventure's that?"

"Living, you know. Growing up. Seeing the world, such as it is."

"You remind me sometimes of a friend I have in Tasmania. Esther Chapman. She has a bookstore too, only a small, very neat one."

"Quite different from here, dear girl."

"Yes, but she's kind in the way you are."

"Perhaps it is you, Rosemary, who inspires kindness. What Miss Chapman and I have in common, then, perhaps isn't books but rather an affection for you."

Behind his head stood an art deco vase filled with tired-looking peacock feathers. The feathers were old, but their purple and turquoise centers set deep spots of color against the faded spines of books.

"The eyes of Argus," he said, following my gaze. "They watch but are benign. They never judge," he added encouragingly.

"I wanted to ask you something. About Walter Geist. I suppose it's because I'm worried . . ."

"The Arcade needs a memory, dear girl, but not a conscience. You shouldn't worry about that old fetch."

"But I am worried. There is something strange going on with him; he—"

"Ha!" Mr. Mitchell chuckled. "The man defines strange."

"No, I don't mean that. There's something else."

I didn't know where to begin. Should I tell him that I used to think Geist hated me? Or that he'd loaned me money, possibly without Pike's knowledge? Or that he stood rather too close to me now on most occasions; that he had put his warm hand on the small of my back? I suspected my own tendency to exaggerate. What, for example, if I told Mr. Mitchell that I used to think Geist was like a creature left abandoned in the Arcade, that I felt bound to him in some way, that I perceived a tie I could barely apprehend? What had I fancied about Geist, and what was real? My imagination had always been overactive; the Arcade had only quickened that inclination.

What should I do about Lillian? Did Mr. Mitchell suspect that I loved Oscar? Did he have any advice for me?

"Yes, Rosemary?" he asked.

I'd been silent a long while.

"Oh," I sighed. "Well, I did want to ask you if you think Mr. Geist is ill. Do you think he might be, you know, sick in some way?"

"The man is not my subject, dear girl, but you know he's not exactly robust . . ."

"Have you noticed him worse, though, lately?"

"In what way worse? Could you be a bit more specific?"

"I wonder if you've noticed his eyes . . . if you think he could be going ... well, if you've noticed that he might be losing his sight."

Mr. Mitchell stopped smiling and looked at me with genuine seriousness.

"Well, you know his eyes are very poor on account of his condition, Rosemary. His eyesight has always been weak. He depends on those fancy glasses and he has that special contraption for accounts. I don't care for the fellow, I may as well tell you, but what makes you think so, dear girl?"

"He's become a bit messy looking and he is usually fastidious. And—" I went on despite detecting an internal hesitation, an inner voice of caution—"he's having me read to him. You know, read out prices in the basement, and even a letter, and I think it's because he can't see them himself. I think he's moving about and doing all his usual things by heart, not by sight."

"A letter!" he exclaimed. He could barely remain sitting, his expression flaring up like the match he'd set to his pipe. What had I said? How had I set him off so completely? Mr. Mitchell tried to calm himself. He removed his pipe from his mouth, returned it immediately, sucked on it in short, sharp breaths, removed it again, then cradled the bowl in his large palm as smoke enveloped him. The mythological eyes stared from behind his head, jaded and sly. Peacock feathers are decadent, I thought, as they looked and looked at me through the heavy air.

Robert Mitchell sharply cleared his throat.

"Have you mentioned reading a letter to anyone else?" he finally asked, his face livid.

"No," I lied; I'd already mentioned it to Oscar. Why did I lie? And to Mr. Mitchell?

"The letter you read to him, who was it from?" he asked, leaning forward, attempting to keep his tone even.

"Oh, you know, an inquiry, books for sale." I was trying to

make the very specific as general, as harmless, as possible. "He's passed on the accounting mostly to Pearl," I added pointlessly.

"It wasn't addressed to him, was it?" he cried, standing up.

I shook my head, frightened of him now.

"Those are letters that should be directed to me! Rare books are not in Geist's purview!" Mr. Mitchell spat.

Trying to contain himself, he bit at the stem of his pipe, then extracted it quickly from his mouth. He was indignant, his petulance apparent. I was confused. Worse, I was disappointed. It seemed he only thought of himself.

"The letter just asked for information, you know, that sort of thing . . ." I said evasively, trying to minimize the damage.

"Well, it might seem that way to you, but inquiries are the Rare Book Room's lifeblood," he went on vehemently. "I'm not sure you understand what's at stake. You must tell me if Geist has you read any letters offering to sell books or papers. You must remember who they are from and tell me. You needn't mention that to Geist. He knows very little about my end of things. Rare books really don't concern him. Or Pike, for that matter, so long as I'm making money. I need those letters. They are not for the unseeing eyes of those who cannot recognize their value. They convey knowledge I can't be without."

His pipe glowed, an orb in his hand, and I worried that he already suspected I'd read about papers to sell. Suspicion always haunts the guilty mind, Chaps used to tell me, when urging honesty over childhood fibs.

"It's nothing really, Mr. Mitchell," I said, rising too, wanting to leave before I was robbed completely of my paternal fantasy.

"A very ordinary letter," I ran on. "Boring even. Not the sort of thing you'd want to know about . . ."

I realized my mistake too late.

"Forgive me, Rosemary . . ." he said dryly.

My face throbbed.

". . . but I hardly think you able to determine what I need to know."

~

Although time passed unnoticed in the Arcade, paradoxically, moments were marked as if by a soundless beat. George Pike manned his platform performing his magical pricing with a regularity to rival a metronome. I imagined him the Arcade's silent heart, keeping time without distinguishing time, like the steady rhythm of unconscious life.

I had little opportunity to speak with Pike, for him to notice me, and I preferred it that way. Immured in solitude, Pike stood on his stage, the wall of books behind him ordered like the ruled lines of a ledger. If Pike were a book, it would be a reckoning of accounts, paid and received, and no one but Geist was permitted to read from the pages of that inventory.

"Rosemary," he called as I passed his platform on my way from Mr. Mitchell to Oscar's section, close to tears.

"Yes, Mr. Pike."

"Where are you going just this moment?" He spoke to the book in his hand rather than to me.

"I'm, um, going to help Oscar this morning. Jack and Bruno are up front, Pearl's at the register, and I know Oscar has that reference library to shelve that came in last week."

"Did Mr. Geist direct you there?" Pike asked, looking at me finally. His tone was very even.

"No, Mr. Pike."

"Have you seen Mr. Geist today?" This could almost have been a friendly inquiry.

"No, Mr. Pike."

"Then he will not have communicated to you what your task is late this afternoon."

Was George Pike actually in a pleasant mood? What was going on? Everything was reversed: Mr. Mitchell was nasty and George Pike was pleasant. I'd tried to avoid Geist, and now I suspected Pike was going to send me straight to him.

"No, Mr. Pike."

"You are to accompany Walter Geist on an important call. He suggested that you go to assist him."

"Me?" I asked, incredulous.

"An unusual privilege, I grant you, Rosemary. But Walter insisted, and today George Pike is generously disposed. It has been suggested that the call is of educational benefit."

After I translated what Pike was saying about himself, my first thought was that he must have made a large acquisition or sold an expensive volume to behave so agreeably toward me.

"You will accompany Walter to the library of Julian Peabody. Do your best to help, and be certain to inspect closely anything displayed. Mr. Peabody is our most esteemed customer."

By which Pike meant the wealthiest.

"Excuse me, Mr. Pike, but wouldn't Oscar or Mr. Mitchell be far better equipped to help Mr. Geist?"

"You argue?" He peered down at me. "Of course they would. They are both acquainted with aspects of the Peabody collection. But George Pike is sending you. Their presence here is more valuable. Just pay attention, be quiet, and do as Walter tells you. Do you not wish to learn?"

"I do, Mr. Pike, but I—"

"Good. Make sure your hands are clean. Don't make a fool of yourself or of George Pike. Best to speak not at all."

He turned from me to the volume he held, took the pencil from behind his ear, and scratched his distinctive filigree in the corner. How could he possibly know its worth after so little consideration?

∽

"*You wanted to* see me, Mr. Geist? It's Rosemary."

"I always know it's you, Rosemary. No need to announce yourself."

He was sitting behind his desk. Deep lines of exhaustion cut shadows in his white skin. I saw the loop of silver chain around his neck disappearing into his pocket, his glasses evidently staying put. I'd managed to avoid him and now it was almost three.

"I must apologize for my abruptness to you the other day."

I said nothing, smarting over Mr. Mitchell's reaction to this very subject.

"You are to come with me today to meet with a collector."

"Yes, I know. Mr. Pike told me."

"Get your coat and I'll meet you at the south door."

"Mr. Geist, why am I going? I don't know anything about—"

"Exactly why you must learn, Rosemary," he said, cutting me off. "It is a special privilege, and you're quite correct—you don't know anything. But there is much I'd like to teach you."

I left the office to get my coat from the ladies' room closet. I checked for Oscar in his stacks but couldn't find him, although he must have long before returned from lunch. Geist would be waiting outside in the snow. I wanted Oscar to know where I was; to tell him more about the letter, about the coincidence of Melville's name reappearing, about Mr. Mitchell's sharpness. About Lillian.

I didn't want to have any secrets from Oscar.

∽

I went to the south door and, for a moment, watched Geist through the frosted window. He waited there, the only person on the shoveled path, his face directed at the ground, his sleek-booted foot kicking at ice.

Geist wore a dark coat of some indeterminate thick fabric, with a collar of ruined astrakhan. The coat's shapelessness made for a particularly pathetic silhouette against the banked snow. A battered hat of the same awful fur as the collar sat ridiculously atop his woolly hair. His smooth boots were distinctive, vestiges of an interest in appearances, and this single sign of care made his overall figure sadder. He bent to wipe the tip of his boot, then rubbed his hand onto his coat.

Watching him, I imagined him dissolving inside his old battered coat and hat, leaving them like lumps of coal piled on the snowy street. I recalled Arthur's remark about old photographs: they fade; it was the chemicals. Geist never seemed to merge with the actual. There was a quality of the chimerical about him.

A passerby stared at Geist's distracted figure, then craned his head backward for what he must have thought was an unobserved stare. Look, an albino! Walter Geist was a measure; his strangeness a yardstick for what is known of strangeness. Not that I could condescend to pity. He may as well have pitied me. I was, after all, a blank page with little enough inscribed on it to impress.

I opened the door. He turned at the sound of my footfall. "Rosemary," he said softly.

"I'm here, Mr. Geist."

"We must take the subway to East Eighty-sixth Street. Peabody's is not far from there."

"Then we should head this way," I said.

Geist walked briskly away from me in the direction of the subway, and I struggled beside him, sinking in snow and slipping on ice. Few sidewalks were shoveled. He seemed to know exact distances, from curb to curb, from street to corner.

I was taller by close to half a foot, and amused myself

with the disparity of our figures: he, short, colorless, middle-aged; and me, tall, young, sanguine. The blank snow only served to exaggerate our differences, like a canvas where I stood out while he receded.

Waiting on the platform together, we were a mismatched pair, a bizarre pepper and salt, but once seated in the subway car, Geist showed a small smile about the line of his mouth. He seemed almost pleased with himself.

I noticed a couple sitting opposite in the car regarding Walter Geist unpleasantly. He was oblivious. Was he stared at everywhere he went?

"Can you tell me about Julian Peabody?" I asked.

"I could tell you a great deal," said Geist. "But I'm not going to. That's not information you'll need today. You won't meet him, probably will never meet him. I myself have only met him twice in more than twenty years of business."

"Is his collection very large?"

"One of the most impressive in the country."

"And he is very wealthy?"

"Tremendously."

I wished I had a better coat, or that I possessed a skirt, or even that I'd dressed in one of my few good blouses. The one Oscar liked, the green one. He'd told me the fabric was called balzarine, a word I'd never heard before. Oscar would know, of course.

My hair was wild, electric with cold, and I would have liked to brush it, to subdue it with an elastic band. Jack, of all people, had made a crack about my farouche quality. Another word I'd never heard, but when I looked it up in one of Oscar's dictionaries, I was quite pleased with the definition. I wanted to think myself both shy and fierce: Arthur's Tasmanian Devil, a harmless creature unless provoked. But I didn't want to look like I lived outside, dragged in off the street. I smoothed my hair with my hand.

"It is Peabody's librarian we'll be meeting. Samuel Metcalf. He is an old friend."

"An old friend of yours?" I asked, watching myself sitting with Geist in the reflection of the dark window opposite.

"You find that hard to believe? That I might have an old friend?"

"No, it's just that I—"

"I have a life outside the Arcade, Rosemary," he insisted. "It might be a fairly solitary one, but it is a life. Bookselling gave it to me."

"Of course, I didn't mean—"

"It doesn't matter what you meant."

His defensiveness was congenital.

"Why doesn't it matter what I meant?"

"Because what you think of me must be of little consequence," he said flatly, and removed his sad hat. His assertion told me the opposite was true, that it mattered a great deal. I was catching on.

The other couple in the subway car whispered to each other. The train rattled along.

"Mr. Geist," I said. "That you say it is of little consequence means that it is. Of some consequence, that is."

"What is?" he said, having lost the thread.

"What I think of you."

He closed his eyes for a moment, and they moved back and forth beneath their white lids. Were they ever still?

"I just meant to say, Rosemary, that I doubt you think of me at all," he said, opening his eyes as he finished speaking.

"That's not true. I actually have considered you at some length." And I smiled. It was, in any case, true.

He turned his head toward me, his eyes quivering in their muscular distress, his mouth sliding into the slightest of smiles. He crossed his legs.

We rode along in silence until a muffled voice came over the speaker system.

"The next after this is our stop," Geist said, picking up his hat and replacing it on his head.

"My mother had a hat shop in Tasmania, you know," I told him, leaning over and straightening the unbecoming article. The fur felt greasy. He didn't shrink from my presumption; in fact he himself straightened up a little under my ministrations.

"The store was called Remarkable Hats," I told him.

"A hat shop in Tasmania seems a very unlikely thing," Geist said. The couple stood up and moved to the end of the car, rocking as they staggered away.

"Unlikely things are often true," I said. "Me being here in New York, for one. We lived above the shop. I helped her there for all of my life. Until she died."

"Ah," he said. "I'm sorry. But then you must know about hats, at least," he finished.

At least?

"I do. And this one's too small for you."

I pushed it down farther on his head, but the hat sat awkwardly, as if finding his woolly hair distasteful.

"I inherited it," he said. "It was my father's."

"Then he had a smaller head than yours."

"We were different in every respect," Walter Geist said. "He was German, you know, and very stern. My father," he added, without affect, "was dissatisfied with me."

At least you had one, I thought, but didn't say. My own self-pity struck me as sentimental when I was with him, and his seemed an extraordinary admission. "Dissatisfied" was such a singular description.

The train slowed to a stop and the doors opened. Geist steadied himself on the chrome pole before he walked out, and I caught the watching couple, the only other occupants of the car, in full, undisguised gape. Look, an albino!

I stuck my tongue out at them before exiting, a step behind the outlandish figure of Walter Geist.

✑ "Hello, Metcalf. Admission, if you please," Geist said into a polished brass intercom set into a sandstone wall. Despite the snow, the cold, he was in a very good mood. Alone with this outside-of-the-Arcade Geist was different than I had anticipated. He wanted to show me things.

The street was absurdly impressive, off Park Avenue, each building more lavish in opulent detail (brass, stone, burnished wood) than its neighbor. I rarely ventured this far uptown even in my few daylong forays across the city, and when I had, it was only to walk in Central Park and didn't include inspecting the imposing facades of wealthy Upper East Side neighborhoods. I knew my limits. I was an intruder in a realm meant for an altogether different species; the rarefied, the recherché.

Peabody's collection was housed in an enormous sandstone structure in the center of the block, as wide as two brownstones. We waited, staring at the heavy wooden door which shone darkly behind an immaculate metal grille. In response to the buzzer, the door opened; slowly, owing to its weight and thickness. A tall man poked his head around the door.

"Walter. Good to see you," he said, unlocking the grille and swinging the gate open. They shook hands.

Samuel Metcalf was thin to the point of emaciation, his movements fluid as if a breeze blew him into motion. Heavy, fashionable
glasses defined his smooth face like an architectural feature, anchor-
ing him to the earth, and keeping his head at least from waving
about as wildly as his thin limbs. And he gleamed. It appeared he
used a great many products; his thinning hair, gelled back from his
forehead, lay flawlessly flat. His skin was moisturized to a waxen
sheen, and the scent of verbena rose up when he moved. Metcalf
was probably close in age to Geist, but preserved to a kind of
specimen-like perfection. A cashmere turtleneck clung to his trim
form, which was dressed completely in black: it would have been
easy to confuse his shadow with his actual self.

"Good of you on short notice," said Geist, a bit skittish. He
seemed to lose confidence as we crossed the threshold. A more striking contrast in figures could not have been imagined, unless it was
Geist's and mine. Metcalf appeared a man at once attenuated and
condensed; Walter Geist, simply the specter of one.

"Yes, yes," said Metcalf, noticing me for the first time. "Do
wipe your feet—the snow, you know. Peabody's particular and the
rugs are worth more than my life." Turning to Geist, he said, "I'd
have thought Pike would come himself, Walter, for something this
notable."

"Well, I am his manager, Sam. He has designated it solely to
my consideration. He's not to be contacted until everything is complete."

"If authentic, you understand, this will be big, Walter," he
said, his voice lowered. "Very big."

"I gathered you would think as much," Geist muttered, as we
wiped our shoes on a bristled mat, set just inside. With the heavy
door shut, Metcalf turned, then ran his eyes over me, waiting.

"Yes, ah, Sam," said Geist, "let me introduce you to an Arcade
employee accompanying me today. My assistant."

"You didn't mention a young lady." Metcalf flashed me a false grin, teeth big and square. He ran his tongue over his lips. In contrast to the rest of him, they were rather full.

"We will discuss this upstairs," he said to Geist softly.

"Rosemary Savage, from Australia," Geist introduced me, as we stood in the grand hallway.

A magnificent staircase led away from us, rising in a dramatic sweep from the foyer. Beautiful objects, sculptures, paintings, a beveled mirror made of hundreds of smaller mirrors, decorated the large entry hall. I had never seen such wealth, such ostentatious ornament, not even in a museum, whose treasures are so often portioned out, white walls interspersed, ensuring that one not be overwhelmed. This was a museum as home, a house where objects jostled each other for attention, where they might be touched and even used, accessible and almost carnal in their appeal, their variety.

"Really?" Metcalf addressed me with some interest as I took in the decor. He hummed in his throat. "Australia. 'That great America on the other side of the sphere . . . given to the enlightened world by the whaleman'! Rather a long way to travel just to work in the fusty old Arcade."

"Even further, actually," I found myself saying, unaware that he'd quoted Melville. "I'm from Tasmania."

"I daresay that makes you rather exotic," Metcalf remarked, smirking.

And indeed it did seem a joke that I might be exotic in this hall of exquisite objects, beside this manicured man. I caught sight of myself in the Venetian mirror, my hair wild and on end, my image refracted a hundred times in its beveled surface. For an instant I was trapped in an awful kaleidoscope, infinitely revealed over and over again, like a crowd of identical Dickensian orphans, reddish-favored and scrawny, raw from too much weather.

Geist, another unfortunate exotic, removed his inherited hat and shabby coat.

"Well," said Metcalf, taking our coats to a hidden closet that opened when he pressed a spot on the wall. "This is certainly the place for curiosities."

"I beg your pardon?" I said, thinking him rude.

"Curiosities, Rosemary," said Geist, turning to me. "Peabody doesn't just collect rare books, he houses a large collection of curiosities. *Kunstschrank*," he said in decorous German. "Art cupboards. Cabinets of Wonder. He is fascinated by the medieval practice of trying to collect up marvels. There's a tradition of such collections, since, I believe, the late sixteenth century, Sam?"

"Correct, Walter. Perhaps, young lady, you'd care to look in some of the exhibition rooms while Mr. Geist and I meet in the library upstairs?"

He was trying to get rid of me. It was clear Geist should not have brought me here, that he'd made a mistake. He turned nervously to me.

"Yes, perhaps that's best," he whispered. "We have several matters to discuss."

I stood, confused and embarrassed. It appeared I wasn't to assist him in whatever way he'd wanted. I was sure then that Geist had come to discuss the letter I'd read him. My eavesdropping on Pike told me that Peabody wanted whatever the Arcade had of nineteenth-century American writers. Melville was haunting me, following me about. Hadn't Metcalf mentioned whales? He hummed again in his throat.

"Let me call for the associate curator, Miss Kircher. This isn't my area, you know. I'm upstairs in the library."

He pressed a button beside an elaborate marble-and-gold console. Deep inside the house a bell sounded, elegantly insistent, while we waited in awkward silence.

A peevish woman appeared, in her late twenties but dressed expensively in clothes more suited to a woman twice her age. Her hair was set severely in a bun, and she was round without seeming fleshy, somehow taut inside her clothing, at once plump and stiff.

"What is it, Mr. Metcalf?" she said, snippish.

"I wonder, Miss Kircher, if you'd keep an eye on our young friend here, while Mr. Geist and I discuss book business upstairs."

"How do you do, Mr. Geist," she said, with a patronizing tone. He nodded in her direction. They were apparently acquainted.

"I have work to do," Miss Kircher said to Metcalf, after giving me the once-over. "Besides, I wish to leave at five."

Neither wanted responsibility for me, and I stood there like the little match girl, fallen into a scene glimpsed through a window, let in from the snowy cold into a world of comfort and warmth. There had indeed been some mistake.

Metcalf glared at her, then turned toward the stairs, his arm on Geist's shoulder, preparing to lead him away.

"Just don't touch anything," Geist whispered to me before he followed Metcalf up the magnificent staircase, clutching the wide polished banister to steady his ascent.

Miss Kircher gave out a cluck of impatience.

"I'll give you a brochure," she said. "It's customary to arrange in advance for a viewing. This is highly irregular," she added.

"I'm sorry," I responded, thoroughly intimidated. "I had no idea."

"Evidently," she said.

Miss Kircher handed me a printed series of panels, brochures designed for visitors to the collection. Above the open double doorway to the exhibition rooms was an aphorism in Latin, painted directly onto the wall: QUANTA RARIORA TANTA MELIORA.

"Excuse me, Miss Kircher." She had already begun to turn away. "What does that say?"

I pointed to the script above our heads and took out my note-book to write it down.

" 'The rarer, the better,' " she said dryly. "Mr. Peabody's motto. *Wunderkammern* celebrate the cult of the extraordinary. It's all in the brochure."

She stared at me standing there, and I felt strangely humili-ated. Miss Kircher clearly thought herself exceptional, although she didn't look like anything special to me. Perhaps it was all a question of confidence. Complacency was a privilege I'd never considered my due, but there was something impressive about it.

"Do not touch any of the objects," she warned. "The rooms are monitored by closed-circuit cameras."

She turned fully on her heel and left me alone in the sumptu-ous foyer.

I walked beneath Peabody's motto into the first of a series of huge rooms, each painted a different color. The first, the largest and the drawing room, was green. Another painted script, close to the high ceiling, read NATURALIA. Glass display cases lined the walls, and some stood, containing a single object, in the center of the room. I had the sense I was being watched. Eyes followed me: the glass eyes of animals (a stuffed bear, deerlike creatures) as well as the brown, pupil-less eyes of formal bronze busts. Watching too were the strange, colorless eyes of a ghastly portrait: a deformed man, a crippled dwarf, naked but for an elaborate ruff around his neck and a pointed hat upon his head. His exposed body looked to be half fish and half man. I shuddered.

No cameras were visible.

I sat for a minute in an elaborate chair, to read, to collect my-self. Horns rose curling from the chair's back, an ordinary object stopped in mid-transformation from chair to mythical monster. A composite. I felt a deep disquiet, yet I was fascinated, understanding fully and for the first time how much a part of curiosity is uneasiness.

The pamphlet outlined the intention behind medieval cabinets: to define, discover, and possess the rare and unique. To inscribe them with a special setting which would also instill in them layers of meaning; meaning enhanced through juxtaposition and even implied in the empty spaces between objects. Not that Peabody had much empty space. I felt slightly claustrophobic, surrounded by too much that was unusual.

Peabody was quoted in the brochure as professing a passion for analogies and correspondences and, I copied down, he claimed this a theme that belonged to magic as much as to cabinets, to a theory of aesthetics. I thought that Peabody must be himself something of a curiosity, and an analogy of my own suggested itself: George Pike, the magus of the Arcade, was the poor man's Julian Peabody.

"Naturalia" simply meant things from nature, and I walked from case to case reading labels. Fossils, ostrich eggs, beautiful shells, unicorn horns (narwhal tusks), stuffed birds, petrified wood, huge seed casings, dried and pressed flora, enormous coconuts from the Seychelle Islands. It was like the gatherings of an ambitious child, a child with a mania for picking up whatever fell at his feet; the sort of child who ransacked bird's nests.

Labels told me that large translucent rock crystals were once considered the petrified tears of ancient gods, "eternal ice" with the power to heal. Red coral branches were believed an aphrodisiac. And a chunk of green quartz the size of my head made me take out Chaps's amulet, my guard against heartbreak, and compare colors. They matched exactly; it was the same stone, labeled here as plasma, believed to improve vision and relieve pain. An equally large piece of polished black opal glimmered darkly, lit inside by flashes of brilliant color—a planet, a black moon.

The natural objects gave way to extraordinary transformations spilling into the next room, ARTIFICIALIA, its walls painted yellow. Man-made creations were combined with the natural in weird hybrids. Twenty or more bizarre vessels and flasks that used shells as the center of elaborate gold and silver sculptures of hens, roosters, ostriches, parrots, mermaids, sea horses, even a crouching satyr who sized me up salaciously with ruby eyes.

A large nautilus shell, forming the mother-of-pearl stomach of a silver sea horse, was actually a cup with a hidden mechanism that moved across a table during some arcane drinking game. Red coral branches sprouted from the head of an impressive golden man: Jupiter, father of the gods. He stood astride an intricate writing box with a hundred compartments and hidden panels, and held another piece of red coral in his hand, a lightning bolt, symbol of inspiration, according to the display card beside the box.

Tall ivory towers, carved and turned to an astonishing degree, thin to the point of transparency, revealed geometric shapes within shapes, a mastery of perspective and craftsmanship that was hard to even comprehend. The ivory carvings seemed to push at the very limits of the visible—a tiny frigate, positioned behind a magnifier like the one Geist employed at the Arcade, seemed to contain infinity itself. Cherrystones were carved with miniature portraits, tens of them, in an aberrant play on scale. And indeed the whole exercise, exhibiting the unusually large or unusually small, was strange. Exaggeration itself produced uneasiness.

All these hybrid treasures, embellishments of nature, were dated from the late 1500s to the early 1600s, and most were originally in the collections of European princes. Peabody clearly considered himself something of a prince, or played one. The brochure boasted that nobility had invented the practice of collecting, formalizing it during the Renaissance to a degree that gave rise to the modern museum. Nobility could buy anything. Knowledge was power, and collections controlled knowledge. Only nobility had access to *Kunstkammern*, just as very few people could experience Peabody's collection.

I walked through to an annexed yellow room and rested on a low leather bench positioned in front of a terrifying automaton, a grotesque devil with the body of a Greek statue. Its head swiveled toward me when I sat. Perhaps the floor was weighted, triggering its mechanism. Thoroughly alarmed, I turned my back to it, but felt its gaze boring into my shoulders. I quickly stood up.

Before me were a series of clocks, armillary spheres, and astronomical devices. I read on panels stuck to the wall that in the cabinet, the fascination with the mechanical, with automata, was another hybrid between art and nature, the re-creation of nature: life in the lifeless, even an attempt to assert life over death. And it did seem that many of the objects were, in a way, memento mori; that collections inadvertently celebrated lost or final things. I wondered if Peabody himself was of a melancholic nature, to have acquired the possessions of other men long dead. But then, how was that any different than the buying and selling of used books?

I wrote down much of what I saw that day, but at eighteen I could parse little personal meaning from Peabody's cabinet, apart from its odd beauty, its startling character. I was impressed mostly by his wealth. All these years later, I have come to know how profound are these echoes, these connections, the mysterious correspondences collectors seek to provoke. I felt them early enough myself, with Foys's wall of drawers, with my own poor trinkets; trying to conjure meaning from bric-a-brac, gluing bits and pieces in a scrapbook. And I'd held on to the Huon box, to Mother's ashes, despite the fact that she was gone from me. Peabody's cabinet of rooms, however, didn't seem exactly personal or intimate. After all, he'd named his collection, according to the bold headline in the brochure, THE THEATER OF THE WORLD.

Miss Kircher appeared as I examined an astronomical clock. I felt her presence, standing near the automated devil, but didn't turn around. She'd probably been watching me on some surreptitious screen. She could wait.

I was inspecting a plate engraved in German set into a mahogany plinth which supported the intricate device. Four clock faces registered the hours, quarter-hours, latitude, and positions of the planets for each day. I saw that Jupiter was ascendant, Mars falling, and that the hour was close to eight, fixing forever the moment the clock had ceased to tell time, at least the time in this century. On the wall panel I read that the clock was made in 1572, but as I looked at the four faces, at the universe depicted, the time it told appeared to be eternal, and its creator immortal.

"Beautiful, isn't it?" Miss Kircher remarked loudly. She had tried to surprise me, perhaps hoping to catch me breaking her directive against touching.

"Everything is beautiful here," I said, hoping she understood I didn't include her. "And what isn't obviously beautiful has its own particular loveliness."

"I'm glad it's not lost on you," she said tartly. "You're very fortunate to see some of these objects. Of course, the collection continues in several more rooms, but I would prefer if you waited in the foyer for Mr. Geist. It is close to five and I heard them just now leaving the library."

The library! I had forgotten as I wandered through the cabinet rooms that Peabody chiefly collected books! I was supposed to have come to see the library.

"Can you tell me what is written on the clock?" I asked her, again my reluctant translator. I was determined to assert my right to learn, to take from her whatever information I could get.

"'Vor mir keine Zeit, nach mir wird keine seyn. Mit mir

gebiert sie sich, mit mir geht sie auch ein,' " she recited, her German exaggeratedly guttural. Her manner gave clear indication that she wasn't about to translate, that she was resolved to hoard knowledge.

But as she spoke, Geist and Metcalf appeared in the doorway and stood listening. They waited for her to interpret, and when she didn't, Walter Geist began, addressing me directly: " 'Before me there was no time,' " he said, and moved through the door. " 'After me there will be none.' "

He stood by my side, speaking almost intimately.

" 'With me it is born, with me it will also die.' "

His voice fell softly into the quiet of the yellow room full of silent clocks. He took my elbow in his hand. Miss Kircher sniffed.

"Yes, well," said Metcalf, humming in his throat and breaking the spell. His was an irritating habit.

"No doubt you are correct, Walter. Evidently we are all clocks! No time like the present, and time for us all to be leaving for the day, you know."

He hummed again.

"I'll see you out."

"Thank you, Miss Kircher," I said graciously, Geist at my side.

"Goodnight, Mr. Geist," she said, ignoring me. I led him back to the entrance. He still held my elbow. Metcalf helped him on with his coat and hat, handed me mine, and we were once again on the snowy street, the heavy door and metal grille closed behind us, the *Kunstkammer* like a dream, an hallucination.

∾

Outside was dark and cold. The moon was a mirror, glossy and silver, sitting just above the rooftops at the end of Peabody's street. The light it cast was strangely false, affected. I didn't know why

Geist had taken me to Peabody's. I considered the letter that mentioned Melville, and knew I needed to go over the entire episode with Oscar to understand its meaning.

Besides, I was starving, having missed out on lunch.

"I will be heading further uptown, Rosemary," said Geist. He patted me then, rubbed my arm haltingly. It was an odd gesture, decidedly too familiar. Was I supposed to help him home? Was that how I could assist him? I didn't know where he lived, or how he navigated himself about at night. He waited, although I didn't know for what.

"Thank you, Mr. Geist," I said, suspecting that he awaited my gratitude. I felt it sincerely enough. Seeing even part of Peabody's collection was in every sense a gift. "Thank you for bringing me to Peabody's. I will always remember it. Always."

"I thought you'd find it interesting," he answered, nervous but clearly pleased. "I wanted you to meet Sam Metcalf, but today wasn't perhaps the most—" he paused, searching for the word— "ideal. Perhaps another day; there are several things I'd like you to see. Upstairs in the library."

I should have asked him why it wasn't ideal, what in fact did he think ideal, but I wanted suddenly to be rid of him; to be rid of a sense of obligation to him. I wasn't sure I wanted to see whatever he wanted to show me, although the very idea of Peabody's library was intriguing. Perhaps Pike would send me one day with Oscar? Or even Mr. Mitchell?

Walter Geist straightened his sloping shoulders.

"He thought you were attractive, Rosemary," he broke out. "Sam said he thought you were very unusual looking."

These two statements seemed to contradict each other, and I couldn't imagine any natural circumstance where the subject of my appearance would arise between them. I was deeply uncomfortable at the thought of a conversation with my looks as its theme. I didn't know what to say. The silence between us was freighted then with an intimacy that hadn't been secured.

Geist seemed on the verge of speaking again but didn't.

Needing to escape, I abruptly wished him goodnight and left him there on the street corner, wavering and hesitant, beneath the distorting glare of the queer moon.

∽

On those expensive streets, the snow was cleared and shoveled. But south, across several avenues, a small plow wielded by a workman was sending up snow in a feathery arc in front of an apartment building. The city at night was a transformed place, inexhaustibly invented anew. I walked across town, thinking, unconsciously reversing my walking pattern, down and across, down and across, and visualized again the contents of Peabody's rooms. I clutched at my amulet from Chaps and thought about frozen tears of quartz, horrible mechanical men, disturbing dwarfs, and Jupiter hurling a red coral lightning bolt. Was that to inspire writing, or because coral was an aphrodisiac?

Was I really unusual looking? Attractive?

The city that night appeared surreal after Peabody's. The cabinet had followed me outside. Streets were multiplied and deceptive—reflected streets, double streets, made-up streets. The map of the city, the one in my mind, appeared only to work properly in daylight. That night the city was a fiction. I walked and walked, forgetting where I was going and why, lost in imaginings, trying to tie together threads of thought.

Where exactly was Peabody's? *It is not down on any map; true places never are,* Melville whispered in my mind, still following me about.

I was impatient to find Oscar and tell him everything I had seen, and I checked my pocket to be certain I had taken the pamphlets Miss Kircher had given me. They were like the flower in Coleridge's poem, brought back from another realm. The pamphlets were evidence, proof that Peabody's was real and confirmation that I had actually been inside the Theater of the World.

PART
THREE

"You went where?!" Oscar said, incredulous.

"To Julian Peabody's. Yesterday with Mr. Geist. Have you been? Do you know him? Oh, Oscar, it was the most amazing place I've ever seen. Like a museum . . . but a house as well. I had no idea anyone could be so rich. The objects, Oscar!"

"That's quite a privilege for someone who has only worked at the Arcade a few months," he said primly.

"Yes, I know. Mr. Pike told me I was very lucky. But Oscar, it was the most wonderful place. Peabody's librarian was there, although he wasn't particularly nice to me. Nor was the woman who works there. But I didn't care. Of course, I didn't meet Peabody himself . . ."

"What was Geist's business there?" he interrupted.

"Well, I'm not entirely sure. They went upstairs and left me. There are rooms that are filled with rocks and eggs and bones and ivory. Polished stones. Amazing clocks as well, and sculptures. An automated devil. Fantastic. I've never seen such things. Ever. Anywhere. Have you been there? There was even a big chunk of my green stone, like this."

From inside my shirt I pulled out the drop of green quartz Chaps had given me at the airport.

"Oh, that," said Oscar, in encyclopedic mode. "Chrysoprase. It's almost worthless, actually. Also called plasma. Once believed to improve sight and relieve internal pain."

"Are you sure? I thought it healed broken hearts," I said, inspecting the opaque stone, disappointed. That's why Chaps had given it to me. Peabody clearly thought it valuable.

"Internal pain, broken hearts—same thing," Oscar said dismissively.

"Does this color remind you of anything?" I asked, naively thinking Oscar might have noticed the stone was the color of my eyes.

"What?" he said, irritated. "Green. It's just green. You haven't told me why you went there, why Geist took you."

"Because he wants me to learn. He wants me to know things and help him. Oscar, the whole afternoon was like a dream."

"Yes, right," he said sarcastically. "The baseless fabric of a vision, I'm sure!" His tone turned angry. "I didn't go to Peabody's until I'd been here close to four years, and even then it was because I had an expertise. And I couldn't see the collection, either, just the library. Peabody has some rare volumes of incunabula, printed on vellum. I know quite a bit about vellum as a medium; it's like a fabric to me. I studied it, in fact, at a job I had in a library before I came here."

"I didn't know you worked in a library," I said. Oscar shrugged as if to imply how very little I did know about him. He was jealous, but I couldn't let him hoard his recondite knowledge, like Miss Kircher. I needed it.

"What is incunabula?" I blurted.

"Exactly my point. Why take you to Peabody's?" He sighed, reciting flatly. " 'Incunabula' refers to books printed before A.D. 1501, using movable type. Very valuable. Peabody collects them. And anything rare he can get his hands on. But it is quite pertinent that you should ask," Oscar continued sardonically. "As 'incunabula' also refers to the beginning of anything, the early, primary stages of a thing . . ."

He paused for effect.

"Like your education."

"There's no need to be nasty. I tried to find you so I could tell you I was going, but you weren't in your stacks. Mr. Geist was waiting outside. I didn't have much time."

"I took an early lunch. I have business to attend to, you know. And then I had to relieve that lazy Arthur in the basement, apparently because Geist was out with you. I hate to work in the basement. I need to remain in my section. I don't like being below ground, and I loathe all those new review books—all those plastic shiny jackets."

"I'm sorry, Oscar," I said, uncertain why I felt the need to apologize.

In a way (not the way I dreamed of) Oscar wanted me as his own. He wanted me in his world, but not in opposition to him. He wanted to limit me to his own investigation of who I was, to the girl he described in his notebooks. Perhaps it was his own reflected image that he loved? Perhaps he loved the Oscar I saw? In any case, I was a captive audience to his knowledge, even if he needed to contain me, in his obsessive hand, between pages.

"So you met the librarian, Samuel Metcalf?" he asked, now feigning a casual disinterest.

He sat up on his tall stool.

"He's quite well known, you know. He makes a lot of himself. Terribly vain, although not without his expertise. He always claims he is distantly related to Herman Melville. Probably why Peabody hired him in the first place. Did Geist tell you that?"

"No, he didn't," I said, startled at the consistent recurrence of Melville. How preoccupations insist themselves—how they pursue one! Whenever I land on an interest, I always wonder whether I discovered it, or the other way around.

"It's very odd that Melville would come up," I told Oscar. "It's as if he's following me. I'm surprised that Geist didn't mention it."

"Why is it odd?" Oscar scoffed. "Just because you've been reading *Moby-Dick*? Just because you've encountered our own Redburn? You imagine every reasonable coincidence odd."

"No, I just mean because of the letter. Well, I have to start at the beginning. I came to tell you about it yesterday, but I was upset about Lillian. I have to tell you about Lillian as well."

"Start with Melville, if you don't mind," said Oscar impatiently. "The letter?"

"Mr. Geist had me read a letter for him, but it was addressed to Mr. Pike. I didn't find out who it was from because he snatched it from me before I finished! The letter said something about a manuscript. A manuscript that the Arcade would be interested in and could help authenticate. A rare manuscript by Herman Melville."

"What? Are you mad?"

Oscar jumped from his stool and grabbed me by the arm. He led me like a child back into a narrow eddy made by the confluence of stacks and pools of books on the floor. It was as if he'd constructed a dam of volumes inside his section. I hadn't noticed it, but then it sometimes seemed the Arcade rearranged itself in fresh configurations after everyone had left for the night.

"It's really important, right?" I asked.

He looked furtively around.

"Rosemary, think! There are no manuscripts of Melville's that remain undiscovered," he whispered emphatically. "Tell me exactly what happened and what was in the letter."

I recounted as accurately as I could what little I remembered, relishing the fact that I knew something that held Oscar's attention so intently. I had knowledge he wanted for a change. I particularly reiterated the words "cannot honorably account."

I wanted to give him something with all my heart, and here was a suitably clandestine offering. I wanted, above all, to give him back something on the order of what I felt he'd given me. I didn't consider that what I had to offer was priceless.

"I didn't even finish the letter!" I told him, describing how Geist tore the letter from my hand. "But I assume that whoever wrote the letter has stolen what they have to sell."

"This is hard to believe, Rosemary."

Oscar's ascetic face had transformed. He looked thunder-struck, his magnificent head cocked, his hand against his brow.

"I need more information," he said, more to himself than to me.

"There are lots of rare papers up with Mr. Mitchell," I said, slightly bewildered at Oscar's intense reaction. "Is this that much more significant? Is it because it might be stolen?"

"You must tell me everything that Geist has you read from now on and whether he corresponds with or sees Samuel Metcalf again. Metcalf's father is a retired antiquarian dealer. He used to own a store in Saratoga Springs, in upstate New York. Metcalf has expertise in handwriting analysis, in the accurate dating of papers. His father taught him, and this is in part how he comes to be employed by Peabody. His skills are quite exceptional."

"Do you think Metcalf's father has somehow gotten hold of a manuscript?" I asked, confused.

"I doubt it. He would go straight to Metcalf without going through the Arcade. Peabody is Melville's largest private collector."

My own eavesdropping had told me as much.

"Except for the fact that it can't honorably be accounted for,"

I reminded. "Maybe the Arcade provides a kind of front of respectability."

Oscar sneered at this. "Pike's business is hardly beyond reproach, Rosemary," he pointed out.

He took out his notebook and began to scribble down details.

"How long were Geist and Metcalf upstairs at Peabody's? How long were you alone?"

"An hour, or nearly two. It was dark when we left."

"Geist has something," he said. "And he wants to get his hands on it, but he needs Metcalf. And he wants it kept secret—evidently, even from you."

"Mr. Mitchell can authenticate things, though. Why would Mr. Geist need Metcalf?"

I might as well not have been there. What I'd told Oscar had seized him, animated him in a way I didn't recognize. I wanted back my languid companion, tossing off details about subjects that fascinated me—fascinated me because *he* knew them. Each piece of knowledge Oscar gave me was like a talisman. If I collected enough of his fragments, I'd be able to piece together a true Oscar, an Oscar made of something tangible, something I could keep. I knew reading the letter to Geist was significant, but I couldn't have known then how much would turn on it. At the time, I was less interested really in Herman Melville, or manuscripts, except insofar as they could deliver Oscar's attention to me.

"You know," I said. "I wouldn't have read the letter but for Mr. Geist's problem. I wanted to talk to you about it. I think he's going blind, I think he's—"

"He is legally blind already," said Oscar, cutting me off, absorbed in other thoughts. "It's not uncommon in albinos. He's been gradually losing his sight for the last few years. He covers it well, but it's gotten worse lately."

"You already knew?"

"For heaven's sake, Rosemary, who could miss it? We're all complicit in ignoring it. I'm surprised it's taken you this long, you're usually fairly observant."

"Fairly"? Was that a compliment?

"Pike doesn't care as long as the accounts are in order and the Arcade turns a profit. As long as there's no theft, at least that he doesn't have a piece of. Mitchell is only interested in himself—in oiling his customers and fattening up the Rare Book Room. The rest of the staff despise Geist so much they probably wish far worse fates on him than blindness."

"Have you said anything to him? Do you think we can help him in some way?"

"I'm not interested in helping him. Why would I be? I have my own concerns. Besides, Geist is private. If he can manage, what difference does his blindness make?"

"Oscar, he works in a bookshop!"

"Don't be so dull, Rosemary. There are all sorts of ways to live. Use that imagination of yours."

"I can't imagine not being able to see," I said.

Dull? I wasn't dull! It was proximity to Oscar that made me thick and slow.

"That's not what I meant. In any case, I want to find out about this Melville business." He looked at his watch. "I'm going to make a phone call during lunch. Perhaps I can get to the library this evening."

He began to retreat from the reservoir of books. Here was my chance. He'd have to include me in his next investigation.

"Can I come with you?" I said breathlessly. "To the library?"

"Why?"

"Because I want to know about it as well. You gave me *Moby-Dick* and now I'm curious. I want to learn about Melville too. Come on, Oscar, you wouldn't even know about any of this except that I told you."

"So?"

"I mean, I gave you the information, so can't I help you find out about it? Please?"

"It may turn out that I don't want to know any more than I already do." He hesitated, his eyes widening. "But now that I think of it, there are possibly things you are in a position to discover that I cannot."

∽

"Where are you off to, girl, prettying yourself up like that?" said Pearl, teasing me as I stood before the mirror in the bathroom.

I was going to the library with Oscar. I would be alone with him. I would watch him think, stroking his dark hair flat against his beautiful head.

"Oh, nowhere," I said.

"Well, thanks for nothing," said Pearl, a little hurt. "And here I went and got a name for your friend, and you won't share with me."

"You have something for Lillian, Pearl? Already?"

"I ain't got time to waste, and I could see it was important."

"It is. It is important. Oh, thank you."

"Well, don't thank me yet. I just got the name and number of a person who works with an NGO. That's non-governmental organization, girl. Don't know if they can help, but it's worth a try. Mario's calling them himself today. Give them a heads-up. Here."

From her enormous handbag filled with musical annotations, Pearl took a piece of folded paper. I took it, read the details, and put the paper in my own bag.

"Pearl, I can't thank you enough for this. I'll find Lillian after work tomorrow and give it to her. Maybe her brother can call."

"Why don't you go by there tonight?" said Pearl slyly. "Or are you too busy?" She smiled.

"All right," I said, surrendering the news. "I'm going somewhere with Oscar."

"Not on a date!" shrieked Pearl. She clapped her hand over her mouth, her painted black nails lining up along her cheek like strange punctuation.

"No, of course not," I said hastily. "Not a date. We just have a plan to do something together."

"What could you possibly be doing with him?" she said. "Remember what I told you, girl. That is not a man that loves women. Listen to me now. I'm not joking. I'm just drying out from those tears the other day, and I don't want no more."

"I know. I heard you the first time. We're just, well, we're just . . ."

"Just what?"

How much could I tell Pearl? Oscar had been so mysterious, and then I didn't know much myself. Secrets separate people. All of a sudden I had information—to tell, to hide.

"Look, Pearl, we're just going to the library together. I was asking him about some stuff I didn't know, and he's going to help me look it up."

"The library!" Pearl burst into raucous laughter. "Now I know that's true. Ain't nobody else in the world that would be true about except Oscar. Going to the library's his idea of a night on the town!"

I laughed with Pearl but realized that even though all indications suggested otherwise, I did imagine that an evening with Oscar at the library meant something. We had an interest to share—Herman Melville, of all things. I freshly fantasized Oscar's golden eyes upon my skin like sunlight through a window, warming me. I pictured us sitting together in a library, an open book between us—one another's best.

Pearl calmed down. "Lord," she said, growing serious. "I'm glad to see you laughing after the other day."

She collected her handbag and checked her makeup in the mirror.

"Tell me what happens with Lillian. I'll meet with her if you think it'll help."

Pearl waved a long finger at me, its black nail a sharp comma.

"I'm going to a big audition. For real opera! I'm perfect for it, you know. A coloratura. You wish me luck, Rosemary. And you better be sure and tell me about the library. We girls got to share."

Pearl put on her coat and kissed me on the cheek.

"It's good to have dreams, girl, but just be realistic. That Oscar ain't got nothing to give you."

"He does, Pearl. I know it's not what I might hope for, but he knows everything."

"Nobody knows everything. You can bet there's a world of things he don't know. About women, for one thing. Just be clear what you want, Rosemary. I'd hate to see your heart broken, although, Lord knows, it's bound to happen."

"Don't worry about me, Pearl. You'll have to meet Lillian—she worries all the time as well."

"She got a real reason to. You have her call, okay? Mario and me, we'll try and help."

"Good luck," I called after her.

She laughed. "Same to you!"

❧

The grand main branch of the New York Public Library wasn't open after work that evening, but Oscar also frequented another branch farther uptown, housed in a large modern building.

As we emerged from the subway into the cold night, I deliberately walked close beside him, and warmed myself with imagining that a casual observer might mistake us for lovers. Snow was piled in filthy clumps on street corners, and patches of the sidewalk were slick with ice. After a short block we arrived at the smaller library.

It was clean and orderly. The architecture—concrete, glass, and steel—was aloof and spacious. The interior lights were bright; every aspect the antithesis of the Arcade. I knew books to be objects that loved to cluster and form disordered piles, but here books seemed robbed of their zany capacity to fall about, to conspire. In the library, books behaved themselves.

Oscar had known the night librarian for many years; he was one of the Civil War buffs who regularly prowled Oscar's own stacks. After a call from Oscar earlier in the day, several books had already been pulled from the shelves, stacked neatly behind the returns desk. The librarian had also collected photocopies of articles to save Oscar time. He knew the favor would be remembered and returned. For the librarian, it was an investment in his own collection.

The place was all but empty of readers. We took the books and papers to a carrel in the rear of the open room. Alongside the desk were floor-to-ceiling windows, an exterior wall of the library, that looked down Broadway toward the lights of Midtown. I had never been on what Americans called a date, but sitting in a private study space with Oscar, for me, defined its meaning. I was on a date whether or not Oscar would indulge the fantasy. I had willed myself into a deluded trance.

Oscar set to work. Solemnly, taking out a pencil and one of his notebooks, he laid them on the desk. He flipped index pages, running his fingers down columns absorbedly.

I felt a little giddy. Looking to Oscar's right, I studied all the well-behaved books shelved neatly and subject to repressive regimentation. George Pike's desire for the mild boredom of alphabetical order seemed modest, charming even, compared to this civilizing uniformity. There are some enterprises in which a careful disorderliness *is* the true method, according to Melville, and he had swum through libraries.

I thought again of Peabody's, and how it too had insisted on a different way of looking at things, a way I was sympathetic to, an alternative aesthetic. Mine had been transformed by the Arcade and by the people in it, and the library's contrary example just confirmed that aesthetic. The Arcade, and now Peabody's, combined to tell me that there was life in objects, in books. It was all about having eyes to see the true meaning of things. As Pike proved daily, books held a kind of magic, an apparent as well as a hidden value.

I looked at the spines of several biographies of Melville and wondered what productive, purposeful action I could take. Oscar quickly became so absorbed in his reading that when I looked across at him a few minutes later, it was as if he were trapped inside a cast of himself; his own aliveness flickered only in the movement of his eyes.

"Oscar," I whispered, startling him. He'd forgotten I was there.

"What?"

"Can I help? What should I look for? Do you think I should just start reading one of these?"

I pushed at the heavy books on the desk, hardly disguising my reluctance. But I did want to help. I wanted our search to be a common one, a shared interest; I just didn't know what I was searching for.

Oscar sighed. "Why don't you start with these articles. Or read this book of letters and see if they tell you anything about any novels of Melville's that you've never heard of."

The only one I had any knowledge of was *Moby-Dick*. There was evidently *Redburn* as well, but all I knew then was that Mr. Mitchell had ironically borrowed the title to bestow upon a thief.

"We're looking for something that's lost," he said. "A book that was lost."

"Well, if it's lost, and people don't know it's lost, what am I supposed to notice?"

"Here, read this book of letters. Just read and tell me when you find something interesting. It's called research. The idea is that you don't know what you'll find until you find it," he added, irritated.

I began to read, and after a while, to enjoy myself. Perhaps an hour passed. I read the introduction, which summarized Melville's biographical details: the early death of his father; his subsequent employment in a fur and cap shop of his brother's, then as a teacher; his escape to sea and his ultimate return in his early twenties. His early fame as a writer was founded on somewhat risqué adventure novels, and when he wrote what he wanted—for example, in *Moby-Dick*—he fell from popular favor, faced financial ruin, and withdrew to New York City. For nineteen years he worked six days a week as a customs inspector, writing poetry at night.

Occasionally Oscar would scribble something in his notebook. His nearness was distracting. He smelled incredibly clean.

But as I read on, I too became absorbed. The book of letters contained several Melville wrote to Nathaniel Hawthorne, and although I knew relatively little then of either writer, I was quickly taken with Melville's enthusiasm, with his patent need to communicate to someone he admired, someone he loved. He had, I recalled, dedicated *Moby-Dick* to Hawthorne—"In token of my admiration for his genius." And I discovered that Melville had hired a private room at an inn in Lenox, Massachusetts, near both their houses, to celebrate the publication of *Moby-Dick*. Hawthorne was his only guest.

I already knew that Melville's voice in *Moby-Dick* was often ecstatic, but turning to these letters, his tone was ardent, intimate.

His letters to Hawthorne were passionate and compelling. Responding to a letter of Hawthorne's praising *Moby-Dick*, Melville returned: "I felt pantheistic then—your heart beat in my ribs and mine in yours, and both in God's." I adored this sort of dramatic declaration and longed to make such pronouncements myself. I wanted to be a pantheist too, along with Melville. I wanted another's heart beneath my ribs—Oscar's. I was eighteen years old and ready to see yearning in everything. I actually blushed when I read: "Whence come you, Hawthorne? By what right do you drink from my flagon of life? And when I put it to my lips—lo, they are yours and not mine."

At that age, I didn't know exactly what Melville meant except that when my hand went to my own lips (as it did while I read on), I wanted them to be Oscar's lips. When I felt my heart, when my hand brushed my own breast, I wished that hand were Oscar's. Surely this wasn't what Melville intended? I knew it wasn't, but whatever he did mean, it excited me. "I feel that the Godhead is broken up like the bread at the Supper, and that we are the pieces."

I was just awakening to passion, and Melville's letters made me want to be passionate too; generous and unrestrained in my affections. And yet, loneliness was also something I recognized, and Melville's loneliness was poetic, even heroic. He wanted to believe Nathaniel Hawthorne knew him as no other. He felt for him an "infinite fraternity of feeling." Infinite! "Knowing you persuades me more than the Bible of our immortality."

He told Hawthorne: "You were archangel enough to despise the imperfect body, and embrace the soul. Once you hugged the ugly Socrates because you saw the flame in the mouth, and heard the rushing of the demon,—the familiar,—and recognized the sound; for you have heard it in your own solitudes."

I looked across at Oscar with longing: "embrace the soul." Melville wrote to Hawthorne that with him as a companion, "I am content and can be happy." Contemplating Oscar, I thought I knew what Melville was getting at.

And yet, Melville must have realized that Hawthorne might think him a bit crazy, or at least overwrought, for he qualified in the same letter: "Believe me, I am not mad . . . But truth is ever incoherent, and when the big hearts strike together, the concussion is a little stunning."

Oscar and I have big hearts too, I told myself. I even felt a little dizzy.

As I read on, another letter caught my attention, and I marked it with the leaf of the book's cover. Coincidentally, it was written on my mother's birthday, August 13, almost a hundred and thirty years earlier, in 1852, than the moment I was reading it.

I wanted to tell Oscar I'd found a letter written on Mother's birthday. Did he know how much I missed her? I wanted to tell him that I'd found something lost. Her birthday, given back to me in someone else's letter. Did Oscar miss his own mother as much as I did mine?

He was less than an arm's length from my side. Did he know how much we shared? I could touch him if I reached across the distance between us.

I found something lost, I wanted to whisper. Love! He loved his friend. There's so much love sent through the mail, Oscar. But he was in his element, engrossed in an investigation.

What did Melville mean about immortality? Hearts beating beneath another's ribs, hearts striking together? Interchangeable lips pressed to a flagon of life? "Oscar," I longed to whisper. I wished I didn't adore feeling his name on my lips, inside my mouth. "I found something," I wanted to say. "I found who Melville really loved."

Oscar was framed against the night. The scene beyond the wall of windows revealed the tremendous city, cold and hilled with snow. Only a few weeks before I'd seen the first inklings of snow. With Oscar. I wanted any and all discoveries with Oscar. I wished it had been Oscar who had taken me to Peabody's and not Walter Geist. That it was Oscar who placed his hand on me, who stood too close to me, who needed me to help him, rather than Geist.

But I knew even then that he would have been happier tracking down whatever obscure facts he wanted, without me. Collecting information was his occupation; it was remembering that would become mine.

I barely knew what I was looking for. What record could there be of something truly lost? I had been looking for an empty space and here I'd found it filled with all this urgent emotion. With immortality!

As if he hadn't said enough to Hawthorne, Herman Melville raved on in a postscript:

> P.S. I can't stop yet. If the world was entirely made up of Magians, I'll tell you what I should do. I should have a paper-mill established at one end of the house, and so have an endless riband of foolscap rolling in upon my desk; and upon that endless riband I should write a thousand—a million—billion thoughts, all under the form of a letter to you. The divine magnet is on you, and my magnet responds. Which is the biggest? A foolish question—they are One.

I felt I should remove this book of letters from the library so as to read it at home, in private and alone. "All under the form of a letter to you," I mouthed silently.

◦◦◦ For Nathaniel Hawthorne's part, he had written a diary entry recording a visit from his passionate friend to his small red house in the Berkshires: "Melville and I had a talk about time and eternity, things of this world, and of the next, and books and publishers, and all possible and impossible matters that lasted pretty deep into the night." There had been mutual feeling then, even if Hawthorne's was measured and restrained beside Melville's unstoppable outpouring.

Turning back then to the letter I had marked, the one written on Mother's birthday, August 13, but in 1852, I read:

> *My Dear Hawthorne,*
>
> *While visiting Nantucket some four weeks ago, I made the acquaintance of a gentleman from New Bedford, a lawyer, who gave me considerable information upon several matters concerning which I was curious.—One night we were talking, I think, of the great patience, & endurance, & resignedness of the women of the island in submitting so uncomplainingly to the long, long absences of their sailor husbands, when, by way of anecdote, this lawyer gave me a leaf from his professional experience. Altho' his memory was a little confused with*

regard to some of the items of the story, yet he told me enough to awaken the most lively interest in me; and I begged him to be sure and send me a more full account so soon as he arrived home—he having previously told me that at the time of the affair he had made a record in his books.—I heard nothing more, till a few days after arriving here at Pittsfield I received thro' the Post Office the enclosed document.—You will perceive by the gentleman's note to me that he assumed that I purposed making literary use of the story; but I had not hinted anything of the kind to him, & my first spontaneous interest in it arose from very different considerations. I confess, however, that since then I have a little turned the subject over in my mind with a view to a regular story to be founded on these striking incidents. But, thinking again, it has occurred to me that this thing lies very much in a vein, with which you are peculiarly familiar. To be plump, I think that in this matter you would make a better hand at it than I would. Besides the thing seems naturally to gravitate towards you——

Here the book indicated a torn line, the words illegible.

I thought it uncommon that one writer should be trying to impress upon another an idea for a novel. But apart from the coincidence of the date, the letter seemed far less interesting than others Herman Melville had written to Nathaniel Hawthorne; less a discovery than the letters of such high feeling.

Oscar had not so much as shifted his position. I looked around the empty library: quiet, humane. Beyond the tall windows, the winter night was bright with illuminations—reflections of light off snow. A dreamlike quality made me feel slightly disoriented, at once drowsy and paradoxically alert to subtle turns.

I took up the book and continued:

The very great interest I felt in this story while narrating
to me, was heightened by the emotion of the gentleman who
told it, who evinced the most unaffected sympathy in it, tho'
now a matter of his past.—But perhaps this great interest
of mine may have been largely helped by some accidental
circumstance or other; so that, possibly, to you the story may
not seem to possess so much of pathos, & so much of depth.
But you will see how it is.—

I could see Melville wanted Hawthorne to take it up; wanted
him to feel the emotion of the story. What was the story? I skimmed
ahead and read the lawyer's diary page enclosed within Melville's
letter.

It was, in its details, a simple, perhaps even a common, story.
Melville wanted Hawthorne to write about a woman named Agatha
Robinson (or Robertson in the lawyer's, a Mr. Clifford's, diary
page). Agatha's was a story of deep longing; of abandonment and,
Melville suggested, of remorse. Clifford's diary page laid out the
particulars:

It appears that Robertson was wrecked on the coast of
Pembroke where this girl, then Miss Agatha Hatch was
living—that he was hospitably entertained and cared for, and
that within a year after, he married her, in due form of
law—that he went two short voyages to sea. About two years
after the marriage, leaving his wife enceinte ⟦pregnant⟧ he
started off in search of employment and from that time until
Seventeen years afterwards she never heard from him in any
way whatsoever, directly or indirectly, not even a word. Being
poor she went out nursing for her daily bread and yet contrived
out of her small earnings to give her daughter a first rate

education. Having become connected with the Society of Friends she sent her to their most celebrated boarding school and when I saw her I found she had profited by all her advantages beyond most females. In the meantime Robertson had gone to Alexandria D.C. where he had entered into a successful and profitable business and married a second wife. At the expiration of this long period of 17 years which the poor forsaken wife, had glided wearily away, while she was engaged away from home, her Father rode up in a gig and informed her that her husband had returned and wished to see her and her child—but if she would not see him, to see her child at all events—They all returned together and encountered him on the way to coming to meet them about half a mile from her father's house. Their meeting was described to me by the daughter—Every incident seemed branded upon the memories of both. He excused himself as well as he could for his long absence and silence, appeared very affectionate refused to tell where he was living and persuaded them not to make any inquiries, gave them a handsome sum of money, promised to return for good and left the next day—He appeared again in about a year, just on the eve of the daughter's marriage & gave her a bridal present. It was not long after this that his wife in Alexandria died—He then wrote to his son-in-law to come there—He did so—remained 2 days and brought back a gold watch and three handsome shawls which had previously been worn by some person—They all admitted that they had suspicions then & from this circumstance that he had been a second time married.

Soon after this he visited Falmouth again & as it proved for the last time—He announced his intention of removing to Missouri & urged the whole family to go with him, promising money land and other assistance to his son-in-law. The offer was not accepted. He shed tears when he bade them farewell—From the time of his return to Missouri till the time of his death a constant correspondence was kept up money was remitted by him annually and he announced to them his marriage with Mrs. Irvin—He had no children by either of his last two wives.

Mr. Janney was entirely disappointed in the evidence and the character of the claimants. He considered them, when he first came, as parties to the imposition practiced upon Mrs. Irvin & her children. But I was satisfied and I think he was, that their motives in keeping silence were high and pure, creditable in every way to the true Mrs. Robertson. She stated the causes with a simplicity & pathos which carried the conviction irresistibly to my mind. The only good it could have done to expose him would have been to drive Robertson away and forever disgrace him & it would certainly have made Mrs. Irvin & her children wretched for the rest of their days—"I had no wish" said the wife "to make either of them unhappy, notwithstanding all I had suffered on his account"—It was the most striking instance of long continued & uncomplaining submission to wrong and anguish on the part of a wife, which made her in my eyes a heroine.

Agatha's story struck a chord in me. I thought of Mother raising me alone; of my absent father. I thought about waiting for someone to return. Lillian waiting. Dead or disappeared? Years of waiting compressed into a moment of return, and the impossibility of reconciliation. " 'I had no wish' said the wife 'to make either of them unhappy, notwithstanding all I had suffered on his account.' " Agatha was a heroine. But why had her story so impressed Melville? Why did he want to give to Hawthorne a story of such longing? Why didn't he write it himself? As I read on, it was almost as if Melville was writing Agatha's story himself, in note form at least. In trying to impress the story upon his friend, Melville wrote to Hawthorne in great detail about how the story should take shape:

> *Supposing the story to open with the wreck then there must be a storm; & it were well if some faint shadow of the preceding calm were thrown forth to lead the whole.—Now imagine a high cliff overhanging the sea & crowned with a pasture for sheep; a little way off—higher up,—a lighthouse, where resides the father of the future Mrs. Robinson the First. The afternoon is mild & warm. The sea with an air of solemn deliberation, with an elaborate deliberation, ceremoniously rolls upon the beach. The air is suppressedly charged with the sound of long lines of surf. There is no land over against this cliff short of Europe & the West Indies.*

"Supposing"? Is this what writers suggest to each other? Supposing you write this? For me?

Oscar would know about such things. I would ask him. He would tell me. I glanced over.

He was leaning into his reading, his great head bent forward, as if he looked over an edge where a falling vision drew him down. I hesitated.

"Oscar?" I asked softly.

"Just a minute, I'm following something," he said impatiently. He took up his pencil and scribbled again in his notebook. "Let me finish here," he snapped.

"Sorry. Never mind," I muttered.

I wasn't helping. He didn't expect I would find anything. I took up the letter again and read Melville's postscript:

P.S. It were well, if from her knowledge of the deep miseries produced to wives by marrying seafaring men, Agatha should have formed a young determination never to marry a sailor; which resolve in her, however, is afterwards overborne by the omnipotence of Love.

"The omnipotence of Love"? Did Melville believe love over-came every misgiving, every obstacle? Or only in books? Was it just books that gave people these ideas? Agatha falls in love—a choice that will make her miserable. The sea had delivered her a husband and then, she thought, taken him back. But he wasn't lost at sea. He'd deserted her. Melville added another postscript:

P.S. No 2. Agatha should be active during the wreck, & should, in some way, be made the saviour of young Robinson. He should be the only survivor. He should be ministered to by Agatha at the house during the illness ensuing upon his in-juries from the wreck.—Now this wrecked ship was driven over the shoals, & driven upon the beach where she goes to pieces, all but her stem-part. This in course of time becomes embedded in the sand—after the lapse of some years showing nothing but the sturdy stem (or, prow-bone) projecting some two feet at low water. All the rest is filled & packed down with the sand.—So that after her husband has disappeared the sad Agatha every day sees this melancholy monument, with all its remindings.—

Agatha is Robinson's savior. The prow is left stuck in the sand like a sentinel. Agatha will see the prow of the shipwreck buried, a memorial to her sea-sorrow. Poor Agatha. But what did Melville expect Hawthorne to do with his imaginings? Was Hawthorne rolling his eyes by the time he got to this second P.S.? What is another to do with a fiction of your own making? Wear it like an ill-fitting hat? I scanned the rest of the letter. The second P.S. went on for pages of description, ending finally:

> I do not therefore, My Dear Hawthorne, at all imagine that you will think that I am so silly as to flatter myself I am giving you anything of my own. I am but restoring to you your own property—which you would quickly enough have identified for yourself—had you but been on the spot as I happened to be.

He is restoring to Hawthorne his own property? I could make no sense of this.

The final page added yet another postscript: more details, more suggestions for the story, more of Melville's assurances that "if I thought I could do it as well as you, why, I should not let you have it." If Hawthorne didn't write the Agatha story after this, then Melville wouldn't have had much choice but to write it. He had invested it with such value.

I looked over at Oscar. He was engrossed in his reading, his hand resting on the top of his head as if it hurt, as if the effort at concentration might lift his sculpted head from his shoulders. "Oscar?" I wanted to whisper in his ear. "I've found something."

It seems to me now that giving Hawthorne the story was a way to bind him to Melville, to join him, through the gift. Identifying a story of longing and loss was a way for Melville to communicate something of the same order to his famous friend. And then the whole thing appeared akin to a present I could give Oscar. An arcane quest was a gift he would really want to have.

"Oscar?" I said again, laying down the book of letters. I reached across and tugged his sleeve, determined now to interrupt.

"What is it?" he responded, exasperated.

"Did Herman Melville or Nathaniel Hawthorne ever write a novel about a woman and a shipwreck? About a woman being abandoned for many years? A woman deserted by her husband? A woman named Agatha?"

"Did you say 'Agatha'?" Oscar asked, his golden eyes round with astonishment.

He put down his pencil.

"Yes, I've found letters about a woman named Agatha Robertson with lots of detail, like you'd put in a novel. All sorts of imaginings that would make up a story . . ."

"Well, what do you know?" Oscar said to the air. "The world is bound with secret knots."

"What precisely have you found?" Oscar asked.

"I'm not sure," I replied. "But I've been skimming through letters from Melville to Nathaniel Hawthorne, and there's this long one where he's trying to push a story on to Hawthorne as an idea for a novel. But it seems to me that Melville is the one who really wants to write it."

"About a woman named Agatha?"

"Yes, but that was her real name, he would have changed it. He heard about a real story from a lawyer he met, a Mr. Clifford. And Clifford sent him a diary page with notes about the family. Do you know of a novel of Melville's about abandonment? About the resignation of women?"

"There's something in the index of this biography listed as 'the Agatha Story,' and I've made a note here."

He drew his notebook closer on the desk, inspecting his own neat printing.

"Here it is. I thought perhaps it referred to a short story. Also this reference in a letter between Melville's sisters to a work called *The Isle of the Cross*, which I've never heard of. The year . . . let me check . . . is 1853." He drew his hand across his head.

"Would his sisters know about his work?" I asked.

"They lived with Melville and his wife at the time. So did his mother. Both sisters were his copyists, chiefly Augusta. It was common practice to have neat copies made and the only way was to copy out the entire manuscript by hand. Besides, Melville's hand-writing wasn't very good, full of spelling errors. He had terrible eyesight; his eyes were weak from a childhood bout of scarlet fever. He supported them all with his writing, so his work was his sisters' work, too."

Geist's letter had been written in a beautiful hand. Whose? I thought of lovely looping copperplate, of Melville's sisters dutifully copying pages and pages of manuscript. The patience and endurance of women. Agatha wandering the shoreline with the prow embedded, resigned and abandoned.

"Oscar, you said 1853? This letter to Hawthorne is from the year before."

I handed him the book, opened at the page. Oscar checked his notes.

"In one of the postscripts he writes to Hawthorne that Agatha should wander the shoreline thinking about her husband who has disappeared," I told him. "And that the old prow of his shipwreck is stuck in the sand. Perhaps rather like a cross?"

"Show me that passage," he demanded.

I watched his face closely as he read. His head loomed close to mine, and later I was sure I'd dreamed his nearness. After a minute he sat back. He addressed the air again in a soft, excited voice.

"This biography suggested that there was something unexplained about Melville's development. He was a terrible failure, you know, after tremendous early fame. *Moby-Dick* wasn't a success, and he immediately wrote another book that was a public scandal. That was *Pierre*, in 1852, the year of this letter. Critics called him insane."

He wasn't mad, I thought. Intense feeling is liable to be misunderstood. "Believe me, I am not mad . . . But truth is ever incoherent, and when the big hearts strike together, the concussion is a little stunning."

"He was deeply in debt," Oscar went on. "After *Pierre* there is a break and then short stories started to appear in magazines more than a year later, in a different—one might say an almost resigned—style. Something had changed in him."

I must have looked blank, for Oscar tried to explain. "Remember *Bartleby*? You must know *Bartleby! The Scrivener*, for heaven's sake! The point is, he taught himself something with every book. It seems plausible that there was a book in between."

"Well, if you think that might be true, here's a description of a possible story. A story he was clearly interested in." I pointed to the book of letters in his hand. "A woman is deserted by the shipwrecked sailor she had nursed back to health and married. Melville says he was interested in patience, in endurance. In perseverance and remorse. The prow in the sand is almost like a gravestone. I'm going to take this book out and read through all the letters."

"Melville must have felt he knew something about endurance himself by then," Oscar remarked, seemingly to himself.

We both sat perfectly still for a full minute.

"It's not possible that Walter Geist has stumbled upon a copy of *The Isle of the Cross*?" Oscar asked his doppelgänger, his surprised reflection, staring at him from the blackness of the library window. "Is it?"

We searched through other correspondence; Oscar requested a biography of Nathaniel Hawthorne, which was promptly located. We had to hurry before closing hour, at ten, and the curfew lent a feverish quality to our search. I checked out the book of letters, determined to read them alone in bed. We had discovered a great deal; and while the actual meaning of much of it eluded me, I was thrilled by the search's numinous quality, and by sharing it with Oscar.

Hawthorne, the biography indicated, had briefly worked on something called *The Isle of Shoals*, and Melville for a while had even wanted to use that title for the Agatha story. Apparently he discarded it, the "shoals" part at least. I continued to scour the book of letters I had checked out, and I would later find a far more subdued letter from Melville, written a few months after the passionate ones that so impressed me. Inexplicably, something had shifted between the friends:

> *My dear Hawthorne,—*
>
> *The other day, at Concord, you expressed uncertainty concerning your undertaking the story of Agatha, and, in the end, you urged me to write it. I have decided to do so, and shall begin it immediately upon reaching home; and so far as in me lies, I shall endeavor to do justice to so interesting a story of reality. Now Melville will undertake the writing of the novel for Hawthorne, because Hawthorne urged him to it. The gift will run the other way.*

But there was no doubt now, at least, that Herman Melville had written another novel, now lost, called *The Isle of the Cross*.

∽

"*What do you* think it all means?" I asked Oscar as we left the library and walked toward the subway.

It was after ten; we'd been together for close to four hours. Oscar was silent.

"Why don't we just talk to Mr. Geist about what we've

found out?" I suggested. "And see if we can help the Arcade get the manuscript?"

He came to a halt and turned to me.

"Has it occurred to you that Geist does not want the Arcade to acquire a priceless manuscript? A manuscript that may well change certain assumptions about a great American master? That may be stolen, in any case? That perhaps Geist has other plans for it? That he shouldn't even have knowledge of it, as the letter was addressed to George Pike?"

I couldn't respond. It was hard to think when I was so excited, and it appeared that even Oscar was in his own form of high spirits: drunk on research, exhilarated by arcane details.

"I'm starving," he said abruptly. He was always surprising me. "I'm going in here."

Oscar walked as if directed into the doorway of a diner that showed a neon OPEN sign in the window. His pronouncement was as much invitation as I was likely to get. I followed. We sat in a red vinyl booth, opposite each other. (Together! In a restaurant!)

An ancient waitress with heavy black-rimmed eyes appeared. "Coffee?" she rasped out.

"Eggs, scrambled. No toast. Tea," said Oscar with an unconsciousness that implied all his consideration was focused on something not present, on entirely mental preoccupations. The waitress turned to me and waited impassively, pulling up her bra strap through her uniform.

"Same, I suppose," I said, unable to imagine what I might enjoy eating. "I'd like milk in my tea. Please."

"It's on the table," she said perfunctorily.

I was afraid to break the spell I had willed upon myself. Two glasses of water were banged down in front of us. The ice cubes rattled.

"What did you mean, Oscar, about Mr. Geist having his own reasons for keeping the manuscript a secret?"

"I think it only reasonable to suspect his motives," he said, sipping the water. "He snatched the letter from your hand, didn't he? And he organized to meet with Samuel Metcalf at Peabody's shortly afterward. And he didn't include you in the discussion or even mention the letter again."

The torn corner was still in my pocket. I fingered it as if it were the missing piece to a complex puzzle, confirmation of all I didn't understand.

"What's Metcalf's story of supposedly being related to Melville?"

"One of his chief articles of proof for that relationship is that he comes from the small town in upstate New York where Melville's mother lived briefly."

"Lansingburgh?" I'd learned this detail from that night's reading. Maria Melville had rented a house in Lansingburgh, near Albany, when the family was short on money.

"Exactly! You see, you learned something quite particular before you knew you'd have a use for it. Only one of Melville's four children married, Frances, and she had a child who married a Metcalf. But there's no reason to believe their common name is anything but coincidence."

"The envelope Geist had was blank, so the letter must have been hand-delivered to the Arcade. Mercer can't have brought it in, but wouldn't we know if Samuel Metcalf had been there?"

"Julian Peabody is one of the few people Geist has access to with the resources to pay what such a treasure could be worth. If it's authentic. And Metcalf is the key to both things. Peabody's acquisitiveness is a kind of mania. But if what the letter indicated is true or real, if we can believe in it at all, then such a manuscript should be housed in an institution, a university or a great library, where scholars can study it."

"But the Arcade could sell it just as well to Peabody or to any institution."

"Yes, but not for a commission that cut in Geist, and possibly Metcalf, and not without providing an 'honorable' provenance. No university or library is interested in stolen goods of such a potentially public variety. And Peabody could lock it away for as long as he cares to. Besides, there are things that have a price so high they can never be sold."

Our eggs arrived. Oscar fell upon them like a man starved.

"You mean that if Geist sells the manuscript, without Pike's knowledge, he could get a percentage?" I asked, desperately trying to follow.

"It could be that he and Metcalf will split it. But then, of course, they will be cheating not only Pike, but Peabody, stealing from both employers."

"But the letter was sent to Pike. What does Mr. Geist need that kind of money for, anyway? Surely the author of the letter will contact Pike, or might even mention it to him? Why don't we just tell Mr. Pike?"

"We won't do any such thing! Look, I haven't figured everything out, Rosemary. 'Open-eyed conspiracy his time doth take'! Give me a few days to think about it."

"Sorry." I watched his mouth open and close over a forkful of eggs. "I'm going to read the book of letters and perhaps that will help."

His jaw moved beneath papery skin.

"It is an odd detail that Metcalf may know about the manuscript through Geist," he said with his mouth full. "The author of the letter then can't be Metcalf's father."

I told Oscar everything I could remember about the visit to Peabody's. He listened to me in a way I found thrilling. I told him that Metcalf had been surprised to see that I accompanied Geist, and that he'd wanted to occupy me with the cabinet rooms. He'd said to Geist that this would be big, so he certainly knew that he had something his employer would want.

Oscar had finished his food before I'd touched mine, so intent had I been on relating all I could recall. He sat distractedly looking out the window into the night while I ate my tepid eggs in silence. He asked for the check and painstakingly counted out his share. It hadn't occurred to me that Oscar might be cheap.

"Your share is two dollars and ninety-seven cents," he said, anxious to leave. "Including tip."

I finished my tea, feeling the evening's end moving away from me. I wanted to grab at its tail and hold on. We walked from the diner, pausing to cross the street.

"I have a lot to think about," Oscar said. He walked ahead and turned, obviously in something of a hurry to get away.

But I had waited, and for me it had come to this. The evening possessed an imagined design, and I thought my will played a part in bringing it about. That wanting alone could give me Oscar, standing before me at the mouth of the subway entrance.

I leaned almost imperceptibly toward him. He seemed not to notice, or care, fumbling in his pocket for a token.

Desire was drawn like a wire through the cold evening air.

A light wind lifted my hair. Car horns griped, distracting him. I leaned in again, feeling subject to laws that were nonetheless obscure to me. An inch from his great face, his cheek a curve of living plaster, my mouth opened slightly, remembering his mouth as he devoured his food. His jaw moving that day in my dirty park when I'd kicked a condom under the bench. His face looming close in the library. His lips as he drank his tea. "And when I put it to my lips— lo, they are yours and not mine." My whole being leaned into him.

I would kiss him.

"Stop it! Stop it!" he hissed between his teeth, appalled. His yellow eyes were wide with horror. "Stop!" He reared his head away from me. "Stop!" He actually pushed at my shoulder, shoving me.

"What is wrong with you! What are you doing! You're not to

think like that, Rosemary! Do you hear me?" His voice was bitter and high. "Rosemary!" There was outrage in his voice. "Have I not been clear? Have I? Understand something: I am not interested, in anyone, in . . . in that way. I'm not . . . Don't be stupid!"

He spoke to me as to someone who lacks basic comprehension. There was pity in his voice, but sharper still, disgust. He recoiled from me as if stung. As if I had deceived him. Warm tears on my cold face woke me as smartly as a slap. I staggered against a heap of snow, slipped, and fell hard on the icy sidewalk. My bag flew off my shoulder. My hands scraped the pavement.

Oscar retreated down the subway stairs without another word.

∽

I'd fallen with all the weight of humiliation. I scrambled for my bag, collecting up the book from the library, my wallet, my keys. I saw immediately that I had been stupid, and greedy. Wiping my face on my coat sleeve, I stood, feeling a bruise deepen on my hip. I thought I had deserved to fall, deserved to hurt myself. I was wretched.

I determined then that I would walk, painfully, abjectly, all the way downtown to my apartment. The penance would remind me that I'd been thoughtless. I had no right to such things. No cause to demand.

Oscar. It didn't matter that I'd been warned by Pearl, I had deceived myself. It was my own fault. The fault of a girl who had loved the likes of Pip, Darcy, Knightley, Mr. Rochester (all the usual suspects) without genuinely registering their common quality—they were fictional. The Oscar I loved was invented as well. The Melville investigation had intoxicated me. His wild letters, his fabulous metaphors—magnets, interchangeable hearts in breasts. Oscar was nothing like Herman Melville. Nor was he Ishmael. And he wasn't a subject of my imagination. In the face of every indication of disinterest, I had pressed myself on him.

I actually believed then I deserved what I got.

I felt my own strangeness as I walked through the city; a recognition dogged me: how little I knew, how little I understood. Yet, unlike the night I walked from Peabody's, a hollow certainty filled my navigation of traffic lights. I was a sleepwalker, moving mindlessly around clusters of people in some places, down long, empty blocks in others.

But I was actually awake now, and no longer in a trance.

In Midtown, theatergoers poured out onto the street in a sleepy procession, blocking Times Square, stranding themselves on the concrete traffic islands, adrift in the oceanic city. I walked on, holding my hip, through dubious neighborhoods and equivocally residential ones. Snow-covered shrubs outside a few prewar apartment buildings. My feet were numb in cheap boots. I was limping by the time I approached the Thirties, with many blocks to go before I reached my cold apartment.

Chaps told me once that to be free is often to be lonely—can she have meant this?

Before I understood exactly where I was, a familiarity with the buildings, with the penumbra of shadow around a ragged, ill-lit awning a block away, told me I was close to the Martha Washington, close to East Twenty-ninth Street.

I would stop in and see if Lillian was still awake. There were things more important than this, than me. I remembered the note in my bag that Pearl had given me earlier. It was important to see Lillian.

⌇

She was behind the reception counter, slumped in a chair, asleep. The television blinked on without sound. The earplugs had fallen onto her chest. I touched her gently and she woke in terror.

"*Vive Dios!*" she yelled.

"Lillian, it's me."

"What you are doing here?" She was disoriented from sleep and fright. "You scare me! Do not surprise me like that."

She sat up and straightened her clothes, smoothed her thick hair. She switched off the television.

"You have come back, Rosemary? You will stay here again?"

"No. No. I was just out walking and I thought I'd see if you were here."

"I am always here. Where else I be?" She rubbed her eyes awake. "It is funny, like I'm dreaming. I think it like the night you arrive. In the summer storm. That different girl from Tasmania. Remember? That younger one."

"I'm the one who's been dreaming," I muttered.

She looked at me more closely. "What is the matter?" she demanded.

"Nothing," I lied. "I just wanted some company. I was out, and I was just walking home."

"You have been out with a man?" she guessed.

"Yes, but it wasn't that sort of thing," I said, repeating Oscar's words. "Not like that at all. I went to the library with a friend, to look up some information."

"Then why you look so sad? You have been crying. Why you are so cold?" She touched her hand to my face. "You need more clothes on."

Lillian stood up to fully inspect me. "Your side is wet. Did you fall in snow? You must be careful, I know. We are not used to this weather. Our blood is thinner, remember, I tell you? Sit down here." She gave me her chair behind the counter, pushing me into it.

"You are not all right. I can see. Tell me what happen to you. Someone has hurt you? Tell me."

"No. I'm not hurt," I said, my eyes filling, spilling tears.

Lillian fussed over me, moving a small space heater nearer my feet. "Take off these boots. They are wet through. You are worn out," she said, helping me with my boots.

"You stay here, I think. Your place is still cold? You will catch cold. You need to sleep."

I looked up into her concerned face, ashamed that she should be so solicitous of me, with all her genuine pain. Although, just then, mine was real enough. I felt a fool.

"You stay here," Lillian urged. "I make a room up for you. Free. No charge. I tell my brother. You can go to sleep."

I couldn't help myself then.

"I was sleeping," I blurted out, my voice breaking. "I was sleeping. And I was dreaming about someone, that's all."

The hot tears again; an embarrassing sob.

"All a stupid dream," I spluttered. "And I just woke up. A little while ago. Tonight."

"And you want to dream again," Lillian said, soothing me, patting me. She knelt beside the chair and wrapped her arms about my shoulders, resting her head against mine.

"I know," she said. "I always want that too."

I spent the night at the Martha Washington. Lillian lent me a night-gown and tucked me into bed, a heartbreaking echo of Mother's tending to me that I hadn't considered in years, even when she was alive. As Lillian pulled the blanket up to my chin, she hummed a sad song and I wondered if she felt a parallel echo, if she remembered tucking her own Sergio into bed as a small boy.

My side ached. Lillian sat with me until I slept, deeply and without dreaming.

I awoke early, alone. I washed up in the grimy bathroom along the hall. Renovations hadn't picked up at the Martha Washington in my absence. The whole place was halted, stopped in some other past. A new decade was less than a month away, the city was changing, repairing itself, but not at 29 East Twenty-ninth Street. Lillian had mentioned that her brother had trouble getting his money out of Argentina, that the situation in her homeland was no better. Before she resumed her post at reception I gave her Pearl's note, with the name and phone number, and told her I'd check in with her later that day. Lillian patted me as if she were sending me off to school.

I set out, limping slightly, on my familiar walk from the Martha Washington to the Arcade. But habit had done its work, and the short distance had none of its former surprise; the city had now lost its fresh daylight distinction. Once you know your way about, that earlier experience of discovery can't be restored; a completely unknown New York was irretrievable. The dirty park appeared, almost indistinct from its urban surroundings under snow, part of the landscape now, not more than a reminder that it had served as my natural clock, marking the passing of seasons. I drew a sharp breath. I had to get to the Arcade, to work. I would have to see Oscar. I would have to apologize. I would have to grow up and keep my fantasies to myself.

Winter was harder than I'd imagined.

CHAPTER

SIXTEEN

∾ W alter Geist was the first person I saw when I arrived at the Arcade. He and Pike were almost always early; Mr. Mitchell, almost always late. I watched Geist stumble against the pile of books waiting to be shelved at the base of Pike's platform. He darted a quick look around to see if he'd been observed. Somehow he knew I was there, although I hadn't spoken.

"I wish to speak with you in the office," he said. "Please come upstairs, Rosemary, as soon as you have hung up your coat."

He looked ill and anxious, like a crustacean drying outside its shell. Now that I was there, I felt a little like he looked: in need of nourishment.

I had already removed my coat and held it in my hand. I was wearing the same clothes as the day before, a whitish salt stain marked my side; but Pearl was the only person who would notice such details. Beneath my black trousers a large bruise had appeared, tender and sore to the touch. So much for Chaps's green amulet— internal pain, heartbreak, same thing, Oscar had said.

Geist went up to the office.

Pike was on his stage speaking into the telephone, cutting the air into squares about the size of pages with his free hand. The re- ceiver he held in his other was comically large; even the telephone at the Arcade was an anachronism. Most of the antiquated technology in the place was broken, but the old phone worked. Pike didn't want to take root in the century where he found himself, particularly if it meant replacing any objects that served perfectly well as they were. I wondered if Geist was included in that impulse. He couldn't be serving perfectly well.

"You are utterly incorrect, Mitchell," Pike was saying with some vehemence. "Wrong. As usual. I will mention it to him, but I'm certain you are mistaken. All correspondence is accounted for. Spare the Arcade your conspiracies! And you're late again!"

He slammed the heavy Bakelite receiver onto its cradle. He noticed me at the base of his stage.

"Do not listen to the conversations of George Pike, Miss Savage. Commonly called eavesdropping. Don't be common."

Did he know I'd done it before? I blushed.

"Oh, I'm sorry, Mr. Pike, I was just on my way, um, to the office. I'm sorry."

"Are you quite well?" he asked, more curious than concerned.

"Yes, I'm fine, Mr. Pike. Fine."

"Good. Not floating today. After you see Mr. Geist, you are to work in Oscar's section for the entire day."

"In Nonfiction?" I was thrown at the prospect of so quickly having to confront Oscar. I hadn't a clue how to handle it. What should I say? Would he even speak to me? I must have looked shocked.

"George Pike directs you to Nonfiction. Is there a problem?"

"No, sir. I—"

"Oscar will not be at the Arcade today," he said. Relief flooded me. "You must try and manage as well as you can with his regular customers. Business is brisk! Christmas is coming!"

He spoke these declarations to the surrounding air, then tilted his head slightly in my direction.

212

"George Pike advises caution with regard to shoplifters. Thieves love this time of year. They see a gift in everything, even where there are none. Purchases, not presents. All eyes!"

He gestured to his own face and opened his eyes comically wide. Had Redburn been back in? How many others were there? Clearly his paranoia took the shape of legions of robbers.

"Yes, Mr. Pike."

I would have to make up with Oscar, but not today.

I hung up my coat in the bathroom, where the GEORGE PIKE WILL NOT TOLERATE THE THEFT OF MONEY OR BOOKS! sign shouted at me, needlessly reiterating its author. I climbed the stairs to the office at Geist's request, slowly, my hip hurting and the rickety railing no brace on that side.

∽

"*You wanted to* see me, Mr. Geist?" I said, after waiting a moment at the door.

Geist was holding a paper no more than an inch from his face.

It seemed impossible that he could read anything held so close. "Ah!" he exclaimed, and threw the paper onto the cluttered desk. I wondered why he didn't use his magnifier, why his pince-nez glasses stayed in his pocket, the attached chain glinting. Perhaps he'd given up.

"Come in, Rosemary," he said, shifting his small body in his chair, leaning forward. "I need your help."

"Yes, Mr. Geist," I said, without enthusiasm. Now that I suspected him of plotting against Pike, against the Arcade, I didn't know how to behave with him. Could it really be true? Did he want to draw me into it?

"Mr. Pike wants to hold a small gathering to celebrate the season. Nothing fancy. Or expensive. Wine and cheese. Just the staff, an hour before closing." He waved his delicate hand in the air as if it were more articulate in such matters than he.

"Do you have a specific date in mind?" I asked, relieved that this was the only sort of help he wanted for the moment.

"Well, we're closed on Christmas Day, so how about Christmas Eve?"

"Two weeks from today, then?"

"No. Is it?" He seemed confused, and sat back. "Is it really?"

He rubbed his face with both hands and left them there for a long moment, holding his head in his hands.

"Time is running out, Rosemary," he said enigmatically. His hands dropped.

"Running out?" I asked, and approached the desk. He really wasn't well. "Mr. Geist, what's the matter?"

"The matter?" he repeated. "It's all running out, Rosemary. Time is a burden, don't you think? Being a clock, as Metcalf said. Remember? At Peabody's? Sit down, will you?" he asked. "Please?"

"But Mr. Geist, I'm supposed to relieve Oscar. He isn't in today."

I sat anyway.

"I know," he said. "His first absence. The most reliable of employees. Remarkable, really, that in five years he's never been ill."

I felt guilty then, thinking, rather foolishly, that Oscar was absent due to my behavior. Geist was visibly exhausted, and fell silent. His vacillating eyes were restless, averted in their peculiar way, their motion preventing any direct engagement. He sank into himself.

"Are you not sleeping well?" I asked, nervous to be sitting with him without conversing. And I was concerned. I found him poignant, whatever his secret plans, his strange wants. I realized that I couldn't believe this frail man was a thief; it seemed mad to suggest as much.

"I am an insomniac, Rosemary, since you are good enough to inquire. It is a symptom that much crucifies melancholy men, as someone once said," he sighed.

Crucified? By sleeplessness? I thought at once of Agatha, the prow stuck in sand. Perhaps he wanted *The Isle of the Cross* to relieve some crippling debt? I couldn't forget Mother's insomnia, brought about by indebtedness, and how it had destroyed her health.

"Have you seen a doctor?" All I could think to say.

He gestured with both hands, beautifully, like the spreading of wings, then let them fall on the untidy surface of the desk.

"I have shifted my allegiance," he said, cryptically, after a long while. "In the end, I've no wish to be a janissary, lickspittle and cowed."

He turned his face away from me.

"I don't accept my position, you see. Envious of everyone, and secretly enamored. I want something of my own."

I couldn't follow him, but leaned forward to listen to his sibilant words more closely. I called myself to attention. I must attend, I thought, attend. Oscar would want to know what he was telling me. I would need to remember everything he said. What exactly was wrong with him?

"I'm a stranger always, Rosemary," he went on quietly. "Apparent enough, I know. There are always anomalies, and I am one."

I guessed he meant that he was always outside of everything, an oddity—which was true, but in a way true for me as well.

"I could say the same about myself, you know, Mr. Geist. I often feel I'm a kind of exile. A fish out of water."

He brightened at my words, at the idea that I might think myself like him in some way; misplaced and analogous. Once he'd tried to have me admit my ordinariness, and here I was trying to reassure him of our resemblances.

"Rosemary, I want to speak to you of something other than myself," he began, leaning forward. "There is much that you can do for me. When we went to Peabody's, when we met Sam Metcalf—"

Jack Conway appeared at the door, thumping rudely on the wooden frame.

"Sorry to interrupt," he said, his Irish brogue cheeky and not at all sorry. His look was inquisitive.

"What is it?" Geist demanded, furious.

"Pike's after you, Geist. He sent me up to get you. Problem with a customer. In the basement." He pointed downward with both index fingers.

"All right," Geist snapped. "Rosemary, I—"

"It's all right, Mr. Geist. I've got to go to Nonfiction."

Jack waited in the doorway until I stood up and walked out onto the landing. "Having a nice chat?" he then muttered to me. "If you're looking for company, you needn't stoop to nutty old Geist."

He raised his eyebrows suggestively.

"What?!"

"Always happy to oblige a lonely girl, meself," said Jack, shaking the broken handrail. I went on ahead of him. "I'd have a go, you know," he whispered behind me into my hair. "Any time you say the word, Rosemary. Come 'ere, you know what the word is, don't ya?"

His hand swooped forward and grabbed at my bottom, causing me to trip.

"Careful there. I'll have a hold of you if you fall!" he laughed.

I jumped the last two steps down to the main floor, the pain in my hip flaring up sharply.

"Not interested, Jack," I shot back, my face hot, disgusted by him.

"Rather play out Beauty and the Beast, would ya?" he said beneath his breath. "Or is it the blind leading the blind, up the garden path? Enjoy a bit of a tease, do ya?"

He raised his head in a dismissive way, his shiny scar another kind of insult. Who was he to call anyone a beast?

Walter Geist was behind us then, on the stairs, and barked at Jack to get to the paperback tables at the front of the store. I doubt he'd heard Jack's insults, but I was pricked by them, and considered, with quiet dismay, that he might not be the only person they had occurred to. I knew that Geist longed to confide in me, and knew too that I'd rather he didn't. Whatever he told me, I was bound to confess to Oscar. I would offer Oscar anything that intrigued him now, by way of apology, to make amends.

At least I had a day's reprieve with regard to Oscar. I wandered through his section, missing him. Was he thinking about *The Isle of the Cross*, about Melville and his story of remorse, or about me? I felt confused and humiliated by my feelings; by Jack's innuendo; by Geist's confidences. I ran my hand along the shelves of Oscar's Psychology section, too despondent to look inside any of the volumes. Perhaps something a bit more oblique than the workings of the mind. How about the soul? Embrace the soul. I wandered over to Philosophy, despite feeling unphilosophical, and randomly selected a book, shelved at eye level. I quickly read something incomprehensible about how the shape of intelligence is time, a thin line that only presents things to us one by one. I closed it with a thump. What nonsense!

Mr. Gosford, the collector with seemingly unlimited credit, appeared in the corner of my eye, and hoping to avoid him, I hid behind the stack. I wasn't up to answering any inquiries. I couldn't find again the eddy of books Oscar and I had retreated to, together; and seeing Gosford rounding the corner of my hiding place, I ducked behind Biography, down the alley of Military History, only to come out exactly at the place where Oscar usually sat, waiting to greet customers, and scribbling in his notebook.

Nonfiction remained a maze to me, but, momentarily free of Gosford, I could privately pretend to be Oscar. Upon his tall stool lay a small book of poetry. I picked it up and sat to rest my sore hip. I'd never sat on his stool before; as far as I knew, no one else had, either. It was his throne, and not particularly comfortable. I opened the book to the page held in place by the cover flap. Several lines were marked, in pencil, in the center of the facing page. I looked around. Had a customer left it? Had the book been left for me? Or for Oscar?

Who knows now what magic is;—the power to enchant
That comes from disillusion. What the books can teach one
Is that most desires end up in stinking ponds . . .

Another line, sharply underscored, close to the bottom, seemed directed even more pointedly at me. At least I took it that way. Poetry stumbled upon never seems accidental.

All we are not stares back at what we are.

What was I to make of this? Surely a deliberate act, leaving a poetry book in Nonfiction, and on Oscar's stool of all places. I turned the book over and decided to return it to its proper place, the shelf I had first begun to organize the day I walked into the Arcade, six months before. I slipped from Oscar's stool and went to Poetry.

I recalled my first meetings, with George Pike, with Walter Geist. Everything seemed so inevitable then, my future opened like a book I'd been waiting to read. That Pike should have employed me so readily was an act of magic. On that day, the whole Arcade had appeared a creation drawn exactly to the specifications of my need.

That this sort of thinking would be proved false is apparent only now. Despite how much the Arcade satisfied me, how much it taught me, I hadn't found it on a wish. Life is more complicated than that, marked by suffering that can be neither relieved nor, in some cases, even understood. There is little sense that it comes one by one, in a line of time—all at once heaped in a knotted tangle is more like it.

Before I shelved the book, there at the start of Poetry, I plucked a single hair from my head and laid it into the crease where the pages joined. I was marking a place: all of my self stacked in one auburn column. I fancied it a message of my own for whoever had left the book on Oscar's stool. The strand curled on the white page like a copper wire; a single thread that could tell the tale, that could show the way.

I'd read the message, even if I couldn't decipher it. And there I was, inside a book, ready to be shelved back at the place I'd started, cryptic as the poem. Oscar's rejection had served to tell me what I was not, what I couldn't be to him. I read the lines again. Did books really say that most desires end up in stinking ponds? Not the ones I had read. Books were the very source of desire. But then, perhaps that was precisely the point?

Chapter

Seventeen

⁓ Arthur lumbered over from Art, rousing me from my daydream. He looked at the cover of the book I'd taken from Oscar's stool.

"Auden, is it now, my Tasmanian Devil? *The Sea and the Mirror*. Don't tell me you are to become the Arcade's next poet! Have you contracted that special illness of the ear—verse?"

"Oh, don't start, Arthur," I said, without energy or interest in banter. I'd been content drifting.

"Not like you to be short so early in the day, TD," he said, feigning hurt. He pointed to the book. "He's a hero of mine, you know. This is his riff on *The Tempest*."

The mention of Chaps's favorite play brought her to mind. I missed her, missed taking for granted that someone loved me implicitly and without agenda. Someone absolutely certain who I was, having had a hand in my making.

Arthur shifted his weight from foot to foot and watched me. His breath was sour and labored; his bulk like a punitive suit over what I imagined was a secret, slender self. Another Arthur was trapped inside, as his eyes confirmed when he smiled at me.

"I'm happy for a chat, TD—if you'd like to have one," he offered. "You know you're my favorite, and I don't have many—at least not here."

He was solicitous, even if I wasn't ever convinced of his earnestness. I felt homesick, and in the absence of Chaps would have liked to visit Mr. Mitchell. But after the last occasion, I couldn't be sure of him, either, at least to provide the solace I craved.

"I'm supposed to work in Oscar's section," I told Arthur. "He's absent. I found this book there on his stool and thought I'd return it."

"Ah, the Eternal Return!" Arthur quipped, above my head. "Oscar's never been absent before," he said then, and rubbed his vast stomach thoughtfully. "Let alone leaving Auden about."

"I don't think he did leave it there. Someone else must have."

"Probably right," he said. His stomach made a squelching sound. "Oscar's not one for poetry, unless it's bound in silk or vellum."

"Why is Auden your hero?" I asked, forcing the small book back into the press of spine-out-only volumes. It was like trying to squeeze music back into an accordion. I gave up and rested it across the tops of other books.

"Oh, you know, art is queerness and all that. I relate," Arthur said. "Except I'm not a poet and the only art I make these days is the kind I usually eat. Oh, and the kind I sell packaged up in books." He was trying to be flippant but sounded resigned instead.

"What does that mean, Arthur—'art is queerness'?"

"Just an idea." He waved a thick hand. "I think Auden meant that whenever there's a gift there's a guilty secret, a thorn in the flesh. Both things are given at once, and the nature of one depends on the other. I studied him, you know. When I was confused, and young, and ashamed to be myself. When I still thought I might write."

He smiled sadly.

"That was long before I came to work here, TD."

Auden's idea struck me as profound in an obscure way. Queerness and art—a guilty secret. I thought of Oscar and the previous evening. The letters from Melville to Hawthorne and the story of Agatha. Perhaps "longing" was just another word for "queerness"? And "queerness" another word for a way to manage, a means of making sense. Less about sex than a kind of wit. As I stood thinking, Arthur touched my shoulder, bringing me back.

"What is it, my Tasmanian Devil?"

"What do you think Oscar's gift might be?"

"Oscar?" Arthur sighed. "Hard to say. He is so secretive. I've had long talks with him over the years only to realize afterward that they were monologues. He just listened. That's a gift, I suppose. He's very clever. But his gift is not for love, if that's what you're asking me. Not for loving anyone, I can assure you. Not women. Not men."

"Really? No one? That seems incredibly sad."

"Only if you want him to love you back," Arthur said, shifting his weight again from foot to foot. "And that is less his problem than yours. Or even"—he looked mournful—"mine."

He waved in the direction of Oscar's stacks.

"Oscar has his Nonfiction. His fabrics. His precious notebooks. I think, Rosemary, that you're a very romantic girl."

"I think I am as well."

"For a fragile sort like Oscar, romance is an extravagance. An impossible demand."

He patted my wild hair.

"Enough chatting! Will you help me move some stock? I've got a box of Goya monographs that you wouldn't believe. I'll show you them—art opens the fishiest eye, you know. Fantastic stuff. But perhaps you know him already? *The Sleep of Reason Brings Forth Monsters*? Or *Saturn Devouring One of His Children*?"

"No," I said, shrugging. Arthur, too, wanted to educate me. "They don't sound very cheerful."

"'About suffering they were never wrong, the Old Masters.'" He threw a heavy arm across my shoulders. I smelled his sweat. "Come and I'll show you Goya and then we'll move him up front. Pike thinks they'll go for Christmas, of all things!"

He squeezed my arm.

"You're a big strong Australian," he said. "And your back can bear much more than mine."

Arthur's stomach gurgled audibly, and he clapped his hand over it. "Speaking of devouring . . . my God, I cry out for sustenance!"

"I'm hungry as well—I'll run across the street and bring you a sandwich."

I hadn't eaten since the night before with Oscar in the diner. I saw him again sitting across from me in the red booth, meticulously tallying the cost of his eggs, distracted and excited about Melville, about the possibility of *The Isle of the Cross*.

I was starving.

"The stomach is a tyrant," Arthur said, cheered at the prospect of food. He handed me a crumpled, damp ten-dollar bill retrieved from his pants pocket.

"Mine demands fealty, Rosemary. Roast beef with all the extras. It's on me, only hurry!"

❦

As I *returned* with sandwiches through the south door, Mr. Mitchell appeared, about to ascend the stairs to Geist's office. We hadn't spoken since I visited him alone and blundered through my disastrous admission about reading a letter to Geist. I felt awkward now, not quite believing anymore in his benign goodwill.

"Oh, Mr. Mitchell. Hello. I don't often see you outside the Rare Book Room."

"You found me, dear girl, but I was looking for you. I thought you might be up in the office."

"Why would you think that?" I asked.

"I thought Geist would be up there and that you might be, well, assisting him. You do spend a great deal of time assisting him."

"He's in the basement. I just picked up a snack for Arthur and me. I have to work in Oscar's section today. He's absent."

"Indeed, how unusual. Gosford told me as much a short while ago. He was prowling around here, after some Nietzsche. Can't imagine why. I have a first edition," he ran on distractedly, "but it was too rich for his blood, and I wasn't about to budge on the price, not today at least . . ."

"Well, anyway . . ." I said, and turned to go, but Mr. Mitchell stopped me.

"What is it, Mr. Mitchell? I have to give this to Arthur, and he's desperate."

"Actually, I came to apologize for my outburst the other day. About Geist having you read to him. I'm sorry, Rosemary. Insensitive of me, you know, and selfish."

I forgave him immediately, in fact realizing I had hoped that he would forgive me, although I'd really done nothing. With all that had gone on since then, I just wanted him to be kind. I counted on his kindness, and as with Oscar, I would do anything not to have him angry with me. But I couldn't tell him about *The Isle of the Cross*. That belonged to Oscar.

Mr. Mitchell lowered his voice and said with some urgency, "Do keep an eye out, though, won't you, dear girl." He pointed to his open eye, and scrunched up the other as if he were peering through a spyglass. He looked like an elderly pirate.

"And come and see me with any questions you might have about letters, won't you? No need to wait to escort a customer, just come up and visit. If there are any more letters, I mean. Anything you might be privy to." He added resentfully, "Anything Geist gets his hands on."

"Yes, of course, Mr. Mitchell," I reassured him. "Of course I will. No need to apologize, I know how much the Rare Book Room means to you."

"Alas, it is my life!" He looked around theatrically, as if to solicit sympathy. "But as I well know, and as Mrs. Mitchell reminds me regularly, '*Habent sua fata libelli.*'"

My lack of comprehension apparent, he paraphrased. "Latin, dear girl. One of my battle cries—'Books have their own destinies'! I'm sure it's true. I believe it. And I mustn't be greedy about what comes my way . . . how it comes my way. I'm sorry. Do say you forgive me?"

He took my hand and patted it. His florid face inclined toward mine. He was behaving conspiratorially, but as long as I was included, I didn't care. I remembered Pike telling him he was wrong on the telephone . . . utterly wrong. What could Robert Mitchell possibly be wrong about?

"Of course," I said. "There's nothing to forgive."

"And you will think of me, won't you? With regard to any letters? Any information?"

I nodded absentmindedly, wanting only to eat my sandwich.

"There's a good girl," he said, taking from his pocket his unlit pipe and biting down on the stem.

∽

"*Weren't you wearing* the same clothes yesterday?" Pearl asked slyly, as I walked into the ladies' bathroom, our regular meeting place, later that afternoon. "Don't tell me you didn't make it home last night? Tell me it isn't true!"

"I didn't, Pearl. Don't ask me about it, all right?"

"All right," she said. "I won't ask what happened last night, if you don't ask me about my audition."

"Oh, I'm sorry, Pearl." I'd forgotten all about it. "I'm sorry I didn't ask. Really, though, how did it go?"

"It was a disaster, girl." Pearl sat heavily on the ruined sofa. "I had a little thing prepared, from Handel's *Orlando*. You know, I can sing the countertenor as a mezzo-soprano. Women are sometimes cast in the lead. It's a travesty role, and I certainly know all about those. Anyway, I thought it would be good to do something a little unusual. But I blew it. I choked. I might as well face it—I can't have everything."

"What happened, exactly?"

"It's my voice, Rosemary. All the stuff I've been taking. The hormones. It's all changing, like in the fairy tale. *Mutabor!* I'm Pearl!" She waved her arm in a gesture of transformation, but her face was desolate.

"I want to change, I'm not confused. But I didn't count on losing the voice. It seems like I'm always having to lose one thing to get something else." She pointed between her legs, embarrassing me.

"And I'm not talking about that," she added.

"You mean you can't sing? But Pearl, I hear you in here all the time. Your voice is so beautiful."

"Oh, it's all right for some things, but not for the demands of opera. Not anymore, anyway. Not if you know anything about the voice."

Pearl crossed her legs and inspected her orange nails. She sighed.

"You know, that part was written for a castrato. Figures," she said sarcastically. "I've only got another couple of months to go before the operation. I'll just have to focus on that." She looked up at me. "There'll be even more medication after the surgery."

"Will you have it in New York, Pearl?" I asked. "Can I come and see you?"

"Of course you can visit, girl. I'm counting on it. But not in New York. At Johns Hopkins. Baltimore. The place is excellent. I've been a couple of times for interviews already. Mario's paying for the whole thing, you know, even all the counseling I've been having the last year."

"You mean a psychiatrist?" Pearl was the sanest person I had met in New York. "Does it help?"

"Well, it's helped with some things," she answered vaguely.

"Like what?"

"Oh, like the fact that now I'm an orphan, like you. Only my family is all still alive—I'm the one that's dead!" She smiled with some bitterness. "But I've never had any doubts. That's just the way it always was for me, Rosemary. I never should have been anyone other than this here old Pearl girl." She grabbed her own breasts affectionately, and I wished I felt as familiar, as comfortable, with my own body.

"Of course not," I said, not really knowing what to say.

"The body's got to match." She pointed to her temple. "It's all got to match and it has to really be mine," she added. "See, I'm not gay, like Arthur, you know. I'm a woman, same as you. Only there was a mistake, and that's what has to be fixed."

"Of course," I said again.

I didn't really understand, but I believed Pearl and believed what she knew about herself. In a way, I even envied her. She was so certain, so wholly active in the process of her own becoming. For her it was all so literal, a pragmatic problem. She made me think about my own body, and whether I could claim it as credibly, as fully, as she asserted her womanliness.

"Geist and Mr. Pike will have to sort out the register when I'm gone. It'll take a few weeks to recover, plus I'm thinking of having a bit of other work done at the same time!"

She laughed and indicated her beautiful long nose, and pouted out her vermillion lips.

"Oh, don't, Pearl!"

She laughed. "Mr. Pike has been wonderful to me about it all, right from the start. I have a lot to be thankful for, Rosemary. There's Mario for one thing, my own true prince. And there's always been a place for me here at the Arcade."

"What will Mr. Pike do, do you think?" I asked. "When you're away, I mean?"

"Who Knows?" she cracked. "All these weird men? Perhaps they'll put you up there in front," she suggested. "Customers would love it!" And she laughed again. "No more surly Pearl."

"But I'm not good with money," I said, alarmed. "I can hardly manage my own. And you're far more patient than I'll ever be. Besides, I like floating. I want to work on the floor, with the books."

"With Oscar, you mean," said Pearl, imitating my accent, and clasped her hands to her breast in a mocking plea.

"Pearl," I sat beside her and lowered my voice. "Can I talk to you? I need to tell you something. I tried to kiss him last night, Pearl."

"You did not!" she said loudly. "After what all I told you!"

"I did, Pearl. I got caught up and I tried to kiss him." I visualized his face, twisted with disgust. "And he was horrified and ran away. And he didn't come in today, the first time ever."

She tried not to smile, and I tried not to cry. She put her arm around my shoulders and chuckled quietly. My problem wasn't Pearl's idea of tragic.

"Well, Rosemary, girl, these things can be very complicated. And I should know."

She sat forward.

"Look here," she said, taking my shoulders and forcing me to face her. "I'm not certain what Oscar's problems are, but don't make him *your* problem. Girl, you're young and gorgeous and you just got to find you a man that loves women. My God, hundreds of men are in here every day. Lots of fish in the sea, and all that."

The deformed fish-man portrait hanging in Peabody's collection rose up involuntarily in my mind, and I shuddered at the memory. One thing was certain: the men that frequented the Arcade weren't looking for women—for all their patent desire, it was books they lusted after.

"They don't want a woman, Pearl. It's just like *The Aspern Papers* in here!"

"For heaven's sake!" Pearl said impatiently. "Get out a bit then and look around. It isn't that hard. Just watch me and do what I do! I ain't never had no trouble!" she boasted, sitting up straighter and sticking out her formidable breasts.

We laughed together. Pearl pushed my hair behind my ear in a sisterly gesture.

"Listen, let's us girls have a drink together tonight. To cheer ourselves up. Just the Arcade women, out on the town. We could go to a bar I know." She waved her long nails at me.

"Well, I need to check in with Lillian after work. I told her I would. Will you come with me? I want you to meet her."

"Sure I will, girl. Did you give her the number?"

I nodded. "She said she'd call. I slept there last night, Pearl. After Oscar ran away. I needed some company, and Lillian is, well, she was my first friend here."

"You never told me why you even went to the library with Oscar in the first place, Rosemary."

Pearl stood up then and checked her makeup in the mirror. "Just asking for trouble," she added. "What were you looking for anyway?"

"Oh, it doesn't matter now. It doesn't even seem important today."

Pearl looked skeptical, watching me in the mirror.

"Well, I guess it's up to you what you share and what you don't," she said. "But don't go complaining to me about being lonesome."

CHAPTER
EIGHTEEN

Lillian was, as usual, positioned behind the reception desk, intent upon the television, the wire running from the set to her ears. Pearl and I stood smiling at her profile for a full minute before she turned, flinching as if we had materialized.

"Rosemary!" she said, shouting, forgetting she had her ears stopped up.

"Lillian." I leaned across the desk and took out the earplugs.

"This is my friend Pearl. From the Arcade. Remember, I told you about her? Pearl Baird. The one who gave you the phone number?"

"Yes," she said. "Nice to meet you. Lillian La Paco."

They shook hands.

"You are really Pearl?" she went on tactlessly, studying Pearl's hand, her polished nails. "But you are a man?"

"That's the trouble with people," Pearl said to me. "Always judging a lady by her flaws."

"Lillian, please," I said, leaning over the counter to admonish her. "That's not your business to ask."

"I mean no offense," Lillian shrugged, as if she couldn't imagine that Pearl would take any. "I just notice, that's all.

"I have to thank you, Pearl," she said, standing up and leaning over the counter. "I made a call today and I speak to a man at this place you give me. I will go after Christmas to talk with some people. With a lawyer. They speak Spanish there and I tell them about Sergio. They know already about Argentina. They have workers there, they tell me. I thank you for this, Pearl. I will see them—I tell my brother already. But I have no hope."

"You don't need to thank me," said Pearl. "But try to be optimistic. Perhaps they can help. Hope is something that's hard to live without."

"That is true," Lillian said simply. "But here I am—living. You must understand, I have called names and phone numbers, like you have given me, **many**, many times before. I have had meetings, sent papers, walked with the mothers in the Plaza. In protest, you understand? I have tried to find Sergio for years. I am grateful for your help, but I have no hope."

Lillian said this in the most matter-of-fact way. Her aristocratic face showed the ravages of all that she hadn't said, all she hadn't described. Chaps told me once that aging was a process of exchanging hope for insight, and it occurs to me that Lillian had made this exchange well before her time. I could see Pearl's admiration for her. They liked each other, despite a rough start. I felt my circle expanding even in this small way. We all smiled, slightly hesitant to change the subject, but wanting to.

I was moved by these two women, so different but alike in a way that was difficult to quantify. Perhaps the patience, or even the resignation, that marked their lives made them appear similar. It may well have been as simple as the fact that I loved them both, and felt that affection palpably, as I stood with them, together for the first time.

"How are you today?" Lillian asked, turning to me.

"I'm all right," I said, chagrined. "Fine. A little embarrassed about last night. Thanks for letting me stay here. It made all the difference."

"You are a young woman with things that are sometimes in your head only. Not real. This is not always a bad thing, Rosemary. It is to be expected. But it will hurt you sometimes." She gestured toward her heart, then reached across the counter to touch my face. "Not to ever feel embarrassed," she said.

Pearl watched Lillian, her eyes warm.

"Pearl and I are going to go out for a drink tonight, Lillian. To cheer ourselves up."

"Can you come too?" Pearl asked. "Do you have to stay here?"

"I cannot go," said Lillian. "But thank you for asking me to come. My brother needs me to stay here. Maybe someone will check in tonight. He is busy with many other things."

Pearl glanced around the shabby lobby, the closed-off sections, a ladder leaning against the wall behind the front entrance. I had to agree with her dubious expression.

"How about we go and get a drink and bring it back here?" Pearl suggested. "We'll keep you company."

"But I have wine here!" said Lillian, jumping up and slipping through a door, the side entrance to the old shuttered restaurant that had once made the lobby of the Martha Washington quite lively. At least it appeared so in the few faded black-and-white pictures that hung behind Lillian's desk. Men had evidently been permitted in the restaurant during the thirties, even as they weren't ever allowed as guests at the hotel, and stood with their arms around women, smiling out of the photographs.

Lillian came back with a dusty bottle of wine and three glasses. I took the glasses down the hall to the bathroom and rinsed them. By the time I returned, the bottle was open and Pearl and Lillian were engaged in a half Spanish, half English conversation.

"I picked up a bit of Spanish from the boyfriend before Mario," Pearl said to me as I set the three glasses on the reception counter. "Mostly curse words, I'm afraid."

"Just maybe one drink," Lillian said. "Or my brother will be angry."

"How will he know?" Pearl asked.

"Is he here, Lillian?" I said, remembering that I'd only ever seen him on a couple of occasions.

"No. He is out, but he will come back later, and if he finds me drunk and asleep . . ."

"If you're drunk and asleep, you won't give a damn, a *maldecir!*" finished Pearl. "Or even notice!"

"Salute!" said Lillian, raising her glass and laughing. "I drink to not giving a damn. *No me importa un comino.* To no longer noticing!"

We all toasted such a sensible, unlikely idea, our three glasses clinking. Then we toasted the holiday season; then Pearl's impending surgery; then Lillian's upcoming meeting with the human rights lawyer; then to me finding a suitable man. Not too old, they both agreed—and nothing like Oscar, Pearl threw in.

"Sex is what you want," Pearl declared, making Lillian laugh behind her hand. "Sex, sex, and more sex!"

The bottle was empty by the time we finished toasting to me.

Lillian wanted to get more wine, but I realized how weary I was. My head swimming slightly, I stopped trying to follow the Spanish-and-English jumble of conversation, and thought about heading home.

"Ladies!" I interrupted. "If you don't mind, I think I'll walk home. I'm very tired and I haven't been to my flat since yesterday morning." It felt as if I'd been gone for a week.

"What about more wine?" Pearl asked.

"I've had enough," I said blearily. "But could we get together again?"

"Of course."

"How about Christmas Day?" I suggested. "At my place. We don't have to work, Pearl—the Arcade is closed. It will be my first without my mother. I could use the company."

We agreed that Lillian would check with her brother, and that Pearl would check with Mario. I was reminded that I had no one with whom to check—and felt equally relieved and disconsolate.

The women kissed me before I left them together at the Martha Washington's reception desk, chatting away like a couple of gossips. We were all a little tipsy and affectionate with each other, and I thought that what Lillian and Pearl had in common, apart from me, was their unimaginable experiences: experiences painful enough that, when seen in another's face, they amounted to real recognition.

ॐ

When I *returned* to my apartment, a package from Chaps leaned against the door, colorful Australian stamps optimistically lining the top right-hand corner. A Christmas present! I still had her other little parcel waiting to be opened, and here she'd sent another. But this one wouldn't wait.

A gift of a different kind waited inside: miraculously, the place was warm. The radiator hissed reassuringly, like the murmurings of an intimate. The heat was almost tropical, and, missing Australia, I took up the Christmas present from Chaps, tearing it open at the edge. Inside, wrapped in tissue, was a beautiful red blouse made of sheer fabric, delightfully impractical. Perhaps Chaps had forgotten that it was winter in New York? She included a Christmas card and a note full of questions. Why hadn't she heard from me? What was I reading? Had I met anyone I liked? Had I considered burying Mother's ashes or, better still, sending them home to her? How was the Arcade?

I put on the blouse at once. I hadn't bought new clothes since I arrived; extra money was nonexistent, after I paid Jack the rent and bought food. My small Arcade salary was reduced even further, paying off the loan to Geist. I'd been forced to buy boots and a heavy coat when winter came, but had to make do with the cheapest I could find. Consequently, the gift from Chaps possessed the aura of luxury. The fabric was almost transparent, and I was a little surprised that Chaps would send me a gift that was, well, revealing.

I thought with an ache that I'd love to ask Oscar what the shirt was made of. Have him consider me in it, touch it, and think for a moment before he told me about the fabric's derivation. Catching my image in the old oval mirror, a young woman in a bright blouse returned my gaze, a great mane of hair around her head. She wanted tidying, I thought, but she was pretty, if too ardent, a little too intense looking—a bit much, as they say. I wanted to tell the girl in there to lighten up.

I took off the shirt.

Walking about in my bra, the apartment cozy for the first time since I moved in, I absentmindedly set two large pots on the stove to boil, forgetting that if I had heat I most likely had hot water. I turned on the bath expectantly and, after a great choking spurt, steaming rust-colored water shot out. I dropped a fresh bar of soap into the brownish water, and it sent clouds swirling through the rust. Once the tub filled, it looked like a huge cup of milky tea.

Taking off the rest of my clothes, I inspected the bruise, brown in the center, yellow at the indefinite edges, a ragged circumference of color intense against my freckled skin. It was an autumn leaf pasted to my flesh.

An insignia of humiliation.

I sank into the warm, cloudy water, my pale body rising as I relaxed. Between my legs, the triangle of ginger-colored hair collected soap suds, a small island in the rusty water. What Pearl would undergo to have a body that resembled mine! My nipples floated pink above the water and I pinched them gently, feeling them stiffen. Sex was what was wanted; Pearl was quite right.

Only experience would give me the knowledge of my own body that I craved. I wanted someone to love me. To desire me. And I didn't want to wait.

My hands ran over my body as I tried to imagine they were someone else's. Oscar's hands. A man's hands. *Your heart in my ribs and mine in yours.* My hand passed between my legs. I saw Oscar's mouth moving, and lay fully into the water, my head thrown back like one of Arthur's nudes lost in a landscape of skin. Golden eyes flashed above me. With one hand across my breasts I stroked my nipple and, unwittingly, furtively, a vision of Geist's feathery fingers fluttered into my mind.

I sat up, dismayed. Where had that come from? I didn't want Walter Geist to penetrate any fantasy of mine, and the idea of his white hands on me was more than disconcerting. I had an apprehension of his intentions, but it was the stealth of my own imagination that shocked me.

I primly finished washing myself and got out of the bath.

Later, lying in the hot alcove, I picked up the book of Melville's letters I'd taken out from what I considered Oscar's library. I wanted to read again the passionate missives penned to Hawthorne. "The divine magnet is on you, and my magnet responds."

The letters struck me differently than the night before, when I'd discovered them. Perhaps it was the absence of Oscar, but the letters seemed a little mad, as indeed did parts of *Moby-Dick*. Herman Melville seemed to know a more frightening loneliness than I could ever imagine. The sort of wild emotion I had had a glimpse of in Lillian; the sort of desperate melancholy I sensed in Walter Geist.

I had read that Melville's father had died in a paroxysm of despair over bankruptcy. Was that the sort of despair that ended Mother's life?

There was a letter in the library book that Melville had sent to his editor and friend Evert Duyckinck in 1849. The letter remarked upon the decline of a mutual friend, a poet, Charles Fenno Hoffman, who had become "deranged."

> Poor Hoffman—I remember the shock I had when I first saw the mention of his madness. —But he was just the man to go mad—imaginative, voluptuously inclined, poor, unemployed, in the race of life distanced by his inferiors, unmarried,—without a port or haven in the universe to make.

This seemed to describe a good many people I had met in New York. In fact, it describes me at the time, with the exception that I was happily employed.

> This going mad of a friend or acquaintance comes straight home to every man who feels his soul in him,—which but few men do. For in all of us lodges the same fuel to light the same fire. And he who has never felt, momentarily, what madness is has but a mouthful of brains.

I set the book aside, inexplicably disturbed. The hot apartment hissed and ticked with unfamiliar noises. I was restless. I would have liked to speak to Mother, as I usually did, but something restrained me. I hadn't breathed a word of what had happened the previous evening to the Huon box, or mentioned why I'd been out all night. I felt guilty and rebellious that I didn't address even a shortened version of events to Mother. The box of ashes sat with silent opprobrium, covered by the orange scarf, on the floor against the far wall.

I kicked off the blanket and lay naked in the transparent heat. Eventually I slept, and dreamed of a dark, nameless lover, virtually insane with desire. His eyes burned, gleaming like great full moons, as he rose above me.

∽

Oscar was on his stool when I approached him, writing in his notebook. My stomach hurt at the sight of him, his sculpted head bent over his task. He didn't glance up until I was close, and then he met my eyes evenly.

"Oscar," I said, my voice weak.

"Hello, Rosemary." His tone was as level as his gaze, without a note of the conciliatory.

"About the other night . . ." I began lamely.

"I think I have been clear. I prefer not to discuss it."

"I'm sorry, Oscar—"

"I don't want an apology, Rosemary," he cut me off, his long hand raised, calling a halt. "It will not happen again. I need your assurance, in fact, that it won't. That you will not impose upon me again, in that way."

There was no misinterpreting him now, no casting him in a role of my invention.

I shook my head. "No, Oscar," I said. "And I am sorry. Truly. When you weren't in yesterday, I—"

"Don't imagine that had anything to do with you," he said bluntly.

Any illusion I might have had that he was troubled by my attempt to kiss him, to touch him, was no more than vanity.

"I took a rather large risk yesterday," he said determinedly.

I thought it was I who had taken a risk.

"What do you mean?" I asked.

He looked at me steadily.

"I went to see Samuel Metcalf at Julian Peabody's."

He stood up then in an exaggerated way, imperiously, and I followed him back into his stacks, to the eddy of books I hadn't been able to find when I mooned about his section on my own, trying to avoid customers. He struck something of a pose, one arm thrown against a shelf, his notebook in his other hand. I sensed Oscar loved the drama of this particular chase, and needed me to witness his cleverness. I was his audience, his only votary.

"Needless to say, Rosemary, Metcalf was more than surprised to see me."

He had taken the day off to track down more details about Melville. My behavior was barely more than an annoyance, and although it was certainly unacceptable, he wanted to forget my repugnant advance. I saw at once how absurd, how ridiculous it was to have thought otherwise.

"I'll tell you what I've found out, but you must be discreet." He stared at me with some firmness. He meant more discreet than I had been with him. "That means not telling Pearl, or Mitchell, or anyone."

I nodded.

"Geist must not know that we've been researching *The Isle of the Cross*," he went on. "Metcalf will not tell him, under threat of me revealing it to Pike. I take you into my confidence because I must have your word that what we've discovered remains a secret. I suspect that Mitchell has a clue something's up. I don't know how, but he was sniffing around my section this morning, under the pretext of telling me about shoplifters when you know that Redburn fellow hasn't been sighted for weeks."

I didn't say then that I had told Mr. Mitchell about reading a letter to Geist, although I should have. But I especially didn't want to mention it, now that I'd made up with both of them. I thought it wouldn't matter; and after all, I hadn't told Mr. Mitchell anything about the letter's contents.

"Metcalf admitted to an agreement with Geist after I pretended to know all about it. I tricked him into an admission." Oscar bobbed his head slightly, clearly pleased at his own cunning. "He actually sat down when I said the words *The Isle of the Cross.* He hasn't seen the manuscript, but Geist assured him that he would. He seems to think that it is not in Melville's hand. As you will recall from our research, that's probably because Melville's sister Augusta made the clean copy for his publisher. I am researching this through the main library. They have copies of Augusta's letters there. I've seen her handwriting." Oscar paused to rake his hand over his head, stroking flat his dark, thinning hair. "Incidentally, her hand is quite beautiful," he added.

Copperplate, I imagined, a beautiful looping script. Oscar was thinking out loud rather than conversing with me, but I hung on his words, on the aliveness of his interest and the thrill of sharing it with him. Even Melville's letters now seemed part of an intimate discourse of our own. It was as if, in some distorted way, Oscar had become their subject. Melville had written to Hawthorne:

> It is a strange feeling—no hopefulness is in it, no despair.
> Content—that is it; and irresponsibility; but without licentious
> inclination. I speak now of my profoundest sense of being . . .

"I still have no idea who wrote the original letter to Pike," Oscar developed. "And if I can believe him, neither does Metcalf. But it will be extremely difficult to keep the information a secret the more people know. You saw yourself how easy it was for us to determine that there was a lost novel, and that it was called *The Isle of the Cross.* Anyone with the time and the interest could ascertain as much."

"I've been reading that book of letters," I told him. "And there must be a copy in Peabody's library. He'd know all about Agatha."

It bothered me that Metcalf, or anyone really, should read those letters. It was ridiculous, but I felt proprietary about them.

"But I'm still confused, Oscar. Why would Metcalf want to cheat Peabody? Or Mr. Geist steal from Pike?"

"Money isn't a sufficient motive for you?"

"But they'll both lose their jobs if it's discovered. Jobs they love, that are their lives."

"Probably one of these psychology books would theorize some nonsense about fathers, or failed adoptions." He waved his arm at the shelves dismissively. "But I've found money is most often ample incentive. As well as all the cloak-and-dagger business. Collectors—and remember, they are both collectors—love all that secrecy. Conversely, perhaps fame, too, has something to do with it, at least on Metcalf's part. Whoever announces this find will become known for it. Of course, they'll have to fabricate a means of 'discovering' it." He stared past me thoughtfully.

"Who has it, Oscar?" I whispered.

"What's interesting is that Metcalf's father actually did find some original papers of Melville's some years ago. They were in a trunk in an attic. In a house in Lansingburgh. Remember Lansingburgh?"

He half-smiled at me, the name of the town a fragment of the useless information I had collected, now useful again. It gave me great comfort, that small smile. It made me feel that I could at least have this Oscar, the one that wanted to teach me things, that included me, if only peripherally, in his enthusiasms, a secret sharer of his intrigues.

I just had to keep my hands to myself.

"Hard to believe, I know, that still happens, but people bring in books here every month that have turned up in the same way, in a trunk or found in a drawer. My own theory is that if *The Isle of the Cross* is written in Augusta's hand, then the manuscript is the copy Melville submitted to Harper Brothers, which they rejected but didn't return. I'm looking into that."

"I really don't want to think that Mr. Geist is a thief, Oscar. I'm not sure I can believe it. Perhaps he has a plan to surprise Mr. Pike with the acquisition. To give the Arcade a windfall."

"Don't be childish, Rosemary. Think about it. Geist doesn't have much time left. He can't continue on here indefinitely. He can barely see; he is sick with some kind of illness. His behavior has become as bizarre as his looks."

"He told me he was an insomniac," I said vaguely.

And that time was running out. I recalled Geist's weariness, and how he'd murmured about being envious, and secretly enamored, of everyone. Motivation enough, it seems to me now, to try to grab a piece of something for himself, to hold on to value denied him.

"Insomnia's the least of it," Oscar said. "Albinos are plagued with all sorts of illnesses, because their immune systems aren't strong."

Of course, he'd know, albinos having been one of his research subjects. I felt awful for Walter Geist. It was all so complicated and unclear. What would he do if he didn't work in the Arcade? Who would care for him if he was truly ill? Was George Pike close enough to him to assume a familial obligation?

"There's something else you should know, Rosemary. As it concerns you directly." Oscar ran his hand over his dark hair.

"Yes," I said. "Why do you hesitate?"

"Metcalf told me that he thought Geist brought you to

Peabody's in part to—to show you off to him," he said, speaking rapidly.

"What do you mean, show me off?" I said. Exhibited like one of those strange displays? Metcalf had said I was unusual looking. Attractive.

"Apparently Geist implied some sort of "—he looked down at his notebook, as if for confirmation—"some kind of relationship between you."

Was this a question? Was Oscar actually asking me this question? He looked into my face.

"I didn't think so, really," he said quickly. "But I mention it because it's something to think about. To consider. You might be part of Geist's motivation. He may intend to include you in his dealings with Metcalf. When your name came up, I remembered the loan. When you asked Geist for an advance on wages? You told me that he insisted it was he, and not Pike, who loaned you the money. Perhaps Geist imagines that if he has a great deal of money, if he can sell this stolen manuscript, he'll have something to offer."

I knew what he would say next.

"Something to offer you, Rosemary," he finished.

"Something to offer me in return for what?" I asked aloud, suspecting that I knew the answer even as the question hung in the air.

"Well," said Oscar, with evident distaste. "Men want things from young women. But my point is, Rosemary, you can find out what Geist's plans are. You can . . . encourage him a little. And you can tell me what he knows already and whether he has the manuscript to hand."

"You mean you want me to tell him that I know about *The Isle of the Cross*?"

"Of course not," he said. "But you did read him the letter, and there's more you can do. There's more you can know. Draw him out. You must know a way to indicate that you'd like to help him."

"And by doing that I'll be helping you?" I asked him.

Oscar placed his hand on my arm in one of his characteristic gestures of inclusion. His rare eyes looked at me unblinkingly. I felt their heat warm my skin. We stood together in that aspect for a full moment. He had forgiven me.

"Rosemary," Oscar said. "I trust you'll tell me whatever you discover."

⌒⌒ Set on my mission for Oscar, the following week I descended alone to the basement to find Walter Geist. More on Herman Melville—that's what was needed, and to discover how much Geist actually knew about *The Isle of the Cross*. I found him beneath the brilliant bare globe, his head in his hands.

"Mr. Geist, are you all right?" I asked him, approaching the counter.

"Are you alone, Rosemary?" he said, raising his head and leaning toward me.

"Yes. I just thought I'd come and see if you needed anything."

Remembering what Oscar had suggested, I added, "If you need me."

"That's kind of you," he said, looking slightly puzzled. "I'd actually like to finish the conversation we were having, before we were interrupted by Conway, the other day in the office."

"Yes," I said simply. "I'd like that."

"You should be careful, Rosemary. Jack Conway is not the sort of fellow to spend any time with."

I was struck with how everyone in the Arcade was always warning me off everyone else, and I wondered if he'd heard Jack proposition me on the stairs.

"I don't spend time with him, Mr. Geist," I assured him.

"Good."

I leaned across the counter toward his stooping figure and we were quiet together. I heard furtive footsteps within the maze of stacks, customers searching out spoils. The low ceiling, with stacks meeting it, always made me feel like stooping. It was as if the basement insisted Geist's posture upon its visitors.

"Do you have plans after work this evening?" he asked abruptly, and I started at the non sequitur. His hand disappeared into his pocket and jiggled at loose change.

"This evening?" I repeated. Was he asking me out? Would Oscar want me to go and be his agent?

"This evening? Um, no, Mr. Geist, I have no plans. Well, I have to see about the wine for the party you asked me to arrange, but I can do that tomorrow."

"Excellent," he said, standing a little straighter. "We can finish our conversation over a cup of coffee." He smiled to himself.

"Excellent," he repeated. "I'll meet you at the south door. At six."

"At six? Can you leave then?" I asked him. "Don't you usually stay later?"

"This evening I will leave at six," he said, with some purpose. "I'm not an indentured servant, you know. Pike doesn't own me. I am, after all, the Arcade's manager."

I *returned upstairs* to Oscar, perched on his stool, in Nonfiction.

"Have you seen Geist?" he asked, reading my expression.

"I'm to meet him outside at six," I answered. "He wants to finish the conversation we began in the office, before Jack interrupted. I know it's about Peabody's. He was going to tell me something about why we went there."

"Good. Good. Don't mention our research at the library," Oscar coached. His enthusiasm depressed me. "Let him tell you what he's found out. Just listen."

"All right, Oscar," I responded. "I know."

"Take your notebook," he said. "And write down anything you think you won't remember."

"I can't sit there writing down information!"

"When you can, I mean. Immediately after. Whatever you remember."

"You'd be surprised what I can remember, Oscar."

"Good," he said encouragingly. "Surprise me, then."

∽

At six, I stood out on the street corner, inspecting the dirty snow and thinking of the way the scene was reversed. The day Geist took me to Peabody's he waited outside, while I watched from the window in the south door. Something else was reversed, but I didn't see it then.

Presently Walter Geist came out in his ridiculous winter coat and hat, and I called to him so he'd know where I stood on the cleared footpath. He walked over and suggested a coffee shop in the next block. He walked close to my arm, coat sleeve to coat sleeve, matching my steps as we headed along the avenue.

The hostess seated us away from the window, and we hung up our coats on tall hooks that rose on a thin post beside the seats. Geist slid into the booth and placed his hat beside him. Sitting opposite him, I couldn't help but reflect on the evening spent with Oscar. That other scene silently replayed itself. Here I was in a diner opposite another man, only days after that earlier humiliation, but how far from that nervous excitement I felt! I must do this thing for Oscar.

"Rosemary," Walter Geist began at once. "Do you know who Herman Melville was?"

I flinched. "Yes, of course I do, Mr. Geist. I've been reading *Moby-Dick* for ages. Oscar gave me an old paperback edition as a present."

"Did he?" he asked, his tone hard to read. "It's not a book I care for."

"Really," I said. "I'm completely taken with it."

His head moved back as if I'd struck him.

It was, I realize now, insensitive of me. After registering the chapter on whiteness, I didn't need to ask Walter Geist why *Moby-Dick* was a book he hated. Melville had equated whiteness with annihilation, with abomination.

"You will perhaps remember that letter I had you read to me," Geist pushed on. "It mentioned Melville? From a person interested in selling a manuscript."

My face flushed to the roots of my hair. "Of course I remember," I replied, the torn corner of the letter still in my pocket, itself a stolen token. "You snatched the letter from me before I'd finished it."

"I did. I wasn't thinking, Rosemary. I apologize, but I needed time to think about what the seller was putting forth. It seemed inconceivable at the time. I went to Peabody's with you to discuss it with Sam Metcalf, my friend. He is very knowledgeable about nineteenth-century American writers. They are of particular interest to his employer."

Walter Geist drew an envelope from his coat pocket. "Sam sent me this yesterday." He passed the envelope across the table. "Open it. It is a newspaper article he thought would interest me, but it was evidently reproduced from microfiche."

The envelope contained a thickly folded document. It opened

into a complete newspaper sheet, reproduced on stiff photographic paper. Indeed, the type was small and even blurred in some places, but the headlines were quite clear. I marveled at how much type was crowded onto a nespaper page in 1855, the date printed at the top, beside the masthead: THE NEW YORK DAILY NEWS.

"I'd like you to read it to me."

"Of course, Mr. Geist. But I could have done that at the Arcade."

"Do you find it unpleasant to sit in a coffee shop with me?" he asked keenly. Defensiveness was the cardinal quality of his disposition, and it was painfully easy to upset him.

"No, Mr. Geist, not unpleasant at all."

"Well, then."

His strange eyes vacillated unceasingly. They looked raw and hurt. A heavy silence ensued while his articulate hands fidgeted, making little motions of anguish.

"I'm sorry, Rosemary," he began again. "The whole thing makes me nervous. It's just that I have no experience with . . . with such things."

I thought to ask him what sort of things he meant—I wasn't a thing, after all—but remembered Oscar's admonition to find out all I could. To just listen. And perhaps the thing he had no experience with was deception.

"There's a lot here. What is it you want me to read?"

"You understand, Rosemary, that this is between us. I must have your word. This is a highly unusual situation, I grant you, but I must know that whatever I ask you to read remains between us."

Here was another suggestion of Oscar.

"Why only between us, Mr. Geist?"

"You will come to understand why. I must trust you. I do trust you, but you must trust me also. I want you to know how important this is to me. The letter you read for me is a key to something I have long been waiting for."

He had already given me his trust, and I was inwardly horrified that he would grant me it so readily. Advice that Chaps had given me as a child returned, and I faltered at the extent to which I was discounting it. "Love all, trust a few, and do harm to none," she used to say. I couldn't love all, I answered in my mind. I didn't know whom I trusted, but I did know that I loved one in particular.

At the bottom of the page was what appeared to be a feature section with the heading "Ambrotypes." Herman Melville was the article's subject.

"Here's something on Melville in a separate section. What is an ambrotype, Mr. Geist?" I asked, never having heard the word.

"In this case, I gather it is the title of a biographical sketch," he answered. "But the word itself refers to a type of photograph. That would suggest this was a series of sketches."

"The reporter's name is Thomas Powell."

"Ah," Geist said. "That's interesting. I recall that Powell was something of a scoundrel. He obtained various jobs for newspapers based on connections he claimed to have with famous writers. Dickens was one, I think—a particular favorite of mine . . . Ah, here's our waitress. Coffee?"

"I'd rather have tea," I answered, scanning the photocopy.

"Of course. One tea and one coffee. Black for me," he said.

I took up the paper and began to read the article. Powell mentioned that few authors were, as he put it, "more suddenly popular than Herman Melville." Later, I would copy down a few details in my notebook for Oscar. For myself, I made a mental note to ask Arthur about ambrotypes.

" 'Ten years ago Melville was unknown to the public; he is

now one of our most successful writers, although his prestige has been considerably damaged by his unfortunate attempt to load his graceful narrative with metaphysical speculations.' "

I stopped when the waitress returned, and after adding milk to my tea, I took a sip. The tea went warmly down my throat, and after I swallowed, I smiled. Walter Geist sat taking in my every gesture with his swimming eyes. I could hear him breathing. It struck me that I knew exactly how he felt. To be out with someone you want to be with, sitting in a booth in a diner. Consider what Geist and I shared: unrequited affection for someone essentially unsuitable, not to mention indifferent, to our romantic fantasies.

"When you are ready, Rosemary," he said. "Do continue. I enjoy listening to you read."

"Thank you, Mr. Geist," I said, warmed somewhat to the task, and to him. I was seeing him freshly. I knew what it felt like to be humiliated, I had a bruise on my hip to prove it, and I wouldn't have wished that on him. The echo of my evening with Oscar was palpable, not just because of the obvious parallels, but the mood felt vaguely familiar as well.

In the newspaper article, Powell had included a physical description of Melville, and I was curious to know what the passionate man, so enamored with Nathaniel Hawthorne, had looked like.

" 'He is a handsome gentlemanly man. Very kind and courteous, and a most agreeable companion—having more the ease of the traveler than the dogmatism of the author. In person he is a little above medium height, and dresses very carefully.' " Like Oscar, I thought, with his neat black pants and handmade white shirts. Handsome and gentlemanly. It was Oscar who had given me Herman Melville, and they were starting to merge in my mind.

"Rosemary," Geist said, interrupting. "What I want to know from this article concerns Melville's work, not his appearance. What he looked like is of no interest to me."

I scanned the article and continued reading aloud, inclined toward Walter Geist's face. He listened with rapt attention, leaning across the table.

" 'It may seem impertinent to reflect upon an author's undeveloped powers, but we are afraid that he has laid the brightest of his gifts at the footstool of that great tyrant—the world—who insatiably craves more, and of a better quality. We conclude our rough, but we hope candid, ambrotype by mentioning that he once named to us the plan of a work which he has not yet carried out. It was intended to illustrate the principal of remorse, and to demonstrate that there is, very often, less real virtue in moral respectability than in accidental crime. Some men save their conventional reputation by living up to a decent average of legalized vice, always simmering up to that point but never boiling over; while some are entirely virtuous and truthful all their life, until some sudden and uncontrollable impulse carries them at one bound over the height, and they perish eternally.' "

"Ah," said Walter Geist thoughtfully. "That's it, of course. The work on remorse."

"Remorse?" I echoed, but he didn't respond.

The theme of *The Isle of the Cross*. Geist, then, had already discovered this. I supposed that Metcalf had told him when they met upstairs in Peabody's library, and had probably read him the Agatha letters addressed to Hawthorne. But why had Metcalf sent him this article? It seemed to carry an implied warning. For what *was* news, and what I couldn't wait to tell Oscar, was Melville's notion that an uncontrollable impulse might carry a virtuous, truthful man over the top. That is, if the scoundrel Powell was to be believed in relating an actual conversation he'd had with the author. Was this what Melville thought had happened to Robinson when he abandoned Agatha for seventeen years? Wasn't this what was happening to Walter Geist? Keeping the manuscript a secret, stealing from George Pike, might carry him over the height. Except that it wasn't entirely a secret. He was sharing it with me. Trusting that I would keep it concealed.

"You see, Rosemary," Geist continued, "I have learned from Sam that a novel with this theme was lost. This is what has come to my notice. I want you to help me find out as much about it as I can. That will help me to . . ." He paused, searching for the word. "That will help me to evaluate it."

"So that you can buy it for the Arcade?" I asked, aware that even my sham naïveté appealed to him.

"What I intend to do with it must remain between us," he said meaningfully. "For now, I hope this is a fascinating puzzle that we can share, and that you will keep my secret."

He made to move his hand across the table to clutch at mine, but in the process upset his coffee, sending the hot liquid spreading toward his shirt, beginning a stain there across his chest, as he bent over the table. "Ah!" he yelped, and I quickly tried to mop the spill with paper napkins pulled from a chrome dispenser clustered at the table's end, along with its family of salt and pepper, sugar, and milk.

"Ah!" he repeated, more than flustered. "I am appalling! A clumsy fool! How can you bear a minute of me!"

"It's all right, Mr. Geist," I said, astonished at the vehemence of his reaction, the napkins wadded up in my hands. "It's an accident. Just an accident."

He clutched at my hands then, preventing me from cleaning up the coffee, and pulled my right hand violently to his mouth. I felt his teeth press hard through his lips into my palm.

"Mr. Geist . . ." I stammered, wrenching back my hand, aghast. I had snatched it back as suddenly as he had pulled the letter from me in his office. He grimaced as if I'd slapped him.

From the corner of my eye I saw the waitress approaching, only to turn away at our awkward tableau.

My palm was wet and I wiped it on my trousers.

"I have to go now, Mr. Geist."

I quickly stood, grabbing my coat from the hook, assuming a friendly, unaffected tone I didn't feel.

"Thank you. Thank you for the tea."

I wanted to forget about helping him with the Melville search, and forget about being a spy for Oscar. Walter Geist was far too serious. This wasn't a game, after all, like the Who Knows? game we played in the Arcade.

"Thanks very much and I'll see you tomorrow. Okay? I'll see you at the store. Bye."

He was silent. I left him seated there, the brown coffee stain spread across his breast like a mark of obloquy.

∽

I told Oscar everything, of course, except that Walter Geist had passionately kissed the palm of my hand. I told him about Powell's "Ambrotype," and that the unnamed work the article referred to was intended to illustrate the principle of remorse—ironically, a principle I was experiencing in some measure.

"Well," said Oscar. "That wasn't so hard to find out."

"No," I told him. "Mr. Geist wants to confide in me."

"I've no doubt he finds you very appealing," he said dryly, well aware of what Geist wanted.

"Let me tell you what I've discovered in the meantime. It's very interesting, and along the lines of that decent average of legalized vice that you noted from the newspaper article."

Oscar went on to tell me, in a rather convoluted fashion, how publishing worked at the time of Melville's fame. It appeared that an author financially subsidized his own work, but perhaps none more so than Herman Melville, particularly after the spectacular failure of his psychological novel *Pierre*—the book that prompted reviewers to call his sanity into question.

Originally, his publishers, Harper & Brothers, split the profits fifty-fifty with Melville, after publishing costs had been recouped, and any advance of moneys was subtracted from those anticipated half-profits. But the Harpers actually charged their authors interest on those advances, and even though *Typee* and *Omoo* had made money, Melville had run up a considerable debt to the firm once his sales slumped. Because *Moby-Dick* was a commercial failure, the Harpers were nervous of Melville and no longer regarded him as valuable. With *Pierre*, the brothers demanded an impossible contract, hoping he would decline. Melville accepted, however, on the terms of twenty cents in the dollar, rather than the previous fifty after costs, which meant that *Pierre* would have to sell two and a half times as many copies in order to earn the same share, a share that had already proved inadequate. *Pierre*, too, was a commercial disaster.

"So publishers were thieves in Melville's day," I observed. "Just as Mr. Pike is considered crooked to some people today. But what does that tell us about *The Isle of the Cross*?"

"I'm getting to that, Rosemary," Oscar replied, stringing out his story. "You see, Melville wrote to the Harpers offering them another book. Let me tell you exactly," and he consulted his notebook, furiously turning back pages that I could see were dense with tight, obsessive handwriting.

"Here it is: 'In addition to the work which I took to New York last spring, but which I was prevented from printing at that time, I now have in hand another book.' "

Oscar looked at me as if what he meant was obvious.

"Sorry?"

"He says 'in addition to,' so that implies he hadn't destroyed the book he had brought to them that spring, which was *The Isle of the Cross*. He still had it, even though he was prevented for some reason from publishing it."

"What prevented him?"

"I've no idea. It may have been libelous, because Agatha and Robinson were actual individuals. It doesn't matter, in any case, why. The point is he told Harper & Brothers that he still had it. He was trying to negotiate with them on the half-profits basis he'd had before *Pierre*."

"So you don't think the manuscript could be the copy that Harper and Brothers kept? You think it is Melville's original?"

"That's just it. It's very unlikely that it's the copy submitted to the Harpers, but not because they wouldn't have kept it."

Oscar was so absorbed in the details now around *The Isle of the Cross* that he assumed an air of propriety about the items. His fascination with the details surrounding the lost novel had about it the quality of an infatuation, and I was envious that these long-past events held him in thrall in a way no present person could.

"I found out," he went on, "that the Harper & Brothers offices were burnt to the ground in December of 1853. Six buildings were left in ruins!" His expression was oddly triumphant.

"Melville thought he'd been wiped out, and most of the copies of his books and unbound sheets were destroyed in the fire. It was a terrible loss for him, and practically ruined him financially, on top of the ruin of his reputation because of *Pierre*. He was already deeply in debt. The Harper brothers were merciless and charged him extra costs. As if the fire were his fault! In fact, they charged him twice, because the production costs had already been deducted from the printings that were lost in the fire."

Oscar appeared outraged on Melville's behalf, but of course he sold used books every day whose authors never saw a penny of what Pike pocketed. Even the new review copies that Walter Geist sold from the basement left an author out of any profits, because they had been sent, to garner publicity, to journalists and reviewers who hadn't paid for them, but sold them nonetheless to the Arcade, collecting a quarter of the retail price.

That it was hypocrisy for Oscar to be indignant on Herman Melville's behalf didn't make him any less attractive to me. But it did make me think about George Pike's vast holdings and what little they owed to the creation of literature. The Arcade certainly served collectors and readers, but not those foolish enough to be writers.

"Oscar," I asked him seriously, "what would you do with *The Isle of the Cross*?"

"I've told you before. It belongs in a library or university collection—in the Houghton Library at Harvard, maybe, with Melville's other papers. Or in the Berg Collection in the library here, along with his letters."

He continued with some passion. "I would give it to them, of course! For free. The lost book is not a piece of commerce, Rosemary. Don't you see how Melville was victimized by commerce his whole career? In any case, I'd do anything to prevent Peabody from having it. That would be like putting it in a chest and sending it to the bottom of the sea. It's the endless appropriation that offends me. The man is an emperor of objects."

This sounded very odd coming from someone who daily worked to satisfy collectors.

"I really don't see that it makes that much difference who has it," I said. "Either way, it will be published. People will be able to read it."

"There's no guarantee of that," Oscar snapped. "Peabody is just peculiar enough to hoard it with his curiosities and deny he even has it."

"What makes you say so?"

"I know collectors, Rosemary. Far better than you do. There is something in exclusivity, you see, that nourishes the likes of Peabody. You're from Tasmania," he threw out. "You have no understanding of the hierarchies of things."

But he did. The core of his nature and the secret of it was that he saw these hierarchies, and saw, too, that they didn't include him. *The Isle of the Cross*, then, was a way to thwart all he'd been left out of, even as he had no interest in sharing himself. He knew exactly how much he'd been excepted from, for he'd kept an account of it in his notebooks. It was a record of revenge in that sense, a ledger of losses. But in striking out, he only struck himself—Julian Peabody was exactly the type of abstruse individual that Oscar Jarno was. They differed principally in that Oscar was without means, at least in the pecuniary sense. By way of compensation, he had long ago made knowledge his currency of worth.

∽

"*Arthur*," I *called* into the Art section, only to nearly trip over him, seated on the floor with his legs splayed out in a corner, a large book in his lap, his oversized head drooped backwards in sleep. A thread of spittle ran from an upper tooth to a lower one, vibrated, then snapped with his shallow exhale.

"Arthur!" I went to him and shook his shoulder.

"What?!" He jerked his head up and slapped his own fleshy cheeks. "What is it, TD! Oh, I was quite out. Quite unconscious. I was dreaming—a fabulous dream. I hate to leave it. Oh . . ." His forehead furrowed in his attempt to remember. "I dreamt the store was a museum, and I was the only living thing that moved inside it . . ."

"Never mind that, Arthur, if Mr. Pike catches you, or Mr. Geist, you'll lose your job, dozing away in the middle of the afternoon!"

"Just a catnap." He struggled to his feet, waving his fat hand at me for assistance. "Think of it as contemplation," he puffed as I pulled on his arm. "I do," he said, standing and out of breath. He straightened his rumpled shirt down over his belly.

"I came to ask you about something," I said, bending to retrieve the book he'd left on the floor and handing it to him. He tucked it away on a shelf.

"You're always asking questions," he pouted. "Why don't you *tell* for a change?!"

"Me? I don't have anything to tell," I muttered.

"Is that right?" He smiled and wagged a finger at me. "Nothing to tell? You've been seen, you know."

"Seen?" I colored. "By whom?"

"Don't you mean *with* whom?" Arthur teased.

"I . . ." Confusion silenced me, and I was afraid to give anything away.

"With Walter Geist, of course. Reading to him, in a coffee shop!" Arthur crowed.

"Who saw me?"

"That's neither here nor there, TD. You're not without your admirers. I must say, though, yours is an odd choice."

"I haven't chosen anyone!"

"Well, do be careful, or at the very least, be kind. Walter is . . . well, let's just say that in a melancholy place he is most melancholy. Don't lead him on," he continued. "Don't be too devilish . . ."

"Stop it, Arthur!" I objected, embarrassed. "He just needs my help. And stop gossiping about me!"

He put his hand to his chest in fake horror at the accusation he'd been gossiping.

"I came to ask you about photography," I added, changing the subject. "It's your expertise, isn't it?"

"One of them." He smirked.

"Do you know what ambrotypes are?"

"Of course. They come after daguerreotypes in the evolution of photography. They were briefly more popular because they were cheaper. I can show you a reproduction, I'm sure. If you're interested?"

"Actually, I am."

Arthur ambled over to his favorite spot and extracted a book on the history of photography, chatting all the while.

"An ambrotype was less expensive because the image was reproduced on glass rather than copper. Both used a solution of silver nitrate, but when you see one you can tell the ambrotype from the daguerreotype, and even the later tintype, because they have a slightly three-dimensional quality. It's the glass. And they're fairly pale, too, almost whitish."

He opened the large volume and, after checking the index, pointed to a rather ghostly image of a Civil War soldier.

"The Civil War made them very popular, you can imagine, because ordinary people could afford an image of their loved ones."

He looked intently at the soldier's portrait.

"Handsome," he remarked. "It's a one-of-a-kind image, without a negative, and appears reversed, as in a mirror."

I inspected the incredibly youthful face of the Union soldier. He looked to be about my age, and the ambrotype gave him the bleached-out, slightly wavering look of a person already in the process of vanishing.

Arthur leaned in. "Poor chap," he said. "He was probably killed shortly after this was taken."

He closed the book and returned it to the shelf. "Ambrotypes eventually fell out of favor," he said. "They were too fragile, of course; glass shatters. Tintypes took over, and then, ubiquitously, paper."

He waved his thick hand about, gesturing at the mountain of paper, at the Arcade, which surrounded us.

"Paper," he repeated, yawning broadly. "The stuff of all our dreams."

⌒⌒

"*How are you* doing with that book of letters? Any more information on Agatha?"

Oscar was now buttonholing me during the day, searching me out in the Arcade, a reversal I delighted in. That I might have information he wanted amounted to something like a progression in my aspiration to be like him, and I felt mature, and even assimilated into the mysterious composition of the Arcade. Standing in the History aisle of Oscar's section, I handed him my own notebook, opened to the section I was maintaining on Melville's letters.

"I copied this one out last night," I told him. "Melville wrote this after the long letter with all the story details."

Oscar took the notebook from me, and I watched his yellow eyes move back and forth across the page as he read.

> *Monday Morning*
> *25th Oct.: 1852*
> *My Dear Hawthorne—*
> *If you thought it worth while to write the story of Agatha and should you be engaged upon it then I have a little idea touching it, which however trifling, may not be entirely out of place. Perhaps, tho', the idea has occurred to yourself.—The probable facility with which Robinson first leaves his wife and then takes another, may, possibly, be ascribed to the peculiarly latitudinarian notions, which most sailors have of all tender obligations of that sort. In his previous sailor life Robinson had*

found a wife (for a night) in every port. The sense of the
obligation of the marriage-vow to Agatha had little weight
with him at first. It was only when some years of life ashore
had passed that his moral sense on that point became
developed. And hence his subsequent conduct—Remorse &c.
Turn this over in your mind and see if it is right. If not—make
it so yourself.

"He's got quite the sense of humor, doesn't he?" Oscar commented.

"Well, yes," I agreed. "But what do you mean in particular?"

"Oh, just that 'peculiarly latitudinarian notions.' I gather Melville was pretty broad-minded himself, having been a sailor as well."

"I don't think that means he approved of Robinson's behavior, if that's what you mean, abandoning Agatha like that."

Oscar handed me back my notebook with an irritated look. "Does it occur to you that Melville might have sided with the runaway husband? That perhaps the appeal of desertion was a subject that interested him?" he asked.

"Well, no . . ."

"No? Perhaps he wanted to run away himself, back to sea. His wasn't a wholly happy marriage, you know. And obligations of one sort or another were driving him mad. Perhaps he hoped Hawthorne would recognize something in that, too. That he might see the allure in running off as well."

Something struck me then about the confidence of Oscar's assertions.

"How old were you when your father ran off, Oscar?" I asked him frankly.

"Don't make this about me," he replied, clucking impatiently.

"I can see this is just how your imagination leads you astray. It can be banal, Rosemary, to always see one thing in another. You know, everything isn't a key to everything else!"

"I wasn't even born when mine left," I told him. "Like Agatha's daughter. And she was almost my age when she did finally meet him."

Oscar said nothing to this, but looked as if he found me tedious. He straightened a few volumes along the shelf behind my head.

"People deceive each other, Rosemary," he said, with sufferance. "Sometimes without even intending to. What can appear malicious might, in fact, just be fecklessness. Perhaps *that* is the story of *The Isle of the Cross!*"

"Well, we don't know anything for certain," I replied, sensing him tiring of me. "But I think it's a story about women and how they endure."

"Oh, they endure all right," Oscar said, his voice droll. "As if enduring were some unrivaled accomplishment."

"Well, what is it if not an accomplishment?"

He confused me. Hadn't his own mother persisted and, against various disadvantages, raised him well? Hadn't my own? And wasn't that worth something? Besides, I knew the power of Lillian's example.

"What's the accomplishment exactly? Living? Put it this way," Oscar went on. "What isn't transient? Who doesn't lose, one way or another?" He looked at me sharply. "Things endure, not people, Rosemary. That's what dealing with collectors has taught me."

Mother's voice spoke in my memory, telling me again that nothing lasts; that eternity isn't even a human thing. She endured in me, of course, as Oscar's mother did in him, but I hadn't the voice for such assertions then. Silently observing Oscar, I did comprehend, finally, that he was more than capable of cruelty. The diffidence that fascinated me was in fact a kind of disability. I had imagined his remoteness a counterweight to my intensity, but there was a want to him, an exigency, I was only beginning to see.

"Let's just leave motivation out of the whole thing," he wound up. "It's incidental, in any case. Have you seen Geist about? Has he told you any more?"

"I've been helping him, but no. Nothing more."

"And you haven't mentioned this to anyone else?"

"No."

"Good. I'm going to the central library this evening. I'm following a line of inquiry that I hope will end with whoever has the manuscript."

I knew I couldn't accompany him. I couldn't even ask.

"I suppose I should just stick with the letters?" I said, wanting some direction from him; wanting him to tell me what he wanted me to do for him. My own interests weren't practical. I was fascinated now with the story of Agatha, as much as with giving Oscar what he wanted.

"Yes," he confirmed. "You should stay with the letters, but see if Geist has anything more to add. I'd like to know the exact nature of the deal between him and Metcalf. That would be extremely helpful. After all, the subject of the novel is less the point than the fact that it exists. I need to know who has it."

A customer headed toward us, calling Oscar's name in an ingratiating tone. He answered in kind; an actor responding to a cue. He turned, addressing me over his shoulder, reverting to his normal voice.

"You might want to consider the whole thing from a man's perspective. One's own point of view, Rosemary, is inevitably limited."

─ ∞ ─

I sat that evening in my rescued armchair eating bread and butter and considering that there might be more to the Agatha letters than

I had supposed. I was interested at first because of the passionate way Melville had written to Hawthorne, but now I suspected Herman Melville had something to tell me about a story that resembled my own, that he could actually reveal something of myself to me. His influence felt almost paternal. In my own life, I'd assumed abandonment an active, even malicious act, whereas perhaps Oscar had a point. Was there another version? And was it Melville's? Perhaps "fecklessness" described more impulses than I had ever wanted to admit. Perhaps I owed my very existence to fecklessness?

I made some tea and returned to my chair, taking up the library book. I went back to the long letter that Melville first sent to Hawthorne, the one written on Mother's birthday, August 13, 1852, which accompanied the lawyer's account (the "Diary"):

> In estimating the character of Robinson Charity should be allowed a liberal play. I take exception to that passage from the Diary which says that "he must have received a portion of his punishment in this life"—thus hinting of a future supplemental castigation. I do not suppose that his desertion of his wife was a premeditated thing. If it had been so, he would have changed his name, probably after quitting her. No: he was a weak man, and his temptations (tho' we know little of them) were strong. The whole sin stole upon him insensibly—so that it would perhaps have been hard for him to settle upon the exact day when he could say to himself, "Now I have deserted my wife;"

Well, I thought uncharitably, perhaps the day he married another woman would have been an exact enough day for Robinson to acknowledge desertion! But I had to reckon with the idea that weakness, rather than premeditation, might apply, and I recalled the letter I'd shown Oscar. Melville had suggested Robinson's sense of obligation to Agatha was at first no more than a sailor's. Yet, as his moral sense grew in him, its development resulted in remorse, etc. So we all grow, learning how to behave from the behavior of others. But can remorse ever assuage the impact of such thoughtlessness? That Agatha suffered was a fact regret couldn't alter.

I returned to the original letter. Herman Melville had an extraordinary amount to say about a story he was at first intending to give away to Hawthorne, and the insistence wrapped around his particular gift was more than curious. If Agatha's circumstance were a common fact in Melville's day, why had it awakened such a lively interest in him? Certainly, the letter to Hawthorne was filled with enough fictional detail to suggest a deep interest in the tale. Or was Melville simply determined to make the gift as appealing as he could, relating every item as inducement to take the story on? Melville's letter even qualified:

> *Many more things might be mentioned; but I forbear; you will find out the suggestiveness for yourself; & all the better perhaps, for my not intermeddling.—*

Nonetheless, he couldn't help himself, and continued:

> *Young Agatha (but you must give her some other name) comes wandering along the cliff. She marks how the continual assaults of the sea have undermined it; so that the fences fall over, & have need of many shiftings inland. The sea has encroached also upon that part where their dwelling-house stands near the lighthouse.—Filled with meditations, she reclines along the edge of the cliff & gazes seaward. She marks a handful of cloud on the horizon, presaging a storm thro' all*

*this quietude. (Of a Maritime family & always dwelling on
the coast, she is learned in these matters.) This again gives food
for thought. Suddenly she catches the long shadow of the cliff
cast upon the beach 100 feet beneath her; and now she notes a
shadow moving along the shadow. It is cast by a sheep from the
pasture. It has advanced to the very edge of the cliff, & is
sending a mild innocent glance far out upon the water. Here,
in strange & beautiful contrast, we have the innocence of the
land placidly eyeing the malignity of the sea. (All this having
poetic reference to Agatha & her sea lover, who is coming in
the storm: the storm carries her lover to her; she catches a dim
distant glimpse of his ship ere quitting the cliff.)*

What if Hawthorne didn't want to begin it that way? What if
Hawthorne's own imagination suggested an entirely opposite version of Agatha's plight? A different interpretation of the same facts,
just as Oscar's differed from mine? But Melville didn't rest with
mere scene setting—he wanted to provide outlines for characters:

*The father of Agatha must be an old widower—a man of the
sea, but early driven away from it by repeated disasters. Hence,
is he subdued and quiet & wise in his life. And now he tends a
lighthouse, to warn people from those very perils, from which
he himself has suffered.*

I could see how the story had captured Melville's imagination,
but I still couldn't reconcile the idea that all he was doing with such
details was restoring to Hawthorne property that "belonged" to
him. Yet, just as I wanted to share the search for *The Isle of the
Cross* with Oscar, and even as Geist wanted to share it with me,
perhaps Melville wanted Hawthorne to write it *with* him—so as to

have made something in common. He even referred to what "we" must do in explaining the details:

> After a sufficient lapse of time—when Agatha has become alarmed about the protracted absence of her young husband & is feverishly expecting a letter from him—then we must introduce the mail-post—no, that phrase won't do, but here is the thing—Owing to the remoteness of the lighthouse from any settled place no regular (male) mail reaches it. But some mile or so distant there is a road leading between two post-towns. And at the junction of what we shall call the Light-House Road with this Post Road, there stands a post surmounted with a little rude wood box with a lid to it & a leather hinge. Into this box the Post boy drops all letters for the people of the light-house & that vicinity of fishermen. To this post they must come for their letters. And, of course, daily young Agatha goes—for seventeen years she goes thither daily. As her hopes gradually decay in her, so does the post itself & the little box decay. The post rots in the ground at last. Owing to its being little used—hardly at all—grass grows rankly about it. At last a little bird nests in it. At last the post falls.

There are no letters for Agatha.

The radiator ticked, expanding with heat, a rival to the green clock, and I felt I too was waiting for something, sitting there in my small apartment. It was nameless, the sense of apprehension, other than to call it waiting. But the feeling had as much to do with a folding-over of time—which seemed to bring Melville's letters to me in the very moment of their writing—as the sense that there was no single moment but the moment enfolding me, sitting in my chair, reading his letters.

By November 1852, Melville had asked Hawthorne to return all the correspondence concerning the Agatha story, including the lawyer's diary page that he'd forwarded with his first letter. He hoped his friend wished him well: "I invoke your blessing upon my endeavors; and breathe a fair wind upon me."

Finally, he would write the story of Agatha himself.

PART
FOUR

"All right, dear girl," Mr. Mitchell said with mock seriousness. "Here I stand, your slave, a poor, infirm, weak, and despised old man. Put me to work!"

He was the first to appear for the Christmas Eve staff drinks that Geist had asked me to organize. Wearing a red vest buttoned over his large torso, with his peaked white hair and purplish nose, he could have passed for a dissolute Santa Claus in street clothes.

I handed Mr. Mitchell some of the plastic cups that Pearl and I were setting out on the counter at the front of the store, after we'd covered it with a vinyl tablecloth. Mr. Mitchell promptly knocked over the cups and they fell to the floor. He made a motion to pick them up, but had trouble even bending over. His ruddy face deepened its color in the attempt, and his breath quickened.

"Ah," he said, panting slightly. "Too much lunch today, dear girl. I've contracted Arthur's indigestion."

He rubbed his chest with his large pink hand.

"Don't bother, Mr. Mitchell—Pearl and I have it all under control," I said, picking up the cups myself.

Pearl had moved on to setting out cheese on a plastic tray, occasionally skewering a cube with a long nail (red and green for the season) and popping the cheese into her mouth. She had arranged the crackers in a circular pattern.

"You can see I'm completely worthless outside my Rare Book Room," he went on. "A fact Mrs. Mitchell often repeats. I can't change a lightbulb, dear girl." He was clearly proud of his uselessness.

"Let me pour you some wine," I offered. "While we're waiting for the last customers to leave."

There were a few lingerers, and Jack and Bruno were doing their aggressive best to round them up. Pearl had closed the register promptly at six, but there were always stragglers.

"Ah, rotgut, I see," Mr. Mitchell said, reading the wine label as I poured. "Quite the cure for what ails me. Pike is nothing if not beggarly."

He took a large swallow of red wine.

"Abominable," he said, smacking his lips and holding the opaque plastic cup up to the light. "Or perhaps 'odious' is a more apt description. Best to check with a true oenophile. Here's one."

He grabbed at Bruno, who heaved a shopping bag up onto the counter.

"More plonk," said Bruno. The bottles clinked together in the bag. "They dropped it off at the south door. Where do you want it?"

"Just there is fine. I thought they'd sent less than I ordered," I said, taking out the bottles, and guessing that the wine store had recognized the shortfall. I'd had to buy the cheapest wine because of the tiny fund Pike had approved for holiday refreshments. Besides, I didn't know the difference.

"Come here, my Slavic comrade. Let me pour you some of this ghastly stuff. I started in early, as the Rare Book Room was empty by five, no scheduled collectors."

"Don't mind if I do," said Bruno. He filled a cup to the brim, and raised it to Mr. Mitchell.

"To literature," said Bruno, his wide face ironic.

"Indeed," said Mr. Mitchell, a little breathless. They both emptied their cups. They were determined to be drunk quickly, and first.

"I had settled on 'odious' for this beverage, but clearly you're the expert," said Mr. Mitchell.

"I think 'foul' covers it," said Bruno, belching loudly.

"I defer to you," said Mr. Mitchell, wavering slightly. "Let's agree on 'unspeakable.'"

They refilled their cups and toasted the unspeakable, drinking the wine as if it were water.

"Steady on there, Mr. Mitchell," I said. "You've got to get home in one piece. Bruno's the one with a head start—he usually begins drinking first thing in the morning."

"So young and so untender," Mr. Mitchell said, chucking me under the chin.

"Hey, girlie, come on and have a drink with us," offered Bruno, leering, and touching my sleeve.

"Nice shirt, very sexy," he commented, and nudged Mr. Mitchell, who was inspecting the cheese.

"Back off, Bruno," said Pearl, from the other side of the counter.

"Rosemary is looking rather captivating this evening," Mr. Mitchell said. "That blouse becomes you, my dear."

"Thank you," I responded, blushing deeply. "It's a gift from my friend in Tasmania, Miss Chapman."

"Evidently a woman of some taste," said Mr. Mitchell, popping a cube into his mouth.

I half-filled two cups, passing one to Pearl.

Jack appeared then and helped himself to wine.

"What, no beer?" he said, pouring the wine. "Well, here's my comfort," and drained his glass. He promptly refilled it, along with Bruno's and Mr. Mitchell's. His girlfriend, Rowena, was tapping on the window, waving at him from the street side of the latched glass doors, hoping to be let in.

Jack went to unlock the door. They kissed, roughly and noisily, at the threshold.

"Staff only," Pearl whispered to me. "I can't stand that French poodle."

Pike appeared then, smiling in his guarded but beneficent way.

"George Pike wishes happy holidays to all," he said in his high, odd voice. He had put on his suit jacket for the occasion, straightened his tie, and appeared dapper in a slightly threadbare fashion.

"Would you like some wine, Mr. Pike?" I asked.

"Never touch the stuff, Miss Savage. George Pike is a teetotaler."

"Unlike the rest of us," said Mr. Mitchell, too loudly.

"One's health is to be considered," said Pike, addressing Pearl, deliberately looking past Mr. Mitchell, at whom the comment was directed. "And one's comportment."

"Alcohol amends both, in certain cases," muttered Mr. Mitchell sarcastically. "Care's an enemy to life."

"Life is short, art long," quipped Arthur, shambling over from his section, joining in. "Time for a drink?" He had a sprig of holly stuck behind his left ear and seemed unusually cheerful. "This side means I'm available," he told Pearl and me, pointing to the holly. "A seasonal specialty, like plum pudding." A plum pudding was exactly what Arthur's head resembled with its festive garnish.

Oscar followed a moment later, his hair neatly combed, but otherwise without concession to the occasion in his crisp white shirt and black trousers.

"Looking very devilish in that blouse this evening, TD," Arthur remarked. He leaned across the counter, investigating my shirt. "Why, that fabric is almost sheer, you cheeky thing. And scarlet!"

"It's a type of lawn," said Oscar, barely looking up from the cheese. "Probably meant to resemble organdy. It costs less, but it's unusual to dye lawn a shade so deep. Must be the result of a process called kalamkari—repeated dyeing."

Arthur shrugged at me as if to imply that Oscar was a lost cause, and that I should ignore him.

"The point is," said Pearl, always protective, "that you look fabulous, girl. Very Christmassy."

I was embarrassed. "Where is Mr. Geist?" I asked, hoping to change the subject.

"Why do you ask?" Arthur grinned.

"Walter is in the office, tallying the day's accounts," said Pike. "He will be here shortly."

"Let's hope that's all he's up to," Mr. Mitchell said in a low, malicious voice. His cup was empty again, and Jack promptly refilled it as well as his own. But his remark had drawn Oscar's attention. He studied him.

"Robert," Pike said sharply. "Hardly the time or the place for your paranoia."

"I told you before what he's been up to," muttered Mr. Mitchell belligerently. " 'A bitter heart that bides its time and bites.' You'll see!"

He was drunk now, and red-faced.

"Robert!" Pike took the cup from Mr. Mitchell's hand, leaning across him and handing it to Pearl, who disposed of it.

"He's probably up there with that device of his reading my mail and yours," Mr. Mitchell threw in, a wheeze in his low voice. "Selling the place out from under you!"

"Enough!" said Pike, turning his back on him.

Not everyone had heard the exchange, but Oscar hadn't missed a word. He stared across at me with cutting inquiry in his eyes.

Reading his mail? Who else knows? his glare demanded. Who else have you told? What kind of game are you playing?

I shook my head in dismay and silently willed Oscar with my expression to rest assured, I hadn't told Mr. Mitchell anything. He knows nothing about *The Isle of the Cross*, I mentally projected. Oscar returned my pleading gaze with what I recognized as contempt.

He was certain I'd betrayed him.

❦

Walter Geist appeared, looking haggard, and Pike addressed him with false joviality.

"Walter! Here you are—last is commonly best! Are the day's earnings worthy of this celebration?"

"Not a bad day," murmured Geist, his face downcast.

"Excellent!" cried Pike, his thin voice hollow-sounding in the empty Arcade, tinny under the vast domed ceiling. Now all the staff were clustered around the front counter, all drinking and chatting with the exception of Pike and Oscar.

Mr. Mitchell, wobbling slightly, glared at Geist, his face a mask of drunken hostility.

Oscar moved toward him, taking his arm, separating him from the clustered group we formed. I watched as Oscar whispered fervently beside Mr. Mitchell's ear. I sipped my wine, oblivious to the conversations around me, fixed upon Oscar, on his silent accusation.

It's a mistake! I wanted to yell across the heads of the staff. He doesn't know what you think he knows. I haven't told him anything. He knows nothing about the Melville novel. Nothing. It is our secret. Ours.

But something else was seriously wrong.

As if in slow motion, I watched astonished as Mr. Mitchell began to topple backwards, his hand clutching his chest. He was falling heavily, with the tremendous force of his weight, stiffly as a tree. Oscar tried to catch him, his face stunned and blanched, but Mr. Mitchell was too much for him. The others turned only at the sound of collapse, and we all ran at once to where Mr. Mitchell lay panting on the Arcade floor. Oscar tore off the old man's tie and opened his vest and shirt, while George Pike pushed everyone back.

"Give him air, give him air!" he yelled shrilly. He seemed momentarily distraught.

Pearl leaped over the counter in one swift motion and put her ear to Mr. Mitchell's sweating chest. He tried to speak but couldn't.

"Call an ambulance!" she barked at Oscar.

He ran to Pike's stage and could be heard calmly directing an ambulance to the store.

Mr. Mitchell rallied slightly when I brought a cup of water to his lips. He mouthed something inaudible, perhaps "dear girl."

In the frightening minutes that followed, all sorts of fugitive, irrational thoughts filled my head. If Mr. Mitchell died, I would have to return to Tasmania. I wouldn't be able to bear it. It would be an indication of my bad faith, my poor character. I would have killed him in some way. Murdered him. I had upset the balance of the Arcade with my presence. Secrets were pernicious and I wanted nothing to do with them; I couldn't keep them, in any case. Oscar must have whispered to him that I was untrustworthy; that I was deceitful and false.

A policeman was knocking heavily on the glass windowpane and an ambulance light flashed red outside on the avenue. Jack ran to open the double doors wide, and a stretcher was wheeled in, Bruno and Jack taking Mr. Mitchell's feet while the two ambulance men managed his shoulders. He was conscious, although clearly in pain, and before an oxygen mask was clapped over his face, he waved feebly and tried to speak. Pike was at his side and took his hand. He walked beside the stretcher and climbed after it into the ambulance. Passersby had gathered to gawk, and we all moved outside briefly, standing shaken in the cold night. Snow was falling lightly, in between a chill rain, dissolving where it fell on the salted sidewalk.

"Walter! Walter, take care of everything!" George Pike called before the ambulance doors slammed shut and the siren keened.

We turned back into the Arcade. Bruno locked the doors against the crowd gathered outside a moment after Oscar, his coat on and buttoned, slipped out. He vanished before anyone had a chance to notice him gone. Except for me.

∽

"*Mr. Mitchell will* be fine," Walter Geist assured everyone, raising his voice slightly. "He's had these episodes before, and he recovered."

I took a deep gulp of wine to steady my nerves. Pearl was doing the same. Bruno, Jack, and Rowena were huddled together and had a plastic cup in each hand. A laugh rose up from inside their circle as they mumbled to each other, apparently not terribly unsettled by what had gone on, or perhaps too drunk for it to sink in. Arthur sat down on a stack of overstocks at the end of the counter; the holly had fallen from his ear. Pearl patted him on his broad back.

"Oh, I'm all right," he said to her, his mouth filled with remaining cubes of cheese. "Just famished."

Looking around, I fancied that I was the only one upset. I was terrified that Mr. Mitchell was dying, and thought it despicable of Oscar to have snuck off—and cowardly of him not to give me a chance to explain. What had he whispered to Mr. Mitchell? Where had he gone?

"Rosemary," Geist called to me, gesturing to the air with a raised hand from some feet away.

"Look out," Jack said as I passed his little group. "The beast beckons."

Bruno and Rowena snickered together at what was apparently a shared joke at my expense, and Geist's. I wondered if it was Jack who had seen us together in the diner.

"The Ghost of Christmas Present calls and you go running," Bruno slurred into my hair, his breath fetid.

"What is it, Mr. Geist?" I asked, flustered. My head throbbed from the cheap wine. I felt slow, removed from myself, unable to focus. Did Oscar leave so abruptly because he was furious with me?

"In Mitchell's absence, the Rare Book Room will have to be locked up, the lights turned off, his briefcase and keys collected and returned to his wife."

"I can't take care of the Rare Book Room!" I blurted out, shocked at the suggestion.

"I'm not asking you to," he said, without impatience.

Geist appeared impossibly composed, or perhaps just depleted. "I merely ask that you accompany me up there when everyone has left. You must help me. Please start to straighten up this mess. I need you—" he hesitated—"I need you to make sure I haven't missed anything, and then I want you to deliver the briefcase to Mitchell's building. His wife will be at the hospital by then. I'll call her now."

"Of course," I said. His sensible directives calmed me.

I collected the plastic cups, plates, and napkins and tied them up in a large garbage bag. I hugged Pearl goodnight.

"I've got to meet Mario or I'd stay and help," she said, putting on her coat.

"It's fine," I assured her. "I'll finish here with Mr. Geist and then I'll drop off Mr. Mitchell's stuff. It's the least I can do. See you tomorrow, right? Lillian's coming around four."

"Great," said Pearl, kissing me. "I'll be there. Don't worry, he'll be all right. I'm sure of it."

The others departed grumbling, the few remaining bottles tucked under their arms, determined to continue their drinking elsewhere. Arthur blew me a kiss after struggling into his coat. I closed the front door, turning the bolt and pulling across the metal guard.

Walking back toward Pike's platform, I heard Walter Geist on the old telephone, speaking softly to Mrs. Mitchell, telling her what had happened, giving her the address of the hospital nearby. He spoke with real kindness. Listening at the base of the stage to the exemplary way he used his voice to ease made me consider how contradictory were his dealings with me: translating the inscription on the clock at Peabody's; his enigmatic remark about his insomnia; clutching my hand and putting it to his mouth. I had embarrassed him by ignoring his urgent gesture, and felt ashamed and immature for disregarding what it must have cost him to make it.

He hung up the heavy receiver, seemingly collected, but then he slipped on the two short stairs descending Pike's stage. He recovered himself, grabbing my arm in place of the banister on his way down.

I steadied him.

"Thank you," he said.

We held each other by the forearm for a moment, his face averted.

"Always helpful, Rosemary Savage," he said to the floor. "What would I do without you?"

"You would manage, Mr. Geist," I said lightly.

"No. I can't anymore. Not without you," he declared in a dignified way.

We walked together through the Arcade to the elevator near the entrance, and it occurred to me that I was glad of his company—masculine company, after all. Oscar had fled without letting me explain, without wanting me to explain. And what if Mr. Mitchell died? I wouldn't be able to bear it. Geist leaned a little against my arm and I wasn't repelled.

"The Albino is as well made as other men," even Melville conceded.

We rode up to the Rare Book Room in silence. The cranky cage stuck when I tried to open it, and we had to squeeze through a gap just big enough to admit us individually.

"See if you can find Mitchell's briefcase," Geist said, feeling for the switch and turning out the light in the first enfilade of small rooms that made up Robert Mitchell's domain. "And also a large bunch of keys."

"All right," I answered. "But leave the lights on, or I won't be able to find anything."

I walked to the main room, drawing a deep breath full of the vanilla scent of lingering pipe smoke. The smell, the soft, ashy film that coated everything in the room, asserted Mr. Mitchell's continued existence. His desk sat across a corner, shelves behind and to the side of its cluttered surface. The peacock feathers watched as I bent to look around the desk for his case. A bunch of keys hung from his chair by a long red ribbon. I found the case and dropped them into the top.

It was then, as I bent at the waist, that I felt his presence.

Walter Geist approached me from behind. His hand, when it lay lightly on my back, did not startle me. He had touched me there before, after all. I straightened and turned to face him.

He stepped away, standing against the shelves of volumes Mr. Mitchell liked to keep closest to his desk, the most fragile ones. Geist moved back to open a space between us, to show he did not threaten me; to see if I would pull away rudely as I had in the diner.

He was giving me room to decide. It was a subtle motion, indicative of him, and I knew at once that what would pass between us was inevitable.

"I absolve you of your debt," he said, rather formally.

"My debt?"

"The loan you borrowed. It's canceled. Void. There won't be any more deductions from your pay."

"You mean I paid it off? Already?"

"I mean, Rosemary, that you have no debt. You are free and clear."

"Thank you, Mr. Geist," I said.

I took a step toward him. I remember that it was me who stepped forward. It could only have been me. I cannot explain it.

Geist raised his arm and placed his hand upon my face, his fingertips beside my eye, his palm along my cheek. I considered his beautiful fingers. The strangeness of him then was no more than his maleness.

The eyes of the dusty peacock feathers watched, canny and decadent, spies for Mr. Mitchell. But they do not judge, he'd told me so himself.

"Mr. Geist . . ." I wanted to speak to him: not to protest, but rather to ask him what he thought. His swimming eyes were inscrutable.

"Shush," he said, supposing resistance. Expecting it. "I know," he said. "I know that I am ugly and that you, Rosemary, you are beautiful, and for this difference I am sorry. I couldn't be more sorry."

He spoke in a whisper, with tremendous delicacy, as if to soothe a frightened animal. I wasn't frightened. It was unsettling, this intense closeness, but I wanted it, and was more curious than dismayed.

"I am old as well, but I can give you something, Rosemary. Something no one else can."

"What? I don't want anything from you," I said. It was a lie, although it felt true enough to say.

I placed my hand over his, my face limned now, on one side, by both our hands.

"I know you don't want anything from me," he whispered. "That's why I have it to give."

I wanted him to continue speaking, to not stop speaking to me in his hushed, layered voice. It was hypnotic to be spoken to this way, his voice thick with emotion.

"I do not know how to speak of this. This feeling of our likeness, and of our difference. I want to tell you all sorts of things, everything, but I don't know how to speak to you. I have—" he hesitated—"I have little experience with women. With speaking of my feelings," he murmured, then rushed on, his words rustling against each other, tender and quick, a little giddy. "A moment," he said. "Perhaps this is a moment where poetry is called for . . ."

"Poetry?" I said, confused. The wine, worry over Mr. Mitchell, Geist's intensity, made my head spin. What was he talking about? The poetry book left in Oscar's section? Had he left it?

He pulled me closer.

"Let me tell you this, Rosemary," he whispered into my ear, his hand across the back of my neck, beneath my hair. His other hand pressed into my back, splayed as it had been against the covers of books when I'd watched him in Oscar's section, when for a fleeting moment I'd seen his dignity and thought him almost attractive.

"Let me say this to you, Rosemary Savage." His breath soft, his hand behind my neck pulling my ear to his mouth. "'Only as I am can I love you as you are.'" His odd diction was deliberate, precise. "Do you understand?"

"No. I . . . Mr. Geist." My own voice sounded far-off.

His hand moved from my neck and down. He held my breast beneath his hand and a low sound hummed in his throat. Heat rose inside my body, and his other arm drew me to him. I was taller, and for a strange moment his woolly head lay beneath my chin, his face resting on my breast. I wondered if I should do something, touch him in some active way, but I wanted to be acted upon. I wanted to know. And I wanted this fresh heat to continue.

"I hear your heart," he said, his ear to my breast. "You are full of life."

"Mr. Geist, I . . ." He lifted his head and brought my face forward to kiss. I did not push him away. I was moved by him. Excited. And I liked this closeness, this quiet. I felt a melting in me. I wanted tenderness, wanted desire to seep down. I wanted this with Oscar, and saw him there, standing in the room of my mind, surrounded by books, standing precisely where Geist stood.

It was Oscar there with me.

He pressed his mouth to mine and I felt his even teeth through my lips. He did not know how to kiss, any more than I did. He simply held my face to his, mouth to mouth. He breathed in deeply, enraptured, as if holding handfuls of flowers or leaves to his face, breathing me in. His hands found my hair and he brought handfuls of that, too, to his face. He breathed and breathed as if I were made of air, and I felt myself become that quality—light and essential. It was how he saw me.

"Understand, Rosemary," he said urgently. "Because I am the way I am, ugly, dull . . ."

"Shush," I said in turn, quieting him now. I would not hear of his hurt.

"Understand, because of these things, I am freed," he went on. "To love. You will not encounter this again. It is true, I know it."

There was nothing to say to this certainty. I felt the truth of it even while I knew it had little to do with me. He wants life, I thought, but so do I. His was waning. Although I didn't know for sure, I felt it. For all his ardor, I could smell it on him: senescence.

And he seemed more concerned with the scent of me, with the closeness of me, than with union. More interested in feeling me there than seeing me, and for that matter, less about me than about the aliveness, the actuality of my body. He undid the buttons of my blouse and lifted my breasts from their confinement, pushing my bra down to my waist. His light hands moved, from my shoulders, bare now, to my breasts, in gentle searching motion. A man's hands on my body was what I'd longed for. His touch was exquisitely mild, his face lost in an expression of marvel, his eyes closed to any other reality.

But he saw me, I'm convinced of it, even while I know he could see little but light and darkness. He saw me without looking.

Then Walter Geist leaned his small body against my thigh and I felt his sex stiff through his clothing.

He quickly undid his belt, unbuttoned his trousers, and, taking my hand as he had taken it in the diner, pressed it to him.

The instant my hand closed around him, a shudder ran through his body, and he cried out in anguish, falling away from me against the shelf behind him. Several books fell at once; a single volume balanced on the edge for a moment, before it too fell.

Abruptly conscious, as if shaken awake, I stood starkly separate.

In my palm I held a puddle of milky liquid, a small pool of him, white as his body. I stared at my cupped hand, astonished. My own melting had been sharply checked, closeness cut off like a book slammed shut.

"Rosemary," Geist whispered, hiding his face against the shelf. Another book fell. "Rosemary."

I stared at my palm, at what I held of him, repelled by its texture. I felt slightly ill. I was without a handkerchief, so I shoved my hand into my pocket, wiping the stuff against the lining. I picked up my red shirt, pulled up my bra, and hurriedly dressed. My pocket was wet against my thigh, and quickly cold. I pushed the shirttail down behind the lining to add another layer. Then I remembered the fragment of paper, the corner of the letter, ruined now for sure. I had wanted to keep it, the clue to a riddle I still didn't understand. Oscar had said he was a thief, but it was the sadness of the man I'd finally grasped. It overwhelmed me.

Geist was fumbling with his trousers, his back to me. He appeared to be whispering in another language—German, or possibly nonsense.

"Mr. Geist," I said, my voice uncertain. "Are you all right?"

He turned around, his trousers buttoned, his belt buckled.

"Yes, yes," he said. Then, with unaccustomed familiarity: "The proper question is, Rosemary, whether *you* are all right."

"I'm all right," I said, feeling bile rise in my throat. I bent to pick up the books that lay around his feet. My hands trembled as I reached for them.

"But," he asked delicately, "unsatisfied?"

"I'm all right," I answered, collecting the books. My knees shook as I straightened to stand.

Mr. Mitchell would know if the volumes weren't put exactly back in place. He would know they had been knocked from the shelves. The lining of my pocket, the tail of my shirt, stiffened and stuck to my skin. If I wasn't ashamed of what had passed between Geist and me, why did I care what Mr. Mitchell thought? I had to pick up the books. Rare books knocked to the floor! Geist thought he was giving me something, but he wanted to bind me to him with a gift. He imagined we shared the secret of the Melville manuscript, and that now we shared this secret intimacy; but I wanted none of it. I couldn't begin to address his loneliness, and felt only despair at what I'd glimpsed of it.

His manner became increasingly agitated. "Stop—don't worry about those!" Geist said, realizing I was determined to pick up the volumes, trying carefully to shelve them. The books were delicate, their old polished leather scuffed and nicked. They were so beautiful, objects of such antique glamour. One sent a brittle page spinning down like a pressed leaf. I tucked it back in gently, horrified at the damage.

"But Mr. Mitchell will know," I choked. What if he dies?! "I know he will, and he'll be upset. I don't want to upset him."

"Just leave them!" Geist demanded.

His anger froze me. "I can't just leave them," I said, astonished.

"Why not?!" he cried in exasperation. His anger seemed to come from nowhere that I could fathom. He looked about wildly, as if unsure where I stood.

"Ah! Goddamn books! They're just books, Rosemary. Things! They don't live, they don't breathe! Ah!"

He flung his arm to knock more books from the shelf but missed, nearly falling, and once again I caught him.

He appeared utterly undone at that moment. His hands fluttered in a gesture of hopelessness. His shoulders slumped.

"I can't see them," he said, finally, leaning against my shoulder. "Don't you know I can't see them?"

"Yes," I said, and let him go, pushing him from me a little. I straightened the last of the volumes in the case behind him. I needed to get him out of there before he did more harm.

"Yes," I told him again. "I know you can't."

"I'm blind," he spat out.

"I know," I repeated. "Everyone knows."

I read somewhere that for some the loss of sight can come almost as a relief, but for Walter Geist there was nothing redemptive in blindness. It wasn't a romantic rest from the uses of the world, from the accumulation of knowledge. For him, it was the end of what sustained him.

We left the Rare Book Room together that evening in silence. I helped him close up, brought him his shabby coat and ill-fitting hat, and left to get my own. When I returned to the office, he was fussing over a thick envelope he removed from a drawer in his desk, carefully securing it in a leather pouch he zippered shut and slipped inside his coat. His hand rested on my shoulder as we descended the stairs. He gave me the keys and I locked the south door, setting the alarm with the code he recited to me. We stood outside on the street, sleet falling between us, and he held on to my arm as if I might escape. I longed to.

"Rosemary, there is something I must do tonight. Something very important to me," he said keenly. "And I hope it will be important to you."

I made no reply. I didn't want him to tell me. I didn't want his secrets and knew I couldn't keep them, that I was bound to tell Oscar whatever I knew about *The Isle of the Cross*.

"I have an agreement with that seller," he went on. "An agreement to acquire the manuscript by Herman Melville. It is worth a great deal of money. There is need for tremendous discretion, however. I don't have much time . . ."

"Please, Mr. Geist, really, none of that has anything to do with me."

"Just listen. I can't continue here; in fact it is best that I don't. I was supposed to meet him this evening a short distance from here, and I'm very late now because, well, because of Mitchell's attack. But I want to tell you that soon, shortly, I will be leaving the Arcade."

"That's not my business, Mr. Geist, I don't—"

"But it does concern you. You'll understand when I tell you. I concern you, don't I?"

I gave no answer. Sleet stung my face. I clutched Mr. Mitchell's briefcase across my breasts like a shield. I was cold, and my stiff pocket and shirttail itched my thigh. I wanted to go home, to bathe, to forget what had passed between us. But I knew I wouldn't forget, and that he wouldn't, either.

"Rosemary, let me come to you later. I will come to you later this evening. Then I can tell you everything."

"No," I said flatly. "No. You can't."

"I'll explain it all to you then, I promise. I'll come to you later, at the Martha Washington." He wasn't listening to me at all.

"No, I . . ."

As I shook my head, he leaned in and kissed me, missing my lips, his mouth hitting my chin with an awkward bump. I was appalled at what it implied—the attempted kiss almost as intimate as the exchange in the Rare Book Room because of what it assumed. Walter Geist was appropriating a continued intimacy. Without waiting for my response, he turned and made his way to the corner, heading downtown, recklessly crossing the avenue without even pausing. How was he going to make his way? It was almost as if the admission of his blindness had made him even less cautious.

"No," I called weakly, but he didn't hear me. The icy sleet fell like sand, hissing as it hit the pavement. He walked quickly, slipping a little, his silhouette distorted between streetlights, an apparition appearing and disappearing in pools of light along the dark avenue. At a traffic light he found the curb and stood waving wildly at passing cars. A taxi stopped.

"No," I called again, uselessly. "Mr. Geist!" I called as he got in. "I don't even live there! Listen to me!"

But he was gone. I had a grim sense that he had taken something from me, that I'd lost ground in a way that had to do with my very self, with my autonomy. He had murmured about giving me something, but instead I felt bereft. It was as if, in wanting to give me whatever he thought he could, he were simply reminding me of my obligation to him.

Mother came into my mind, as if she'd witnessed the whole transaction, but I willed her away. What would Chaps have made of any of this? Where was Oscar? I trudged to the subway. Underground was bright, dry, and warm, and I was relieved to be in a crowd. My head ached, but I clung to the dutiful errand of delivering Mr. Mitchell's case. I wanted to be responsible for an act that was thoughtful and decent. Returning it, I fancied, was a task that would invoke Mr. Mitchell's well-being, his health. It meant he wouldn't die.

The Mitchells lived on the Upper West Side, and although no one would be home, at some point he'd want his papers and his keys, and he'd want to know, too, that the Rare Book Room was safely locked, awaiting his return. I worried about the fragile volumes that had been knocked to the floor. He'd blame Geist; he hated him for reasons that weren't entirely clear. What were they rivals for apart from George Pike's approbation?

In the subway car the scene in the Rare Book Room played over in my mind. My skin burned with the memory of Geist's hands on me—with the heat of sensation, with the startling experience of another's touch. White, feathery hands had ranged over my skin. Caresses staved off something, and I had wanted more. But it had been Walter Geist and not Oscar Jarno there with me. There was shame to be had in that, a complicit shame that it was Geist who'd held my ear to his mouth and whispered . . . poetry! It was a line from the book I'd shelved. The same poem that ran: "All we are not stares back at what we are." Poetry—now the secret symbol of an imagined affinity.

The subway car rattled on. Perhaps my emptiness came with the loss of no longer wondering. The end of guessing at clues, of puzzling at Geist's motives and actions. He'd become too real, and had broken out of the cabinet I'd kept him in. He was a man, after all, and not a curiosity. He had demands. He wouldn't be explained away or, as Oscar would have it, investigated out of his humanness. I was sickened by the thought that he'd tell me everything Oscar wanted to know about *The Isle of the Cross*. He'd give it to me if I asked him. But what did I owe in return?

The fragment of paper in my pocket was glued to the lining and tore into confetti when I peeled it from the fabric. Extracting the pieces one by one, I collected them in my palm. Then I dropped them and watched as they fluttered to the dirty floor. Just bits of paper, after all, blank and meaningless.

I'd never know who sent the letter.

I came out of the subway close to the library where Oscar and I had spent the evening, near the place where I'd fallen on the sidewalk. My bruised hip no longer hurt, but I felt an ache all the same. How much had Oscar's rejection prepared me for Walter Geist?

Walking west toward the river, the sleet now a cold rain, I miserably considered again the night I'd learned about *The Isle of the Cross*, about Agatha, abandoned and betrayed. About the passionate Herman Melville and how I'd wanted to be passionate too, pantheist too. I saw Oscar's face twisted with disgust, and just that evening, with contempt.

The Mitchells' apartment building cornered Riverside Drive, and a uniformed doorman sat in the warm lobby, out of the cold. He looked close in age to Mr. Mitchell but was trim in a tailored jacket with brass buttons and epaulets. After introducing myself, I handed him the damp briefcase.

"That's very good of you, miss," he said as he took the case. "Mrs. Mitchell ran out of here about two hours ago in a state. Called her a cab. He's downtown, Beth Israel."

"Yes," I acknowledged. "Hopefully he'll be fine," I added with forced optimism.

What if he dies?

"He doesn't look after himself," the doorman confided, eager to share what little he'd observed of the Mitchells' private life from his limited perspective in the lobby. "They've lived here for thirty years, and it's only her that ever takes a walk. He comes in here with an open book in front of his face. He wouldn't even recognize me! A big man like that, reading all the time; he needs exercise."

"Do you think so?" I said, a little uncomfortable with the man's assertions about Mr. Mitchell. I wondered if he knew that he drank. "Don't die, Mr. Mitchell," ran around and around in my mind like an incantation.

"You can think too much." The doorman tapped his temple.

He was a fool, but he'd alarmed me, and mention of the hospital had given me an idea.

"Well, goodnight then," I said, edging toward the door.

"Goodnight then, miss. And thanks again for this." He patted the briefcase fondly, as if it belonged to him and was finally back in his possession.

I had the disturbing sense that once I was out of sight, the doorman would rummage through Mr. Mitchell's papers, not out of malicious intent, but from idle curiosity. Curiosity about the lives of others one observed often enough, daily even, but whom one could never really know. The city brought you right up close to people, but that didn't mean you saw them clearly. I'd wanted to snatch the briefcase back, catalogue its contents, and remove anything private or valuable.

∽

I *returned to* the subway, the incantation running through my head, and when the train stopped at Fourteenth Street, I impulsively got off. I knew the hospital was a few blocks away, and had passed it many times on my walks. If Mr. Mitchell was dead, I had to know. I felt it would determine everything for me. Seeing Mr. Mitchell alive would break the spell I felt myself under. If he knew about *The Isle of the Cross*, if Oscar had told him, I could confess my deception, and perhaps out of fondness he would forgive me.

I found the hospital entrance on First Avenue and walked into the emergency room, lit with scalding fluorescent light and smelling of disinfectant. A woman sat behind a curved reception counter. A screen beneath its rim threw a bluish tint onto her brown face.

"Can I help you?" she asked, as I stood before her.

I was silent a moment, overcome with emotion, with all that had happened that evening.

"Who are you looking for?" She was a little impatient.

"My father," I let out, my voice breaking.

"What is his name?" she responded mechanically.

"Robert Mitchell," I said, trying to collect myself. "He had a heart attack earlier this evening."

"Let me check," she said, and tapped at the keyboard in front of her.

"He's still here in emergency," she said.

"Can I see him?"

"You'll have to check with the nurse, through those double doors." She pointed to the other side of the large lobby, scattered with people slumped in chairs.

∽

"*Yes?*" *asked a* nurse standing in the hallway on the other side of the doors.

"I'm looking for Robert Mitchell," I said. "The receptionist said he was still in emergency."

"Are you a relative?"

Tears fell from my eyes then, so fervently did I want to claim him.

"He's my father," I repeated.

"Of course," she said. "You just missed your mother."

"My mother?" I asked uncomprehendingly. She turned and pointed along the hallway to a curtained cubicle at the end.

"Just ten minutes, then you'll have to go. He's all right," she said. "He'll most likely be released tomorrow after tests."

Taking in my stricken face, she leaned in. "Angina," she added, as if I'd understand exactly the symptoms. "Not a heart attack."

Mr. Mitchell appeared to be sleeping. When I laid my hand upon his, his eyes opened at my touch.

"Dear girl!" he said, blinking. "What are you doing here?"

"I was so worried, Mr. Mitchell. I couldn't wait to find out what happened."

"Ah, always impatient for knowledge, Rosemary Savage. At least you're consistent."

"The nurse told me your wife just left."

"I sent her home to sleep." He yawned, his mouth uncovered.

"I'm to see my own cardiologist in the morning. No point in keeping everyone up."

He watched me with a puzzled expression, clearly wondering at my appearance. In his hospital gown he looked immensely old, the skin at his neck hanging in yellowish folds, his pupils large and dilated inside milky eyes.

"I thought you were going to die," I whispered.

He closed his eyes and smiled slightly. "Not this time, dear girl, not this time." When he opened his eyes again, they glistened. "I will, though—that much is certain."

He sighed heavily, and I caught the faintest scent of vanilla, replaced quickly by the ammonia smell of urine.

"I've been lying here thinking about Rilke, for some reason," he went on. "Odd what comes back to you in times like this. I have a perfect presentation copy of *Duineser Elegien* in my little room, and I was reviewing its details in my mind—1923, original salmon boards, dust jacket . . ."

His white hair stood up from his head in peaks like a crest of soft feathers.

"I suppose you may as well sit for a minute," he said, waving his hand at me.

"Thank you."

I pulled up a metal chair beside the high bed.

"It's nice that you came," he went on tiredly. "That presentation copy . . . I was amusing myself with the line: 'Which of us hasn't sat anxiously before the curtain of his own heart? Up it goes.' "

He chuckled deeply in his chest, coughing a little.

"In my case, I actually thought the curtain was coming down on my heart." He smiled. "Who would be brave enough to exist, eh, Rosemary?"

The only concentration of color in his face was in the veins webbing his large nose.

"Do you think you're brave, Mr. Mitchell?" I asked.

"There's no evidence of it," he said simply. "Are *you*, dear girl?"

"No," I said. "I'm not brave."

My thoughts went to Walter Geist and I knew it would have been braver to refuse his advance, to repudiate whatever fleeting pleasure I'd taken from that closeness. To tell him what I already knew. But I wasn't honest enough to be brave, and there isn't any-thing courageous in pity. I wanted to confess to Mr. Mitchell the whole Melville business, and confess as well the duplicity of us all.

"I'm not brave at all," I repeated, ashamed. "I told the nurse just now that I was your daughter."

"That's a rather brave admission," he said, a bit thinly.

"I wish it were true," I said.

"But it isn't true, dear girl. I left my only children behind in the Rare Book Room, and a wise father knows his own child . . . I miss that perfect little volume . . ."

I suddenly started, sitting up straighter. He would know; he would see the books that had been knocked to the floor.

"Don't worry, Rosemary," he said, turning his head toward me, mistaking my alarm. "I will be fine and released tomorrow." He patted my hand.

"Yes," I replied. "I'm relieved to know that."

"You don't look it, if you'll forgive me saying so."

"It was a shock, you know, this evening. I was so worried about you," I ran on. "I took your briefcase up to your apartment building before I came here. It's awful out, sleeting. It's Christmas Eve, my first without my mother. I'm just tired . . ."

"You must go, then."

"I will in a minute."

"That's thoughtful of you to take my things. I'm glad to know they are safe. Who closed up the Arcade? Pike, that rascal, fancy him riding here with me? The man is still unpredictable after forty years. Still a mystery."

"Mr. Geist and I . . ." I stammered. "I helped him close up."

"I've no doubt you did," he said quietly. "Geist would be lost without you."

"What do you mean, 'lost'?"

"The man is besotted with you. You're the blind one if you can't see that."

"I have a sense of that, now."

"Now?" Mr. Mitchell's birdlike face inquired quizzically.

"I know he is fond of me," I allowed.

"A word of advice from a very old man, Rosemary, then you must go and let me rest."

He pushed himself back against the stacked pillows and winced.

"Keep to the sunny side, dear girl. Disavow perversity. It isn't your color. If you're attracted to unsuitability, then I wish for something more, shall I say, more conventional for you. Don't be a martyr to your imagination."

For a moment I didn't know whether he was speaking of Geist or Oscar, but I couldn't press him to be explicit. In any case, it applied equally to both.

"The man's not altogether right," he went on. "He's fit for treasons. I've known he was up to something, and I'd hate for you to be involved . . ." His voice trailed off, losing strength.

"I don't think myself perverse, Mr. Mitchell," I said vaguely.

"Nor do I. But perhaps no one is entirely free of its attraction."

"I'm not really following you."

"Ah, then, let's forget it. I'm exhausted and I hate advice

from any quarter, most of all my own. We need our powerful se-crets, yes?"

"Secrets?" I asked him guiltily.

"I'm not asking for them, just acknowledging they exist."

I wasn't as gracious; I had to ask. I had to know where I stood with both of them. I leaned against the bed.

"What did Oscar whisper to you before you had the attack?"

"Ah, there, you see? Secrets. In truth, I don't recall, dear girl, and for the moment I don't care. Something has fallen from me and I feel lighter for it."

"What do you mean?" I touched his hand again, mottled as an old binding.

"Can we survive without the things of this world?, Rilke asks me."

"And what do you answer?"

"Alas, I cannot," he smiled. "There is only this world. I'm not fit for eternity."

When I finally made it back to my apartment it was after two. I let myself in and immediately ran the bath, opened up a tin of soup to heat, and sat in my old armchair as the tub filled. I was wide awake now that I'd seen Mr. Mitchell, now that I knew he wasn't going to die. Seeing him had quickened my own sense of aliveness. And perhaps something had fallen from me as well. Callowness, or at least a degree of guilelessness.

In the oval mirror opposite I tried to determine if I appeared changed; if kissing Geist, if having his hands on me had altered me visibly. That same ardent girl stared back, a shadow across her green eyes. I clutched Chaps's amulet at my throat.

What had Geist seen when he touched me? Who was it he desired? I thought of him walking off into the night. Going where? To purchase *The Isle of the Cross* with money that didn't belong to him? To meet Samuel Metcalf? What had he hidden in his coat? He said he wanted to give me something, but I wanted nothing more from him. He'd wanted to come to me later, but now I didn't owe him anything. I'd never told Geist that the money he'd loaned me was to help me move, but did he really just assume I'd been living at the Martha Washington for all these months? I'd made a life for myself, and the girl who stared back wore the face that life described. But was I any less an accumulation of bric-a-brac than that younger Rosemary who'd arrived from Tasmania last summer?

From the back alcove I fetched the Huon box, and sat back in the armchair, settling it on my lap. It was time, I thought, to fill Mother in on what had been going on. But as my hand ran over the smooth heartwood, I couldn't speak out loud or find my voice. She was too far from me, irretrievable now. I had been silenced in some way, and had to see the box for what it was—simply a memento, an object that denied oblivion—and to see, too, that in speaking to her, in addressing her, I'd wanted to deny her death. Perhaps, after all, I should send the ashes home to Chaps, allow the box, allow Mother, to be buried and to rest.

I set the box aside, and instead took up her picture from the bookshelf. The black-and-white portrait confirmed her distance from me. She'd been my age when the photograph was taken, and it showed her present in a life I knew nothing of, that knew nothing of me. We'd never resembled each other, but I was hidden somewhere in that image, waiting for her future. I was in there somewhere.

If Mother hadn't died, I would never have traveled to New York, wouldn't be living in the small apartment I'd made my own, sitting in that chair on Christmas Eve, reflected in my old mirror. The Arcade—my life as I inhabited it—all was contingent upon Mother's disappearance.

Her death had called me to my self.

For the rest of my life, I would miss my mother, but I somehow knew that night, that first Christmas without her, that I'd have to learn to accommodate the great favor her death had brought me. It was a gift that brought with it obligations—to live as best I could, and to remember. But the realization that her death had given me freedom, that this was what the dead bequeath the living, stunned me.

I'd neglected to watch the tub, and it had filled and over-flowed its sides, spilling down onto the floor and pooling in rivulets between the wooden boards. I jumped up and turned off the faucet, wiped my wet eyes on my sleeve, and grabbed a towel that quickly soaked through when spread across the floor. I stripped off my trousers, red blouse, underwear, and used the bundled clothes to soak up the rest. Everything would have to be washed anyway.

I stepped into the tub and lay back, immured in the warm wa-ter. Embraced.

∽

"*Merry Christmas!*" I said to Lillian, hugging her at the door.

She was the first to arrive on Christmas Day, closer to two than our agreed-upon four o'clock. I'd had a couple of hours' sleep and was up and out early buying groceries from the small bodega three blocks away, the only store open in my neighborhood. I'd tried to fix up something vaguely festive, and had some meat from a can warming in the oven, vegetables peeled and boiling, and a stale pound cake I intended to dress up with some ice cream. I'd spent my entire food budget for a week. Lillian stood on the threshold weighed down with a shopping bag. She looked distressed.

"I am glad to be here with you. But first I must tell you that a strange man came to the Martha Washington looking for you last night."

She had no time for pleasantries; she handed me the bag and took off her coat, throwing it onto the armchair.

"I was afraid that might happen," I said.

"It was very late, after midnight, and the hotel was closed. He rang and rang the night bell. He wanted you. A taxi waited for him."

"It was Walter Geist, the manager of the Arcade."

"Yes, he told me that. He is albino," she said, unnecessarily. "Very strange. He cannot see?"

"He's ill, Lillian, I think. I'm so sorry he disturbed you. I never told him I had moved."

"That's good, you never told him. He acted crazy and was very angry. Better that he wake me up than he come here and bother you. He did not believe at first that you were not there. What does he want from you?"

"I'm not entirely sure, Lillian."

"Well, think why he wants to see you at midnight!" she said, impatient with my evasion.

"He is involved in something not altogether honest. And I know some things about it, and him, that I wish I didn't."

Lillian moved her coat from the armchair and sat down heavily.

"Be clear, Rosemary. Don't tell me lies by not being clear. A man wants to find a young woman late at night. He acts crazy when she is not there. Just tell me what is going on. The truth."

"I'm not sure I can tell you just now," I said, stung by her words.

"This is the man you went to the library with? When you stayed with me, when you were so upset?"

"No. That was Oscar. Oscar is my friend."

"The friend who make you cry? This man, Geist, was desperate to find you. I tell him I don't know where you live. I lie to him, and I do not like ever to lie. But this man scare me. He is in love with you?"

"I don't know."

"You have some idea?" Lillian demanded.

"He wants my help. He can't continue on at the Arcade and he needs me to help him."

"Help him with what?" she asked. "Do not get drawn into this, Rosemary! You are a child, and this man he is *extraño*, *misterioso* . . . I don't know the English word."

"I don't think he will be at the Arcade much longer, Lillian. His sight is a problem now. Everybody has ignored it, but it's worse than it was, and he is pretty much friendless there, except for Mr. Pike. I'm the only one who helps him."

"Do not have a fantasy of saving. This I tell you, I know. You need to take care of yourself. He will be okay or not—it's not up to you. Anyway, there are always blind men who take care of books. You remember, my Borges, he was blind by the time he was director of the Biblioteca Nacional. And he was not even the first blind director! This Geist can manage and without you."

"My friend Oscar told me that whether Geist could manage or not, it wasn't anyone's business. That there were all sorts of ways to live."

"Well, that is true. Blindness has its gifts and should not be made pathetic. But this is something else. This man has an injury, in his heart. Have you given him ideas you care for him? Does he want sex from you? Are you frightened to say no? If he thinks he loves you, he might . . ."

"I'm not frightened, Lillian!" I said, cutting her off. I didn't want her speculating about Geist's sexual interest in me. It was apparent enough now. And I wasn't frightened of him, but I was confused and uncertain. I thought I'd know how to behave once I knew exactly what he'd do next—and once I could straighten things out with Oscar.

"Is it money? Is he stealing? You could be involved," she went on. "You are not a citizen. Not legal. You could be in trouble."

"I haven't done anything!"

"I know, but stay away from him. He is disturbed. I am afraid, even in America. You don't know what can happen. I told you what can happen!"

"Lillian, nothing's going to happen to me."

There was a knock at the door. Lillian jumped up, startled.

"That will be Pearl," I said. "Calm down, and please don't bring up Geist with her. I'd rather just sort it out myself."

"No. You need advice about how to manage strange men," she said, resolved. "Pearl knows him, yes? Ask her about him!"

The knocking continued.

"Ah, I see his face," she said, agitated. "*Embrujada*, like a spirit. Pearl will know if he is a danger."

"Lillian, I'm old enough to take care of myself," I said.

"You are a child! And you forget I am a mother," she replied, pointing an admonishing finger at me. "Do not forget."

"I haven't forgotten that at all," I said, putting my arm around her shoulders. I kissed her on the temple.

Pearl knocked louder on the metal door.

"All right!" Lillian waved her hand impatiently, and half held me, half pushed me away. "We will talk later. Let her in!"

I opened the door and there was Pearl, leaning in the door frame, dressed from head to foot in a fluffy white fur coat and matching hat.

"Merry Christmas!" she sang, and sauntered in, twirling about in her coat as if she were on a catwalk. "I thought I'd never be able to make my entrance!"

"It's not that cold out, is it?" I teased.

"Isn't it fabulous? It's my present from Mario. He's with his ex-wife today and his kids, so we had our own little party last night."

"It's beautiful, Pearl," I said. "Although, you know, I don't really approve of fur."

My strange identification with the lifeless pelts piled in the backroom of Foys (that grim sepulchre) had left me queasy about fur since I was a child. It took forty rabbit skins to make a fine felt hat, how many in a coat?

"You look like a snow queen," said Lillian, her face frowning. "Or maybe a polar bear."

"Thanks very much, you two! Is frankness a trait of the Southern Hemisphere? But there's something else . . ."

Pearl extended her large brown hand with its red and green nails. There was a ring on her finger: a dark opal with two tiny diamonds on either side.

"A ring!" Lillian and I exclaimed. We inspected Pearl's hand, Lillian standing up for a better look.

"Is it an engagement ring?" I asked.

"Well, no," Pearl said, clearly emotional. "But it means a lot to me. I've got to get through the operation first and then we'll see. One thing at a time."

"Well, it's lovely, Pearl. Congratulations. Mario's a lucky man."

"I'm the lucky one," Pearl smiled.

"Very nice," said Lillian, screwing up her eyes for a closer scrutiny. "Those little ones are diamonds?"

"The big stone's an opal," said Pearl, holding her hand away from her and admiring the ring from the distance of her arm's length.

"Opals, they are bad luck, no?" asked Lillian offhandedly.

"Do you mind?" Pearl demanded, dropping her hand. "It's my birthstone, Lillian—for October."

Lillian shrugged and sat back down in the armchair.

"That's just an old wives' tale, you know, started in England last century when opals were discovered in Australia," I told them. I'd heard the story from Mother once on our way to Sydney, on a buying trip. It was her way of explaining to me that value was a thing imposed.

"Opals became very popular, so diamond dealers spread the rumor that they were unlucky and brought misfortune, because they didn't want opals to compete with them and lower the price of diamonds. I think they actually took the idea from a book by Sir Walter Scott."

"Interesting," said Lillian. "So the bad luck is a lie only?"

"That's right, just a rumor that protected the price of diamonds. In Julian Peabody's collection I saw a huge black opal, like a globe of the world. Shakespeare called them the Queen of Gems."

"Well, that's appropriate," Pearl observed. "And aren't you the fount of information!" she went on, turning the ring on her finger thoughtfully. "You could almost pass for Oscar Jarno."

"Really? Do you think so?" I still wanted nothing more than to sound like Oscar. To be like Oscar. "I suppose there are a few things I know," I said, a bit smug.

The two women looked at each other across me.

"Do you know how to feed your guests?" asked Pearl, taking her furry coat and hat into the alcove. "And how about a Christmas drink? You've fixed this place up very nice, girl. Love all the colors, and all your funny bits and pieces."

"Thanks, Pearl. I'm so glad to have you here."

I was very glad of their company, and relieved not to be alone. I felt safe with my two friends, and protected in a way that I didn't think I needed. I spread a blanket on the floor and invited them both to sit down, as I was without a table or chairs.

"A Christmas picnic!" said Pearl enthusiastically, crossing her legs and sitting.

Lillian held back, still disturbed, I could tell, by my vague accounting of Geist and why he'd shown up at the Martha Washington after midnight on Christmas Eve. But she pulled out a bottle of wine from her shopping bag and expertly opened it with her pocket knife. I retrieved mismatched glasses from the cupboard and set them on the blanket, and lit all the little votive candles I had about the place. Lillian had also brought cheese and nuts and Argentine chocolates for dessert. I'd been so taken up with my own concerns I hadn't bought either of them anything. In any case, I had no money for gifts. I apologized as I sat down.

"You're feeding us," said Lillian. "That is the present."

"Besides," said Pearl, "after last night, who could think of going out for gifts?"

"What do you mean?" asked Lillian quickly, glancing at me.

"Didn't Rosemary tell you?" said Pearl.

"Tell me what?"

"Mr. Mitchell, the gentleman who runs the Rare Book Room at the Arcade, had a heart attack."

"He's all right, Pearl! I went to see him at the hospital last night."

Both women looked at me with surprise.

"I know he's all right," Pearl said, clearly bewildered that I'd go to such trouble. "I called Mr. Pike before I came over. You really went to the hospital?"

"Yes," I said. "You really have Mr. Pike's home number?"

"Of course," said Pearl, not without some pride. "He has me do the banking these days. He always wants to know about money."

"Mr. Mitchell didn't actually have a heart attack," I told her. "But he does have angina and last night was a serious episode."

"But he'll be all right," Pearl confirmed.

"My husband, Emilio," said Lillian softly. "He died from his heart."

"Oh, I'm sorry," Pearl responded.

"He never have that trouble until our son was taken," she added wistfully, her mood shifting. "Christmas is not so good for me."

Lillian stood up then and went into the alcove. Pearl and I looked at each other.

"Perhaps this wasn't such a great idea," I said quietly. "Perhaps Lillian should be with her brother."

"Not at all, girl," Pearl said. "It's right that we're all here together. We need each other. Remember, us girls got to stick together?"

It was what Pearl had said to me when we first met in the Arcade bathroom. She patted my hand. We sat in silence, trying not to listen to Lillian's subdued weeping behind the curtain of Indian silk.

"What happened to Oscar last night?" Pearl asked, sipping her wine.

"He left as soon as the ambulance did," I said. Rushing off to where? I wondered. What was Oscar doing on Christmas? Investigating, no doubt, like every other day.

"Any trouble closing up with Geist?" asked Pearl, with false nonchalance.

"Trouble? No," I lied. She heard something in my voice and turned to me curiously.

Lillian returned and seated herself on the blanket, her eyes gleaming in the light thrown by the candles. "I am better," she said.

We smiled gently at each other, and sipped our wine together. I served up the dinner, and the three of us ate in companionable silence.

∽

"*I have a* small present for you, Rosemary," said Lillian, finishing her meal, standing and taking her plate to the sink. From the shopping bag, she pulled out a wrapped gift and handed it to me. I thanked her and tore off the paper.

Inside was a jar of lavender bath salts, and a small leather wallet from Argentina.

"Bath salts are perfect, Lillian, because I've been taking baths ever since the heat came on."

"I remembered your bath," she said. "It has feet!" She pointed to the claw feet of the tub, perhaps remembering the night she'd told me about Sergio, when he'd seemed to rise from it, restored to life, as she spoke to him in Spanish.

"To give a wallet is good luck," she said, showing me the various recesses in the soft leather. "Money will come to fill it!"

"I hope you're right," I said, and thanked her again. "I could use it."

Geist wanted to tell me about money, about coming into money, and it was because of his loan that I had this cozy place of my own. Perhaps the wallet had better stay empty. Money caused trouble—but then so did the want of it. I cleared away the plates and poured more wine.

Pearl had a gift for me as well, and I could tell immediately that it was a book. A book is always a gift, Chaps would have said had she been there. I still had her little wrapped parcel, but here was a present I didn't hesitate to open. Removing the wrapping paper revealed a paperback of Ovid's *Metamorphoses*. Pearl had found it on one of the Arcade's front tables, the title something of an inside joke between us.

"I should be giving this to you, Pearl," I said, and kissed her. "Thank you."

"Well, we're both changing," Pearl said.

"You're right," I told her. "We're both changing."

"Everything changes," said Lillian, shifting her position, her legs elegantly folded to one side. "Everything changes all the time."

Pearl and I exchanged glances.

"Only sorrow stays the same," Lillian added. "Only sorrow."

Our festive mood evaporated. Lillian stared off at the brick wall where the flaking mirror hung, her aristocratic features in profile lit by twinkling votives. She was drifting away from us in her thoughts, and I felt her leave us even as she sat there on the blanket.

She would return to Argentina and bury her son, finally, I

knew it at that moment. I thought of Mother, of sending the Huon box back to Chaps, who missed us both, and I knew too that I'd send Mother's ashes to Tasmania, just as Lillian would return to her home.

"My mother used to tell me to remember that nothing lasts," I said, catching Lillian's melancholy and holding on to it like a token of her.

"Sadness lasts," she said. "It comes to fill up every empty space." Her hand went to her heart.

"Now, girls," Pearl said abruptly. "Let's not be maudlin just because we've had some wine!"

She caught up Lillian's hand into her own larger one. The dark opal glimmered on her finger.

"I have a present for you, Lillian. Only it's not wrapped." She turned to me. "It's from that piece I had prepared, you remember? From *Orlando*? He's healed from madness by love. This is a *lamento*."

With that Pearl stood up, and after self-consciously clearing her throat, proceeded to sing in a sweet, tremulous voice. The sound filled my small apartment with its beauty, both contradicting and asserting Lillian's claim about sadness. Pearl's was a sad song, but she filled every empty space with her lovely rich voice. The sound was whole and alive and gave shape to melancholy, changing it before our eyes into something ineffably beautiful, something we wouldn't forget.

CHAPTER TWENTY-THREE

"Good morning, my Tasmanian Devil," said Arthur, lumbering out of Art. "You and I should know better than to show up on Boxing Day. From the looks of the place we're the only ones who did!"

"Mr. Pike must be about somewhere, Arthur, I saw him opening up," I answered, following him back into his section.

I'd actually shown up earlier, but had waited across the street until I saw Pike arrive. I was on the lookout for Walter Geist, and wanted to come upon him in my own way, as well as Oscar, for that matter; but it appeared that neither had arrived. I didn't like skulking about, but that's exactly what I'd been doing. I was caught now between Geist and Oscar, and feared the discovery of my actual duplicity almost as much as Oscar's accusation.

"How are you, Arthur?" I asked him, nervously looking around, reluctant for the Arcade's day to begin. I hadn't taken off my coat and, for the first time, would have liked to turn on my heel and return home.

"I'm fine," Arthur said. "Always better for a day off. Although I'm glad to get back to Art. Glad to find all my friends waiting for me between the covers." His fat hand patted a tall stack of monographs piled on the floor. None of the Goya had sold for Christmas, I noticed.

"I saw Mr. Mitchell at the hospital, Arthur. He's going to be fine. Turns out he has angina."

"Just the venomous malice of his swelling heart, was it, then?" Arthur asked, making light. "Nothing too serious, or uncharacteristic."

"It's not funny, Arthur. Don't make a joke," I said, irritated. "I thought he was going to die!"

"It will take more than a few drinks too many to knock off that old bird," Arthur said.

He didn't care for Mr. Mitchell, but as I was fond of them both, I let it go.

"I wanted to ask you something, Arthur."

"More questions! Which is it—photography again, or Oscar?" he asked, raising an eyebrow that wrinkled his wide, flat forehead. "Because I'm happy to answer anything about the former, but unraveling the enigma of the latter I must decline."

"No," I said, slightly embarrassed. "It's not about Oscar."

"Good, because I don't have any answers for that one."

"Do you know a line of poetry that goes: 'Only as I am can I love you as you are'? Do you know who wrote it?"

"Ha! That you ask *me* indicates you know the answer," he said, smiling.

"You mean it's Auden?"

"Of course," he said. "From the book you were reading the other day."

"I wasn't really reading it," I said. I'd hoped the line had come from elsewhere.

"Apparently you *were* really reading it." He shrugged.

"Oh, well, just a few bits," I conceded.

"As bits go, that's a rather memorable one," Arthur remarked.

"Perhaps that why I remembered it," I lied.

Geist murmuring it into my ear, his hand around the back of my neck, beneath my hair.

I'd left a single strand inside that book, marking a place. For whom I hadn't known. I didn't want to believe that it was Walter Geist who'd left the book there, perhaps looking for poetry to recite to me. To use on me. Surely he couldn't see well enough to have underscored the lines? It was hardly romantic. And why leave it out on Oscar's stool? In Nonfiction?

"I daresay you remember that line," continued Arthur. "Indeed, appear haunted by it, because it's very beautiful. And although beauty is accidental and ephemeral, it is also unforgettable."

"I'm not haunted, Arthur . . ." I began, unbuttoning my coat. "I'm not a bit haunted."

George Pike began yelling at the top of his voice for Pearl: unusual enough to rouse our attention, for Pike rarely shouted.

"That's not a good start to the day," Arthur commented, sighing. "Foul weather for us when he's cloudy. Can't be a shoplifter— it's awfully early and very quiet . . ."

Pearl hadn't come in yet, so I dashed to Pike's platform to see if I could help.

"Pearl's not in, Mr. Pike. Do you need something?" I offered.

"What! Not in!" He was extremely worked up. "The bank's just called!" He spoke above my head to the empty air.

"Were you calling me? I'm here, Mr. Pike," said Pearl, breathless and running to the platform. In her new coat and matching hat, she looked swathed in fluffy snow. She mouthed her thanks to me for attending to Pike.

"Pearl Baird, why does the balance not match my calculations? Does not match your previous report?" George Pike sputtered.

"What do you know about a bank draft, a transfer of funds from the general account?"

"Nothing, Mr. Pike. I made the usual deposit Christmas Eve. Walter gave me the cash pouch himself."

"That's not what was asked!" he snapped.

"I'm trying to understand what you are asking," Pearl said patiently.

"Miss Savage," Pike said, noticing me standing at the base of his stage, listening. "Yours is an unbecoming habit. Excuse yourself!"

"Oh," I said, withering under his glare, certain that the problem involved the zippered pouch Geist had taken with him, hurrying off into the night.

"I'm sorry—I was just on my way to hang up my coat," I stammered apologetically.

Pike descended his platform and gestured for Pearl to follow him to the office. She quickly handed me her coat and hat.

"Hang this up for me, will you?" she asked, shoving the fluffy white things on me. "I've never seen him like this."

She followed Pike up the rickety stairs to the landing of the reeflike structure, hard by the ceiling in the rear. They disappeared into the office. Was Walter Geist up there? Was he hiding? Would he be revealed a thief?

"Rosemary."

I jumped, and turned quickly around.

It was Oscar, his golden eyes cool and distant.

"I must speak with you," he said firmly. "Now."

"All right," I replied, finding my nerve. "I want to talk to you too, about several things. You're mistaken about the other night, you know—I haven't said a word to Mr. Mitchell, I swear, Oscar."

He listened impassively. Pearl's fluffy things trailed from my hands, and I had yet to remove my own coat.

"Listen, I have to hang this up for Pearl. I'll meet you in your section. I'll come straightaway."

"I'll wait at my stool," he said, nodded curtly, and I watched his straight form disappear into the aisle marked Criticism.

I'd tell him about Geist and what happened on Christmas Eve. Not everything, of course, but I'd tell him that I suspected Geist had taken money to secure the purchase of *The Isle of the Cross*. Then he'd believe I hadn't disclosed anything important to Mr. Mitchell. Then he would believe he could trust me. I imagined Oscar writing it all down in his notebook. It was vital to me that he know I hadn't betrayed his confidence, even as it meant betraying Geist's.

❧

I entered the ladies' bathroom and opened Pearl's locker, opposite the ruined vinyl couch. I hung up her coat, stroking the soft fur for a moment, imagining how many white rabbits had gone into making it.

"Poor things," I said out loud.

"Rosemary."

Walter Geist was sitting on the sofa, lying across its torn arm. I hadn't even noticed him. He looked dreadful.

"Mr. Geist, what are you doing in here!" I cried, going to him and crouching beside him. He wore his ancient coat, as if preparing to leave at any moment. His hat lay beside him.

"Waiting," he said, his voice faltering.

"Waiting?"

"Waiting for you."

"My friend Lillian told me you went to the Martha Washington on Christmas Eve."

"Why didn't you tell me you weren't there?" he broke out. "I wanted to come to you later! I told you I would!"

"Mr. Geist, you didn't wait for me to tell you," I said, although I could have made him hear me. "You rushed off."

I could have told him, but I didn't try hard enough, and we both knew as much. He looked frightful, as if he hadn't slept or changed his clothes since I'd left him on Christmas Eve. He'd been waiting, or hiding, for some time.

"Let me help you up, Mr. Geist—you shouldn't be here in the ladies' bathroom."

I made a move toward him, but he clutched at my arms and pulled me down on the couch. I lost my footing and fell beside him; he held me there.

"Listen to me," he rasped. His breath was bitter and his expression fervid; his eyes moved back and forth in their ceaseless vacillation. "I want no more misunderstandings, Rosemary. Listen to me closely." His grip tightened on my arms.

"I have secured the lost novel. I obtained it from a man who cannot sell it for its true value because he himself stole it. I intend to sell it to Julian Peabody for eight hundred thousand dollars. Sam will authenticate it, although I know in my heart it is Melville's. I know it. I have agreed to give Sam three hundred thousand dollars of his own employer's money. Do you see, Rosemary? The rest is mine. Do you follow? I quit the Arcade. I won't be Pike's shadow any longer. I am my own man." He spoke in a fevered rush, overwrought and gripping me through my coat sleeves.

"Mr. Geist, please stop now . . ." I tried to pry his hands from my arms. "Calm down." He was distraught, and I was frightened.

"Where were you?" he whined. "It was your job to be there. I wanted to come to you later . . ."

He brought his face close to mine and I pulled my head away. His grip tightened.

"I want you to stay with me, Rosemary. I will pay you . . . Don't you see? I will give you anything you want to stay with me. Are you listening to me?!" He shook me with shocking force.

"Mr. Geist, stop! Stop it! I'll scream!"

I had to get out of the bathroom. I had to get away from him. I broke free and stood up, leaving him panting from exertion, but the sight of him froze me to the spot. His head flopped against the wall.

"Rosemary," he whispered, spent. "I'm sorry."

I stood above him, appalled. He was pitiable, and I didn't know what to do. I had to think. I wanted to help him; I wanted to get away from him. I needed to tell Oscar what he had done, but there was a way in which I felt responsible. The night in the Rare Book Room, I had stepped toward him. I was complicit, and complicity meant that I'd assumed a sort of charge.

"Mr. Geist," I said, as evenly as I could. "You have to get up. You must go and speak to Mr. Pike."

"Didn't you hear what I said? Don't you understand?" he asked, picking his woolly head up from resting against the wall. His neck looked thin and incredibly white, too fragile to support his head.

"I understand you," I said cautiously. "I understand you perfectly well. More than you realize. I heard what you said and I know about *The Isle of the Cross*."

"You know?" he asked, astonished, sitting himself up a little straighter. "How? How?"

"I researched it, after I read the letter to you."

I let him think the knowledge mine alone.

"After I read the newspaper article I knew Melville's subject. And I found a book of letters. I've read the Agatha letters to Nathaniel Hawthorne."

"Then you know he completed it and you know it was lost!" he whispered passionately, his head nodding as if confirming something to himself.

"You are clever, Rosemary," he said. "I always knew you were clever. Well, it has been found! You know what it will mean to discover it?" He brightened in a wild way.

"I know enough to know there is no value you can place on it," I told him.

"Well, I know its exact value to me. What it can vouchsafe for me isn't a bit arbitrary. Its price is what I have told you. As for Peabody—he will pay and I'll be done with it. He will do with it as he pleases and be damned . . ." He muttered on to himself.

I wanted to tell him that Oscar believed an institution should have it; a library where scholars had access to it, not locked up, another object in Peabody's cabinet. But Geist was still murmuring to himself, and in any case, all that mattered to him was that he could secure something like his freedom. Hadn't he told me he was his own man?

"Quite the deal, don't you think?" he rambled on. "Pike couldn't have managed it better himself. Cash in hand was all the seller wanted. And to keep it anonymous. Still don't know his name. That's all to the good. He has no understanding of its worth . . ."

"You mean you don't even know who has it?" I repeated, incredulous. "You don't know who wrote you the letter?"

It was as if he couldn't hear me.

"Mr. Geist," I asked, frightened now to upset him but upset myself. "Who has the manuscript? Does Metcalf have it now? Have you seen it?"

"You know I cannot do that, Rosemary," he said with a strange smile, the admission of his blindness like another intimacy between us.

I shuddered. He bent toward the floor.

"It is here," he said simply, reaching beneath the sofa.

Walter Geist pulled a thick brown-paper parcel tied around with crimson string from beneath the couch, and sat back, his arms crossed over it, holding it to his body.

"I have it here, Rosemary." He assumed a sort of parody of his former managerial comportment, an unctuous tone I'd heard him use on collectors, but now he was entirely sincere. "I have it here," he said. "For you!"

I could have wept for him then, so utterly vulnerable did he seem, so full of hope.

"Take it to Metcalf," he went on. "I've been waiting for you. We'll forget about missing each other. There's still time. I want you to collect the money."

He rocked a little, the package a fulcrum, the center of his equilibrium. It wasn't possible. He really wouldn't even try to understand.

"Mr. Geist," I said, speaking to him slowly and deliberately, for I began to sense how disturbed he was, although even then I couldn't fully reckon with what he intended.

"How did you pay the seller? Who was it that found this?" I asked him evenly.

He smiled up at me sightlessly, from his position crumpled in the corner of the couch, his arms tightened about the package.

"I took money from the Arcade's account," he said, almost matter-of-factly. "Only Pike's or my signature is accepted for withdrawals. Pearl made up the difference when she gave me the cash deposit."

"How much did you take?"

"One hundred thousand dollars only," he said, rocking again as he spoke, clutching his accomplishment. "Don't you see how I've managed it? But you mustn't worry about that. Pike mustn't worry. I've only borrowed from him. I have it planned. I'm not a thief, you know. I will return the money to him and still have made money. Lots of it. Four hundred thousand, in fact. I will pay you, Rosemary. You won't need to work here either. I can give you whatever you want. To attend me . . ." He trailed off.

"To attend you?" I asked, baffled by his choice of words.

"I don't imagine you love me, Rosemary Savage," he said. "But I can give you something."

Whether illness or madness held him, I couldn't disguise my chagrin.

"I told you before, Mr. Geist. I don't want anything from you," I said, moving toward the door.

"You're not well." I tried to soften my tone. "Let me help you, as I have done before. It's not too late to tell Mr. Pike what's happened. Just tell him that you've acted on his behalf, that you have a ready buyer in Metcalf for Peabody's library."

I knew the folly of this. Pike would never accept a deal he hadn't negotiated, let alone accept that he'd been robbed by his most trusted employee. Geist had been a fool. In losing his sight he had lost his way.

But Oscar and I were fools as well. We had avidly followed the trail of something that was beyond our control, never supposing the outcome. Reading Melville should have taught me as much: we all pursue a phantom. Walter Geist sat holding his.

"Take it," he said suddenly, indicating the package but still clutching it. "Keep it safe, Rosemary. Take it to Metcalf and I'll wait for you. Don't give it to anyone else but Metcalf. He expects you. Then come back and help me."

"Help you, Mr. Geist?" I was trying to think what to do.

If I snatched the parcel from his hands I could give it to Oscar, waiting for me in Nonfiction. He would believe then that I hadn't said a word to Mr. Mitchell. But that would mean deserting Geist entirely.

"Help me, Rosemary," he said simply. He reached a pale hand toward me, unseeing. "Rosemary, you can stay with me."

If I grabbed the parcel from him at that moment I wouldn't have to hear another word.

"Why have you never called me by my name?" he went on.

"Why? Can't you say my name? I know you cannot love me, I don't ask you to, but you can help me as you have done here since you came to the Arcade. Everything changed when you arrived."

He pulled himself up to stand, the package under one arm. If I pushed him, if I shoved him hard, I could snatch it.

"I need you," he said, plaintively stretching out one arm in my direction.

I stood flattened against the wall, incapable of volition.

∽

Pearl pushed open the door and walked into the bathroom.

"Rosemary, I've been looking for you!" she said. "Mr. Pike needs me to go to the bank, and then to try Geist's apartment. He's not answering the phone. What's the matter?"

Her eyes traveled from my face to the other figure in the anteroom.

"Lord!" she yelled. "What are you doing in here?"

She turned to me for a response as Geist wavered on his feet.

"He's been in here all along," I said quietly. "But Pearl—"

"You have to come with me, Walter," she said sharply. "Come with me to Mr. Pike." She took another step toward him. "Whatever has happened, it can be sorted out."

"No!" he brought out, and retreated to the corner between the sofa and the scuffed wall.

"Please, Mr. Geist," I said. "I will come with you to Mr. Pike."

He clutched the brown-paper parcel. "Stop it," he said in a harsh rasp. "I've told you what to do. You have an obligation."

Pearl looked at me dumbfounded. "Rosemary?" she asked.

What he'd said woke me into action. "Pearl, perhaps if you go and tell Mr. Pike that we're here, that would be better."

Confused, she shook her head.

"It's all right, Pearl, we'll wait here. Go and tell Mr. Pike."

We exchanged looks and she understood she was to bring the Arcade's proprietor immediately.

"And get Oscar," I whispered to her.

She left the bathroom.

"Come on, Mr. Geist," I said, moving toward him now, certain that I needed to take the manuscript from him. He'd been carried over the height. It was stolen, after all, secured with stolen money. He was correct to remind me of my duty. But it wasn't to him. It was only proper that I take *The Isle of the Cross* from him. Oscar was the person who should decide what to do with it.

As it happened, I didn't have to take it from him. He gave it to me.

"Here," he said, pressing the parcel into my hands. "I understand what you're doing. Go quickly, before they come back. Take it to Metcalf. Tell him it's from me and collect the money. It's ours, Rosemary. That money is for us."

I took the parcel, moving toward the door.

"I don't want the money, Mr. Geist," I said, with all the scrupulousness I now felt, now that I held the manuscript. "I don't want any of it. I can't be whatever it is you want. I'm sorry about all this. I'm sorry about what happened between us. But it was a mistake, you see. An accident."

"Accident?" he echoed. "There's been no accident."

CHAPTER

TWENTY-FOUR

"Are you in there, Walter?" called Pike furiously, opening the door, slamming it against the wall.

"Go!" Walter Geist cried.

"What in God's name is this about?" Pike shouted angrily, standing on the threshold, an odd propriety preventing him from entering the women's bathroom.

"Come out this instant! George Pike will not stand here and wait. Absurdity! Come out immediately!"

He was livid, and made no attempt to control his voice or his temper. Oscar stood behind Pike, Pearl at his side, his eyes fixed on the package in my hands.

"Walter, what are you doing?" Pike said, and stepped gingerly inside. Geist's distress was evident, and he shrunk visibly into the corner of the anteroom. Pike shook his head, appalled at the state of his manager, his anger dissipating into a fastidious disgust.

"I've no wish to speak with you," muttered Geist to the floor, his head down. "I'm not your subject."

"Mr. Pike," I interrupted. "Mr. Geist isn't well."

"That spectacle is apparent, Miss Savage," said Pike viciously. He stepped forward and roughly took Geist by the arm. "Let's go up to the office."

"Rosemary!" cried Geist. "Please go. Now!"

"She's not going anywhere, Walter. Miss Savage, come along," Pike directed, a scowl on his dull face.

"Yes, of course," I answered.

Pike propelled Geist from the bathroom and I followed, the manuscript beneath my arm. Oscar pulled me away from the strange pair as they passed.

"Is that it? Do you have it?" he whispered into my ear fiercely.

Pearl searched my face for a clue as to the nature of these bizarre proceedings.

Walter Geist's woolly white head swiveled around, trying to locate me. "Go!" he cried up to the huge domed ceiling of the Arcade, where it reverberated pathetically.

I was silent.

"What the hell is going on?!" Pearl demanded. "What's wrong with him?"

"Rosemary," Oscar said, and put a finger to his lips, indicating discretion.

The three of us hung back and watched as Pike and Geist ascended the stairs to the office. The Arcade's proprietor had his hand firmly in the center of his manager's back, rebuking him all the while, an unforgiving father reproving a recalcitrant son.

"Tell me," insisted Pearl, "what's going on, Rosemary? I gather from Pike that the cash account is a hundred thousand short. Geist can't really have taken it! He wouldn't steal from Pike."

"He did, Pearl," I said wearily.

I turned to Oscar. "Geist stole the money to buy *The Isle of the Cross*," I told him. "He paid a hundred thousand for this."

His golden eyes locked onto the parcel.

"Geist told me to take it to Metcalf. He stole from the Arcade account to pay the seller in cash; the only other condition was anonymity. He told me that Peabody has agreed to pay eight hundred thousand for it, of which Metcalf secretly takes three. Geist planned to pay Pike back and keep the rest, although he didn't think he'd be discovered before he could return the money. Something went wrong with his plan."

"And what was that, Rosemary? What went wrong?" Oscar asked, studying me intently.

I couldn't answer. Perhaps if I'd been at the Martha Washington the night Geist had been looking for me . . . But I wasn't there, and he didn't know where to find me. The truth was, I didn't know why it hadn't worked. The whole thing was doomed from the outset, determined as it was by Geist's desire to possess not *The Isle of the Cross*, but his freedom—as well, perhaps, as me.

"Geist gave that package to you?" asked Pearl. "Is it the money? Did he steal it for you?"

"No, it's not the money, Pearl. Oscar, it's the manuscript. Although, of course, Geist hasn't seen it. He's blind."

Oscar ran his hand over his dark hair skeptically. "Who did he buy it from?"

"I don't think even he knows," I said.

"How can he not know? Do you mean that the seller stole the manuscript from another collector?" Oscar said, shaking his head in disbelief. "That he stole it and sold it to Geist anonymously?"

"That's what he told me."

"I have no idea what you two are talking about," interrupted Pearl. "What's *The Isle of the Cross*? Rosemary, fill me in. Why did Geist say you had an obligation to him?"

"Not now," I said.

"What obligation?" asked Oscar.

"Here," I said, echoing Walter Geist. I gave him the package, just as it had been given to me. Oscar stood holding it with both hands, momentarily fixed to the spot.

"It's for you," I said.

"Will one of you just tell me what's in the package?" Pearl asked, indignant now with not understanding. She'd watched our exchange, following in confusion, from the sidelines.

Oscar solemnly walked to his stool in Nonfiction, Pearl and I following like acolytes. He placed the parcel on his stool and carefully untied the crimson thread.

"Odd," he said to himself. "Cotton ribbon like a lawyer's binding. The proverbial red tape . . ."

The brown paper was thick and otherwise unfastened once the tape was removed. Oscar gently opened the paper and stood staring down into the unfolded envelope of wrapping.

"Well?" Pearl said. "Is it whatever you thought it was?"

Oscar's face was impossible to read; his phlegmatic nature rendered it a mask. I watched him in profile as I had done the night in the library when we'd discovered the details of *The Isle of the Cross*. His magnificent head bent forward as if peering over a ledge. He reached into the wrapping and withdrew a thick ream of paper.

"It's a trick, right?" said Pearl. "Whatever you thought it was, I'm sure that's not it!"

The paper was blank and starkly white.

Oscar held the ream of paper and his golden eyes slowly rose from it to my face. "Where is it, Rosemary?" he asked contemptuously.

"It's a fraud? A fake?" I sputtered. "It's not there?"

"*The Isle of the Cross* is not a fake, Rosemary," spat Oscar. "But the charade you've been carrying on might be considered one."

"What are you talking about?"

"Where is the real manuscript?"

"Oscar—I know no more than you do!"

"Oscar," said Pearl, "Geist gave her that parcel. He had it in the ladies' bathroom."

"Where is it, Rosemary?" Oscar repeated.

"I don't know. I swear. Geist left me on Christmas Eve and I didn't see him again until this morning. I swear."

"Have you seen Mitchell?"

"Well, yes, I went to the hospital, to see if he was all right."

"And you told him about *The Isle of the Cross*? You gave it to him?"

"No, Oscar." I pleaded with him to believe me. "I swear on my mother's ashes, I swear, I haven't told a soul."

He moved toward me and I stepped back, frightened of him, of the awful menace in his eyes.

"What a waste of time you are!" he hissed. "You stupid, ignorant girl."

He turned, throwing the ream of blank paper violently into the air, and stalked from Nonfiction toward the rear of the store.

The sheets of paper floated to the Arcade's dirty floor, scattering.

Pearl put an arm around me.

"What have you gotten yourself into, girl?" she said gently.

Desperate, I made to follow Oscar, but Pearl instinctively held me back.

He disappeared from view, hidden by the stacks, but in a moment we watched him run up the stairs to the office. After he entered, shouts rang from the interior in a heated exchange that continued for some minutes. I broke from Pearl and stood beneath the office at the foot of the rickety stairs, trying to make out the raised voices. Walter Geist seemed not to speak at all; for all his defensiveness he was silent in defense of himself.

"I don't know how you're involved in this, Rosemary, but I'd stay out of it," Pearl said, standing behind me, her hands on my shoulders.

She'd followed, and pulled me into the circle of her arms, away from the stairs. She tugged me to Pike's platform, and we stood together on his raised stage, our attention drawn upward to the office.

George Pike and Oscar Jarno appeared a minute later on the landing, Pike holding Oscar's arm as if he'd hauled him from the interior. Their shouts resounded across the vast Arcade, the ceiling a chamber that returned their emphatic exchange.

"This is not your concern!" Pike's odd high voice commanded. "He's not in his right mind. He's broken the law, but you are not—"

"Just let me tell you! I'll explain it to you!" Oscar shot back at Pike. "Or I'll make him tell you!"

Geist appeared on the landing, stooped and disoriented. Oscar went at him, shouting into his face. He yelled that he was an imbecile. That Oscar knew all along what he'd been up to. That he wasn't fooled and where was the real manuscript? Where had he hidden it? Who had really written the letter? Where was the novel?!

"You gave it to her, didn't you? You gave it to Rosemary!"

Walter Geist didn't appear bothered by Oscar shouting at him, until my name came up. He kept his head lowered as if resigned to attack, and a slight smile played about his mouth.

As Pearl and I stood on Pike's stage, our arms around each other, customers too were watching below the landing of the office, immobilized by the scene, as theatrical as anything the Arcade had ever presented.

Oscar, maddened by Geist's smile, shoved him hard in the center of his chest.

The loose rail snapped as Geist stumbled against it, and he plunged down, landing with a sickening snap, crumpled and unmoving near the sheets of scattered paper.

Pearl and I rushed to him. George Pike reached him first.

"Don't move him!" Pearl shrieked.

But Pike held his head in his hands.

Walter Geist's eyes were open and still.

∽ For months afterward, Walter's form fell again and again in my mind's eye, a rag man tossed over the broken rail. Arthur had once shown me a painting by Goya: four girls held the corners of a blanket and tossed a straw man up into the air, his arms and legs in curious relation to his limp body, contorted into parody. I saw him over and over against the vault of the ceiling, floating with his shabby coat open, his smile flickering a moment before he fell. He dropped again and again to the floor of the Arcade, all strewn about with empty pages. For months, a hovering vision of him would come upon me unbidden. He haunted me.

His ridiculous hat, the one his father left him, remained on the ruined sofa in the anteroom of the ladies' bathroom until I took it home to my apartment. Chaps used to tell Mother and me that a hat wasn't like a book—people didn't need hats. I kept his, however, added to my collection of bric-a-brac. Over the years, I've even put it on several times. It fits me perfectly.

George Pike closed the Arcade for a single day to mourn his manager, but there was little mention of the episode in the weeks that followed. The police concluded the death in the Arcade was an accident, brought about when Pike confronted his manager with the evidence of misappropriated funds. They suggested Pike should

have called them in first, if he suspected Geist a thief, or at all unstable. But if George Pike felt remorse over the outcome, he never
showed it, and because he was as impossible to read as the city itself, I can't know what he lost, personally, when he lost Walter
Geist. I choose, however, to believe that he never forgot him; that
in his own way Pike valued Geist's memory.

Of course, everything changed.

∽

Oscar Jarno vanished from my life, and from the Arcade, as palpably
as Geist did. He disappeared the day Walter fell, slipping out unnoticed in the chaos that had followed.

Over the ensuing weeks, I began an investigation of my own.
I located the address Oscar had listed as his residence from the scant
employment files Geist kept. But the building Oscar's old application listed on West 125th Street had long been abandoned. I tried to
locate his tailor, but couldn't find one who hand-made shirts to the
sort of specifications I knew Oscar demanded. No tailor I spoke
with recalled so distinctive a customer.

There was a mailing address on the old form, a post office box,
and I wrote to him, sending several long letters, telling him everything I'd never been brave enough to say.

Reading them now, I see I assured him that no one held him
responsible for what had happened. But some letters one really
writes to oneself; some letters just describe what it is we hope will
be returned. My letters to Oscar are pasted into my scrapbook, their
envelopes stamped in red capitals where the post office marked
them Undeliverable before sending them back to me.

I've lost the days that immediately followed Walter's death
and Oscar's disappearance but I know that on New Year's Eve,
alone in my apartment, I briefly considered opening Chaps's small
present, still resting near my scrapbook on the bookshelf. I even

took it up and stroked its beloved blue paper. Surely this was my worst moment? But something prevented me. Perhaps it meant more to me that her gift waited, that it remained to surprise. I set the package down and took out a few almost transparent sheets of airmail paper. I wrote to Chaps instead. I told her as much as I could. Then I walked into the alcove, got into bed, and pulled the covers over my head.

I was asleep before a new year, and a new decade, began.

When Chaps wrote back—immediately, as I knew she would—her advice was simple. Everyone can master a grief but he that has it, she said of Walter Geist's death. I wasn't certain if she meant his grief or mine. I knew I couldn't master grief, I wasn't interested in trying, but I did want to learn how to live with it with equanimity. After all, I owed grief something. It is woven into that year, into me, as intricately as a thread in one of Oscar's precious fabrics.

I stopped writing in my notebook after that. The narrative just falls away. I didn't have the heart to follow Oscar's example anymore. If I were to truly emulate him, I think I'd have vanished as well.

∽

A month after Walter died, George Pike uncharacteristically began a game of Who Knows? He had hired several new staff members, and when the call first went up, I imagined Pike wanted to introduce them to the pastime that served to train staff in the enigmatic search of the Arcade's vast contents. In the absence of Oscar and Walter Geist, the Arcade's collective memory was impoverished by an immeasurable degree.

"What's the title?" I asked Bruno, not having heard the game's beginning. I'd escorted a customer to the basement, where a new store manager, a Mr. Angelo, quickly processed review copies beneath the brilliant single globe, without needing any assistance from me.

"Who the fuck knows?" said Bruno, already slurring his words, although it was only early afternoon.

"Pike started it," muttered Jack. "Didn't catch the title."

They'd lost interest in the competition, in playing Who Knows? There seemed little to gain now in mastering the contents of any given section. Besides, Pike's paperback fellows were never really interested in helping customers. Arthur wasn't anywhere to be seen, so I walked toward George Pike's platform, but froze when I saw who stood beneath it, conferring with the Arcade's proprietor.

"Ah, Miss Savage," Pike said, calling me over. "We are looking for a volume. You can perhaps assist?"

"I'll try," I said.

"The title again?" Pike asked the thin man. I caught a whiff of verbena as he turned.

"*The Isle of the Cross*," said Samuel Metcalf. "By Herman Melville."

"That book does not exist," I told him flatly. "As you know perfectly well."

"I know nothing of the sort," Metcalf said accusingly.

"You are familiar with the work?" Pike leaned over the rail bordering his stage, his attention fixed intently upon me for the first time in my entire experience at the Arcade.

"What do you know about it, Miss Savage?"

"It is a lost novel by Herman Melville," I told him, ignoring Metcalf. "Written in the fall of 1852 and completed the following spring. The novel was based upon an actual story of desertion, of abandonment. Its theme is resignation and remorse. Melville submitted it to his publishers, but for an unknown reason was prevented from publishing it. The only copy may have been lost in a fire that destroyed Harper & Brothers' offices late in 1853. The novel has not survived, Mr. Pike, and Mr. Metcalf knows as much. It is a disgraceful sham that he comes here asking for it. Ask him what he means by pretending he doesn't know it was lost."

"How dare you! Pike, you're surely not going to let her speak to me that way?" Metcalf said, his thin limbs waving wildly. He turned on me then. "I think you know where it is, and I came to the Arcade to find it. It is owed to me."

"It is not in the Arcade," I said, unafraid of him. Metcalf was playacting, trying to rattle me. "You are owed nothing."

"You are certain of this fact, Miss Savage?" asked Pike scrupulously. "The novel is not in the Arcade?"

"Yes, Mr. Pike. Absolutely certain."

"Your knowledge is impressive," he said, astonishing me with the first, and last, compliment he ever paid me. "There is nothing more you wish to add?"

"No, Mr. Pike. There is nothing more."

"Thank you," he said, dismissing me.

I walked away, but Metcalf pursued me, frustrated by Pike's acceptance of the simple truth. He grabbed my arm and turned me to face him.

"I thought you cared about him," he said villainously. "He would want you to give it to me. He wanted Peabody to have it."

"You don't know what he wanted."

"I know you were his lover, Miss Savage. Which puts you in rather closer proximity than anyone else to know what he did with the manuscript."

I fell back from him, shaken. "I was not his lover," I whispered.

"Hardly spoken with the strength of conviction," Metcalf observed. "In any case, where is the manuscript?"

"I have no idea."

"Oscar has disappeared and you're the only person who knows the details of its discovery."

"It was not discovered," I told him. "It was a hoax. Mr. Geist was deceived."

"By you, certainly!" he spat.

I felt dizzy then, confronted with this accusation, as if Walter Geist himself rebuked me.

"He gave it to you, didn't he?"

"It was a counterfeit," I repeated. "The whole thing was a fraud."

"A fraud at the rate of eight hundred thousand dollars," he said. "Who has the money, then?"

"You're not out of pocket, Mr. Metcalf. And in any case, that's only the price," I said, shaking him off. "It doesn't approach the cost!"

"I want that manuscript!" he demanded. "I'll do anything to get it. I'll have you fired, for a start."

I turned and walked out the south door; I had to get as far away from him as possible. The collector in him sickened me.

Out on the street, without my coat, I tried to catch my breath. I felt as if I exhaled loss with every gasp, briefly visible in the cold air, evaporating into the February afternoon. I leaned against the Arcade's windows.

"Are you all right?"

A man approached me, bundled in a dull brown coat, its collar turned up against his ravaged cheeks. It was Russell—Thomas Russell, I remembered—who'd once given me his card, offering me a job whenever I was ready to jump ship.

"Rosemary, isn't it?" he inquired kindly. "Are you ill?"

"No," I said. "I just got a bit of a shock."

Lovers? Were Walter Geist and I lovers?

"Things not going well at the Arcade?" Russell asked. "I read about that tragic business with the manager. Were you friendly with him?"

"Yes," I told him, feeling my eyes fill. "We were friends."

"That's hard, then," Russell said simply.

We fell silent, and I noticed my breathing even out. I blinked into the bright daylight, glad to be outside the Arcade.

"Do you remember offering me a job, Mr. Russell?" I surprised myself by asking him. "A job making books?"

"Yes." He smiled, and the pitted scars on his cheeks creased and pleated. I found his devastated face oddly reassuring.

"You must have finished *Moby-Dick* by now," he said.

"I have," I answered. "And you didn't really spoil it for me."

"I didn't?"

"Well, as you remember, one does survive the wreck."

He studied me closely. "Not going back to Australia?"

"No."

"Do you still have my card?"

"Yes," I told him. "Are you still an editor?"

"I am," he said. "Call me, Rosemary. I'll see what I can do."

∽

Just when New York was a world of winter, I was reminded that seasons change, and spring, of all things, began to send out emissaries of what was to come. Each day lasted a little longer, and as a consequence I resumed my evening walks. Buds appeared on the shrubs in my dirty park, stuck to the branches like tiny brown nuts. The trapped plastic bags, ubiquitous to city trees, filled with warmer, snowless air, making them less melancholy than they had once appeared. Perhaps it was I who had changed, despite, or maybe because of, all that had happened.

I visited with Lillian often, and we spoke of quiet, unimportant things. We kept each other company. I never told her about the letter Geist had me read, or about *The Isle of the Cross*. Pearl knew something of it, of course, but as I never discovered who had written the letter offering Melville's manuscript, it remained a conundrum I couldn't well explain. To this day, I wish I had the torn corner, my flake of paper snow. At least then I'd have proof the letter had actually existed; testimony that Walter Geist hadn't invented it himself or that something more tangible than desire had set circumstance in motion.

Finally, one March evening I made my rambling way to 104 East Twenty-sixth Street, preparing myself for an encounter I had long postponed. I'd learned the address from the letters inside the library book I'd never returned, and I counted it remarkable, really, that my pilgrimage lay so close to the Martha Washington.

Of course, it wasn't what I expected; nothing ever is.

I shouldn't have been surprised that Herman Melville's house had disappeared, absorbed into the city's endless reconfiguration. But my disappointment at finding only a plaque, only token evidence that he'd once lived on the block, made me realize how much I'd wanted to stare into the windows that Herman Melville had gazed out from. I waited on the street for a while, loitering about as if he would appear rounding the corner on his way home from the Customs House, as he'd done for nineteen years. Or was I waiting for his counterpart: an immaculate white shirt picked out sharply in the dusk, even from a distance?

Standing that evening, on East Twenty-sixth Street, I watched a fingernail moon rise in the blue twilight, little more than a pale shell. The moon was waxing, I recall, growing whole again, setting an example.

∽

Pearl would be leaving for her operation, so Pike had engaged his ancient sister to run the front register. She was Pike's double in anachronistic appearance (absent mustache) and equally Victorian in her reserve. But unlike her brother, Ethel Pike was incompetent. Pearl trained her for two weeks, amid complaints and exasperated asides. George Pike didn't seem to care; the performance of his mysterious pricing hardly abated, despite frequent interruptions. Once Pearl was away, only Arthur Pick and Mr. Mitchell would remain to keep me company, to continue my education.

I called Thomas Russell and, after several interviews over the course of a few weeks, was offered a position as intern at the publishing house where he worked, for thirty dollars more a week than I received at the Arcade. One hundred dollars a week!

"You're on your way, girl," Pearl said, when I told her.

I'd arranged for Pearl and Lillian to meet at my apartment for dinner, to send Pearl off with our best wishes. Lillian was late.

"I don't know how you can say that, Pearl. I think all they want me to do is copy stuff. Maybe make coffee."

"Well, you're out of the Arcade at least, and into the larger world."

"I'm going to miss it, Pearl. It seems like I'm always leaving home," I said. "And I'll miss you terribly."

"I'll be back in a few weeks." She waved her hand dismissively. "Besides, you'd said you'd visit me in the hospital!"

"I will," I assured her. "I'll take the train down."

"You'd better," she smiled. "We girls got to stick together."

I returned her grin, glancing over at the green clock. Where was Lillian?

"Mr. Pike is giving me half wages for the weeks I'm away," Pearl told me. "Isn't that amazing?"

It certainly was amazing: Pike parting with money to ensure Pearl's return.

"Do you know what Mr. Pike said when I gave him my notice?" I asked her, wincing at the memory.

"What?"

"He said that he wasn't in the habit of hiring young women and that I personified all the reasons why he wouldn't hire one again."

"Well," said Pearl, who had a soft spot for Pike, even without the half wages. "It's understandable he feels a bit sorry for himself."

"I feel sorry myself, Pearl. For disappointing him."

While we waited for Lillian, we talked over what Pearl was about to undergo. It felt momentous, her transformation, and we fell silent, after a while, in contemplation of it. In the quietness, we both started when Lillian banged on the metal door of my apartment.

"It is Lillian!" her muffled voice called through the door as I went to open it.

"I know it's you," I said, kissing her in greeting after unlocking the door. "Who else would it be?"

"Sorry to be late," she said, as she bustled in through the doorway carrying her usual bag filled with offerings. She looked distracted and upset.

"I fight with my brother," she announced. "He is very angry with me. He tell me to stay."

Pearl stood up from the single chair in the room and after helping Lillian off with her coat pushed her into the old armchair. "What happened?" she asked.

There was an expectant pause as we waited for Lillian to fill us in. She twisted her hands in her lap. "I brought some wine," she said incidentally.

"What happened, Lillian?" I asked, repeating Pearl's question.

"Rosemary," she said quickly, "I am leaving. I am returning. To Argentina. I go next week."

Pearl moved to me instinctively, and without another word I burst into tears. As water ran down my face, I had the presence of mind to notice that my tears fell freely and without sobs; without the resistance that makes crying painful.

"This really is a farewell supper, then . . ." Pearl said.

Lillian nodded, her own eyes shining.

"I assume," Pearl asked, with a coquettish grin, "that you've brought another bottle of that fabulous Mendoza stuff?"

Lillian gathered up her big leather bag and drew out a bottle. Pearl took it. I went to Lillian then, crouching beside the armchair, leaning against her. She held me, each of us laughing a little as well. I think we both remembered the night I showed up at the Martha Washington cold and dejected and crying over Oscar. The night she'd tucked me into bed.

"You know," Lillian told me, her mouth against my ear, "you know why I go. I should not have left at all, Rosemary. It was wrong to leave. It was my duty to stay. So now I go back to bury Sergio, properly. You know it is right, child."

I nodded into her shoulder. Pearl left us to ourselves, fussing with the bottle and glasses at the sink against the brick wall. I took off my green necklace and put it around Lillian's neck. It wouldn't protect her against heartbreak, any more than it had me, but I wanted to give her something I loved.

The rest of the evening was spent sitting again on the blanket on the floor. We talked about books and music and when I would meet someone suitable. We avoided all hurtful subjects. And while it occurred to me that all my mothers were leaving, this time it was different.

I would stay.

∽

I sent Mother's ashes home to Chaps, packed tightly inside a box, cushioned all around with a great deal of paper. At the post office, the clerk made me spell "Tasmania" twice as he filled in the customs form, suspicious that I had invented the parcel's destination. He thought it was a made-up place, taken from a book or a fairy tale, until I pointed to a map of the world behind him on the wall. The island of Tasmania declared itself, looking like a scrap torn off the corner of Australia. The clerk chortled. "To think," he said, shaking his head, "to come all that way . . ."

"Yes," I said. "To think."

I considered it no more than a white lie when I signed my name to the customs form, certifying that the contents of the box contained only a gift for the recipient. (I couldn't very well have declared the box contained Mother's ashes.) In the Estimated Value column the clerk scribbled a zero. Gifts were valueless, he advised me, unless I wanted to insure it.

As I left the post office, I felt immeasurably older for the single year that had passed. I had written as much to Chaps in a letter I'd enclosed with the Huon box. I'd written that I was leaving the Arcade for a better-paying job, and that I was sending Mother's ashes back because she would know what to do with them, and because it didn't seem right for me to keep them with me anymore. New York was where I lived; Mother had just been visiting.

My last day at the Arcade was April twenty-fifth. Only Pearl knew it was my birthday, and she was in Baltimore recovering. There wasn't a single person I knew in all of New York who also knew it was Anzac Day, or even what the day commemorated. Unless, of course, Oscar was somewhere in the city.

Mr. Mitchell had invited me up to the Rare Book Room during the afternoon. Struggling with the cranky elevator cage, my heart hurt thinking of Walter Geist and Christmas Eve, when we stood together beside Robert Mitchell's desk. I hesitated at the elevator and listened as Mr. Mitchell closed a deal.

"This copy is exceptionally fine, aside from a minor repair to the corner of the last leaf. There's a bit of close trimming which has affected some of the letters in the headline. But the price takes that into account—I've reduced it, because I know George Herbert is something you'll want. You've got to branch out from Donne, to vary your collection. Notice the folding cloth box with morocco labels," Mr. Mitchell cooed. "*The Temple* is one of the landmarks of English poetry. Look, here's 'Redemption,' 'Affliction,' 'Vertue'— some of the most widely anthologized poems in the English language. Colloquies of the soul, man, from 1633!"

"Are you sure you can't do better than forty thousand dollars? Should you query Pike?" the customer asked, and I could tell in his voice that he'd already decided to take it.

"I'll leave you with George Herbert for a minute," Mr. Mitchell said, his timing impeccable. "A friend has just arrived I must see to."

He walked through the enfilade of rooms to where I stood at the elevator.

"Rosemary," he said, the smell of vanilla as comforting as the arm he threw about my shoulders.

"He's going to go for it," I told him softly.

"Yes, of course, dear girl," he whispered. "I have him pegged."

"How do you remember all that?" I asked him. "What's been anthologized and what everyone wants . . ."

"Remembrance is nothing more than quotation, of course. But

I'm just in the middle of things here, Rosemary. I'll have to come down at six and see you off properly."

"No need, Mr. Mitchell," I said. With Pearl away, I hadn't planned on any formal goodbyes but this one.

"It's not like I won't be seeing you. I'll be back—and soon."

"I'll be right with you!" Mr. Mitchell called through the doorway, at once trying to attend to his collector, as well as to me. His priorities were clear.

"You won't forget an old man, Rosemary?" He bent to kiss me and I put my arms around his neck, hugging him: the father I still hadn't found.

"I'm to have lunch with Arthur next Friday, after my first week of work. I'll stop up then."

"Watch out for those publishers, dear girl." He smiled, his head cocked. "A pack of thieves."

I left him to his customer, to Herbert's *Temple*, and he walked back through his suite of rooms.

"Rosemary for remembrance!" he called, over his shoulder, as I pulled the cage closed.

∾

I *arrived at* my apartment while it was still light with a bag of expensive cherries I'd bought at a specialty store. They weren't in season, but cherries were what I wanted on my birthday, on the first anniversary of Mother's death. The heat had gone off again in my apartment, well before the days were even warm. It didn't matter, I simply left my coat on when inside felt wintry, although I missed the murmurings of the radiator, and especially a hot bath.

I took from my bag the small book of Auden's poetry—a goodbye present from Arthur—to add to my bookshelf. Poor Arthur can't have known the ambiguous sentiments it evoked, and I wondered if the strand of my hair had fallen from its pages while some casual browser thumbed through its contents. Perhaps it was coincidence after all that Walter Geist had whispered a line from this very book, rather than having left it for me to find. Perhaps it was mere happenstance that in the vast Arcade it was this book that had appeared on Oscar's stool. Where was Oscar? I asked myself for the thousandth time.

I leaned Auden up against the dog-eared *Moby-Dick*. The collection on my shelf had expanded, and would only continue to. My eyes ran over my few Arcade purchases, coming to rest on the small bluish package lying unopened on the bottom shelf.

It was time.

The parcel Chaps had pressed on me at the airport all those months before lay there, waiting for me: a birthday present after all. I had saved it for a desperate moment but had managed this far without it. Now that I'd sent Mother's ashes to Chaps, it was as if her small package would assuage, a little, that irretrievable loss.

Walter Geist floated for not more than an instant in my mind's eye, his coat falling open behind him.

The little package had met me here. A book is always a gift, Chaps had said. I needed her. I needed to believe in Esther Chapman, alive and consistent. Chaps, who loved me. Who would take care of Mother's ashes, properly, reverently. Esther Chapman, who had sent me to New York. Would her present tell me why?

I fell into my old armchair and held the small parcel in my hand for a long time. Wrapped and obscure, it was as enigmatic as any object in Julian Peabody's cabinet. The city hummed outside in a low continuum that had become a kind of silence. With my fingernail, I carefully peeled off a piece of tape that held the familiar paper closed, trying not to tear it. Its very color was like an image of Chaps, and I pictured her wrapping this present for me in her tidy little store. I would glue the paper into my scrapbook later, to keep it safe.

Before I removed another piece of tape, before I saw inside the wrapping, I experienced an immense hallucination. Staring down at the bluish parcel in my lap, my eyes blurred, and I closed them upon a waking dream.

Sitting in my rescued armchair, fully conscious, I had a vision that Chaps had given me, at the airport the day I left Tasmania, a copy of *The Isle of the Cross*, and that it lay now, beneath the paper, there in my lap, waiting only for me to unwrap it.

My entire journey in New York was a thread that met its end. Unwrapping the book would uncover what I possessed all along. The gift I'd brought with me was the one Walter Geist had pressed into my hands, and that in turn I'd given Oscar. It was absurdly sensical, a trajectory that ordered every event to this moment, wrapping it up inside Chapman's Bookshop paper. There it was in my lap: a secret that told me that nothing is truly lost, but is simply replaced.

I opened the book. An elegant frontispiece depicting an enchanted-looking island faced the impressive title page. It could have been my island state. The thick, rough-cut pages of *The Isle of the Cross* turned beneath my hand. An epigraph from Shakespeare established Melville's theme:

> O, I have suffered
> With those that I saw suffer! A brave vessel
> (Who had no doubt some noble creature in her)
> Dashed all to pieces! O, the cry did knock
> Against my very heart!

Miranda was evidently Agatha's model, but it was Melville's art, not Prospero's, that conjured the storm. Across the sea of space and time he set the wild waters in a roar. The storm rose; thunder and lightning struck Agatha's island, wrecked the ship, and delivered her a faithless love. Her own love would save him, recall him to life. But he abandons her and their child. She waits. She walks the coastline and waits for the sea to give him back.

I read on and on, the words crowding fast like a single, streaming sentence. I held every lost thing in my hands, restored between the covers of his book. I knew what Melville wanted to say about pity, about longing, about the omnipotence of love. What the nature of our obligation is, one to another. The *Isle of the Cross* I held wasn't a paean to remorse, but a liberation from it. It was Melville's other masterpiece, and I recognized its absolute value. I glimpsed, fleetingly, the full measure of his soul.

It was like being given the ocean.

The vision dissolved in the tears falling from my eyes, vanishing as completely as it had emerged, fully formed, from my imagination. Oscar had told me that the world exists to end up in a book; this one, *The Isle of the Cross*, had disappeared again into the lucid air.

Alone in my small apartment, I sat stunned in my rescued armchair. The city hummed. The faucet dripped into the claw-footed tub. The green clock ticked. I recognized myself, reflected in the oval mirror, red hair standing about my face as if from shock, and I pulled my coat tighter, shivering. It was Anzac Day—my birthday. A day of commemoration—of mourning. The first day of my twentieth year.

The parcel still lay in my lap. Inside its dear blue paper was Chaps's actual gift, warmly pressed upon me in departure, ten months before.

The wrapping opened easily to reveal a small leather edition of *The Tempest*, her favorite play. When I was a child living above Remarkable Hats, Chaps would boast that in teaching me to read, she'd endowed my purposes with words. But there were no words for what I felt.

I smoothed the paper flat, picked up the volume, and kissed the scarlet leather binding. I held it up to the light, the gilt-edged pages glimmering with promise. On the inside cover, in her fine neat hand, a gentle cursive, Chaps had written:

> For Dearest Rosemary, on the day of her beginning:
>   "I shall miss thee,
>   but yet thou shalt have freedom."

It was what I'd been given. It was mine to keep.

"*They lard their* lean books with the fat of other men's works" is certainly true of me. Shakespeare is in evidence throughout the novel in much of what Esther Chapman advises, in some of Robert Mitchell's dialogue, and scattered within Rosemary's observations in instances too numerous to cite.

The Melville "Agatha letters" to Nathaniel Hawthorne, excerpted in chapters 13 and 14, were taken from the transcribed text reprinted in *The Letters of Herman Melville*, edited by Merrell R. Davis and William H. Gilman, published by Yale University Press in 1960, a book currently out of print. The original letters are in the Melville Collection, Harvard College Library. Further insight into the Agatha correspondence, and other biographical information on Melville, was obtained from *Herman Melville: A Biography* by Hershel Parker, a work of unprecedented scholarship, in two volumes, published by Johns Hopkins in 1996 and 2002. Parker also published an article that was helpful, "Herman Melville's *The Isle of the Cross:* A Survey and a Chronology," in *American Literature*, volume 62, number 1 (March 1990). Also of use were *Herman Melville: A Critical Biography* by Newton Arvin (Grove Press, 2002); *Melville: A Biography* by Laurie Robertson-Lorant (University of Massachusetts Press, 1998); and *Hawthorne: A Life* by Brenda Wineapple (Random

House, 2003). During a late revision, Andrew Delbanco's remarkable *Melville: His World and Work*, published by Alfred A. Knopf in 2005, was an inspiring influence. Quotes from *Moby-Dick* are taken from the Everyman paperback edition, which employs the Northwestern University Press text. Other short quotes and fragments are taken from *Whitejacket*, *The Confidence Man*, and *Redburn*.

Permission to quote from W. H. Auden's poem *The Sea and the Mirror* is granted by Edward Mendelson, William Meredith, and Monroe K. Spears, executors of the estate of W. H. Auden, and used with the permission of Random House, Inc. I have taken several ideas from the introduction and notes by Arthur Kirsch in the Princeton University Press edition of the poem, published in 2003. *The Tempest* quotes are from the Pelican Shakespeare Edition, edited by Peter Holland (1999).

In chapter 9 Robert Mitchell and Oscar Jarno quote from Walter Benjamin's essay "Unpacking My Library," which appears in *Illuminations*, published by Schocken Books, 1969. Oscar's lengthy quote, also in chapter 9, is from Goethe's *Wilhelm Meister's Apprenticeship*. Mitchell quotes from Browning's "Caliban upon Setebos" in reference to Geist on page 277. Details on the condition of albinism were taken from information produced by the National Organization for Albinism and Hypopigmentation (NOAH).

Lillian La Paco's story is a fictional composite of actual abductions that took place in Argentina during the "dirty war" from 1976 through 1983. Estimates vary as to the number of the "disappeared," but most range between ten thousand and thirty thousand individuals. I have relied on details recounted in the testimonies of the Mothers of the Plaza de Mayo, as told to Matilde Mellibovsky (a founding member) in *Circle of Love Over Death* (Curbstone Press, 1997).

Inspired by the work of Jorge Luis Borges, I have used several texts apart from *The Book of Imaginary Beings* (Penguin Modern

Classics edition, translated by Esther Allen, Suzanne Jill Levine, and Eliot Weinberger) which appears in chapter 6. Various ruminations on the nature of time are taken from essays in *The Total Library* edited by Eliot Weinberger (Penguin Classics [UK], 2001): specifically, "On the Cult of Books" and "A New Refutation of Time," the latter essay using as its epigraph the German quote that Geist translates on the clock in Peabody's rooms in chapter 12. I have also used a variation of a line from Borges's short story "Shakespeare's Memory," from *Collected Fictions* translated by Andrew Hurley (Viking, 1998), on page 348.

The Rilke quotes that Robert Mitchell speaks in chapter 21 are taken from *The Duino Elegies*, translated by Gary Miranda (Azul Editions, 1981). General information on cabinets of curiosities, as well as the description of certain images and objects, is taken from *Cabinets of Curiosities* by Patrick Mauries, (Thames & Hudson, 2002). Various descriptions of rare and expensive volumes were taken from a catalog published by Lame Duck Books in Cambridge, Massachusetts. A conversation about manuscripts and fraud with Isaac Gerwirtz, curator of the Berg Collection at the New York Public Library, was invaluable, and I thank him for his time. The Goya painting Rosemary recalls Arthur showing her is *The Straw Manikin (El Pelele)*, 1791–2, Museo del Prado, Madrid.

In the end, books aren't one's life; people are. This book is dedicated to Michael Jacobs, who has made my writing life, and my life otherwise, possible, meaningful, and challenging. I thank him for, and return, his love, and thank him always for our own Matthew and Emma. I am indebted to all three for their forbearance, and for keeping steady the center of my life.

I would like to thank the Bennington Writing Seminars, in particular Askold Melnyczuk, Douglas Bauer, Martha Cooley, and

Alice Mattison. Sheila Kohler has been more than generous with her time and her consideration of early drafts of this work, and I am grateful to her. My thanks to Liam Rector and Priscilla Hodgkins for my ongoing relationship with the Seminars.

Bennington also gave me Joanna Anderson and Judy Rowley, dear friends and writing companions, who have helped me more than I can say. I thank them for their fine intelligences, their good hearts, and their continuing company.

I thank Elaine Koster for her early and steady support, for her professionalism, and for her kindness. My great thanks to Deb Futter at Doubleday, a pleasure from start to finish, and the best instinct I ever went with.

Most especially, my thanks to Nuala O'Faolain for the deep pleasure of her acquaintance; and for his sustaining friendship, Mark Stafford. Thanks also to: my sister, Jai Simmons, Jane Otto, Daniele Menache, Maria Kargman, Brenda Marsh, Guillemette Bowler, Douglas Glover, Julia Dorff, William Vandegrift, Lillian Ferrari, and of course, Jack.

P.S.

Ideas,
interviews
& features ...

Q and A with Sheridan Hay

Did you enjoy writing *The Secret of Lost Things*?
Writing is difficult and takes time and discipline but it is intensely satisfying. When I look up after a day of concentrated work and realize that I've been enfolded in an envelope of time – hours pass in one attenuated moment – that is what I really enjoy and I came to that eventually with *The Secret of Lost Things*.

***The Secret of Lost Things* feels like a fairy tale or fable at times, at other times a compelling detective story. Did you consciously use different genres?**
I was conscious of trying to write a sort of personal fable – one girl's 'myth' of her beginnings – and that the structure of the *Bildungsroman* was a form I wanted to employ. An exemplar of the form is *Great Expectations*, and I've always been taken with Dickens's ability to make 'types' wholly compelling as characters. One doesn't really question, for example, the 'believability' of Miss Havisham remaining in her wedding dress or not throwing out the cake after half a lifetime! I am interested in the emotional impact of theatrical 'reality' – the staged piece that none the less moves one to tears. So there is an element of the theatrical in the novel – the characters are playing, to some extent, 'roles' in Rosemary's play, and the Arcade is both theatre and bookshop. The 'mystery' element owes less I think to a detective genre than to my interest in Borges

and playing around with truth and ideas of history.

Melville was brilliant in his manipulation of different forms and very early on was moving between genres. In *Moby Dick*, he made a new form using combinations of established forms, which is interesting to me.

Did you like using factual material in the novel?
I love letters and what they communicate and what they leave out. Letters are the best kind of history because they record thoughts. It was only as I sat with the material over a couple of years that I saw how Melville's lost novel and its theme of abandonment and remorse could amplify Rosemary's story of becoming herself. The factual elements of Melville's story, research into the lost novel, as well as things like the cabinet of curiosities and the arcana of collecting, meant that I couldn't wait to get to work each day, that there was always something interesting to find out about and to find a place for.

'[Australia] That great America on the other side of the sphere . . . given to the enlightened world by the whaleman.' What was it like to come from Sydney to New York? Do you miss Australia and will you ever return to live there?
After more than twenty years in New York, I think what I miss about Australia has less to do with what I might find if I lived there ▶

‘ My mother died just as I began the novel and for some time I felt that in describing Rosemary's fictional anguish, I was describing my own. ’

Q and A with Sheridan Hay *(continued)*

◄ again than with what lives in my imagination. At 46, I've lived away almost as long as I lived at home. There are great advantages to being an expatriate but I'm never sure if the underlying sense of loneliness and isolation I occasionally feel describes my nature or my displaced condition. I have family in Australia, so I will always return to visit but I've made my life in America and have an American family of my own. In that sense I think the children of an expatriate become her roots rather than the more conventional way one's parents root one to geographic place. Both my parents are dead and that changed profoundly my idea of Australia as a home to return to.

Rosemary says of her mother's death, 'Her death had called me to my self.' Have you any personal experience of such grief?
My mother died just as I began the novel and for some time I felt that in describing Rosemary's fictional anguish, I was describing my own. I had a feeling throughout that my mother was keeping me company as I wrote, and the sense of loss that pervades the novel is perhaps its most autobiographical element.

Oscar is an original and intriguing character. Did you want his ending to remain enigmatic?
Oscar, in part, stands outside the action of the novel, so having him 'escape' its ending is intentional. Oscar is not touched by the lives of others but is driven by a fascination with his own subjectivity. I see this less as narcissism than as retreat. He will turn up in

a situation that suits his purposes. I think there are people who find intellectual immersion and the accumulation of knowledge a way to remain beyond the realities of emotional demand. The fact that Rosemary imagines he can return something on the order of affection to her is an indication of her naivety, and her optimism.

What does Rosemary learn during the course of the book?
Well, Rosemary learns many things but mostly she learns how to live free of the projections of others and a bit closer to the notion of her own truth. She is on the way to learning the hard lessons of resilience and independence, and we have to assume she gains them as the narrative is told in retrospect and the older and wiser Rosemary looks to this particular year and its experiences to illustrate those gains. She learns that the way through grief is to remember and to live as best she can. It is her imagination that saves her.

Apart from Rosemary, who is your favourite character in the novel?
I love all of them – you have to like your characters to spend so much time with them. Lots of people have mentioned finding Geist either disgusting or repulsive but I find him neither. To me he is heartbreakingly lonely and isolated. Rosemary's encounter with him is an encounter with otherness, and he stands, in a way, for the inevitability of such reckonings. A sexual encounter appeared to be the most dramatic way to depict his ▶

> 6 Rosemary learns many things but mostly she learns how to live free of the projections of others and a bit closer to the notion of her own truth. 9

5

Q and A with Sheridan Hay (continued)

◀ utter remoteness: his complete incapacity. That incapacity is something he shares with Oscar, only it takes a different form. I know the scene in the rare book room is disturbing; it would have little impact if it wasn't disturbing. But it is Geist who is revealed in that scene rather than Rosemary. It is his suffering that we discover. Readers have told me that they love Lillian and especially Pearl. I imagine that's because they are both capable of loving. All the characters are flawed and sort of in disguise – each has something to 'give' Rosemary (almost like tasks in a quest) but it isn't necessarily something she can anticipate – or want!

The theme of memory is threaded throughout the novel. Rosemary's name is the symbol for remembrance. And the Arcade functions because of the booksellers' use of memory. Do you think new technologies will necessarily alter our use of memory for the worse?
I know they will from my own experience. Memory is internal not external and the process of recall is idiosyncratic and entirely human – that is the point of the Who Knows? game in the novel. My way of writing is associative and depends on reading and the experience of reading. If the novel fetishizes books as magical objects, then it is certainly no more than the computer is perceived by some as an object of enchantment. Perhaps both things are true, but I wrote an old-fashioned novel because my ideas about these things are, I suppose, conservative. I don't want to

witness a transition from the medium of books to some other technology and I don't see why that should be the case. It isn't either or, but both serving different purposes.

I do feel that technology is having its impact on bookselling and publishing, and the novel is an intentional homage to a sort of life I feel has largely passed from the culture. It is that feeling that makes the novel have a fairy-tale aspect – that it in part takes place in another time where things were done differently. But that elegiac quality might be intrinsic to the pastime of selling books itself: it is a business forever in decline, and its demise has been predicted for as long as I can remember.

There are many eclectic references in the novel: to Shakespeare, to Auden, to Borges and of course to Herman Melville and Nathaniel Hawthorne. Do you see any parallels between being a writer and being a 'collector' like Peabody?
Absolutely. I like to think about the Australian species of bowerbirds – they build an elaborate nest and fly around looking for shiny bits and pieces to decorate the nest and make it beautiful. If you ever find a nest, it's full of bright things like tin foil and bottle caps, the odd earring, shells and even berries: sometimes hundreds of dramatically coloured objects that the bowerbird sorts through obsessively. I think my writing style is something like that. I'm on the lookout in everything I read, I see, I hear, for 'shiny bits'. I keep copious notes on these bits of treasure and look through my pages of fragments before beginning writing each day. That ▶

> ❜ That elegiac quality might be intrinsic to the pastime of selling books itself: it is a business forever in decline, and its demise has been predicted for as long as I can remember. ❜

Author photo © Marion Ettlinger

LIFE
at a Glance

BORN

17 October 1961 in Sydney, Australia.

EDUCATED

At an all-girls boarding school in Bathurst, NSW, and finished high school in Sydney. Master of Fine Art in literature and fiction, Bennington Writing Seminars, Bennington College, Vermont.

CAREER

About fifteen years in publishing as, among other things, a bookstore clerk and buyer, a sales representative, a marketing manager, a publicity director, and finally an editor – at various houses including Penguin, HarperCollins and Simon & Schuster.

Q and A with Sheridan Hay *(continued)*

◄ way my mind is working on associations, on the stuff of my preoccupations, on things that caught my eye in another context, while I concentrate on moving the story forward. This is exactly like collecting objects except that I'm the only one who values the bits I've found. They don't have any other value until they're strung on the thread of story.

Are you working on another novel?
Yes, an historical novel set in the middle of the nineteenth century in America and England. The novel's protagonist is a very minor historical figure, an obsessive and an unreasonable woman. She was a writer. I've been researching the book for a year and am now writing the first draft. ■

Top Ten Books

Moby-Dick
Herman Melville

Middlemarch
George Eliot

Villette
Charlotte Brontë

Love in the Time of Cholera
Gabriel García Márquez

Anything by Henry James but especially
*The Golden Bowl, The Spoils of Poynton,
The Bostonians, The Ambassadors*

The Great Fire
Shirley Hazzard

The Vivisector
Patrick White

The Complete Poems of Emily Dickinson

The Rabbiter's Bounty: Collected Poems
Les Murray

Of Heroes and Tombs
Ernesto Sabato

A Writing Life

When do you write?
From around 9 a.m. to about 3 p.m. four days a week. Weekends I just 'visit' the work for a few hours.

Where do you write?
In a studio beneath my house that was formerly a storage area. I have to leave the house to enter the room.

Why do you write?
Because it is the most personally satisfying thing I've found to do with my time.

Pen or computer?
Both. Pencil for marking up books and taking notes, and drawing up ideas. Computer for when I'm organizing a narrative.

Silence or music?
Silence.

What started you writing?
An overwhelming desire to.

How do you start a book?
With a compelling idea/image/person that won't go away and starts to accumulate and draw other things to it.

And finish?
The end of this novel came halfway through and I just had to put it away and get on with the middle. I don't think you know until you get there the *way* it ends, even if you have an idea about *how*.

Do you have any writing rituals or superstitions?
I take Thursdays off and spend them in Manhattan, and the break in the pattern of days *makes* the pattern, the rhythm. I don't have the space here to list all my superstitions.

Which living writer do you most admire?
This is difficult. There is much great writing I admire – Gabriel García Márquez, José Saramago, Javier Marías – their work is incredible. But to take the question somewhat differently, I have to say J. K. Rowling, not because of the Potter books in and of themselves (although I admire them) but because I've seen the impact her message has for children: that reading is a way to independence, to knowing your own mind. She has created a generation of young readers alive to allusion and complexity and I think she has done all writers a great service.

What or who inspires you?
Reading inspires me. Specifically, Henry James and the consciousness transmitted in his novels.

If you weren't a writer what job would you do?
A teacher of literature.

What's your guilty reading pleasure?
I love to look at catalogues. I suppose it's just shopping, really, while lying down . . . ∎

6 I don't have the space here to list all my superstitions. 9

How I Came to Write

by Sheridan Hay

THERE USED TO be an expression, English in origin, that describes a person as 'Penguin-educated'. It describes me. (I gather the expression came about because much literature, once hard to get at, became easily accessible in cheap Penguin paperbacks.) Penguin-educated means, in my case, that I didn't attend college and educated myself by reading as many books as I could. Like Rosemary, a bookstore was my first university. This had as much to do with a lack of funds as with a desire to hang about reading books. When I finally did go to college (at forty) I found myself a natural student. After years in bookstores and publishing, I knew how books were produced, sold and marketed, but I wanted to know how they were written.

I wanted to write them myself.

I went to graduate school and became completely taken with nineteenth-century American writers, for reasons I still don't fully understand. Herman Melville was one of them.

I think it's fair to say that I fell in love with him. He died in 1891 so this didn't bother my husband – well, not too much. Melville died in obscurity at 72 in New York. He had spent much of the last twenty years of his life writing poetry in the evening while working as a customs inspector on the docks of Manhattan. He is as enigmatic a figure as any he created in his own fiction.

But what does reading a lot of books and falling in love with dead men have to do with becoming a writer?

I took my desire to write seriously and went to school to study the craft. Education is, of course, transformative. But perhaps the most immediate means of self-transformation happens when one falls in love. Falling in love is an act of the imagination, which is obviously just the thing to exercise if you want to become a writer. As an imaginative act it's hard to beat. This is what I needed Melville for – to be able to imagine myself 'different' within the confines of a fixed identity. But I was used to doing that – imagining other 'selves' – from reading lots of books.

Books, specifically novels, persuade us that consciousness is valuable and that the 'self' is worthwhile. I was trying to make a new 'self' – one that wrote fiction. I needed a hero who truly struggled, and in Melville I found one. There is a generative quality about his work (a quality I admire too in Shakespeare). Both writers also share an aspect best called mythopoeic. What they have made gives life to the making of other things. Their work engenders the work of others. And this is what reading any good writer can do.

Of course, 'falling in love' with a writer is an act of substitution. What I was really smitten with was writing. I needed to be passionate about it, and Melville served as a guide to the kind of passion that leads to commitment and discipline. There are, of course, many other writers who do the same. Hundreds of them live on my bookshelves.

The best of reading is that novels can address us on a level that is below ▶

❝ Rosemary is who she is because of what she has read – and the other people she meets are similarly taken up with ideas gleaned from literature. ❞

How I Came to Write *(continued)*

◄ consciousness, and can communicate the subjective reality of another's mind. When reading a novel, we don't wonder what someone is thinking, we *know*. And knowing another subjective reality is, itself, transformative.

When I came to write *The Secret of Lost Things*, I tried to dramatize this idea of a 'self' constructed from reading – a character that has absorbed the literary consciousness of others. Rosemary Savage has a slightly archaic diction. Her voice is full of allusions and quotes and references to Shakespeare, Auden, Borges, Rilke and, of course, Melville. Rosemary is who she is because of what she has read – and the other people she meets are similarly taken up with ideas gleaned from literature.

In the Arcade, books are the objects of desire – but this is just another way of saying that the novel is about desire – about wanting; collecting but never actually 'having'. That desire is to want, not to possess. And that value and worth exist in relation to desire, as a measure of it. Books are the perfect metaphor to express this quality of the unrequited because what a book is and does is extraordinary as well as ordinary. Something invisible is made actual – something imagined can be held in the hand, can be 'published', which is to say, transmitted. It's an ordinary object that remains the same after it has been consumed. It is the consumer – the reader – that has been altered, and sometimes, as with me and Melville, transformed.

Books – and in this case, a bookstore – are familiar and obvious metaphors. We think of a face to be 'read', we 'turn a new page', we 'start a new chapter' in the 'story' of our life. It's commonplace for such metaphors to describe the self and the pattern, the 'narrative', of life. 'Don't judge a book by its cover' is an admonition that suggests there may always be something more inside, if we 'read between the lines'.

In the end, it may be that this 'self' we make through reading is largely fictional, in every sense. But then perhaps we remake the world – or write the book – every day through imagination, through consciousness. And a book – like this one in your hand – is the evidence of that living creation. ∎

If You Loved This,
You Might Like . . .

Possession: A Romance
by A. S. Byatt
Winner of the 1990 Booker Prize, this is a
complex and compulsively readable novel.
Both erudite and passionate, it is an
incredibly moving love story about the affair
between two literary academics and the
Victorian poets who are the subject of their
research.

The Thirteenth Tale
by Diane Setterfield
A gothic tale in a modern-day setting, *The
Thirteenth Tale* is the story of the life of an
elderly famous writer, as told to her bookish
biographer. Filled with references to
nineteenth-century novels and with a pair of
sinister twins at its core, this is a captivating
mystery.

84 Charing Cross Road
by Helene Hanff
This is a fascinating and moving series of
letters between an outspoken New York book
lover and a restrained English antiquarian
bookseller between 1949 and 1969. A
delightful and charming story, shot through
with wit and warmth, it was the basis for a
highly successful film of the same name
starring Anthony Hopkins and Anne
Bancroft.

The Dante Club
by Matthew Pearl
In Boston in 1865, four American scholars must find a way to stop a series of gruesome murders based on the descriptions of punishments in Dante's *Inferno*. This is a page-turning literary thriller, filled with wonderful period detail.

The Old Curiosity Shop
by Charles Dickens
First published in 1841 to great acclaim, this has a fairy-tale quality and a wonderful comic feel despite its bleak and tragic central story. Worth reading for its brilliantly drawn cast of grotesques alone.

The Secret History
by Donna Tartt
This international bestseller has a spellbinding plot, filled with blackmail and violence: the misfit narrator becomes embroiled in a dark murder story when he makes friends with a group of eccentric students at an exclusive New England college.

Find Out More

Melville: His World and Work by Andrew Delbanco

www.aba.org.uk – The Antiquarian Booksellers Association

www.inprint.co.uk/thebookguide – a guide to secondhand and antiquarian bookshops and book fairs in the UK.

The Book of Lost Books: An Incomplete History of All the Great Books You Will Never Read by Stuart Kelly – an entertaining anthology of literary 'losses' through the ages, for example all of the Marquis de Sade's unpublished manuscripts or Philip Larkin's diaries.

BOOKSHOPS TO VISIT

Sheridan Hay's favourite bookshops

The Strand Bookstore, 12th Street and Broadway, NYC, where Sheridan Hay worked for nine months – 'The Arcade resembles a wildly exaggerated memory of that time but it does not exist.'

The Corner Bookshop, 1313 Madison Avenue, Manhattan, NYC

Gleebooks in Sydney, Australia: www.gleebooks.com.au

London bookshops

Hatchards – booksellers since 1797:
www.hatchards.co.uk

Heywood Hill – new and antiquarian books
in the heart of Mayfair:
www.heywoodhill.com

Foyles – a famous London bookshop on
Charing Cross Road: www.foyles.co.uk